The Wedding Guest

The Wedding Guest

Anna Gilbert

St. Martin's Press New York

Design by Basha Zapatka

Library of Congress Cataloging-in-Publication Data

Gilbert, Anna.
    The wedding guest / Anna Gilbert.
        p.   cm.
    ISBN 0-312-09935-5
    1. Young women—England—Fiction.   2. Aunts—England—Fiction.
I. Title.
PR6057.I49W4   1993
823'.914—dc20   93-23121
                                                             CIP

First edition: September 1993

10 9 8 7 6 5 4 3 2 1

The Wedding Guest

THE TWO BEAUTIFUL Findon sisters had been blessed with all the advantages of a prosperous provincial background in the early years of the twentieth century, the last golden age in English history. Their niece, Elinor, had been enthralled as a child by her father's stories of his boyhood in the family home, Hoodman House.

But by the time she went to live there with the aunts she barely knew, the Edwardian age was over; the Great War had changed the world; and Elinor was to find that some other event, closer at hand and more personal, had overshadowed the closely interwoven lives of the two women with whom she had thrown in her lot. Her growing suspicion that the quiet surface of country life may be deceptive failed to prepare her for the appalling truth it concealed. In confronting evil, she was forced also to confront urgent moral problems, only partially resolved.

Throughout her ordeal the house itself plays a sinister part; but in the romantic garden of neighboring Winkblade, Elinor finds not only solace but love—and the promise of lasting happiness.

§§§§§§

. . . Standing among the cool reeds, I felt the first thrill of an unfamiliar pride. I alone, witchlike in my unholy knowledge, knew all the secrets and could use them or not as I chose. Beyond my shadow the pool sparkled dangerously; air and water blazed with diabolical fire.

It lasted no more than a minute, my trespass into forbidden territory. A cloud came; sky and pool darkened; the air felt cool. I was myself again, but not as I had once been. Hoodman House had changed me for the worse: it had initiated me in the power of evil. Its chill threatened my soul. Here on the very brink I must draw back. It was better not to know the dark side of other people's lives, better to leave the past alone. Knowledge might be a weapon, but it was a burden too, like a sharing of guilt. Best to leave still waters undisturbed . . .

1

MY FATHER'S HALF-SISTERS, the two Miss Findons of Hoodman House, were well known in the neighboring town of Bidminster not only as the daughters of a prosperous businessman but also on account of their outstanding beauty.

So I understand from hearsay. Being so much younger, I barely knew them in those days before the war; but my earliest memory confirms all that was said about them and may even have given a hint—children have an instinct for such things—of how very much more there was to be said.

It was in the year 1908 in the bedroom of a London hotel that I saw them for the first time. In the soft light of the shaded lamp, through the lingering mists of sleep, they hovered into view: indistinct, unreal, a vision of gold chains and brooches and perfumed silk.

"Your aunts are here, Elinor!" Drifting from sleep to waking, I felt my mother's hand on my brow. "They've come to say good-bye."

They had perched themselves at the foot of my bed, one on either side: Aunt Kelda and Aunt May.

"How do you do?" I said and hesitated to say "good-bye," though that was what they had come for. It seemed too soon.

They laughed.

"There now! So polite—and she's still half asleep."

"Dear little Elinor! It was a shame to wake her."

The mist thinned into a shimmering haze about the two angels come to bless my bed: young Edwardian angels, their brows fringed, their light brown heads leaning toward me on long lace-swathed necks. They seemed identical, two halves of a single entity, yet possessing twice the power and twice the mystery of one person. It was to be a long time before I saw either of them clearly as a separate individual, if indeed I ever have done.

"We only wanted to wish you bon voyage."

"We'll see you when you come home again."

They leaned nearer. Each in turn kissed my cheek, one the left, the other the right. Dazed, I submitted, having no choice. They rose in a rustle of silk and withdrew. Their silver mesh purses dangled twinkling from their wrists. The door closed. I slept again.

The next day we sailed for India to join my father. When he could spare time from his regimental duties, he used to tell me stories about his boyhood at Hoodman House in the village of Saury near Bidminster, where his younger half-sisters still lived with my grandfather Findon. They were stories of a golden age peopled with countless friends, especially the family of Mr. William Tass, my grandfather's business partner, who were almost like relations. They used to drive out from Bidminster for parties at Hoodman House and picnics in the wild garden at Winkblade, a neighboring farmhouse long empty. In summer they drank lemonade from green-tinted glasses in Mrs. Torgill's shop or ginger beer poured from cold stone jars. In winter they rolled up the carpets for dancing and roasted chestnuts in the fire or skated on Lott's Pool.

At quite an early age I sensed in his voice the homesickness of an officer serving abroad—and grew familiar with the comfortable parlors and well-furnished tables of Findons and Tasses in the last years of the century I had just missed.

"The garden at Winkblade when the lilac was in bloom, and then the orange blossom! It was a trysting place for lovers. We went there to listen to the nightingale. Just an excuse. There never was a nightingale in Saury."

"But you weren't a lover," I would point out, scandalized. "You hadn't even met mother then."

"Of course not. The best part of my life was still to come." And he would put his arm round my mother and kiss the top of her head.

The tranquil happiness of those early years came to an end when my father died in my eleventh year. My mother and I came home to England and settled for the time being at Rosedown Hall in Surrey, the home of friends Colonel and Mrs. Burnett. At the beginning of the war they turned over part of the house to the Red Cross as a nursing home for officers and my mother joined the nursing staff.

The exchange of letters with my Findon relations at the time of my father's death soon petered out. There must have been little inclination on either side to keep in touch, despite the fact that if my mother should die before I was old enough to fend for myself, I must make my home at Saury, a prospect I tried not to think about.

All the same we did sometimes toy with the idea of paying them a visit.

"So that at least you'll have some inkling what to expect, just supposing . . ." My mother's lighthearted tone was reassuring: it made a mockery of the possibility that she would ever die.

"Inkling?" The unfamiliar word intrigued me.

"Some idea. Instead of being thrust upon them some day without even knowing one aunt from the other. We really ought to go."

5

The project remained theoretical until the summer of 1916 when, after a long silence, Aunt Kelda's letter arrived.

"I shall have to accept." My mother studied the wedding invitation. "Your father would have wanted me to go. And it will be a help having other people there."

And so somewhat cautiously, there being no reason not to go, we went.

The weather was hot, the journey long and tiring. The offensive on the Somme had begun a fortnight before and we spent hours shunted into sidings to make way for military supply wagons and slow trains full of wounded soldiers. We arrived at midnight on the eve of the wedding and left early on the day after it.

Weary, heavy-eyed, anxious to please strangers who had known my father, I moved in a state of stupefaction shot through by moments of feverish alertness: moments vivid enough to recur without warning in later years and startle me with strange insights.

And somehow once again my aunts eluded me. There was a good deal of embracing, of being drawn close to satin bodices and slender waists; but they were too busy to talk to me. As for distinguishing between them, naturally under the circumstances there could be no difficulty. My first emotion on meeting them was of surprise—after one breathtaking glimpse of her—that it was not Aunt May who was to be the bride. The surprise lasted only until I identified the bridegroom, Mr. Julius Cade. He was not exactly old but of the indeterminate age that renders a man totally uninteresting to a girl in her early teens; certainly no fit consort for Aunt May even if he could—just—be made to do for Aunt Kelda. Besides, Aunt May, we gathered, was engaged to one of the sons of Mr. Edwin Tass.

My mother mingled with the other guests. I scarcely saw her all day but hung about and did my best to become invisible, finding temporary refuge with my grandfather, a tall thin old gentleman in clothes too wide for him. He sat behind the drawing room door in a brown leather chair, clutching its arms as if at any minute he would gather strength to get up and escape.

"Vincent's little girl?" His blue eyes were dim and tired. His sight must have been failing: I was no longer little.

"Yes, grandfather," I nevertheless said, and that brought our conversation to an end. He reached for my hand, held it for a moment, and smiled. It was the nicest part of the visit.

Among the guests were a good many Tasses. They outnumbered the Findons, of whom—in desperation I had taken to counting—there were only five. Wandering aimlessly into the bedroom where the ladies left their wraps, I came upon a Mrs. Tass. She too had a headache and obviously preferred to be alone. When she had dabbed my temples with eau de Cologne as well as her own, I drifted away.

Even at the time and more so afterward, I recognized the quality of my enjoyment as mediocre and wondered that it should be so: girls are supposed to like weddings. Only later did I realize how preoccupied the grown-ups must have been with the terrible casualty lists, which, in view of the occasion, were never mentioned. The generally subdued mood was further clouded for me by small personal trials—the coarse rub of cotton mittens on my palms; the damp warmth of the garden flowers I clutched all day, not liking to put them down until the event was officially over; the wartime table bare of refreshments usually found at festivities.

True, there were macaroons. The only other young person present, a silent youth who was also a Tass of some sort, sat next to me at the lower end of the table. "Would you care for a macaroon?" he said from time to time, breaking the appalling silence and offering the plate in polite desperation. From similar motives I ate three and wished they had been meringues.

Besides the heat and the headache and the uncomfortable mittens there was something else: a small incident depressing in its effect. It was late in the afternoon. I had come in from the garden. The bride and groom were going no farther than Bidminster that

7

night and had not yet left, but some of the guests must have gone: the house seemed quieter. Loitering in a passage off the hall, I found a door half open, an empty room, a cool hiding place in which to steal a few minutes of privacy. The venetian blinds were down but their wooden slats were open. I sidled into a high-backed chair, ventured at last to lay aside my wilting pinks and gypsophila, pushed back my stiff-brimmed hat, spread my white embroidered dress . . .

Voices roused me. I must have been listening half-awake and now, returning to life, felt my whole body stiffen anxiously. Ears strained, mouth open, I listened. There was no one to be seen, no human being, but looking up, I recognized under a glass dome on the chiffonier a fellow creature, a red squirrel with a hazelnut in its paws. It sat bolt upright, as if it too were listening, sharing my sense of something discordant, unsuitable. A breeze stole through the blind. A low sunbeam isolated the red-brown head from the body. One glass eye glared, startled.

People were talking close at hand. A man and two women? I couldn't tell where they were but from a word or two here and there, from the tone of first one voice and then another, I knew that their talk was deeply serious. There was passion in it and outrage. The moment was one of crisis. Something was said about telling— or not telling.

All at once from an unseen door someone erupted with the suddenness of uncontrollable distress and stumbled across the hall: a woman, one of my aunts? I shrank into the high-backed chair to endure the unpleasantness of it as she groped and fumbled her way with ugly little exclamations of pain like a person wounded to the heart. I thrust my fingers in my ears to shut out the sound of weeping. Weeping at a wedding! When I removed them, all was quiet again. It was over; but the day, already flawed, had taken on a further mysterious gloom.

Still, we had been warmly received, and so adventurous an

expedition naturally gave us plenty to talk about in the train on our way home.

"I always suspected that your father had more in common with the Tasses than with his own family." My mother removed her hat and pierced it thoughtfully with her long hat pin. "Perhaps that's why I got on so well with them. The families have been close friends. Your Aunt May's engagement is very suitable." As was to be expected, her observations had been sharper than mine and more accurately aimed. "That ruby"—she referred to Aunt May's engagement ring—"must have been expensive."

Despite having missed a good deal of what was going on I had certainly noticed the ruby, a surprising stone to discover, like a sudden red eruption on the pale hand that wore it.

"Not that the Tasses can be short of money. And there's a fabulously rich uncle in Kimberley, Mrs. Edwin Tass's brother. Yes, a diamond mine. And he's a childless widower into the bargain." Then after a reflective pause: "I couldn't help feeling—you wouldn't notice it—that there was something odd about the servants. Never mind, I'm glad we went. Very glad." Her satisfaction seemed to exhaust her; she leaned back and closed her eyes. "It went off better than I expected."

Speculating on the kind of disaster we had presumably escaped, I opened the railway tea basket. It had been quietly placed in our compartment by the youth who had offered the macaroons. He had arrived at the house early in the morning, driven us to the station in a pony trap, and waited, attentive but speechless, to see us off.

"As for Mr. Julius Cade"—we turned our attention to the bridegroom—"apparently he's a musician and composes sacred songs. That's how they met. Kelda sings."

I remarked on his highly polished boots and the blackness of his hair.

"A little too black for a man of his age. But there's one good thing, his age will keep him out of the army." In response to some association of ideas that momentarily eluded me she added, "Your Aunt May behaved perfectly."

I sighed appreciatively. A notion of perfection like the radiance of a white light suffused my recollection of Aunt May.

"Her fiancé is somewhere in France. She must have been beside herself with anxiety."

"I heard one of my aunts crying. She seemed dreadfully upset."

"And no wonder. The casualty lists get longer every day and they're printed so close now that nobody can read them without a magnifying glass. Just look"—we were passing through another town—"all these little streets and so many windows with the blinds drawn down."

The woman who wept as she stumbled upstairs must have been Aunt May, whereas for some reason I had thought, had been almost sure, that it was Aunt Kelda. In that thought had lain the worrying incongruity: a bride heartbroken on her wedding day. A weeping bridesmaid was quite another matter, especially when her lover was exposed to almost certain death. Aunt May had contained her anxiety with a sisterly unselfishness beyond praise: the tears had been held back until the wedding was over. And yet there had been something puzzling in the incident. Had it been the weeping of pure sorrow that I had overheard or—as it had seemed—some quite different kind of distress?

"By the way, I spoke to the photographer. He'll send us a print of the wedding group. And that's that." She accepted a cup of tea with a shudder of relief. "I feel easier in my mind now that you've met them."

In the October of that year there came a bulky envelope addressed in my grandfather's shaky handwriting. They had evidently been clearing out cupboards and were sending on papers belonging to my father. The brief covering letter contained nothing more than the hope that we were well and the cryptic sentence: "It was a pity about Cade but we have Kelda back home, thank God."

So scanty an announcement seemed scarcely to justify a letter of condolence and none was sent. Poor Mr. Cade! It had hardly been worthwhile having the wedding for which his boots had been so resolutely polished, his hair so defiantly blacked.

A few months later we heard from a solicitor in Bidminster that my grandfather had died, leaving his estate to be equally divided among his three children. My father's share would be held in trust for me until I came of age. My mother's letter of sympathy to my aunts was never answered.

"Of course we must remember that they're only your half-aunts." Real aunts, it was implied, would have been more responsive. "Still, they're your only relations."

Variations on this theme occasionally occupied our idle moments over the years and more frequently during the last year of my mother's life, which was to be cruelly cut short. She survived the Spanish flu, which claimed more victims than the war itself, but it left her lungs so severely damaged that there could be no hope of recovery. Toward the end she insisted on my writing to Saury. It was Aunt Kelda who answered my letter.

"She writes quite kindly. They really do want you, darling."

"We don't know one another."

"Not yet, but you'll get to know them. They aren't so very much older than you. Well, not as old as aunts usually are. And don't forget—you'll be independent, thank God. Besides your grandfather's money there'll be quite a nice little bit from your father and me when you're twenty-one."

"I know. Don't talk."

"You won't be a guest or under any obligation . . ." Her voice had become a whisper, each breath an act of will. "The house is yours as much as it is theirs. Evidently May has never married. So many women without husbands . . . so many young men gone . . ."

11

Her death left me desolate, indifferent as to where I should go, what I should do. It was fortunate that the decision had been taken for me long ago. Mrs. Burnett asked me to stay on for a few months, ostensibly to help her, and in so large an establishment she found plenty for me to do. We spent our evenings together and she took me to London on shopping expeditions, determined that my wardrobe should be adequate for whatever social occasions Saury and Bidminster might offer.

During that last winter at Rosedown I learned to accept my fate: to look on the next phase of my life as a kind of marking time before the march forward to marriage or a career. Meanwhile, one must belong somewhere and for the time being there was nowhere else to go.

2

I MUST HAVE dozed and woke to find that the train had stopped. A lady was settling herself in the opposite seat. Her companion hesitated at the open door, one foot still on the platform of an apparently deserted station.

"Not a soul in sight," he said. "Shall we risk it?"

"If the alternative is to get out again, yes. Nothing will induce me to stand another second on that dismal platform."

"There's more than a chance that this will take us to Timbuktu instead of Bidminster." He turned and saw that I was awake. "Unless this young lady can tell us . . ."

"Bidminster? Oh yes. At least . . ." Their uncertainty was proving contagious. "I understood . . ."

"Get in and close the window, Aidan. Let's be comfortable. I've always wanted to go to Timbuktu."

They were pleasant traveling companions, a brother and sister in early middle age—Aidan and Harriet Penfold, as I saw from the card she gave me before we parted at Bidminster. She was expensively dressed, self-confident, and disposed to talk; and she had evidently summed me up at a glance: alone, in black hat and gloves, inclined to sit on the edge of my seat. The rest of my situation she soon learned.

"Then you're beginning a new life—and so are we. Venturing into the unknown. Not that we ever do know what lies ahead."

They were house hunting and would settle in rooms in Bidminster until they found what they were looking for. They had known the town years ago before the war.

"Findon?" Mr. Penfold laid down his newspaper on hearing my name. "There used to be a prosperous building firm of that name in Bidminster. Findon and Tass. *The* building firm I should say."

I told him that my great-grandfather Oliver Findon and William Tass had founded the firm in 1850 and that their sons had carried on the business until my grandfather, Oliver Findon II, had died.

"And the third generation?"

I confessed ignorance as to whether any of Mr. Edwin Tass's sons had continued in the business. My own father, having no taste for the building trade, had made the army his career.

"So you'll be living with your aunts." Miss Penfold had effortlessly familiarized herself with my life story. "And you will meet as strangers." Seeing my hesitation in answering—after all, I had met them twice—she went on smoothly, "An interesting situation for you, to know the circumstances but not the characters involved. It's like the difference between reading a history book and seeing a play. Facts are all very well but it's the people who supply the drama."

"Dick Tass!" Her brother produced the name triumphantly, as if he had been struggling to remember it. "Do you remember, Harriet? The boy who did the conjuring tricks at the mayor's Christmas party in the Bidminster Assembly Rooms."

"Good gracious, yes. Prince Charming himself. I never saw a handsomer youth nor any living creature so self-possessed. Most of the tricks went wrong, nothing whatever appeared from the top hat and the hat itself fell to pieces . . ."

"And he didn't turn a hair."

14

"He was so captivating that the children were more interested in him than in what he was doing—or trying to do. We had taken a small niece and watched it all from the balcony. She loved him; they all did, and so did we."

"Do you remember, every time a trick misfired he threw out handfuls of crackers and let loose more balloons . . ."

"Then at the end when they all begged for more, he stood quite still—and serious." Miss Penfold's manner too had changed. "He held up his hand for silence. There was an instant hush. I remember the light shining on his fair hair as he gave a formal bow and said, 'Young ladies and gentlemen, the performance is over. Your magician bids you farewell!' "

"That boy was a loss to the stage."

"Who knows? It was a long time ago. He can't have been more than sixteen or seventeen. You must find out what became of him, Miss Findon. I'm afraid these days one scarcely dares to ask."

We were pulling into the station where they took charge of me, found a porter, and saw me into the branch train.

"It's natural for you to be a little nervous." Miss Penfold bent over me to whisper while her brother was busy with my luggage. "But you'll be in good hands. Your aunts must be well known in Bidminster. Your circle of friends will be already made for you and you'll make others of your own." And as the guard's whistle blew, "I feel sure we'll meet again."

She had bolstered my confidence and that was fortunate. Having secretly expected to be met at Bidminster, I was again disappointed when there was no one to meet me at Saury, no one that is except a man in a peaked cap who put me and my portmanteau into a taxi cab, mumbling something about the train's being late; in which case it was lucky, I persuaded myself, that my aunts had elected to stay at home and so avoid an indefinite wait.

The house was not in Saury itself, a mere hamlet half hidden by blossoming trees. The road beyond wound between fields and copses. Leaning forward to catch the first glimpse of Hoodman House, I saw only sheep and lambs, a barn or two, a pheasant . . . then a twist in the road, a downward slope and at the bottom on the right a gated lane leading between hawthorns to a house about a quarter of a mile from the road. It seemed to face directly into a clump of trees so that only the side elevation was visible with a glassed-in verandah running the whole length of it, like an afterthought to a house too tall for its base, its slate roof too steeply pitched above the high walls. Such was my first fleeting impression before my attention was drawn elsewhere—to the field gate and the figure of a woman standing beside it. One of my aunts?

To claim that I knew at once which of them it must be is to anticipate the extraordinary effect she was to have on me. It couldn't possibly have worked, one would have thought, except at close quarters and certainly not at a distance of several hundred yards. All the same her faculty for arresting the attention without speech or action, merely by being there, affected me from the start, and it seems to me now that I recognized her even before the driver spoke. Not that he referred to her by name.

"She's there," he said, speaking for the first time since we had left the station.

Something in his tone as well as the extreme brevity of the remark puzzled me. It conveyed more than a statement of fact, one that he need not have made: the only person in sight could scarcely be overlooked, even a person so slender, so quietly dressed in gray. The outline of her figure grew clearer as we crept downhill. She stood by the gatepost. Behind her a wild cherry tree spread white blossom. The five-barred gate stood open. In welcome? She hadn't waved—or moved.

Having roused himself to state the obvious, the driver said no more but kept his eyes on the steep incline. The note I had detected—or imagined—in his voice had seemed to express not merely recognition but a restrained wonder in which surprise had

16

no part: he had expected her to be there. He turned in at the gate and stopped. I got out.

"Aunt May?" I said.

She smiled without speaking. Her stillness like her silences was to become familiar but even then I felt no awkwardness, being intent on looking at her almost as if that was what I was supposed to do. But that would have implied some self-awareness on her part and there was none, ever. I had seen her only twice and each time briefly, when I was too young to observe anyone dispassionately, even supposing Aunt May could ever be observed in such a way; but my impression was that she had not changed. There seemed a timeless quality in the picture she made: a picture in which the background of white blossom would need to be renewed year after year but not the central figure.

"Elinor." She bent and kissed me. Her cheek was cool, her hands were cold.

"You've been waiting too long," I said remorsefully. How delicate she was, her face of a smooth unblemished pallor under the coils of pale brown hair. Faint blue shadows underlined her blue eyes. Their expression was serene: they made no appeal, such as mine were doubtless making, to be liked. No such appeal was necessary. Liking, moreover, would have been a hopelessly inadequate word for my response to her.

"You've grown up." Her voice too was cool and light. "And you're more like your mother than ever. How sad it has all been for you! I was so very sorry to hear . . ."

She clasped her hands beneath her breast, as though coming to rest after an interval of activity. On the third finger of her left hand the ruby still glowed, too suddenly red, too heavy for so white and thin a finger. She looked away over my shoulder and up the hill toward the village and beyond. It was as if without any outward movement she had nevertheless moved, so obviously had she left me.

17

I waited, remembered the taxi. To find it still there, black and definite, was startling. The driver caught my eye.

"Will you," I began—it was still some distance to the house—"or shall I . . . ?"

She roused herself.

"Let him go on. We'll walk, shall we?" She smiled and took my arm. "There'll be so much to talk about."

"Oh Aunt May!" I felt a thrill of nervous happiness, as if soaring and yet doubting my power to sustain the flight.

"Not 'Aunt,' please. It makes me feel old. We think of you as our younger sister."

The taxi chugged ahead, startling birds from the hedgerows: finches and sparrows and a blackbird or two. They rose and flounced and dipped and disappeared. We followed, walking arm in arm between the wayside grasses under flowering hawthorn boughs, and in spite of there being so much to talk about, I don't remember talking at all until we came to the garden gate and a woman dressed in black came quickly down the path.

"Elinor! At last! We've been watching for you all afternoon. You remember me? I'm Kelda."

She kissed me without smiling and led me to the front door.

"That'll be half a crown." Having dumped my belongings on the step, the driver confronted us, his eyes directed impartially to the space between our two heads. May had vanished indoors.

"Please, let me. I have it ready." Indeed I had been fingering coins ever since we left the station.

"Oh well, just this once." Kelda dropped her voice as we went into the house. "You gave him more than half a crown. Not another shilling?"

"I'm not sure." In my flurry I could easily have given him an extra florin. Whatever the coin was he had accepted it with a gesture of salute to me and a rather sardonic glance at Aunt Kelda. "And he did have to wait."

18

"He's not used to being paid more than he asks. You've learned London ways—and that's a London hat."

I shed it with my jacket in the hall and followed her through the drawing room to a conservatory, where May was waiting. Tea things were set out on a bamboo table round which were placed three wicker chairs. Kelda went to the kitchen to make tea and brought in the pot herself. Since no servant appeared I concluded that it must be the maid's day off.

Seated between my aunts, with May on my right hand and Kelda on my left, I was able—at last—to give them my undivided attention.

Observing my aunts was to become a habit with me if not an obsession. They were well worth looking at. In age there was less than two years between them, but time, having met its match in May, had avenged itself a little on Kelda as well it might: she was then thirty-two. Her figure was slim, her movements were those of a young woman, her skin was fresh and clear; but even the fairest complexion can barely withstand the deadening effect of unrelieved black and Kelda, I was to discover, never wore anything else.

It was a relief to turn to May in her soft pale gray trimmed with sky blue velvet at the neck and cuffs. In fact I was in some danger of ignoring Kelda. After the restrained warmth of her unsmiling welcome she had lapsed into silence. The smooth flow of talk came from May, so that it was to her on my right that I continually faced, sometimes forgetting the black shape on my left.

The two were very much alike, both delicately pretty. But gazing devoutly at Aunt May (for some reason I have always had difficulty in referring to her as May, though I taught myself to do so) I saw Kelda's features refined, brows more thinly arched, skin more transparent, hair more silkily smooth with lighter tones of honey and gold. How can one define beauty or resolve the mystery whereby a pleasing appearance does more than please—much

19

more? Whatever the secret formula, it had been applied more successfully to one aunt than to the other. Or so it seemed to me on that first afternoon.

When tea was over, May slipped away. Kelda took the tray back to the kitchen, refusing my offer of help. For a few minutes I was alone, and with the sensation of having reached port after a risky voyage, I took my bearings. The conservatory, more precisely an enclosed verandah, faced toward the southwest. On the inner side a door at the far end led into the drawing room and behind me two windows with venetian blinds gave borrowed light to rooms as yet unknown to me. Beyond the potted camellias and hanging baskets of smilax and maidenhair fern there should have been, one felt, a garden, but there was only a narrow fenced-in strip of lawn between the house and an uncultivated field; so that it really was rather like being on board ship, safe for the time being but with unpredictable natural forces lapping at the edge of security.

"Now, then, I'll take you to your room."

I started. Kelda's return had been swift and silent.

"We thought you'd like to have your father's room."

But much as I longed to wash and change there was one question I burned to ask.

"I was wondering if Aunt May—I mean May—is going to be married."

The answer should not have surprised me: situations, I was beginning to discover, were not invariably clear-cut, especially at Hoodman House.

"I don't know," Kelda said. "Probably not."

Her reluctance to elaborate was so obvious that I apologized for having asked.

"It was just that—as she's still wearing her engagement ring, I thought . . ."

"Naturally, and you were right; May considers herself to be engaged—still." With the air of submitting to a duty, Kelda sat down again. "I shall have to tell you about it. May won't want to. The fact is her fiancé was lost in the war, on the Somme . . ."

"But that was years ago."

"It seems a lifetime ago but time means nothing to May now." She looked all at once tired and seemed to slump in her chair, as if a defense had been breached.

As was often to happen I forgot her in thinking of May. Faithful unto eternity! The words came to me as from a divine source. Such fidelity was more than romantic: it was awe-inspiring. No wonder I had felt in her some quality that set her apart. I had been prepared to feel it. "May behaved perfectly," my mother had said, speaking of her conduct at the wedding. Such faultless behavior had so influenced my youthful expectations that I had envisaged my younger aunt as a person very remarkable indeed and I had not been disappointed.

"Had they been engaged long?"

"They were always engaged." It was the sort of remark to be accompanied by an indulgent smile. Kelda wasn't smiling.

"Always?"

"Well, May was only seventeen when she and Dick were officially engaged."

Dick Tass! Of course! The handsome young conjuror at the mayor's Christmas party. Aunt May's fiancé! In my preoccupation with my luggage and the exact location of my ticket as we approached Bidminster station I had failed to make the possible connection. I made it now and found it apt. The youth who had captivated his audience with his looks and charm, with colored balloons and crimson crackers, then bowed and said farewell with grace and dignity, had become the man whom Aunt May had loved; still loved. The poetry and tragedy of his life matched the poetry and sadness of hers. No other man I had ever heard of or could imagine was worthy of Aunt May.

"It's a wonder they didn't marry before he went away."

"He came home twice on leave. The last time was in the

21

spring of 1915." Kelda was speaking slowly and with painstaking accuracy, as if the story were too poignant to tell in haste; as if being of such deep concern to May it must be of deep concern to her too.

"Then it was just at this time of the year that she saw him for the last time."

Kelda nodded. Her expression gave me my first hint of the extraordinary closeness my aunts shared. Fleetingly her face had reflected her sister's anguish as a print reproduces an original work of art; except that sympathy so acute must be as genuinely painful as the suffering that inspired it.

"And ever since, she has kept faith," I breathed, "though she will never see him again this side of the grave."

A tendency to express myself in this way was evidence, if further evidence were needed, of the uplifting effect upon me of Aunt May. All the same, the words were no sooner uttered than I regretted them. They had sounded overdone and tasteless.

"It isn't quite like that." The faint furrows deepened on Kelda's brow. "It's true that she will never see him again. But May believes that she will."

So that was it. That would account for her air of unearthly remoteness. Spiritualism was much talked of at that time. In the prevailing climate of death it offered hope and consolation to the bereaved. The subject had been well aired among the officers and nurses I had hobnobbed with at Rosedown Hall. Not that they believed in it: most of them no longer believed in anything. The paraphernalia of medium, planchette, table-rapping and ectoplasm had generally been dismissed as fodder for the gullible.

Yet some of them, both nurses and men, had strange things to tell: how in an ill-lit ward a night nurse might become aware of an extra bed and in it a corpse not entered on her list; how in the trenches waiting to go over the top, a man might glance aside on the fire-step and find at his right hand a fallen comrade standing as if alive. And intense concentration on the unseen, it was agreed, might in certain circumstances make it visible.

"When I saw her at the gate just now I did feel—that I wasn't the one she was waiting for."

"That was where she saw him for the last time. He had spent the evening here and he left for France the next day."

Kelda's eyes suffused, whether with actual tears or from excess of sympathy I could not tell. As for May, I could now interpret the driver's laconic "She's there." She was, he had implied, invariably there. Remembering his tone, I felt uncomfortable. To the vulgar mind Aunt May's behavior might appear eccentric, even freakish. One couldn't expect him to see it as an example of sublime fidelity.

Could she by revisiting the scene of parting re-create the being she had parted from? Could the convolutions of time in their infinite complexity ever, just for once, spin back a moment from the past? It seemed to me more likely that the sheer power of love could break the bonds of time and space and so bring back the dead. I was at a credulous age.

Upon these wide-ranging speculations Kelda broke in with a simplicity that could not but seem blunt.

"Come along. I'll take you upstairs."

Following her through the drawing room I discovered with a start that Aunt May was there, seated in the window. The bay was also occupied by an upright chair and a table bearing tubes of paint, a pot of brushes and drawing materials. But Aunt May was not using them. She sat on the window seat half concealed by the table so that only her head and shoulders were visible. In the colorless northern light they had the pure outlines and classic proportions of a marble bust: its stillness too. After the warmth of the sunny conservatory the room felt cold.

She turned, acknowledged me with a smile of touching sweetness, and looked away again down the lane toward the gate. I stole tactfully away.

23

3

§§§§§

DEAR MRS. BURNETT,

*You will be relieved to hear that in spite of all my worrying and
fussing about the journey I arrived safely yesterday afternoon. It was very
good of you to offer to come with me but it would have been a dreadful imposition when you have so much to do and there was really no
need . . .*

I dipped my pen in the inkpot and carefully shook off the
surplus drops, making an unnecessarily long pause before going
on, already troubled by an impulse toward concealment that
would have been hard to explain.

*especially after all your kindness to me which I shall never forget and shall
always be grateful for . . .*

That was certainly true; and I was genuinely glad that she
had not come, though not because it would have been an imposition. Of the actual reason I was less certain. The need to distinguish between what was genuine and its opposite, which would

later preoccupy me, remained as yet unacknowledged, like the first symptoms of a serious disease.

I have just got up and haven't unpacked . . .

The open trunk, clothes draped over chairs—did they account for my inability to concentrate on the warm, intimate kind of letter Mrs. Burnett would expect? Or was it just an increasing interest in breakfast? Last night's supper had been a meager affair. With brief messages to my friends at Rosedown and a promise to write again I brought my letter rather abruptly to a close. After all she wouldn't quite understand, even if I could adequately describe them, the indefinable ways in which my aunts were different from other people.

The house was quiet but a glance at my watch told me that the servants must be up. No mention of them had been made the night before and I wondered if Annie was still here. My father had often talked of her: she had taken care of him when his mother died and had become almost one of the family.

I found the kitchen at the end of a narrow passage leading from the hall. It was a vast square room, too lofty to please the eye and with a huge iron range as well as a wood-burning stove with hot plates: on one wall two windows, on another a double dresser with shelves eight feet long rising almost to the boarded ceiling and bearing row upon row of white plates rimmed with green leaves.

My entrance was greeted by a hollow clank from the intricate system of yellowish-buff water pipes festooning the far wall, and presently Kelda came in through the back door, lugging a scuttle of coal. She wore a black sateen apron over a black skirt and blouse and with no more than a brief, "There you are, Elinor," knelt down on the turned-back hearth rug.

"You're laying the fire yourself?"

"I'm used to it. As a matter of fact I like housework. It does

25

me good. I used to fritter away so much time when we had servants."

"Then you have no one . . . ," I began after some hasty mental revision.

"Not for years. Getting rid of them was the best thing we ever did. We sometimes have a woman in to scrub and we usually send the washing out. We do like having the house to ourselves."

"Well, I must say it's a lovely free feeling."

Just the three of us! The novelty of a servantless household appealed to me especially as according to my mother there had been something odd about the Findon servants. What on earth could it have been?

"People don't realize—an indoor staff is simply a burden to a small family. And I take a pride in being able to light a fire with one match." She did so. "We'll have breakfast in here."

It took a long time for the kettle to boil. While Kelda swept the front doorstep I set the table, then went upstairs to make my bed and came down again to find her laying another fire in the drawing room. I had set the table for three, but when we went back to the kitchen, Kelda got out a tray and another teapot.

"May doesn't come down to breakfast. She feels the cold."

"Let me take the tray. Which is her room?"

Aunt May was sitting up, a long braid of honey-colored hair over each shoulder. Her eyes had a fixed and absent look. I had the impression that she had been staring into space and needed a little time to take in who I was. What a blessing it was that Kelda had told me of her state of mind, otherwise I might have thought her manner peculiar. As a matter of fact I did think it peculiar but I had also got it into my head that Aunt May had been singled out by fate for special testing. Hers was to be a trial by ordeal, the trial of a spiritual kind, the ordeal lifelong. With the zeal of an attendant priestess I arranged the pillows, put a woolen stole round her shoulders, installed the tray.

"How kind of you, Elinor!"

26

When at last it came her voice was faint. Her eyes rested upon the tea and toast as on distant acquaintances whose identity she had forgotten. The room was above the drawing room with the same outlook on trees and empty fields from a similar window. It was comfortably and prettily furnished but I thought it cold.

"You must have a fire." The coldness of the house was to become another of my obsessions. I bustled over to the grate and removed the tapestry screen.

"Oh no, Kelda wouldn't like that. It would make more work."

"But there are three of us now, you know."

"No, really. The chimney hasn't been swept for years. I never have a fire even in winter."

"Then I'll bring you a hot-water bottle."

With a certain amount of fuss and a good deal of satisfaction I found one and filled it, though it meant waiting another ten minutes for our own tea.

"You're spoiling me." Aunt May smiled her patient smile as I eased the bottle into position under the covers. "You know just what to do. But then you're used to nursing, aren't you?"

"And I'm going to train as a nurse. It's to be my career."

It must have sounded a little pompous. She smiled again and didn't answer as she attempted to lift the heavy teapot, a task almost too much for her slender wrist.

"Let me."

At the door I turned and saw her take a first listless sip, the cup in her pale right hand; on the other holding the blue shawl to her throat, the ruby clung like a clot of blood.

Gradually, from my aunts themselves—and from others—I learned, not the story of their lives, certainly not that, but enough of its outline to explain their somewhat unusual situation. My grandfather's death had left them accountable only to each other. From the start I recognized their peculiar and exclusive closeness. How could so perfect an equipoise between two people be adjusted to accommodate the presence of a third person? Fortunately it never occurred to me that my coming could alter them: it was I who must adjust without disturbing the balance. To this end it behoved me to listen and watch and learn their ways. There could be something unnerving, I daresay, in the company of an energetic young woman engaged in so single-minded a course of conduct: some strain in being the object of a pair of tirelessly observant eyes; for in those early days it was in their appearance and outward seeming that my aunts interested me most. Naturally enough. What lay beneath took time to discover.

It was an ordered life that I had come to share, quiet and regular as a sisterhood: indeed a sisterhood it literally was, my role being that of the third sister, as Aunt May had said. Our actual relationship was so much less close that the suggestion could have been made only in a spirit of playful pretense. In the same spirit I could submit to it and be charmed by it as an unsuspecting insect might impale itself upon the leaves of the sundew or Venus's-flytrap, lured by their sweetness to become—at first—a willing victim.

"We thought you'd like your father's room," Kelda had said on the first evening. "But there are others if you would prefer one of them."

She took me to a narrow room above the hall and front door. Like most of the other bedrooms it opened onto a wide landing and was next door to Aunt May's. My father had left his mark on it in the shape of sporting prints and school photographs, a case of birds' eggs and another of butterflies pinioned on cork. No time must be lost in removing these masculine trophies and adapting the room to my own taste. I must buy—or find elsewhere in the house—a better carpet, a comfortable chair, a lamp, curtains . . .

"Cushions and things," Aunt May said vaguely when I met her on the stairs the next morning and mentioned the project. "There must be something."

"Yes, of course," Kelda said. "I was going to show you round. I'll just finish these vegetables."

I couldn't wait and rambled off on my own.

It must be said that the appeal of my new way of life had nothing to do with the house. It was almost aggressively without charm, neither attractive in its appearance nor suited to its present occupants: a large double-fronted family house facing north. Iron railings enclosed a small sunless garden and a few overgrown laurels; an iron gate opened onto a rough cart road. House and situation were ill-matched. Hoodman House was a suburban residence that had never come to terms with its country setting.

But it was roomy, substantial, impervious to wind and weather, its walls so thick that once inside with the doors closed one heard no sound from the outer world. The doors were elegantly molded, the stair rails of rich mahogany, the fireplaces wide and handsome, the ceilings decorated with elaborate plasterwork.

Not that I learned all this from my first enthusiastic skimming round its twelve rooms. What I did learn was that there was nothing, simply nothing in the house that I wanted for my own room. For a family house with ample space Hoodman held little in the way of spare furniture. In several of the rooms unfaded patches on the wallpaper bore witness to the removal of large pieces of furniture, possibly as part of a campaign to simplify the housework, which until my arrival Kelda must have been doing singlehandedly—Aunt May was clearly incapable of rough work of any kind.

I paused by an open window. The weather was fine and warm; sunshine and birdsong brought a thrilling reminder that it was spring: a necessary reminder, for there was no denying that the atmosphere indoors was bleak. Ornaments and silver had evidently been put away. Such softening touches must be sacrificed if one had to do the cleaning, polishing, and cooking oneself but it did cross my mind that freedom from the interfering presence of servants might be dearly bought.

It was with some idea of doing my bit toward the restoration of gracious living that I found a china vase in a spare bedroom and filled it with sprays of japonica. The coral-colored flowers should look well against the faded green wallpaper of the drawing room.

Aunt May was quietly at work at her easel. She looked round uneasily as I burst into the room. I had been too abrupt and must remember not to repeat my mistake. In Aunt May the balance of spiritual and physical stresses was so precariously poised that any shock however slight might distress her. Would it be possible with love and care to coax her gently back to the coarse world she had so mysteriously and successfully left?

Seeing myself as the gentle coaxer, I put the vase on a table and went softly to the window.

"May I look?"

She smiled her permission. The picture surprised me. What had I expected? Lilies, soft clouds, a willow tree, a harp, hands symbolically clasped or sadly unclasping—all expressive of a green and yellow melancholy?

Aunt May was putting the finishing touches to a cheerful nursery scene: a blazing fire; on a sheepskin rug two pink-sashed little girls fondling two blue-eyed kittens; a symposium of curls, bows, frilled pinafores. It was a period piece designed to arouse the very response I made.

"Oh, how pretty!"—and more thoughtfully and therefore with increasing surprise—"It's the sort of picture a great many people will like. You're very good at it, Aunt May."

Skill in supplying the masses with what they liked was not an attribute I would have counted on finding in the more ethereal of my aunts.

"You've painted others?" Though unexpected as the product of Aunt May's brush, the little scene was of a kind to be seen in scores of picture books, on chocolate boxes and nursery screens; and my aunt's manner was systematic rather than warmly inspired.

She nodded and languidly added a few touches of burnt sienna to the ruff of a marmalade kitten.

"You should have them framed," I said encouragingly.

Her only response being a murmur of assent I went out, quietly closing the door.

The few pictures I had seen in the house were oil paintings of mountain slopes and waterfalls or engravings of ruined abbeys; but now that my attention had been drawn to the subject I noticed here and there ghostly rectangles on the walls where other pictures must once have hung. For photographs I looked in vain. At a time when every home from stately mansion to humble cottage enshrined the photograph of a serviceman—private, officer, soldier, sailor, airman—framed in silver, velvet, or fretwork—in Hoodman House there was none.

On the whole that first tour of the house left me with the curious impression that its interest lay not in anything there was to be seen but in the things that were not to be seen—or were no longer there.

Dick Tass for instance. He interested me enormously. Surely Aunt May must have a picture of him, a photograph or a locket. If so she kept it hidden away. I took up her breakfast tray every morning and soon became familiar with the contents of her room. There was no likeness of her lost love.

"I keep on thinking of Dick," I remarked one morning on returning to the kitchen. "Dick Tass. The Penfolds made him seem so interesting. You know—I told you—the people I met on the train. Miss Penfold thought him the handsomest young man she had ever seen—and charming too." I repeated her account of his unorthodox performance as a conjuror. "Self-confident," she said, but I thought it sad, the way he bowed and said farewell, considering what was going to happen to him later on."

"Yes," Kelda said after a pause. "Yes, he was all those things."

"It's all right to mention him to you? I mean, just between

31

ourselves. You warned me not to talk about him to Aunt May and of course I wouldn't dream of upsetting her."

Kelda had given me no encouragement, nothing but a slight nod. The look of defeat that had come upon her when she told me of his death and May's strange state of mind had returned.

"I'm sorry. It's painful for you to speak about him. After all you must have known him almost as well as Aunt May did. You must have loved him too. Judging by what Miss Penfold said, no one could help loving him."

I reminded myself that they had grown up together. The two families had been close friends, my father said, and had shared Christmases and birthdays almost like relations.

"Was Dick much older than Aunt May?"

"He was almost exactly my age. We were christened at St. Bartholomew's in Bidminster on the same day." She spoke with the rather naive pride people sometimes feel when referring to important occasions in their lives.

"And he would have been your brother. It must have been dreadful for you all when the news came."

Again she barely nodded, but my relentless sympathy was not to be deflected. The subject was obviously painful to her and must be approached with the utmost tact, though one would have thought that after all this time there could be no harm in talking about it. It occurred to me that in their choice of husbands Kelda might have felt a little envious of the sister in whose radiance her own light had been permanently dimmed. She would have been barely human not to feel outshone by the more brilliant couple, Mr. Cade being as he was . . . Which reminded me:

"I've been wanting to tell you how sorry we were to hear about Mr. Cade. You were together such a short time, and you still . . ." I delicately indicated her black dress, stockings, and shoes and thought she flushed a little.

"Yes, I still wear mourning for the man I loved and always shall until the day I die."

32

There was a hint of defiance in her manner, as if she were trying to convince herself. It seemed unlikely, I thought, in the shallowness of my inexperience, that she could have loved Mr. Cade with such undying ardor. With some remorse I felt the unsuitability of probing further except:

"I do just wonder whether it isn't better sometimes to talk of such things." My only excuse for this smug remark was that I was quoting Mrs. Burnett, who had often comforted the sick and when they died, their mothers. She was a great believer in talking things out. "Rather than keeping it all bottled up and hidden away," I went on eagerly. "Not mentioning people doesn't make them easier to forget."

I put on an apron and absently washed the dishes, knowing that I was right. Hidden photographs and sealed lips might have the desired healing effect on some people but it hadn't worked with Aunt May, nor with me. The reverse had happened. Mr. Cade I could forget despite his widow's funereal appearance, but how was it possible not to think about Dick Tass with Aunt May always there as a living monument to his memory? How was it possible to look at her without thinking that she was thinking of him; or not to look at her when she was so beautiful.

Every day toward sunset when she rose from her easel as promptly as if a voice had called her; when she slipped out of the house and down the lane to stand by the gate to live again the last moments of their parting, it was increasingly as if I lived them too. I used to watch her pass between the hawthorns and take up the position in which I had first seen her. After a time she would come slowly back, a petal or two of cherry blossom on her hair, until all the spring blossom had fallen and it was summer.

The tall trees across the lane grew heavy with foliage, filling the view from our front windows. From the sunless patch of grass outside, one saw their reflection in the long panes, as if the house had nothing inside but moving shadows. The long summer evenings were very quiet. I read and wrote letters in the conservatory until the last of the sun had gone from it. The other rooms were already dark, the passages darker still. It was pleasanter out of doors.

For obvious reasons I avoided the lower reaches of the lane leading to the road. Instead I turned to the right outside the iron gate and soon made the territory to the east of the house as regularly my own as that to the west was Aunt May's. There was rarely anyone about at that time of night, or indeed at any time. When the swallows had ceased to swoop, the bats fluttered from under the trees and rabbits noiselessly occupied the fields.

Before Hoodman House came—so unsuitably—to share it, the cart road had belonged exclusively to Winkblade Farm. The long low house a few minutes' walk farther on had been unoc-cupied for years and was falling into disrepair, but it had a mellow picturesqueness that took my fancy. I made its garden wall the limit of my walks and often found myself thinking of the young Findons and Tasses who had picnicked in its garden and of the nightingale that never came there; and I thought of Aunt May and Dick Tass plighting their troth in this very lane: a troth unbroken by death.

And somehow, whether through solitude or sympathy, a sen-sation of waiting took possession of me too and brought with it a growing tautness of the senses. Sometimes, walking homeward down the lane, I would catch sight of Aunt May walking up it. At such times it seemed kindest to rush indoors ahead of her. After the scented twilight outside, the house was dark and felt larger than during the day so that one's eyes unconsciously sharpened for fear of bumping into something at a turn in the passage or in a dusky corner. Aunt Kelda was usually in the kitchen. We used to call good night to each other. I didn't disturb her but went to bed early, where for a time I lay listening for footsteps on the path or a knock at the door which I knew could never come.

Although I dropped into bed each night worn out by unac-customed housework, I wasn't sleeping well. My dreams, whatever

34

their shape and content, were touched with apprehension: something was going to happen, someone was coming nearer. Lying awake in the early light, I felt his image take on definition: the officer's peaked cap pushed back from fair hair, the khaki tunic, the polished buttons. Unspoken of, never to be seen, he grew more powerful, more persistent, more impossible to ignore.

Once I woke to the echo of his voice. "Not here," it said, "not here," and faded into an infinity of space leaving in my mind a residue of distress; yet it was intimate too, caressing even, as if a tenderness that should have been for Aunt May were being shared with me: more than shared. Given wholly? I lay lost in regret for what had never been. If only I had known him, I could have loved him too.

In the morning I was usually myself again and could at least distinguish dream from reality; could even recognize my state of mind as thoroughly unhealthy. Not that my interest in Dick Tass grew less. As he wasn't to be mentioned in May's presence, I got what I could out of Kelda, and that was precious little until she put a stop to it altogether.

"For heaven's sake stop asking me about him. It can't possibly matter to you what he did or what he thought and said."

She had been sitting with her elbow on the kitchen table, her head resting on her hand. We had finished breakfast. She had eaten little and was heavy-eyed, as if she hadn't slept.

"I'm sorry. I only—"

"I'll tell you what it is." Her vehemence startled me. "You've fallen in love with him too."

"But that's impossible."

"Oh no. With him nothing was impossible." She stopped abruptly but presently, with what seemed a deep weariness of body and mind, she said, "He's dead. Leave him alone. Let him rest."

"I'm sorry. I won't mention him again."

The effect was not what she had intended. Merely to have

spoken of him in so desperate and forthright a way had made him actual. Even though dead? I had sense enough to know that her warning was justified: my feeling for Dick was not only second-hand but morbid, a pallid print of Aunt May's true devotion.

Fortunately, I told myself, it gave me a fresh insight into May's state of mind. Anyone with nursing experience could see that she was sick. So long as I was here (with a flash of joy I remembered that my stay was only temporary) I must find some means of helping her.

But owing to a misunderstanding on my part or a lack of clarity on Kelda's there was one factor I had failed to grasp, and when I did grasp it—well, it didn't make life easier.

4

WHEN THE BELL clanged at the back of the house one morning, it was I who went to open the yard door. My first impression was of a tall, dignified man inappropriately dressed as a tramp. His patched and faded overcoat hung loosely from his thin shoulders like a medieval cloak.

"Good day to you, miss." He doffed his battered felt hat but without haste and with no more deference than was suitable from a gentleman calling on ladies.

While I wondered what to do with him, Kelda joined us, asked him in, and went back to the kitchen. I followed, leaving him to rest on the bench outside the back door.

"It's Sintram," Kelda said in answer to my whispered inquiry. "He drops in from time to time."

It was a tribute to his personality that she should put it like that. He was one of several vagrants who came our way on the long trudge from one workhouse to the next, appeared at the back door to ask for a drink of water and were given tea, bread, and cheese. Their plight was only too common in the early twenties when thousands of men, having fought for a land fit for heroes to live in, had come home to find that there was no place in it for them.

But Sintram was a veteran of earlier wars. He had turned up

one day about twenty years ago and had offered casual labor in exchange for food and cast-off clothing, especially boots. My grandfather had taken to him. By a happy coincidence the two were much of a size, particularly as to the feet. They became to some extent cronies and smoked their pipes together in the backyard. After my grandfather's death Sintram continued to call. Usually we could see people as they came up the lane and so have warning of their arrival, but Sintram had a trick of arriving out of the blue, unseen until the last minute, as he had done this morning. There was a simple explanation for this as I later discovered.

By this time even light work was beyond him and he had little to say as he sat stoically on the bench his friend no longer shared.

"It always gives me a shock," Kelda said as she swiftly cut slices of bread, "to see him in father's old suit. And there's nothing left to give him, not even another pair of boots. You go and talk to him. He's an interesting old man."

He sat with his head resting against the wall. His face, relaxed in the warm sun, was lit by intelligent hazel eyes of a peculiar brightness despite his age.

"You're not from this part of the world. A relative of the ladies, perhaps?"

I explained my presence.

"Your grandfather was a good friend of mine."

His manner was so completely that of a visitor exerting himself to be pleasant that one forgot the stubbled chin, the tattered clothes, and the crude meal—one that he desperately needed, judging by the speed with which he disposed of it.

"And what's the news?" Kelda sat down for a brief rest on the low wall enclosing the rockery. He obliged us with a few items of information: the roof had fallen in at Saury Mill; the housekeeper at the vicarage had broken her arm.

"And Winkblade Farm. But you'll have heard about that.

They say it's to be let at long last—and not before time if it's ever to be fit to live in again."

He had heard the news in the village. Kelda was skeptical.

"We've heard that so many times and it never comes to anything. I'll believe it when the people actually move in."

"Oh, I do hope it's true."

His eyes rested on me, noting my satisfaction. Conscious of having given something away, some hint of deprivation I had been unaware of, I added lamely, "It's such a dear old place," and went indoors to tell Aunt May.

People coming and going past her window! She would see the whole operation of their moving in. It would do her a world of good. I rushed through the house and forgetful of my resolution never to startle her, burst into the drawing room, where my Aunt May was sitting in her usual place at the window, hands folded in her lap.

"News! We've just heard. You won't believe . . . It's happened at last." I paused to give the climax its full measure of drama. "It's about . . . Winkblade." The word died away as I saw the harm I had done.

She had stiffened, as if struck by a lethal charge of electricity. A flood of deep color suffused the faint rose tints of her face so that I seemed to see her features through a purplish red veil. Her eyes widened, seemed immense, altogether different from those eyes of soft and patient blue whose effect on me had been so uplifting. Their expression puzzled me.

"I'm so sorry. I've startled you . . ."

"Elinor!" Kelda appeared in the doorway, took in the scene at a glance and stormed into the room. "What have you done?"

"Nothing, I was only going to tell her about Winkblade."

Ignominiously I turned tail. From the hall I heard them talking in lowered tones but could make nothing of what was said and wandered unhappily down the front path and into the lane.

To my annoyance Sintram was there about twenty yards

away, as if he had heard the gate close and stopped to look back. He waited. I forced myself to speak naturally.

"Is this the way you usually go to Bidminster, instead of through the village?"

"That's right, Miss Elinor. Past the farm and by the path over the fields to the Tile Sheds. It comes out on the road from Upper Saury to Bidminster."

His face was refined, narrow-boned and with a long sensitive mouth. The spare features and luminous light-colored eyes gave him a goatlike look, gentle and dignified.

"You'll have friends here, a young lady like you?" And as I shook my head, "Well, you won't be staying long. Not too long." It was not a question, not exactly a statement, more like a piece of advice, and since it was kindly given, it was tempting to think of it as wisely given too. I felt all at once tearful.

Pulling myself together, I groped in my pocket for the half-crown that should have been there, then remembered I had given it to Kelda to pay the sweep who had cleaned Aunt May's chimney that morning. The lambent eyes, perceptive and kind, had seen my movement and interpreted it correctly. He shook his head, smiled a little, and shuffled away, leaving me to blush over my near blunder. I noticed that he didn't pass the farmhouse but stepped over a low wall and disappeared into one of its outbuildings.

I half expected that Aunt May would have taken to her bed. However when I went indoors again Kelda was waiting for me in the hall with the air of defending the drawing room door.

"Leave her alone, Elinor."

"I have no intention of disturbing Aunt May again," I said with what seemed to me permissible coolness. It grieved me to think that I had upset the very person I most wanted to help and care for, but however clumsy my behavior, it had not been ill-intentioned. Its effect had been out of all proportion to the cause: a trivial piece of local news—as I explained to Kelda.

"It can't have been that," she said crisply as we sank into our usual places with the kitchen table between us. "It must have been something else you said."

"All I said was something about there being good news at last."

"Don't you see what that would mean to her?" Kelda struck the table with her palm in a gesture of despair. "Didn't you realize what she might think the good news was?"

"Well, no, I didn't. And I still don't for that matter."

"The news that she has been waiting for. That he had come back."

"You don't mean—Dick?"

"She thinks of nothing else day and night. Surely you've seen that."

"Of course I have. You told me that she hoped she would see him again some day. People do hope that the dead will communicate with them or even appear but if that were to happen it would be a private experience, wouldn't it, not the kind of thing to be told them by an outsider like an item of news. Suppose it was my mother, for example." The comparison was no sooner made than abandoned. A salutary inward voice reminded me that my mother would never involve herself—or me—in a so bizarre an experience. "It's not as if Aunt May expected him to come back—really come back—in the flesh."

"But she does," was the amazing reply. "That's what she does expect—hope for—long for"—and as I stared in disbelief—"he was reported missing. Didn't I tell you? His death has never been confirmed."

"No, you didn't tell me."

An anxious review of the words with which I had burst in upon Aunt May convinced me that they had been particularly ill chosen. All the same—"It isn't possible. You know that, Kelda. He must be dead."

"Of course he's dead." There was deadness in her voice. "Dead, dead. Nothing on earth can bring him back."

It was a genuine lapse into despair that I was witnessing, and no wonder. How could any reasonable person deal with the hopelessness of such a delusion as Aunt May's. How could it be endured, years of close companionship with someone who had—there could be no beating about the bush—taken leave of her senses?

And yet—

"I suppose"—the thought was tentative, even frightening in its power to shatter the settled state of things and reassemble them in a new pattern, though surely for the better—"it isn't absolutely impossible. One has heard . . ."

What had one heard? A Captain Bowes (the case had been marveled over at Rosedown Hall) reported killed at Arras had been found, astoundingly, to the joy of his grieving relatives, in an army hospital in France. Then there was the more romantic tale of a British private horribly wounded and left for dead who had been found, after his section had been withdrawn, by local people, a French farmer and his family returning to their farmhouse. They had taken him in and cared for him. It was two years after the Armistice when he came home.

"His death will never be confirmed." Kelda was speaking with the bleak certainty of death itself. "Thousands of unnamed dead are still lying on the battlefields of France. Dick is one of those."

It was all very well in the kitchen to think of Aunt May as mildly insane. One had only to see her face to withdraw the phrase as crude and insensitive. When half an hour later I took her the glass of wine and the biscuit she always had at that time of day, her self-control seemed perfectly restored. Not that she had actually lost it. Her only movement had been to press her two hands to her temples, as if to contain an explosive force of emotion. The other changes—the deathly pallor, the hectic flush, the strange look—were the involuntary response to inward stress.

Now as she held the wineglass to her lips, her beauty overwhelmed me, as if I saw it for the first time. Her delicacy, her stillness, I told myself, were not as they had sometimes seemed, the cold perfection of a sculptured bust. Within the exquisite outer form, I thought, resorting once more to the language of romantic poetry, breathed a suffering human heart. Her look of unearthly fragility was that of porcelain not marble and could be shattered by a careless word.

"Thank you, Elinor." The wine had brought a little color to her cheeks. She set down the glass.

"I'm sorry I upset you."

"No, no. It was not your fault, dear. You mustn't reproach yourself. You have brought us so much comfort, Elinor. We can't do without you, you know."

I kissed her cheek. The penitent gesture kindled a light in her eyes, a faint spark in the uttermost depths of their ethereal blue. I knew that it would instantly be gone. She would turn her head. She would look out again down the winding lane as she had done year after year in sun and snow. She would not change. I had learned my lesson. All I could do was dedicate myself to the task of caring for her as for an invalid; and indeed she was suffering a strange malady that nothing but a miracle could cure.

Now that Dick Tass was no longer to be thought of as an apparition he should cease to haunt my dreams. And yet as dread of his ghost faded, a new anxiety took its place. What if Aunt May, unique in every other way, should also be unique in this one tremendous way? What if destiny had singled her out and molded her to become the instrument of a miraculous event? Suppose it really was going to happen and by some strange insight she knew it. There is practically no limit to the excesses of a youthful imagination in solitude at night or in the twilight of a country lane.

If the impossible should happen, in what condition would he return? Not even by a miracle, I told myself somewhat illogically, could he be as he had been. Remembering the shattered wrecks at Rosedown Hall of once strong men, maimed, crippled, their nerves and lungs destroyed by poison gas, embittered, all astray in a world no longer theirs—I almost hoped for Aunt May's sake that he was dead. Waiting could be safer than fulfillment. Things were best left as they were.

But the sensation of waiting persisted and with it despair at the endlessness of it all. I was becoming part of it. The normality of life at Rosedown Hall had slipped away. The outer world was withdrawing. Somehow I had lost the detachment whereby I could view my aunts and their problems with the freshness of an outsider come on a longish visit. Worse still, they needed me. It wouldn't be easy to get away or even to remind them that I wouldn't always be there.

Sometimes I was bewildered by the strangeness of their situation: one so briefly married and so conspicuously mourning a husband she never mentioned; the other promised but unpossessed, neither free nor bound, devoting her days to a man neither known to be alive nor known to be dead. Thinking in this way, I had the uneasy feeling that I had found in Hoodman House as weird a departure from the ordinary as in my childhood fantasies, when I had placed it in the same category of dwellings as the witch's gingerbread house and the palace of the Snow Queen.

5

WHEN DID I first suspect that there was something more: that something was being kept from me? If I went into a room and found my aunts together they were rarely talking. But there was communication between them of some sort. Either what they had to impart to each other had all been said before I appeared or they imparted it without speaking, just as they acted with complete interdependence like the two hands of a clock.

Their unity excluded me and seeing them wordlessly together, I sometimes fell victim to the disturbing fancy that together they actually became a third person, a being more than the sum of its two parts. From whatever was hatched in this silent colloquy I was kept in ignorance. What were they concealing from me? It didn't take me long to find out, or so in my innocence I thought.

My shopping trip to Bidminster had been postponed several times, not from lack of enthusiasm on my part but always because some small inconvenience would have been involved, some hitch in the smooth running of the household that would never have occurred to me if one of my aunts, usually Kelda, had not pointed it out.

At first I was too busy to notice our isolation. When it did dawn on me that I was seeing no other human being than my aunts for days on end, well—the remedy lay in my own hands. If I wanted to go to town, it was just a matter of walking to the station; or I could arrange with the sardonic taxi driver to drive me to Bidminster.

"What became of Annie?" I asked Kelda one morning as we cleared away the breakfast things. It may have been the daunting prospect of yet another day of household chores that prompted me to think with some nostalgia of such domestic mainstays as Annie.

"Annie left," Kelda said curtly but not at once. "Years ago."

"She must have been very old. My father was fond of her. He said she was like a mother to him. That was before my grandfather married again of course," I added, lest any slur should attach to Kelda's mother.

All the same when she offered no more information, I felt entitled to persist. Recalling her earlier remark about the servants—"We got rid of them"—I found it distasteful. Indeed I was finding it hard to keep on good terms with Kelda. Her unaccountable changes of mood were beginning to irritate me. As an adopted sister I had put my shoulder to the wheel, fetched and carried, swept and dusted, paid my share of the household expenses, and had therefore earned a sister's right to know what was going on: or in this case, what had gone on.

"She is still alive?"

"So far as I know." Kelda glanced at the clock as if suddenly aware that the morning was slipping away.

"I should like to see her and talk over old times. Where is she living now?"

"She went to live in Bidminster," Kelda said—and became absorbed in her shopping list.

"Would you like me to do the shopping?" The offer was made automatically. I knew that she would refuse and suggest some reason why I should stay at home while she was out.

"No, thank you, Elinor. The walk does me good and it would

46

be such a help if you would start the stew. Besides, May likes to feel there's someone in the house. You've made a wonderful difference to her spirits, I can tell."

Through the open door I could see Aunt May coming downstairs to begin her day. She moved slowly and quietly with a drifting motion, as if borne on invisible pinions. I could see no difference in her manner, nor in her spirits, certainly no change that I could claim credit for. But at the mere sight of her my irritation faded.

"I was asking Kelda what happened to Annie."

"Dear old Annie!" Her accompanying smile was tender. "Enjoying her retirement, I suppose. So thoroughly well deserved." She passed serenely into the drawing room, having scarcely displaced the air except to leave a faint trace of perfume.

My offers to do the shopping in the village had always been refused. But I had not been slow to visit the shops on my own accord—the post office, the butcher's, Mrs. Green's general shop—and was soon known in all of them. One clang of Mrs. Green's bell as I went in, one searching glance from the other side of the counter and I was placed.

"You'll be the young Miss Findon?"

I know now that her quick glance at my purse was one of mingled hope and calculation, but I was only in quest of biscuits to devour in the privacy of my walk home. I seemed always to be hungry.

On another occasion I popped into the butcher's, attracted by a succulent leg of lamb hanging in the shaded window.

"For Hoodman House?" Mr. Carshott unhooked it doubtfully. "It isn't Mrs. Cade's usual cut. She generally has middle neck or scrag."

Again the sight of my purse reassured him.

"Chump or chine?" he asked more happily, sharpening his knife.

"All of it."

He beamed, found the weather perfect for the time of year, and dispatched his boy posthaste on a bicycle to Hoodman House. Kelda had been astonished and pleased but reproved me for extravagance.

But it was with Mrs. Torgill that I made friends. Not until my third visit to the village did I find her tiny sweet shop, squeezed between two other cottages, its front room equipped with a green oil-clothed table as counter and shelves of green glass jars of boiled sweets and toffees.

Stepping down from the street was like entering a cool sea cave. One peered over the counter into further depths where Mrs. Torgill spread her ample form over a low chair. Rising, she seemed to flounder to the surface like an amiable seal, pale, plump and pleasant, and with a tendency, either physical or temperamental, to sigh.

"I've seen you once or twice," she said when I first went in and ordered a glass of lemonade for old times' sake. " 'That'll be Mr. Vincent's girl,' I said to George, 'or I'm much mistaken.' 'Never,' he says. 'You mark my words,' I says to him, 'she's come here from the south, an orphan, poor girl, Mr. Vincent's daughter.' "

"You remember my father?"

"He could be sitting there still where you're sitting now on that very stool. That's whether I remember him or not. Drinking this very lemonade." She wiped the base of the glass and accepted my three halfpence.

"I know he used to come here. He told me."

"On Saturday afternoons. He'd bring them all, bless him."

"All?"

"The children. His little sisters, Miss Kelda and Miss May— and their friends that came out from Bidminster. They'd come for the day in a brake and play in the fields and paddle in the river while the ladies and gentlemen visited at your grandfather's. I can see them now, the boys in their sailor suits and the girls in their white frocks and sashes—and sure as life Mr. Vincent would bring them here and buy them licorice and mint imperials and coconut lace . . ."

Mrs. Torgill and I sighed in unison as we contemplated these lavish scenes. She was a woman of abundant leisure, thanks to a hardworking unmarried daughter, and of that truly creative turn of mind that finds in other people's lives the very stuff of romance. I don't think she invented. Life itself offered all the poetry she needed.

"There was one wet day—they came in here to shelter, the whole troupe of them with their fishing rods and butterfly nets. Little Master Dick—he was the one that used to entertain them all. Seemingly he and Miss Kelda used to sing duets. They were about the same height. There they stood, just there." She pointed to the spot on the green-painted wall behind me. " 'Now wait for me, Kelda,' he says and beat the time. She watched him, all eyes, and then off they went as sweet as birds . . . And now he's gone. He'll never sing again. And your poor father. We never thought in them days. We never thought. And a good thing we didn't. Some things don't bear thinking about—and it's all so different now."

So sighing and sipping, I enlarged not only my acquaintance with Mrs. Torgill but with the history of my family, adding here and there a mental stitch or two to its tapestry until bit by bit new shapes began to emerge and suggest unexpected patterns.

"You were at Mrs. Cade's wedding," Mrs. Torgill said. "Our Susan was taken on at the House for two days to help in the kitchen. She told me that Mr. Vincent's wife and little girl had come from London or thereabouts."

"Not so little, Mrs. Torgill. I was nearly fourteen."

"A lovely-looking lady, Mr. Vincent's wife, Susan said, in crêpe de chine. And Miss May, the centerpiece. Well, not the bride, but as I've said many a time, Miss May looks like a bride every day of the week. 'Give her wings,' our Susan says, 'and you'd see an angel fit for heaven.' " These sentiments drew forth a deeper sigh than usual and the unexpected corollary; "Poor Miss Kelda!"

"Poor?"

"Oh it's just my way of speaking." Breathing deeply, Mrs. Torgill sank below the surface of the counter and resumed her chair.

Drinking lemonade became one of my diversions. Fathoms deep in Mrs. Torgill's mermaid's cavern, it was pleasant to slip back in time to the days of the old queen. Viewed from the darker side of the Armageddon that cut us off from them, they merged into one long golden afternoon in which the young Findons and their friends stretched their nets to catch butterflies and dropped their lines for fish in a security untroubled by any thought of what must come. Pleasant but sad. An uneasy feeling that metaphorically speaking most of the butterflies and fish had got away and that some of the catchers had become the caught sometimes troubled me when, not always willingly, I went back to Hoodman House.

To revert to old Annie . . . Having failed to find out anything about her from my aunts, when next I went to the village for stamps, I dropped in on Mrs. Torgill.

"Our Susan was asking after you." Mrs. Torgill handed me my glass. I perched on the stool. " 'Fancy Miss Elinor coming to live here,' she says. 'I'd never have thought it.' Well, none of us would."

"Was Annie still at my grandfather's when we came to the wedding? I don't think she can have been. We would have talked to her."

"Annie Thacker? No, there were no regular servants even then. For the wedding they took in this one and that from round about and paid them by the hour."

"You don't remember how long it is since Annie left?"

"Let me think." Mrs. Torgill rolled her eyes upward, as if consulting an unearthly almanac. "The war had started, that I do know because Lucy—she was the housemaid—was walking out with a soldier. It never came to anything. Then there was Mabel— and Annie. They were all given notice, real sudden. Annie came here in a daze, and can you wonder? 'I'm leaving,' she says. 'Come into the back,' I says. 'It's a wicked shame.' Excuse me saying it, Miss Elinor, after all you weren't there at the time nor your mother, and Mr. Vincent would never have treated Annie nor anybody else like that. Of course we always knew that things weren't as they had been up there, but to turn the three of them away with a week's warning . . ."

"When would that be?"

"Well on in the year it would be. Our Susan came in from picking apples. 'Have you all the apples you need up at the House, Annie?' she says. 'There's plenty here this year.' 'I neither know nor care what they need,' Annie says, 'seeing as they don't need me.' And she burst out crying."

September? But in which year? And why was I suddenly curious to know more about the dramatic departure of Lucy, Mabel, and Annie when it was only Annie's present whereabouts that concerned me?

"It wouldn't be more than a day or two after Annie left and went to her niece in Bidminster that Mrs. Cade went away as well. (She was still Miss Findon then.) Yes, she went off to London and was away a good long time. So far as I recollect it must have been January or February before she was back in Saury—and then she was married in the summer."

So it must have been the autumn of 1915 when she went away.

"She must have gone to London for her trousseau."

Mrs. Torgill shook her head.

"There was no talk of her getting married when she went to London, not so far as I know. Any talk I heard was more about Miss Kelda being left on the shelf if she didn't look sharp. It seemed as if she never would marry. It would be near the next

Whitsuntide when the news got round that she was engaged at last to this Mr. Cade, a musical gentleman visiting Bidminster, and she started going to Miss Byrd for fittings. There isn't much Miss Byrd doesn't know about wedding dresses, say what you like about London."

We were interrupted by a gaggle of small children, and while they wrangled over lucky potatoes and lozenges with mottoes, the thread of our conversation was lost.

Coming up from the depths of the shop into the bright day brought in every sense a change of outlook. How different my aunts had been in those days! May had been perfectly capable of running the house for months on end and looking after my grandfather without servants while Kelda was away. Of course she was happy then in her engagement, even though Dick hadn't come home for a whole year before his death. Even so . . . It was the Findons' attitude to their servants that I was beginning to dwell on as a kind of clue to other mysteries of which I was as yet only half aware.

For the time being I could see no further than the obvious fact that it was all to do with money—or rather the lack of it. Walking slowly home I brooded on that unsatisfactory affair, the wedding. The oddity my mother had noticed in the servants had not taken the form of eccentric behavior with plates and glasses; she had sensed their unfamiliarity with the household. It would not have occurred to her that they were hired. All the same I marveled that her sharp eyes had not discovered signs of what I had at last been forced to acknowledge—though at that time it had still been possible to cover up the cracks in the imposing structure of Hoodman House. There had been no telltale patches of wallpaper where solid pieces of furniture had once stood. The chatter of guests had diverted attention from other things, which had since gone from bad to worse.

At first I had supposed that my aunts had disposed of heavy furniture in order to refurnish in a more practical style. Of this I had approved, though it had crossed my mind to wonder whether my third share of the house included a similar share of its contents.

The ban on servants had been put to me as a bold step toward an adventurously modern way of life. Kelda's concentration on housework had seemed a gallant attempt to make the adventure work. The stews and bread-and-butter puddings had been—literally—harder to swallow, but it could be argued that the stew pot could be left on its own whereas the more expensive cuts of meat needed more attention. The unconventional style of living ruled out conventional entertaining, and so there could be no visiting either.

It was uncomfortable to feel that in my enthusiasm for looking after—and up to—Aunt May I had missed certain warning signals, or misinterpreted them: that somehow I had been—manipulated.

When the road took a twist and fell away in a long slope at my feet, I stopped, not yet in a mood to go home, not quite ready to put the stark question to my aunts: "What happened to the Findon fortune?" The question was of vital importance to me. Its answer could affect my whole life.

My resentment centered on Kelda. It was to her that I had blithely handed over most of the money I had brought with me, almost sixty pounds, and yet for all that we were obviously in debt to the village tradesmen. Because she had not been open with me, I now condemned her utterly. Deception hung in the air like dust. The country silence seemed pregnant with unpleasant truths concealed. From the five-barred gate at the foot of the hill the lane curved up to the house, rising offensively from the harmless fields, the sharp upward thrust of its slate roof at odds with the sky.

Five minutes later I arrived home, nervous but resolute, with enough restraint left me to go in by the back door to avoid disturbing Aunt May. Kelda was darning stockings in the morning room down a passage from the hall. It contained little but a table and the high-backed chair she was sitting in.

"There's something I want to know." The harshness of my voice must have startled her. Wariness leapt into her eyes. I faced her squarely. "Are we hard up?"

She gave a gasp. Her shoulders relaxed. It was almost as if she had feared a different question. Not that she liked the one I had asked.

"I don't care for your tone, Elinor."

"And if it's true, I don't like your keeping it from me. It is true, isn't it?"

"Yes." Her face was heavy with resentment. "It's true."

"How poor? Go on, tell me." She seemed unable to speak but made savage jabs at the woolen stockings with her needle. "A third share of everything was to be mine, remember. I ought to have been told what happened to it. Why didn't you tell me?"

I believe she was genuinely at a loss. Habits of concealment had so grown on her that she had forgotten how to be straightforward.

"What happened to the money my grandfather left?"

"Money?" She spat out the word bitterly. "There was no money."

"None?"

"It was all my father could do to pay his way. Very well, you've asked and I'll tell you. He'd overspent and been let down and was owed money he never got—and stopped caring. My mother was insanely extravagant. Money flowed through her hands like water. It's all right for you." She spoke with such rough directness that I flinched. "You've lived in comfort and your father never did anything to help us here, although he had ten thousand pounds left him by his mother."

"My father had no idea that you needed help."

"He took it for granted, you mean, that he'd come in for a share of my father's money—and so did you. Without lifting a finger. It's been different for me. Ever since I was your age I've known what was happening—the debts staring us in the face.

Things weren't as bad then as they are now but I knew we were slipping downhill; and ever since I've been scheming and contriving and skimping to keep up appearances and working my fingers to the bone—"

"But why," I interrupted, "did you have to keep it from *me?*"

Or from anyone, I might have asked, but I knew how painful it must be for women of my aunts' generation and class to come down in the world—even though the world was changing more rapidly than ever before and the old conventions were losing their hold.

"You said—debts."

"There were debts. I managed to persuade my father to sell land, even most of the garden. We paid off most of them before he died—the builders' merchants and so on . . ."

Even more than the distressing facts, her bitterness shook me. The very room was unfriendly and full of tension. When a breeze stirred the venetian blind it made me jump. A feeling crept over me of having been there before in just such a state of stress. Something like this had happened before, here in this room. I almost knew what would happen next.

"Mr. Tass?" I asked. "My grandfather's partner. Was he ruined too?"

"It's years since the partnership ended." Kelda's tone was one of impatient contempt for my ignorance, for all the indifference she had resented in my parents. "The Tasses are very comfortable, to say the least. Trust them to look after themselves."

"But surely your husband"—it was none of my business and yet her private affairs, like every other family circumstance, had become my affair too—"he must have provided for you."

Her look was blank, as if I had mentioned one of the discarded pieces of furniture she now had difficulty in remembering. For a second I wondered if Mr. Cade had ever existed; but I couldn't have imagined the polished blackness of his hair and

55

boots any more than I could overlook the blackness of mourning she wore for him.

Her eyes had shifted, became wary again.

"No, he couldn't. Julius had nothing either."

Then she must have married him for love. No one would have guessed it. There was no hint of remembered tenderness in her manner. Presumably the widow's weeds said it all.

"There's the house," I said in the stupefied way in which people communicate in a calamity.

"There's the house," she repeated. "Oh yes, we have a roof over our heads." She glared round the room, as if planning to blow it apart with the force of sheer hatred.

I too looked round. On the wall opposite the window a beige rectangle with a smaller one above showed where the chiffonier had stood. I remembered it and the glass dome standing on it.

"If there's absolutely nothing else, what have you been living on, you and Aunt May?"

"We've lived," Kelda said with the same suppressed fury, "on seventy-five pounds a year between us and on what May can make from selling her pictures. We managed to find an agent for them in London. He takes them now and again."

"So that's why you stayed so long in London?"

The remark was involuntary, the result of piecing together two items of information. There seemed nothing in my words to account for their effect. Kelda's eyes had darkened, her jaw sagged, her hands shook. It was as if she were inwardly falling apart. With an effort of will she got to her feet and leaned heavily with one hand on the table.

"London?"

The word seemed to have severed all connection with what had gone before. She had lost her way like an old woman whose memory lets her down, or more alarmingly like a woman unhinged.

"You've been gossiping in the village, haven't you? You've come here to pry into my personal life . . ."

Thank goodness, I thought, shaken by her unreasonableness and by a hint of violence in it, she's only my father's half-sister. Thank goodness the relationship is no closer. And with rather splendid calmness I said in a tone of ice, "Whatever my reason for coming, I understand now why you were so pleased to see me. My money has been useful, hasn't it?"

I had my back to the door. A change in Kelda made me turn. With relief I saw that Aunt May had come in—slight and beautiful and quiet. It was remarkable—her gift of bringing light into a room; and this time she brought something else: authority. She was a little taller than Kelda, Kelda as she was now at any rate, head bowed, shoulders bent.

"Yes, Elinor." Her voice had never seemed more gentle. "We are pleased to have you here but not just because we're poor and you have helped us so generously. We love you for your own sake. You must forgive us. We should have confided in you from the beginning—or before you came. But we were brought up, you see, to think of poverty as a crime—the worst of sins." The candor of her smile made me ashamed. Anger and disappointment left me. "Of course we know better now." She turned to her sister, a new inflection in her voice. "We know now that there are much worse sins, don't we, Kelda?"

I hadn't expected her little speech to conclude in that way. It bewildered me for a moment. Kelda had been listening transfixed, had looked up to gaze at the soft curve of her sister's lips as if hypnotized. May's final question, if meant to restore a proper sense of values, seemed to have the opposite effect. With a passion that took my breath away Kelda gave some incoherent exclamation, lost all restraint, and bursting into sobs, rushed from the room. We heard her weeping as she stumbled along the passage and up the stairs. Her bedroom door slammed shut and its thick panels cut off the sound.

The extraordinary thing was that it *had* happened before. I *had* been here in this very room. They must have been talking in the conservatory after the wedding. And I had been right after all. It was Kelda not May, not the bridesmaid but the bride who had broken down on her wedding day. The memory cleared. The voices echoed. "Of course he doesn't know." Had that been May's voice? The outraged protest had come from Kelda. "No. No. You mustn't speak of it. I can't bear it." Mr. Cade must have spoken because I knew that he was there but his words were lost to me—and now he was dead. Everybody was dead except my two aunts—and me.

Shivering slightly, for the incident had been upsetting, I looked at May. Beyond a regretful shake of the head she had shown no sign of distress, disapproval, or concern. How could I have been persuaded that she, in her unfailing stillness of spirit, would ever have been the one to make such a scene?

I sat down on the high-backed chair. Through the half-open blind a sunbeam pointed to the rectangular shape of the chiffonier, to a spot near the top right-hand corner.

"I remember this room." It was all I could find to say in the dreadful aftermath of Kelda's flight. "There used to be a stuffed squirrel."

It had sat bolt upright as if listening, like me, but with a warning glare in its glass eye.

"The squirrel? Yes, I'd forgotten. It was given to me when I was a girl." She glanced absently at the bare wall. I wondered if the squirrel had been sold with the other things or pushed into a cupboard when the removal men came for the chiffonier.

"And I remember Kelda crying like that—on her wedding day," I burst out, feeling once more the disharmony of it, the violence. "Do you know what it was that upset her so much?"

I watched Aunt May's lips part. I caught the gleam of her small white teeth.

"She was overwrought, I suppose. A wedding can be a nerve-racking sort of thing. Brides do tend to cry." She made these observations with a mild regret tinged with wonder and had evidently forgotten the incident.

Perhaps I too had been overwrought. All the same her generalizations about brides didn't satisfy me. They didn't explain my instinctive feeling—at the time—that there was evil at work. Some spirit of malignity had been released and had broken forth again only a minute ago; so that, making the connection and finding it inexplicable, I was almost bound to ask, "But why was Kelda so upset just now?"

There came no reply. May had gone. Without her I was plunged in misery. The past quarter of an hour had changed my relationship with Kelda forever. How could we live together after such a scene. It had been vulgar, degrading.

Finding the house unbearable I went out again. As soon as possible I must pack and leave. After all I had never intended to stay. It was just a question of where to go. Not to the Burnetts. I would rather they didn't know of my predicament, which seemed to cast a slur on the Findons and on my grandfather. On my present allowance of 150 pounds a year I could live in rooms and there was nothing, short of a few inquiries, to stop me from training as a nurse.

But at the moment, I remembered with a shock, I had only a few shillings in my purse. My quarter's income had slipped away. More than once I had been quick, too quick, to offer more than my share to pay for coal, wood, rates—to save Kelda from going to the bank in Bidminster. "Just this once," she had said each time, hand outstretched.

At the front gate I turned toward the road with a vague feeling that it led to other people but I had no destination. The warm day discouraged effort. Besides, without money escape was impossible. My share of Hoodman House included a share in my aunts' predicament. We could none of us leave. With money in my purse I could have abandoned Kelda without a qualm; but not

May. Turning, I could see her slim figure at the window, looking my way but watching for someone else. She could live without me but not without my 150 pounds a year, especially as she grew older. She asked so little, living in nunlike simplicity, eating like a bird. How could I leave her? We must live here together until one by one we all three died.

The lane, winding between the hawthorns, led me to her trysting place. I leaned on the gate, bowed my head, and wept.

Beyond the cherry tree someone moved. Looking up, I saw that it was a man and stared at him with blurred eyes so that his form wavered like that of a ghost taking shape.

He came closer. There was only the gate between us.

"I say"—his voice was concerned—"are you in trouble? I saw you come out of the house. I don't suppose there's anything I can do, is there? But of course you don't know me. My name's Tass."

6

$\mathscr{88888}$

My PERSONAL TROUBLES evaporated. I ceased for an instant to exist except to register amazement that it had actually happened: the miracle of his return.

He was not quite what I would have expected, assuming that any reasonable person could have entertained expectations as to how he would look if he came back: *when* he came back; for here he was, very much—though incredibly—as he must have been when he went away, even to the khaki knapsack lying on the grass behind him. Surely after all he had gone through he should have looked older: should have shown some touch of world-weariness even if he had survived without a scar and, so far as I could see, unmaimed, his light hair unflecked by gray, his fair skin fresh with health. If he was less handsome than I had imagined him, he was handsome enough.

What I hadn't been prepared for among other things was the warmth of my own reaction. As the shock passed and he became real to me, I felt an instant liking—or rather the revival of liking that comes when friends are reunited.

He too leaned over the gate in the leisurely manner of a man with all the time in the world to give to a tiresome girl who was delaying his already too long delayed homecoming.

"You must excuse me. You'll think me . . . I don't know what to say." I found a handkerchief, did what I could to my face, and held out my hand. It was awkward at an acute angle over a five-barred gate; I withdrew it to fumble with the iron latch. He pressed it open. "You'll want to . . . Only I think it would be better if I went on ahead. Don't you think I should perhaps warn Aunt May?"

"Warn?"

"I didn't mean that she won't be overjoyed," I assured him, "but it's bound to be a shock after all this time. But of course you don't know yet—she has never given up hope. She has expected you every day, every minute."

"Oh Lord!" His dismay like everything else about him was unexpected. "Elinor—you are Elinor, aren't you?—let me introduce myself. I'm Clement Tass."

"Not Dick," I said carefully.

"Definitely not Dick. I'm afraid Dick won't ever be coming back. I'm his brother Clem. I should have said so at once."

"Of course," I said, aghast at my own stupidity, "I knew it couldn't really be Dick and I'm terribly sorry about him but"—impossible to explain how the phantom haunting Aunt May had haunted me too; or the relief, the sudden happiness of finding in its place a brand-new person, a normal three-dimensional young man. If the relief had been preceded by a stab of disappointment sharp as pain, there was no explaining that either. "But meeting you here where I always thought of him . . . this is where they last saw each other—where she comes to wait for him."

"So that's still going on, is it? I wonder why." His gaze, having strayed toward the house, returned to me and as if he had come to a decision he pushed open the gate, drew me outside, and closed it.

"But ought you not to . . ."

"Call on them? I don't think so. It was you I came to see. And as far as I can make out you aren't particularly keen to go back just yet. No? Then what about having lunch with me?" He pointed to the knapsack.

"A picnic?"

"A necessary precaution when visiting Hoodman House, to bring your own refreshments. Unless things have changed . . ."

"They haven't changed."

"If only I'd come in the car I could have whisked you off home to my mother's tender care. You could do with it, couldn't you? And she's anxious to see you."

"Me?"

"Very much wanting to. She's been trying to get in touch with you. So, as her letter may have been lost in the post, I've been dispatched as a last resort. Believe me, I wouldn't have dared to go home without news of you."

"Do you mean to say that Mrs. Tass has written?"

"Apparently your mother told mine—at Kelda's wedding—that if anything happened to her, you would come here. We didn't hear of your mother's death, not at the time. I'm sorry, Elinor. But the news did get round to us eventually, just recently in fact. Some people my parents came across at a concert had met you in the train."

"The Penfolds."

"That was when mother wrote to Kelda asking her to bring you to Bidminster."

"And she didn't answer?"

"No." Clem made no attempt to gloss over the rebuff. "I've been away for a few weeks and only came home yesterday. Mother had made up her mind to write to you but we felt it might be more effective for me to come instead. So here I am." He must have noticed that I was put out by my aunt's behavior. "Now, what about lunch?"

"Oh yes. But not here."

"No fear. I know a better place. The old farmhouse up there. But don't worry. There's no need to go past your gate."

63

He pointed to an opening in the hedgerow leading to an unsuspected path sunk deep between high banks and tangled growth.

"I never saw this before."

"Packhorse Way. Nobody uses it now but it must have been the old road to Upper Saury." Clem went ahead, holding aside the sprawling branches. "It was all right for packhorses but not wide enough for wagons—and it flooded in winter."

"There's our house already." The dim green light had darkened as an opaque mass loomed just beyond the trees to the right. "It's a much quicker way and so near our front gate. This must be the way Sintram comes and goes."

"Does the old boy still turn up? He probably sleeps rough in one of the outhouses at Winkblade. He used to be a hero to Dick and me, a sort of ancient mariner who could make your blood tingle with his stories. Do you know that he fought the dervishes at Omdurman? Major Sintram, believe it or not. We never knew why he was cashiered but it can't have been anything criminal or dishonorable. Most likely he refused to obey a rotten command or spoke up about something he couldn't accept. Your grandfather's theory was that he underwent a mystical revelation—an inner voice or something of the kind telling him to put on the mantle of a wandering prophet."

The aspect of the green tunnel was changing. It curved to the left between banks of wild roses and hedge parsley and widened into a grassy glade open to the south. On the right, rough steps in the bank led up to the wicket gate opening on the garden of Winkblade Farm.

It was warm and still and full of flowers. Neglected survivors of cultivation—catmint, valerian, and marguerites—mingled with a horde of wild invaders—cranesbill and willow herb and purple vetches—all sheltered from the north by the farmhouse, long and low, its lime wash blotched and flaking. We found a sunny corner where a disused wellhead and a tumbled wall formed a makeshift arbor.

"I know this place," I said. "My father told me about it. It's like turning back and finding him again." The feeling of familiarity was sweet and sad like one of his fairy tales. "Even when he was a boy it was always empty."

"This is going to be rough, I'm afraid." Clem was unpacking the knapsack. "I didn't cater for a lady. But bread and cheese is farmhouse fare after all."

"And lemonade! You called at Mrs. Torgill's?"

"I couldn't have got past the shop without her seeing me. 'You'll likely be going to Hoodman,' she said. 'Yes, indeed. I'm going to call on Miss Findon,' I replied. 'Then be sure you get the right one,' she said."

"And you didn't."

"Didn't I?" He held out bread and butter on a napkin. "I thought I had. But one thing I do regret. No macaroons, I'm afraid."

"Macaroons? Then it was you—at the wedding. I was half asleep and stupefied that day and didn't catch your name. And the tea basket in the train! We never thanked you properly. Oh Clem, I'm so happy to meet you again . . . I didn't recognize you but I did feel a kind of recognition, like finding a lost relation."

"Thoroughly satisfactory." Clem rolled his jacket into a cushion to serve me as a backrest. "And we can talk. There was so much I didn't say to you the last time we met."

"You said nothing at all. If it hadn't been for the macaroons I would have thought you'd taken a vow of silence."

"I've improved. A good deal has happened since then and there's more to talk about. I've become quite voluble."

He was seven years younger than Dick. Like him he had seen active service although not in the same regiment. For the past two years he had worked in his father's firm as Dick had done before him.

"I hadn't realized—not until today in fact—that your father and my grandfather had parted company."

"It was bound to happen, I'm afraid. The two of them were too different to pull together comfortably."

There had been differences of temperament, aims, and attitudes. Clem spoke respectfully of my grandfather but I had already sensed that the Tasses had put their two generations of prosperity to better use than had the Findons and had acquired education, taste, and, as I later learned, a superior reputation for fair dealing. The two Oliver Findons, father and son, had been practical, limited, fond of a quick bargain. Their tendency to use ruthless business methods must have worried their more scrupulous partners.

"The partnership might have lasted longer if your father had joined the firm. The old man was bitterly disappointed when he broke away. 'I've had him educated like a gentleman,' he used to growl, 'and what does he do? Takes the Queen's shilling and leaves me in the lurch.' "

Meanwhile Edwin Tass, Clem's father, had developed an enthusiasm for the restoration of historic buildings: a namby-pamby line of business according to my grandfather, who would have been happy to pull them down. But Dick at eighteen had been articled to a firm of ecclesiastical architects with a view to founding a new small firm specializing in restoration. The old partnership was brought to a close, amicably enough. It was remarkable that it had lasted so long.

Once free to make his own decisions, my grandfather launched into a frenzy of building, chiefly rapidly run-up terraces for colliers and ironworkers to the north of the county. Labor and materials were cheap; for a while business boomed; but his reputation for both integrity and workmanship were sacrificed.

"I'm afraid the old man over-reached himself. Then when the second Mrs. Findon died, he just let things go."

"My aunts have nothing. I saw from the beginning that they

66

were living very simply but I thought it was—at least partly—because of Aunt May. The normal worldly things don't matter to her anymore and so they don't matter to Kelda either. It was only today that I realized how desperately poor they are—and of course there'll be nothing for me either, from the Findon side."

"And that was what was upsetting you. You were in a state, weren't you? Unfortunately, unlike me, you haven't an uncle in diamonds. Whenever things show signs of going wrong, we congratulate ourselves on Uncle Vernon. We keep him perpetually in reserve—for a rainy day."

"It wasn't just being less well off than I expected to be that worried me but the effect on my life. I realized that I can never leave them and suddenly felt the burden of it all weighing me down. Then finding you there at the gate! I can't tell you what a difference it has made. And this place! As for the lunch!" I scattered crumbs on the flagstones in the hope of enticing a blackbird from the lilac tree. "I wouldn't have exchanged it for a plateful of macaroons. By the way there's something else I have to tell you. Did you suspect—I don't like them. I only ate them because you kept on offering them."

"There's manners for you. You've been remarkably well brought up."

"But the best thing of all is having someone to talk to." And not just anyone, I might have added, but a companion so kind, so good a listener, so closely bound to me by old ties.

"In other words"—he carefully removed a spider from my hair—"things *have* improved. We have progressed. There is hope."

The garden enclosed us: sun drenched, drowsy with the hum of bees. Beyond the wicket gate, between two ash trees, stretched a vista of fields rising to a blue horizon. Close at hand blue tits were pillaging a giant hogweed for seeds, their movements too light to break the deep quiet of the summer afternoon.

"Hope?" I said.

"We knew that things had gone badly with Kelda and May,

financially, I mean. But we never could make out why they cut themselves off so completely. There's no need for them to live as they do, two healthy women still young and with a substantial though hideous house of their own."

"Our own. A third of that hideous house is mine."

"I know—and that should make it easier. You could make them sell it and live more comfortably elsewhere. Yes"—as I attempted to interrupt—"you could. You're entitled either to sell them your share or if they can't buy you out, then the house can be sold and the proceeds shared; and its occupants must bestir themselves to find some gainful employment."

"It sounds wonderful. For me, that is." Girls of my age and background had been liberated by the war and were learning to stand on their own feet, unlike their mothers who had been completely dependent on men; but my aunts, though little more than a decade older, belonged to a different era. "They aren't used to the idea of working for a living and Aunt May is very frail. I could never force her to leave her home. She is so patient and sad. Any sudden change might make her ill—or worse. She might die. You do understand?"

"I understand that you have fallen under her spell."

"And yet," I swept on unheeding, "she is the one who earns a little, with her pictures."

Clem's response was brusque.

"There can't be much demand for those mawkish daubs. Is Kelda still trying to palm them off on a long-suffering public?"

"I hadn't realized it was difficult. They seem the sort of pictures people might like. But I do know that Kelda had to stay in London a whole winter while she tried to find an agent. At least I think that must have been why she went."

It was after all pure surmise on my part. The experience must have been an important one and wounding too, considering the effect on her of the mere word "London," her nervous collapse, her flight upstairs. Could the attempt to sell May's pictures have been so fearful an ordeal or had other factors besides poverty and its problems been involved?

"Come to think of it, it was about that time that everything changed. Until then, apart from stingy meals, life at Hoodman had gone on much as usual. But there was a sort of gap after Dick went away when the Findons simply faded out of sight—then suddenly we were invited to Kelda's wedding."

"Did you know Mr. Cade?"

"Oh yes. Everybody breathed sighs of relief when he and Kelda seemed to hit it off. People were surprised that she took so long to find a husband. According to my mother, Cade was exactly right for her."

A musician's life can be precarious but his special field, the composition of sacred music, placed him almost in the category of a clergyman. It was at a concert in Bidminster that he and Kelda had met.

"We did rather wonder if Kelda was marrying him for his money, although we didn't know that she had so little of her own."

"But he had none either—or not much."

"Really! That was hard luck. A marriage of convenience that turned out highly inconvenient perhaps—as well as being disastrously short."

"There's something I can't quite put my finger on," I said. "Things I don't understand."

But I felt no inclination to dwell on my aunts' peculiar affairs. The present moment seemed heaven sent, a brief recompense for the dreariness of the past weeks and the unpleasantness of the last hour or two.

"It was Dick who would have kept us in touch with your aunts." Clem lay leaning on his elbow and gazing at the peaceful fields between the ash trees over the wicket gate. "Losing him was like a blow to the head—for all of us. My parents have never got over it. But I wouldn't have expected May to be affected as she has

69

been, or Kelda to retreat into her shell. The two of them are like the weird sisters in *Macbeth* except that there should be three."

"There are three. I've been adopted as a younger sister."

"You haven't been there long enough to qualify as genuinely weird. What have you been doing, by the way, since you came?" And when I told him—"So you've been no farther than Saury. We did rather wonder. You need a change and the sooner the better. What about tomorrow? Can you spend the day with us? Please do. I'll fetch you in the car."

We had got to our feet, reluctantly on my part and possibly on his too. He seemed in no hurry to leave.

"Let me show you the house."

"It isn't locked?"

"Yes, but there are ways. As a matter of fact if this place is left empty much longer, it won't be worth locking."

We went up the steps: he slipped his hand through an empty window pane, released the catch inside, and pushed up the sash. We climbed into a white paneled room with china cupboards on either side of the fireplace and candle sconces, their pink shades worn cobweb thin.

"It's still charming. One could live here."

"Seeing it through your eyes, I realize the old place has its points. The firm of Edwin Tass and Son could make something of it for a client with means in search of a rural retreat. Considerable means! The marvelous thing about restoration is the feeling that you're preserving a fragment of the past—saving it just in time before it vanishes altogether, especially now when so much has been smashed up and lost that if we don't hang on to some of the beautiful things, we're going to have to start all over again from the bottom with no guidance from tradition."

"You love your work, don't you. I suppose your brother must have felt the same."

"Dick? No, he wasn't keen. Caring for buildings wasn't his sort of thing. By the way"—we had stepped into the damp gloom of the kitchen—"there's one feature of the place I'd like to show you."

The farmyard at the back of the house was flanked on the east side by a stable and hayloft, and on the west by a washhouse and other outbuildings.

"This." Clem opened the door of an outbuilding in better repair than the others. "The old bakehouse."

On the wall opposite the door a wide chimney breast tapered to the roof. Set in its ancient brickwork about three feet from the ground was a great iron door fastened with a heavy bar. Clem explained how the oven was heated by brushwood and swept clean before the loaves were pushed in on a long shovel. Raising his hand to undo the bar, he hesitated.

"Coming here certainly brings things back."

As children, he told me, they had congregated here; had heated the oven and huddled round it on winter days, made it the base for hide-and-seek, and stored bats and balls in its deep cavity.

"Actually getting inside had to be ruled out after one or two crises. Once you were in with the door closed there was no getting out without help. Dick made the rules—and there'd be Kelda, May, my cousin Mirabel, Paul and Philip Edstone—oh and Thyrza Beck, a red-haired little brat from the Tile Sheds over the fields there." He smiled, remembering Thyrza with affection, I thought. "There was one warm day, like this, when Dick was putting on one of his acts—here—with his hand on the oven door. 'This is Aladdin's cave,' he said. 'Inside is a remarkable object which in due course I will show to you—on one condition'—or words to that effect. Everybody waited, all agog, just as you are now. I must have been about seven or eight years old, the juvenile hanger-on that nobody took any notice of."

"And the condition?"

"We had to guess what it was and the one who guessed right could have it."

"The remarkable object! No wonder you were all agog."

"Oh, Dick was a dab hand at creating drama. He loved an audience and could turn even the dreariest wet afternoon into a party." Clem's eyes clouded but presently he went on: "There was one slight hitch before we started guessing. That was when Thyrza piped up, 'I don't have to guess. I know what's in there. I saw you put it in.'"

"And the game was spoiled."

"No fear. Dick wasn't having that. He was probably furious but he took it in his stride. 'Come here, Thyrza Beck,' he said, 'and stand at my side. If you utter another word, you will be harshly punished but if you keep your mouth shut, we'll let you come with us to the circus in Bidminster next week.'"

"And she couldn't risk the harshness or resist the circus."

"Exactly. People guessed all sorts of farfetched things: jewels, gold coins, food, a Bible . . . My guess was a catapult. That was all I cared about and it was wrong so I gave up. After a while the guessing began to flag and Dick got impatient. He couldn't bear an anticlimax. 'One last guess each,' he said, 'we can't leave the thing here forever.' 'I know,' Kelda said. 'It's an animal.' Then May said in that eerie way she sometimes had, 'It's something dead.' Whereupon, with a flourish of course, Dick opened the door."

"Go on"—as he paused—"you haven't forgotten what was inside?"

"No, I haven't. It was unexpected enough to stick in the memory even without the fuss it caused. Do you want to guess?"

"I know that Dick was an amateur conjuror and what conjurors produce for some reason is usually a rabbit."

"Not so far out. It was a squirrel, stuffed, with a nut in its paws."

"In a glass case?"

"No. It was just sitting there, rather small in the depths of the oven and strange, like a tribal fetish with a crowd of young savages peering in at it and wondering what it meant. Nobody spoke. Then Dick tried to persuade us that he had trapped it himself, but I was pretty sure my Aunt Claudia had given it to him for some reason, probably because he asked for it. Dick usually got what he asked for."

"And the fuss? Oh, I know. They were both right, Kelda and May."

"It was both an animal and dead. Even Dick had a struggle to carry off that awkward situation. 'If it's dead,' some bright soul piped up, 'it isn't an animal anymore!' Kelda claimed that it had been an animal first and couldn't ever be anything else. Then May said in that cool voice of hers, 'When a thing's dead, it's nothing else but dead.' It gave me a peculiar feeling down my spine. We all just stood and gaped at her."

"Was she as beautiful then as she is now?"

"I don't know what May is like now but then—well, one didn't bother to look at anyone else when she was there. And she could always make you do things you didn't want to do."

"What sort of thing?"

"She made me wade into Lott's Pool once to rescue her bracelet. The water came up to my chin. I fell over and nearly drowned. I was scared stiff. It didn't occur to me that I needn't have gone. One simply did as May commanded."

"And of course Dick gave her the squirrel."

"Not at all. He gave it to Kelda."

"But—" My protest went no further, though surprise that Kelda should have been preferred had quickly given way to doubt, then disbelief. Clem had got it wrong. It had happened a long time ago when he was very young. The squirrel had been given to May: she had told me so.

He had raised the heavy bar, the door swung open. There was nothing inside but dust and flaking brick and in the room no trace or echo of the vanished conjuror and his magic. How could there be? A feeling of loss oppressed me. For a moment the group of children gaping at the squirrel had moved closer as I joined the magic circle, bewitched into half-believing that no man alive however kind and companionable could hold a candle to the man who was dead.

Not dead. Only missing. In silence we walked round to the front of the house. In one of those quiet rearrangements of air and light that steal upon a summer afternoon the garden seemed to stir. Leaves rippled in response to a soundless breath lighter than a breeze. A sunbeam found its way through foliage to the wicket gate and fingered its latch. A missing person, I reflected—lost in thoughts much vaguer than the words needed to express them—remained unconsigned to oblivion. He could come and go, untethered by physical limitations. But then so could a spirit released by death. It could be anywhere and of all places surely here. It must have been here that he fell in love with Aunt May. Winkblade had been a meeting place for lovers even when my father was young. Since then there had been others no doubt. Imagination dismissed them as commonplace compared with the two who seemed the epitome of all that lovers are expected to be: the twentieth-century Lancelot and Elaine or Tristam and Isolde, lovely, fair, and doomed . . .

"It isn't true, is it? That the dead are nothing else but dead. They go on affecting us. I don't want to speak of it if it hurts you, but I can understand why May can't accept your brother's death. Without ever having known him, I can't forget him."

"It's a faculty dead people have, Dick more than most perhaps, of coming back when they please though not in the flesh. But he shouldn't be coming back to you. You never came within his orbit. It's that morbid ritual of May's that preys on your mind. What in heaven's name is she up to?"

It was a pity when in all other respects Clem was so perceptive that he should be a little insensitive about May. Perhaps only another woman could appreciate her extraordinary range of qualities: her profound feeling, suppressed out of consideration for others; her graceful yielding to a cruel fate; her wistful submission.

"She loved him," I said hesitantly, "too much to let him go."

"Love doesn't work like that. Whatever it is, you must be got away from it now and again. Tomorrow for a start."

He slammed the wicket, shutting us out of the garden. We went back down the green way and when the dark mass of Hood-man House showed through the trees, scrambled up the bank between their naked roots. Clem waited until I reached the door and with a final wave disappeared.

May was sitting at the sunless drawing room window, still as a picture, her face ivory pale in the green light. It was cool indoors. The hall, lit only by its stained glass panes of red and blue, was dim and silent as a church after the congregation has gone, leaving only one worshipper. Just for a moment, as if on the brink of waking from an entranced sleep, I thought how strange it was, if love was all she lived for, that it had brought no warmth, no light, no consolation to the house.

7

§§§§§§

Mrs. Tass's hair had turned snow white since the day when she dabbed my temples with eau de cologne, but her quiet warmth of manner was as I remembered it. She welcomed me as one of the family.

"I've always wanted a daughter," she said when the first greetings were over.

"Have a heart, mother," Clem said. "Elinor has already been adopted as the younger sister of her half-aunts. She's beginning to be confused as to who she really is."

"But I know exactly who she is. Dear Vincent's daughter. Your father often stayed with us here after his mother died. He was like one of our own. And this is my husband. Here she is at last, Edwin."

Mr. Tass, a gray-haired, heavier version of Clem, put down his book and rose to greet me as we went into the sitting room.

"Welcome, my dear. I'm happy to see you for your own sake but also because you have provided the most delightful excuse for not going to church."

"And Father has many other excuses on which to base a comparison," Clem said.

There were other people in the room: two young men arti-

76

cled to the firm who occasionally spent a Sunday at their employer's house; Mirabel, Mrs. Tass's niece in her twenties who helped with the housekeeping; Aunt Claudia, a middle-aged sister of Mr. Tass who made long visits to Bidminster from her flat in Hammersmith.

"They're getting longer and longer, Aunt Claudia's visits," Clem told me as we strolled out to explore the town. "We're wondering how long it will be before she decides to settle here."

"Will you like that?"

"It would solve some problems. My mother cannot be without company. Since Dick's death she has never wanted to be alone and it takes a houseful of people to fill the gap he left."

I took an instant liking to Bidminster, an ancient small borough of steep narrow streets overhung by half-timbered houses, with the added charms of a ruined castle, a cobbled marketplace, and three bridges over a tree-shaded river. These picturesque features first seen on a fine summer morning combined with the satisfaction of wearing one of the silk dresses Mrs. Burnett and I had chosen in London, with its matching silk hat, helped to raise my spirits to a pitch I had not known since my mother's death.

The Tasses lived at the upper and quieter end of Battle Street, a haphazard row of houses of different periods and many additions drawn by long association into harmony. Their back gardens sloped steeply down to the river—and there under the lime tree we spent an idle afternoon. Beyond the garden walls the town drowsed in the Sabbath hush. The river was empty of craft; the streets were deserted. The chimes of St. Bartholomew's church clock marked the quarters as they passed—too quickly. All too soon it was four o'clock and visitors began to drop in for tea: a young clergyman; Mr. Paley from the bookshop and his daughter; and, to my delight and surprise, the Penfolds.

"Delightful for us too," Miss Penfold said, "but not a surprise. Mrs. Tass sent round a message this morning to tell us that you were here. I told you, didn't I, that we'd be sure to meet again."

Her glance took in my dress, my hair, my face. "A little thinner perhaps. You are well?"

"Very well." I folded my hands palms uppermost in my lap but without any real hope that their roughened state would escape her.

"And you have settled in happily with the aunts?"

She may also have noticed that my manner was more restrained than when we traveled together and chatted with the freedom that sometimes loosens the tongues of strangers on a journey. Conventional replies, which were all I could manage, revealed to me if not to her how complex a truthful answer would need to be. But I knew that her interest though penetrating was sympathetic and intelligent. Weary as I was of evasions and ambiguities, I liked her directness. Had we been alone I might have told her more; instead I asked her how their house-hunting had progressed.

They had found comfortable lodgings and were enjoying life in Bidminster but so far had been unsuccessful in finding a suitable home.

"Every available house is too big or too small; too many stairs; too noisy; not enough room for Aidan's books and papers . . ."

Her brother was immersed in a campaign that would eventually lead to the founding of the Peace Pledge Union. His passionate commitment to the cause of world peace took him frequently to London and involved him in calling meetings, writing articles, and educating a public opinion still battered and exhausted in the aftermath of war. He and Mr. Tass had already drawn their chairs together and plunged into fundamental issues of disarmament and reconstruction.

"Aidan plans to launch a quarterly magazine—*World Without War*—at his own expense."

"And you will help him?" Her quizzical look had implied some doubt as to the wisdom of such an enterprise.

"A little, in a practical way at least. I've bought a motor car and I'm learning to drive it."

The announcement brought a respectful silence on the part of all who were near enough to hear it.

"In that case, Miss Penfold"—Clem brought his cup and settled himself on the grass beside our chairs—"you can range more widely in your house-hunting. If you haven't found a suitable place in Bidminster, you may find something a few miles out of town."

"Do you know, that's an interesting idea. It hadn't occurred to me. Quietness, space—but near enough for me to drive Aidan to the station here and meet him after his conferences and to drive home after concerts and visits . . . We must suggest it to the house agent or even advertise. You don't happen to know of anything suitable?"

It struck me that if Clem, as he himself said, lacked the flair and fascination of his more brilliant brother he didn't lack means of achieving his own ends.

"I do know of something as it happens: a fine old place falling into dilapidation for want of repair. Putting it right would be expensive, but carefully restored, it would make a little gem of a property, for a connoisseur who could afford it. The rooms are well proportioned; a stable could be converted to a garage; one or two outbuildings could make living quarters for servants—and the situation is really delightful."

"You must tell me more about it." Miss Penfold's cucumber sandwich lay neglected on her plate.

I left them to discuss the project while I helped Mirabel to clear away the tea things, but when the Penfolds had gone I scolded Clem.

"You were talking her into it. Restoring Winkblade will take a tremendous amount of money. You said so yourself."

"Not more than the Penfolds can afford, my dear girl. They're from a family of Birmingham arms manufacturers. Business has been pretty good for them in the past few years, wouldn't you say? He's an idealist—genuine, I'm sure. He's cut loose from the family concern and will probably sink most of his money in this peace movement. But she won't. She's a tougher character and won't lay out money without watching where it goes. There'd be no hoodwinking Miss P., assuming that anyone thought of trying to. As a matter of fact Winkblade could be a very nice little investment."

I went back to the kitchen, put on an apron, and began the washing up.

"Audrey has every other Sunday off so that she can go to church at home." Mirabel stood at the table slicing a cold tongue. She had a pleasant open face, was fresh complexioned with thick waving brown hair and inclined to be plump. "Is that what you do with yours?"

"Maids, you mean? We haven't any."

Hands in the sink, I glanced over my shoulder and saw her motionless with a thin slice of tongue on the fork, her round blue eyes thoughtful.

"Good Lord!" With the flat of the knife she steered the tongue to its place on a serving dish. "What will those two get up to next? It's a bit of a comedown I must say after all their airs and graces."

"Economy, I'm afraid. They're very hard up."

"They could have a girl in daily for five shillings a week." Mirabel briskly mixed mustard. "That's a big house. You could give half the day to the kitchen stove never mind the other fires."

I could only sigh in agreement.

"Why should they be so hard up? Mr. Cade must have left Kelda his money" And when I had put her right on this point— "That's funny," she said. "Everybody thought he was pretty well off."

"I wonder where the idea came from when it obviously wasn't true."

"Goodness knows. Bidminster is full of rumors. But it was from Dick that I first heard it. Not that he was talking to me. He said it to May, I remember. It was one afternoon at Saury. 'Cade's rolling in money,' he said. 'He'd make a rich husband for some poor girl.'"

"Then he must have had some reason for thinking so. I mean, he wouldn't have said . . ."

"Oh, he could quite easily have made it up. If he wanted it to be true, it had to be true."

"But why should he want it to be true?"

"Don't ask me." Mirabel scooped mustard into the pot and brought the basin and spoon for me to wash. "People are always doing things I don't see the point of. It's jolly good of you to weigh in like this, Elinor, especially if you're slaving away all day at home. Somehow I can't imagine the Findon girls rolling up their sleeves. Everybody looked up to them at school." (She had been a few years behind them at The Elms.) "They were always chosen to present bouquets and be introduced to visitors and so on." She fetched a towel and began swiftly drying the crockery. "You lived in Surrey, didn't you? At some big house, Aunt Janet said. Didn't you like it there?"

"Yes, very much."

"Couldn't you have stayed?"

Could I have stayed? It seemed to me now that I could. Mrs. Burnett would have liked me to stay. At the time there had seemed no choice: the decision to throw in my lot with the Findons had been imposed on me, not as an instruction or obligation but as a natural migration to seek security with my own kin.

"It seemed the right thing to do, to come to Saury—and they do need me, especially Aunt May."

"Well, after all you do own a share in the house," Mirabel said sensibly after a slight pause. "You may as well live in what's your own."

I noticed the pause and Mirabel's failure to endorse Aunt

May's need of me. The robustness of her views amused me. She was a likable girl but it was clearly beyond her to understand the subtleties of my aunts' situation.

Suddenly—the change of direction took me by surprise—I saw my claim to superiority for what it was, arrogant nonsense. The so-called subtleties were beyond me too. Moreover it was thanks to Mirabel that a growing suspicion had hardened into certainty. Reasonable employers needing to economize would have reduced their staff gradually, giving proper warning. As Mirabel said, people living in the country could employ daily help very cheaply. The banishing of all the servants en bloc in a single week had not been to save expense. My aunts had acted from a different motive. *They had wanted to empty the house of all outsiders and to do it quickly.*

But for what conceivable reason? Abstractedly I followed Mirabel back to the drawing room. It was taken for granted that I would stay for a cold supper and as long as possible after that. The last hour of the evening was given over to music under the direction of Aunt Claudia, who was the family soloist.

"My voice has gone," she confided as we turned over song-books and sheet music, "but I don't give up. Besides, the rest of them are all so much worse."

We chose a few songs suitable for a Sunday evening: "Where My Caravan Has Rested." "Two Eyes of Gray," and "The Lost Chord," and I accompanied on the piano.

"This is a beautiful little thing. A favorite of mine. I expect you know it."

She placed a song on the music rest and opened it at the first page so that I had only a glimpse of the cover with its vignette of green and brown leaves enclosing a solitary tombstone.

"When I am dead, my dearest,
Sing no sad songs for me . . ."

Aunt Claudia's lack of voice was equaled by my lack of skill, but she sang very softly and following her example, I touched the keys lightly. Our muted approach suited both words and music. Besides no one seemed to be listening; we performed for our own pleasure against a background of conversation.

"And if thou wilt, remember,
And if thou wilt, forget."

The sentimental mood was very much in keeping with popular taste at that time, and when we arrived safely at the last bar, I glanced at Aunt Claudia and returned her nod of satisfaction.

"No one had quite his talent for bringing out the pathos of a poem," she said. "But then he was of a poetic turn of mind. Not that he wrote poetry so far as I know but he read a good deal."

"You knew the composer?"

"Very well." She seemed surprised that I should ask. "We met at the home of a mutual friend in Hammersmith and occasionally at musical evenings. It was through me that he first came to Bidminster."

I turned back the page and looked at the cover—at the composer's name.

"He should have been more widely known but there are so many gifted people who never reach out for success. Julius was a sensitive retiring person. When we first met I was struck by his air of loneliness. He was charming in company in a quiet way but there was, I'm sure, a solitude of soul. One feels it in his music."

The solitary tombstone in its wreath of vine leaves seemed to endorse this entirely new interpretation of a character I had evidently underestimated, and I felt ashamed of ever having thought of him facetiously.

"That's why we were all so delighted when he met Kelda. But your aunt will have told you all about their courtship, I'm sure. Girls like to hear about such things."

Cozy talks with Aunt Kelda about her husband had not been a feature of our life at Hoodman House. Was that my fault? Had she been yearning to unburden herself?

"I wonder"—Aunt Claudia lowered her voice—"has Kelda told you how he died? No? Well, it must be a painful subject. One can't inquire. But we never heard what Julius died of. He wasn't a robust man, but his death must have been unexpected—and so soon after they married. But Kelda has been seen so little since she was widowed that there has never been an opportunity of talking to her. Not that one could intrude on the privacy of her grief, but friends can be a great support, and we were all fond of Julius."

I could only listen and nod and feel, as so often where my aunts were concerned, uncomfortable.

"Let me do that." I helped her to straighten the music sheets and stack them in the canterbury.

"It makes me angry, the way we treat artists. They give us so much pleasure and edification and what do we give them in return? Indifference and neglect. They die and are forgotten. Julius Cade was a gifted man, a good man too, and a perfect gentleman. To let him vanish into obscurity without so much as an obituary paragraph in the *Times* is typical of the way we disregard the loftier side of life; and without his friends even knowing that he was ill. In my opinion it was nothing short of criminal."

"Now, who's committed a crime?" Mr. Tass had overheard the last sentence as he passed us in search of his glasses.

"I was exaggerating as usual. It's my way of compensating for a drab personality." Aunt Claudia popped a lozenge in her mouth and smiled. All the same her onslaught on the uncaring public held a grain of truth. Whatever his contribution to the world at large, Julius Cade had made so little impact on the family he had married into that he might never have existed. It was as if, having fulfilled his role as bridegroom, he had quitted the stage and vanished into some subterranean green room—an unsuccessful actor—a neglected artist—a lost soul.

84

"You're very quiet, Elinor." Clem glanced at me a little anxiously as he drove me home.

"It's been a wonderful day." I roused myself. "It's given me a lot to think about."

"I hope we're thinking on the same lines."

It seemed unlikely; and the lines on which my thoughts were hesitantly moving were best kept to myself.

"This isn't the way we came," I said instead.

"It's the road to Upper Saury. We'll turn off at the Tile Sheds and we can have another look at Winkblade before I drop you at Hoodman," he said casually.

For a whole day I had been free of it, and as its tall narrow shape reared itself suddenly in my memory, I knew how much I disliked its dark corners thronged with shadows: its rooms some-times tense with anger and weeping and voices whispering behind closed doors; its empty spaces where there should have been all the clutter of family living—pictures, looking glasses, ornaments. Its life had ebbed away. Its thick walls enclosed a history of departures. For years and years mine had been the only arrival.

Like Aunt Claudia I was exaggerating. Besides, for a little while longer I was still free. It was a new experience to be driven along a country road in an open car on a warm evening by a young man. By Clem. He had already become as familiar a friend as if we had known each other for years. I said so.

"We *have* known each other for years," he replied. "Yesterday wasn't our first meeting. Had you forgotten? I'm only sorry for all the time wasted in between."

The garden at Winkblade in the warm dusk with the yellow arc of a new moon above the ash trees: a perfect meeting place for lovers! If only I could have been there in the old days—before the war! If only I had been born sooner, in time to know Dick! The perfect lover!

But for all the flower-scented air, the soft silence and the young moon, the romantic mood could not be sustained. If that

85

idyllic time had ever existed, it hadn't lasted. The war had changed the world, but something else closer at hand and more personal had dimmed the early brightness of those who had once been young here.

"Elinor." Clem had drawn closer; too close.

"We must go," I said. "It's been a long day."

"Of course. You're tired. I'm sorry, I should have realized . . ."

A few minutes later he left me at our own gate. My aunts had gone to bed. I glanced up at the two windows, first at Kelda's and then at May's. At each, I was almost sure, a curtain moved.

Conforming to the stealthy customs of the house, I went softly upstairs, as if I thought them asleep; but not straight to bed. Instead I noiselessly opened the bottom drawer of my tallboy, eased out my mother's bulky photograph album, and turned the pages to Kelda's wedding group: my mother in gray crêpe de chine and a hat similar in size and shape to a small boat; Kelda in the center; on her left the bridegroom, holding his highly polished hat, his glossy hair raven black; on her right, pale, rapt, slender as a dryad of the trees behind us, May.

I stared down at myself, overawed, clutching my hot flowers. My anxiety had been intuitive, breathed in with the highly charged air. I felt now a similar lack of ease but the focus of my attention had changed to single out Julius Cade, who had married, it seemed, only to die. What had he died of? "Criminal!" Aunt Claudia had said, speaking of the way we treat our artists. Crime. Sin. The words had arisen recently in some other context but I was heavy-headed after a long warm interesting day and could not place them.

I closed the album with one last unbelieving look at Kelda, beautiful and fair in her wedding dress. Could this be the woman I saw every day clad in funereal black as if she mourned not only her husband but the sorrows of the world—or some unspeakable personal woe to be endured in lifelong retirement with only May to share her solitude? Only May and me?

86

It would be too bad, I told myself—and thumped my pillow after a sleepless hour or two—if having been haunted by Dick Tass, I was now to be haunted by Julius Cade. There seemed no way of fitting together the scattered fragments of information that puzzled and disturbed me. I was unwilling even to acknowledge the suspicions they aroused. But it was as clear as daylight, after the to-do on Saturday, that Kelda had something to hide; some guilty knowledge quite separate from the dismal affair of our lost fortune. She had completely gone to pieces.

And how odd it was, how really very odd, that no one, simply no one, knew what had happened to her husband, the quiet gentleman in black who had passed through the annals of the family—had come and instantly gone as a figure flickers across a cinema screen.

"It was a pity about Cade," my grandfather had written, "but we have Kelda home again, thank God."

Was it God who had so conveniently rearranged things? At this point in my attempt to reconstruct the past I lost my way, baffled by inconsistencies too many and too vague to pin down. Besides, what could I do? To demand answers to such questions as I had in mind was surely unwise if not impossible: I was still shaken by Saturday's confrontation. I could only watch and listen and in a silence similar to theirs become ever more like my aunts.

8

A FEW HOURS' sleep restored me to a more normal state of mind. Kelda was making tea when I ran down to the kitchen next morning, pausing for a quick look, satisfactory on the whole, in the hall mirror. We sat down to breakfast. She looked tired, as if the last two days had told on her. On me their effect had been bracing. It had been a mistake to submit to a way of life I had found from the outset depressing. Henceforth I must go my own way and be quite firm about it.

Before I could speak, Kelda said, "I want you to know, Elinor, that I'm sorry for having spoken to you as I did. There are a great many things I'm sorry about"! She stared at her plate, her shoulders hunched. "But most of all for having offended you by not treating you with the confidence you deserve." Each sentence came out slowly but complete. She might have been dictating—or repeating words dictated to her. "Keeping things to ourselves has become a habit with us. We were very young when mother died. Father seemed to us an old man. He took no interest in us and hated to be worried. We used to settle everything ourselves, May and I, and learned to manage without help."

Exactly what had they managed to do without help? I stifled certain wild conjectures that sprang to mind. Besides, the wind had been taken out of my sails. Any sort of command of the conversation had slipped from me. Reasonableness was proving harder to withstand than passion.

"You've had a hard time," I said. "I can see that all the worry has fallen on your shoulders. Grandfather, your husband"—I ventured the word nervously—"and Dick, they're all gone. And not being able to live in comfort has made it much worse."

Her eyes had filled: eyes, I was suddenly reminded, of as tender a blue as Aunt May's, though tenderness, I was discovering, can be intermittent and misleading.

"But now that I know our position, why don't we discuss it thoroughly and try to do something about it?"

"That's what I thought."

"About the house. Don't you think perhaps we should sell it?" I put to her the advantages of living more cheaply elsewhere. To my surprise she nodded agreement.

"If only we could! I dream about it sometimes, pray for it." She had abandoned the dictated script and seemed to speak from the heart. "To be free of it all and all that has . . . all that it stands for."

"Well then . . . ?"

"May would never leave. Never."

"You think not?" It was the one unanswerable argument. "It would kill her, I suppose."

To disrupt the strange pattern she had woven for her life might indeed be fatal. I pictured her lying helpless like a silver birch uprooted by the wind and was dismayed by a fleeting glimpse of myself, tearless, looking on. Even to think on such lines was wrong, like heresy. We never could drag her away nor could we leave without her. And had she not suffered enough? How cruelly it must have taxed her frail strength to support her erring sister all these years: her guilt-ridden sister with whom I was chatting over breakfast in this harmless way!

"A paying guest perhaps?"

Kelda didn't reject the suggestion.

"Someone suitable . . ."

"We could make two of the rooms comfortable. May need never see the person."

What sort of person would creep in and out unheard, unseen? Who would want to live miles from anywhere without electricity halfway up a lane leading to nothing but a derelict farmhouse? Supposing such a rare bird existed, how could we find him—or her?

The thorough discussion of our affairs petered out. I didn't ask Kelda why she had kept quiet about Mrs. Tass's letter. That now seemed a small offense compared with other possible offenses, which under the influence of porridge and toast I was only too willing to shelve.

May listened absently, her eyes on her painting or on the trees or on the winding lane while I prattled about the Tasses. Experience had made me cautious. I could not bring myself to mention Aunt Claudia without also mentioning Mr. Cade, over whose nebulous personality she had cast additional shade. Nor did I breathe the word "London," which had affected Kelda so unaccountably; nor Clem's plans for Winkblade, since news of any change was so distressing to May.

The same restraint threatened my new friendship with the Tasses, which would otherwise have been entirely happy. Clem's arrival had seemed heaven-sent. The company of my father's old friends had restored to me the identity I had seemed to lose. For one perfect day I had become again the girl I was at Rosedown Hall, secure, cheerful, self-assured; and it was with the Tasses that I was to find such happiness as I enjoyed during that unsettled period of my life. But too often I was on my guard and ill at ease. Suspicions I dared not formulate even to myself and could never breathe aloud put weights on my tongue. I was beginning to be ashamed of my family and was careful not to talk about them. In the natural course of events I would have drawn close to Clem, but he must sometimes have found me reserved and distant.

"Clem asked me to apologize for not calling yesterday," I told them on the morning after my first visit to Bidminster. The apology was a formality. It had been too early when he came to fetch me; when we came back it was too late. "He hopes to see you next time."

"Next time?" An inflection in May's voice together with a lift of her eyebrows made me wonder if I had made Clem seem presumptuous.

"If you don't mind, of course."

"We must see him, I suppose." May sighed then smiled, as always suppressing her own inclination, in this case to be left alone. I felt remorseful. "We did think it a little—what shall I say?—unusual that he hadn't called the day before instead of carrying you off on a picnic so"—again she hesitated, seeking the least offensive word for what was beginning to seem Clem's offensive behavior—"so casually."

Casually? He had found me in tears and had come to my rescue. Had I been too easily carried away?

"In a way that was my fault."

May was quick to exonerate me with a gently indulgent smile and a shake of the head.

"No, dear, not yours. I'm afraid Clem was always . . . We shouldn't really have been surprised."

I found myself wondering quite anxiously what Clem had always been. He had seemed to me particularly considerate and kind but I had known him only two days. May and Kelda had known him for most of his life.

A day or two later he did call and at a suitable time, early evening. We all sat in the drawing room, where it was always dusk long before sunset, always cool, not to say cold. Conversation was fraught with pitfalls. The gap in time, so difficult to bridge, was never mentioned except when Kelda asked after his parents and

91

having ignored them for years, was happy to hear that they were well. Clem took a polite interest in May's painting of country folk grouped about a cottage door; and it was from him that my aunts learned of the Penfolds' interest in Winkblade, one of the topics I had been careful to avoid. Remembering May's strange reaction when I had burst in upon her with Sintram's news that the farmhouse might be let, I now wondered if Kelda had interpreted it wrongly: it may not have been the possibility of Dick's return that had brought the hectic color to her cheeks but rather the news of some revelation she dreaded on Kelda's behalf.

"It's high time something was done with the place," Clem was saying.

"It'll cost a great deal of money," Kelda said.

May expressed no opinion, only stirred in her chair and looked down the lane. It was almost time for her evening pilgrimage. I caught Clem's eye.

"You won't mind if I take Elinor for a stroll?"

Two minutes later we had dropped into the green depths of Packhorse Way.

"What on earth has happened to Kelda?" Clem demanded. "She used to be full of life. In that dreary black outfit she reminds me of the raven in Edgar Allan Poe's poem, forever on the point of croaking 'Never more.' And May! She acts as if she simply isn't there. Yes, I know that doesn't make sense. Let's say she has moved aside and let something else take over, something I don't like, if you don't mind my saying so."

He was obviously prejudiced. A pity! I had noticed it at once on the day of the picnic. It must be quite irrational: no one, no reasonable person could dislike May.

"I don't believe you've ever forgiven her for making you wade into Lott's Pool to rescue her bracelet," I said lightly.

"For nearly drowning me, you mean. What she needs is a tremendous shaking up of some kind, a shock that would bring back her ability to feel. How would it be if I rushed down the lane after her and somehow got it into her head that Dick's dead. He's been dead for five years, blown to smithereens. There's nothing left of him at all. Nothing."

His voice shook. He turned away.

"Just saying it makes you suffer. What would it do to her? I don't believe there's anything more powerful and dangerous than words. Isn't it safer to leave certain things unsaid?"

"I thought you believed in candor and open talking." Clem had recovered himself.

"Oh, I do."

"Then I'm quite free to say anything I like?" He took my hand. His manner was playful but his eyes told me that he was in earnest. "Such as that I want very much to see you often, Elinor. As often as you'll let me."

There could be no objection to that, not by any girl in her right senses. During the next few weeks he often drove out to Saury. Sometimes he took me back to spend the evening with his family and I spent an occasional Saturday or Sunday in town.

Mirabel and I became friends and sometimes went to the somewhat misnamed Palace Cinema, a small dark den of a place at the bottom of Castle Street, to weep over Mary Pickford, the Cinderella of the early twenties. At least I wept. Mirabel, though equally absorbed, remained composed. On the other hand she did laugh at the misfortunes of Charlie Chaplin, whom I found almost as sad as the world's sweetheart, though in a different way. He was her favorite, she told me, as we had tea in Blackwells' café after a matinée.

"I can't think why. He's such an unimpressive little man."

"That's why," was the unexpected reply. "I'm sick to death of heroes. If there hadn't been so many of them, there might have been some men left for us to marry." She poured me a second cup of tea with a reproving hand. Behind two palms the orchestra consisting of two young women and an elderly man was playing "If You Were the Only Girl in the World." "Do you know, the day war was declared I was at a tennis party at the Edstones'. There were twelve of us, six men and six girls . . ."

"Oh, Mirabel. I know what you're going to say."

"The only man left is Paul Edstone. He's still shell-shocked and hasn't come out of hospital yet. There'll be a million of us, they say, without husbands."

"You'll find someone," I began.

"It's just possible, I suppose. And I'm lucky in a way. I have plans. You'll have heard of Uncle Vernon. He's my mother's and Aunt Janet's brother. He's something terrific in a diamond mine in Kimberley and the arrangement is that the next time he comes home on a visit he'll take me back as his housekeeper."

"That would be wonderful! But Mrs. Tass will miss you."

"I know. I'd have gone out to South Africa on my own but I felt it only right to wait until things settled down a little after the war and Dick's death."

Meanwhile she was too sensible to be other than content. Life in Bidminster suited her: tea or coffee with her friends at Blackwells', changing library books, organizing flag days and outings for war orphans—and like me she had begun to see a good deal of the Penfolds.

They were hospitably inclined, and the house they rented in Priorsgate had become a meeting place for people who shared their interests. A small force of volunteers addressed envelopes, typed letters, arranged meetings in church halls, and delivered leaflets in the outlying villages, leaving Aidan to collate material for *World Without War*. Discussion groups and meetings to promote the cause of world peace were held in his spacious study on the first floor and were followed by coffee parties in Harriet's sitting room. During those summer evenings in Bidminster or on country walks with Clem and Mirabel I was happier than I had been for a long time.

But at Saury it was different. From time to time Clem dutifully called at the house, escaping at the end of fifteen minutes with undisguised relief.

"Clem hasn't changed a bit." From her seat in the window May watched him on one such occasion as he climbed into his car. The remark, faintly regretful, was directed toward Kelda, who made no response. "Oh, I know he was rather an uninteresting little boy. It isn't fair to expect . . . One cannot help one's nature."

Now that I knew her so well I understood that she must constantly be comparing Clem with Dick. In this case it was evidently social ease that Clem was felt to lack. Personally I hadn't noticed it. On the contrary, I had rather admired his quiet confidence and sense of humor, but there was no denying that both these qualities failed him at Hoodman House. Almost everything he said was unfortunate. He alluded to the garden in the old days before it became a field. "That was before we lost everything," May sighed. His remark that Mirabel had heard from Paul Edstone was a reminder that Dick was still missing. "He just didn't think," May said afterward. His work had been Dick's work: his home had been Dick's. Any reference to either was received with a sad silence.

"I can't stand much more of this, Elinor." We had got ourselves out of the house after a particularly stiff session. "I know now how a bull must feel in a china shop, afraid to move for fear of breaking something. One of these days I'll make some perfectly harmless remark and the whole place will crack and fall apart." He laughed and added, "I hope."

"It never will." We moved out of the shade cast by its gaunt height and stood in the sunshine by the field gate.

"An architect's nightmare." Clem unleashed on the house the frustration he had suffered indoors. "But I'm afraid you're right. Whatever shortcuts your grandfather took in building other people's houses, he built his own to last." We sauntered up the lane toward Winkblade between the open field on one hand and on the other a high hedge hung with wild roses and honeysuckle. "But it's

95

what goes on inside the house that worries me. Is that meant to last as well?"

It was a question I had often asked myself; but for the moment it was the coolness between May and Clem that troubled me.

"May needs sympathy and understanding . . ."

"I understand her." Clem took me by the shoulders, standing in front of me so that I was forced to look into his face. "Let me tell you something. You think you can cure May—and Kelda too for that matter—of this frightful nervous rot that has got into them. Are you sure the treatment isn't going to work the other way round?"

"You don't mean . . . ?"

"Yes, I do. It's more than likely that you'll be the one to change." His eyes traveled over my hair, my face, deliberately but with such gentleness that for some reason I felt tearful. "You're not like either of your aunts . . ."

"Oh I know. They're both so beautiful. Do you think I haven't noticed?"

"Beautiful? Perhaps that's what's always been wrong with them. Pictures hanging on a wall don't have to exert themselves. It's simply 'Here we are. What more do you want?' But when I said you weren't like them, I didn't mean that you aren't beautiful. As a matter of fact there are times when you take my breath away."

"Oh how nice! How very nice that is!"

"Stop purring. I really have something to say. Yes, you're different. Your hair is darker, your eyes are gray, your mouth . . . Well, you're nothing like those two to look at and yet there have been times—this is true, Elinor—especially when you've been talking about May"—he was so serious and hesitant that I felt uneasy— "Times when you have looked like her. As if she had taken you over."

"Clem! You frighten me!"

"I'm sorry, dear. I only want to warn you that if there are to be any changes at Hoodman, they could be changes in you. You'll say it's none of my business, nor is it, not yet however much I want it to be." He drew my arm through his and we walked on. "You're exactly right as you are—and alive to your fingertips. Alive. Please stay that way."

I partly understood his warning. It was as if he knew of those devitalizing moods in which, like May, I turned away from reality to share with her a dream hopeless of fulfillment. Or—what would be worse—he might have sensed the atmosphere of hidden guilt that I was also beginning to share, though with nothing more to go on than hints, guesses, and the suspicious gaps left by things unsaid. Suppose I told him that I was living with—a murderess. There! I had said it to myself and must have given some outward sign of the horror the word evoked.

"What's the matter?" Clem stopped and faced me. "You're looking pinched. Do you get enough to eat?" Then more seriously, "Is something bothering you? Why don't you tell me and let me help. You know I'd do anything."

He had never spoken so openly of his feeling for me. Perhaps he would have said more if he hadn't felt that in the deepest sense I wasn't listening: my innermost attention was directed elsewhere. It was unfair to him. I roused myself and almost reached the point of confiding in him, only to realize once again that there was nothing positive to tell.

"But they'll never want to let you go," he was saying. "And neither will I."

It was he who would be leaving. In September he was to go to Dorset, where he would help to carry out restoration work on a manor house and explore the western counties for such antique fittings—fireplaces, doors, ironwork, sculpture—as could be moved to the Tasses' repository in Bidminster.

"There may be something suitable for Winkblade." We had come to the farm gate where he had left his car. I saw it as a welcome opportunity to change the subject.

"You think the Penfolds are seriously interested?"

"Miss Penfold has managed to rout out the owner already, an old gentleman who has never so much as seen Winkblade. He inherited it as a young man, let it for a while, then decided it was too unprofitable to bother with."

"Then he'll sell?"

"With Miss P. on his trail the poor old chap'll find himself cornered."

"She'll be an interesting neighbor. But I shall miss you, Clem, while you're away."

"I'll be back," he said. "It's hard to keep away from Saury these days!"

When he had driven off I walked slowly home. May had come into the front garden. I saw it as a sign of her sensitivity that her first remark should echo one I had just made.

"You'll miss Clem when he goes to Dorset." She took my hand between her cold fingers. "I'm afraid . . . No, that isn't what I mean: no one must influence you, not even I who love you should do that. Only I wonder if you are growing a little too . . . if you are growing fond of him."

"I like him very much." It was impossible even when she was most aloof to escape the enchantment of her company. Now, her eyes and lips softened by what seemed a special affection for me, she appeared much younger than her years. I realized how lovely she must have been as a girl, how hard it must have been for Dick to leave her, how trivial in comparison Clem's temporary absence would be. All the same it was only fair to add: "He's been very thoughtful and kind."

"Ah! Kind!"

I understood at once the inadequacy of kindness in the emotional scale of one whose love was of the sort poets dreamed of: Clem's liking for me—straightforward sensible Clem—must fall far short of Dick's romantic wooing of May.

"You've been starved of company since you came here." We walked round the house to the conservatory and sat at the bamboo table. Trailing green fronds drooped from the hanging baskets and feathery green ferns rose from blue and white pots. The air was drowsily warm and moist. "I know how much you miss your mother. Such a pity that we saw so little of her—just that one time in London and again at the wedding. Tell me about her."

What could I say through the tears that welled with a suddenly revived sense of loss? May reached across the table and laid her hand on mine.

"I've upset you. And yet I do so wish that I could—in my ineffectual way—to some small extent take her place. Oh, that can never be, I know. You were devoted to each other. You could tell her everything."

It all came back to me: our long rambling talks in the sunny sitting room overlooking the park; its books and pale chintzes; the portrait of my father in full regimentals; the photograph of our bungalow in Lahore with its wide verandah. I heard the clamor of rooks in Rosedown's tall elms and the last echo of my mother's voice before it faded into silence: "They're your only relations, but, remember, you'll be independent . . ."

". . . the rest of her family. We never heard of any brothers or sisters."

"She was an only child like me."

"Did you ever stay with your grandparents? The Anselms. Wasn't that the name?"

"I can just remember my grandmother. She died while we were in India, but we had visited her when I was very young—in Sussex."

"That must have been very pleasant. You liked it there?"

It seemed to me that I had liked every stage of my life until I came to Hoodman House, but I couldn't very well say so.

"There was a big garden with a summerhouse and a stable and horses."

"Your grandmother kept a groom—and a carriage?"

"I suppose she must have done. Yes, of course: we went for drives."

"How sad for your mother to be so far away when your grandmother died! And the house in Sussex? Did she keep it on for a while?" A young ivy stem hung close to her hair. She raised a languid hand to touch it and twist it lightly round her finger where it clung, trapped, unable to break free until she chose to let it go.

"Oh no, the house was sold. Some of the nicer things are still stored at Rosedown with Mother's. The Burnetts are keeping them for me."

"And I suppose"—May spoke dreamily, as if exhausted by the warm atmosphere or by the effort of making conversation—"everything comes to you, the last of the Anselm side of your family."

Perhaps I too was enervated by the moist smell of the imprisoned greenery that dangled and twisted and spread its leaves unvisited year after year by any refreshing breeze. Our talk had been—or seemed—casual, a mere filling in of time before the evening meal, with nothing in it to bring a chill to my heart, a deep loneliness. The reminder of the relatives I lacked not only focused my mind on the only relatives I possessed but also on the ease and frequency with which people died. Suppose Clem should die, leaving me alone with the relatives on my father's side. Strange that I should think of it like that, as if my hope of security rested in Clem.

". . . a blessing that your mother's people were so comfortably off, and your father's mother too . . ."

She was making an effort to be sociable by taking an interest in my affairs, I reminded myself, not making an assessment of what I was worth. Through long disuse she had perhaps lost a little of the skill in conversation she must once have had. With encouragement it would come back. After all, when their mother died it was May who had learned to act as hostess to her father's friends. The mere fact that she bothered to talk to me in this way was a sign

that her nervous tone was improving. I grew less diffident about
disturbing her and we began to spend more time together. Sometimes when I went into the drawing room to dust or lay the fire
she would look up from her work or rouse herself from reverie and
with a look or nod invite me to join her; or she would keep me in
her room when I went to fetch her breakfast tray. Often it was with
an air of pleading, as if my company did her good, though I knew
that she was putting herself out for my sake.

"I was hoping you could find time for one of our little chats,"
she would say or, "Come and cheer me up. Tell me more about
India—or Rosedown."

At first there were things I found difficult to talk about, but
she was so attentive and perceptive that confidences grew easier.

"I've been thinking about you and Clem," she said one Sunday evening. The day had been humid and overcast and she had
gone to her room feeling unwell. I took her up a tray of tea and
found her lying back in her low chair, her hair undone and falling
in smooth waves over her white dressing jacket. She took the cup
with a murmur of thanks, her eyes half closed by their blue lids.
I sat down in my usual place on the ottoman. There had been a
special gravity in her voice—or was it just the depressing effect of
a headache?

"You spend a good deal of time with him. Just the two of you
alone together." She paused. "Tell me, you mustn't mind my
asking, just as your mother would have asked . . . I'm sure she must
have advised you and warned you of such things . . ."

I smiled, remembering my mother's strictures about changing
wet stockings, how long a visit should last, not asking personal
questions or sitting too close to the fire—not the kind of warnings
May obviously had in mind. She had turned her head, as if to look
out of the window though there was nothing to see but trees: no
people, nothing happening.

"When he is alone with you, does Clem behave as a lover,
Elinor?"

I hesitated, and not only out of embarrassment, although the drift of the question was plain. It had been framed in such a way as to make me see Clem from an unfamiliar distance, his behavior distinct from Clem himself like a disguise. A lover? It amused me to see him for a wild moment as the smoldering sheikh whom Mirabel and I goggled at in the Palace cinema. Clem would have enjoyed the comparison.

"You needn't tell me, dear, if you don't want to. I only want to put you on your guard. A girl may not be aware of the passion she excites in a man—or of what may come of it, the sorrow and shame she has to bear alone if she is so unwise as to forget herself. Some men can be trusted not to take advantage, but not all, I'm afraid, not even . . ."

Not even who? I didn't ask. She didn't say, but went on to enlarge upon the theme of men's passions and women's folly, speaking slowly with significant pauses more cautionary than words. I heard her with the amused indulgence the young grant their elders in such circumstances; until as she persevered in her duty to keep me from the primrose path of dalliance, my attention wandered from what she said to her manner of saying it: from the scorching fires of unbridled desire to the passionless lips from which each word fell as colorless as a water drop from a cool fountain.

In some indescribable way the contrast bothered me. If she wanted to talk of love, why didn't she tell me about her own love for Dick and his for her? About how true lovers felt instead of how cads and simple-minded girls should not behave? Puzzled, yet as always fascinated by her, I could almost have registered the point at which she forgot me as she pursued her theme in a strangely single-minded way, unconscious of her audience: it was the shameful laxity of women rather than of men that she harped on with a persistence that in anyone else, any person less fastidious and composed, would have seemed overdone if not obsessive.

All of a sudden, as if in response to some inner prompting, she

102

stopped and looked round the familiar room uncertainly, as if momentarily lost.

"We were talking about Clem." She seemed to rediscover him. In whatever mysterious labyrinth of the mind she had been straying, outwardly she remained unchanged. In all the time I spent with her, throughout all the pain and distress that lay ahead, I never saw her brow furrowed by uncertainty or doubt or anxiety or the soft blue of her eyes darkened by emotion.

"Coarseness," she was saying. "Not what one would expect to find in a well-brought-up and educated man; but there it is, and a sensitive girl will always be aware of it."

"I don't think anyone could call Clem coarse."

Not too abruptly for fear of hurting her feelings, I got up and put her cup back on the tray.

"That's so like you, dear. Such a loyal little friend."

She touched her forehead as if it hurt. I had forgotten her headache. She had tired herself in the quite unnecessary exercise of what she felt to be her duty.

But not without effect. It was in an altered frame of mind that I went thoughtfully downstairs. From such minute drops and delicate touches are our impressions formed that my attitude to Clem had undergone a small adjustment—as, for that matter, had my attitude to May. Ideas lightly rooted in my mind were to spring, when their time came, into rank and bitter growth.

9

§§§§§§

It was on a Sunday that May warned me against the perils of love. Unfortunately that same week brought a misunderstanding between Clem and me, our first, and upsetting to us both. On Tuesday evening we were to go to a concert in Bidminster. Since Clem's encounters with my aunts were irksome to us all, I had got into the habit of walking up to Winkblade and meeting him there instead of waiting for him to pick me up at Hoodman House. I was ready in good time and sauntered up the lane, dressed in almost my best—a pale yellow tussore silk dress and jacket—having stipulated when the arrangements were made on the previous Saturday that the hood of the car was to be up for the sake of my hair.

He was late. It had never happened before. I stood by the wall of the farm yard, my eyes fixed immovably on the distant Tile Sheds where he would turn off the Upper Saury road. All was still. Behind me, its white walls warmed by daylong sunshine, the farmhouse slumbered in the unbroken silence of years. It seemed impossible that anyone had ever lived there or that anyone ever would.

My shoes were dusty! Hastily removing my gloves as if there wasn't a minute to lose, I flicked them gingerly with a handkerchief, shook it, returned it to my bag, looked in the pocket mirror, adjusted my scarf, thought of other scarves, other concerts, other things, until twenty interminable minutes had ticked by. Drifting round to the garden, I stood between the ash trees (ears pricked for the sound of a car) and gazed over the wicket gate in the direction of Lott's Pool (serve him right if he had drowned)— looked at my watch. Half an hour late! When he did come I would simply refuse to go. To creep into the concert halfway through the performance was out of the question.

Prowling round the outbuildings brought no comfort. Removing my glove once more, I lifted each latch and stared disconsolately at the emptiness of stable and washhouse; at a pile of sacks and a rusted tin trunk in one corner of the woodshed. This must be one of Sintram's temporary lodgings, or did he prefer the bakehouse? With difficulty I lifted the heavy bar securing the iron door of the oven and peered inside, then shut it with a clang that reverberated in the surrounding silence with a dreadful finality. To get inside, not that one would want to, was forbidden, Clem said. Once in, if the bar was lowered, there was no getting out.

But Clem was wrong about the squirrel. Dick would never have given it to Kelda: it was May he loved, had always loved. Conversely, May was right—Clem's behavior was sometimes unsatisfactory and this was certainly one of the times.

"Tuesday?" Kelda said. "It's an odd time for a concert. You've mistaken the day. Concerts in the Masonic Hall are usually on Wednesdays. At least they used to be."

Divested of my finery, I spent the evening reading in the conservatory. Kelda was altering a skirt in the morning room. May still wasn't feeling well. I hadn't seen her all day. When I took up her breakfast tray she had called out feebly that I was to leave it outside her door.

The next evening, suitably arrayed once more but with less enthusiasm, I elected to wait at the drawing room window, with no better result: no sign of Clem. Unable to read or occupy myself in any useful way, my whole soul concentrated on waiting, I stared at May's unfinished picture of two girls in white dresses gathering flowers in a garden, one holding out a basket, the other snipping off what could have been a delphinium, a blue flower of some sort. Having no other company, I observed the girls critically. Their faces were conventionally sweet with the rosebud prettiness of a thousand such pictures better drawn than this. Nauseatingly sweet. On second thought it was the same face: the basket holder and the flower snipper were identical. "Mawkish," Clem would have said. *If he had been here!* Their garden held no hint of rain, darkness, or decay: no necessary imperfection. It wasn't true. In every Eden, as I now know and suspected even then, a serpent lurks.

Common sense told me that whatever Clem's imperfections might be, he would never deliberately have let me down or carelessly forgotten. But he could have written to explain or sent a telegram. If an accident or illness had prevented him from writing, Mrs. Tass or Mirabel would have let me know.

May's indisposition lasted several days during which I scarcely saw her. She stayed in her room and came downstairs for an hour or two in the evening. She didn't feel like talking: our little chats were suspended. I read determinedly in the conservatory or took brisk walks. The week seemed endless.

"That must be Clem," Kelda said when on Saturday morning a car drew up outside. We had just finished breakfast. I remained at the table until he knocked, then with a dignified lack of haste walked to the front door; and there he was, smiling, happy to see me.

"You're not ready?"—and seeing my expression—"anything wrong? Don't you want to come?"

"Come where?" was my distant response.

"To the regatta, of course. You hadn't forgotten? What's up, Elinor?"

Tuesday's disaster had indeed banished the regatta from my mind. We dealt first with his weeklong absence. When he had gone home from Saury on the previous Saturday evening, it was to find that an unexpected problem had arisen at Minhayton, where Tass and Son were restoring some almshouses. Someone had to go: he had left early on Monday morning and stayed until Friday.

"But why ever didn't you write and tell me?"

"Write? Well, I suppose I could have done—but I thought..."

"Excuse me," I said coldly, "but that's just what you didn't do. If you'd given a moment's thought to me you might have wondered what I was doing on Tuesday evening. Waiting a whole hour at Winkblade was what I was doing and again on Wednesday in case I'd been wrong about the day."

"My God, Elinor!" He thrust me backward into the hall and stepped inside. "Do you mean that you didn't get my message? She didn't tell you?"

"She?"

"May." He was suddenly furiously angry. "I came round this way to see you on Monday morning, early, because I had to be at Minhayton by nine. May saw me and opened her window. She told me you'd gone to Ransoms' farm."

"Well, yes." The humid weather had turned the milk sour overnight. I had gone to fetch a fresh supply for breakfast.

"I was in a dickens of a rush and couldn't wait, but I asked her to explain that we'd have to miss the concert and that I'd be here first thing this morning to take you to the regatta."

She must have forgotten. Remote in her room with the heavy door shut, she might as well have been dead for all she knew of other people's activities and would have had no idea that in the room next to hers on two evenings I was dressing as furtively as a mouse for fear of disturbing her. She must have been lying down when I left on Tuesday evening, otherwise she would have seen me setting off for Winkblade, dressed up to the nines.

"You know how little contact she has with the world around her," I began, "and this week especially—"

"Don't make excuses. No normal person could have forgotten. She's got nothing else to think about, has she? She sits up there in her ivory tower like a plaster saint, but, believe me, she doesn't miss much, not if it's likely to affect her in any way."

"You're surely not suggesting that she would . . ."

"Deliberately forget? Yes, I am." Clem's angry voice brought Kelda from the kitchen.

"Whatever's wrong, Elinor? Are you two quarreling?"

It hadn't felt like that. Clem's cheeks and forehead were flushed and his eyes resentful but his sternness had not been directed toward me; and yet it separated us. Momentarily lost for words, he glared round the forbidding hall: at the towering oak hallstand with its dozen empty hooks, the dark green heavily embossed wallpaper, the gray-green stretch of carpet, yards and yards of it, its endlessly repeated pattern of scrolls and urns reaching to and mounting the stairs and flowing along the dark passage to the back of the house.

"I'm beginning to detest this place," he said so savagely that my impulse was to spring to its defense.

But before I could begin on so admittedly difficult a course, the atmosphere changed. A movement at the top of the stairs made us all three look up. May had soundlessly appeared. She still wore her long white dressing gown but she had done her hair. It lay in smooth pale bands like sculpture round her head and was drawn into a loose knot at the nape of her neck. She stood quite still, one thin hand resting on the broad stair rail. Instinctively I closed the front door, lest even on the mild summer morning a draught of air might be too much for her. The only remaining light came from the stained-glass window. Its red and blue panes played their usual trick of confusing dimensions and color values and reducing all that was visible to drab shades of umber and gray. Looking up at the elevated figure in white, I felt a faint dizziness.

In such a situation whatever Clem said or did would have seemed crude.

"Why didn't you give Elinor my message?" he demanded loudly.

I flinched from the roughness of his tone. May came slowly down a step or two, pausing, as if needing to rest.

"About your going to Minhayton?" Her voice held a little more warmth than usual, the indulgence suitable for soothing a fractious child. "But of course I did. I wrote it all down the minute you left," she said, coming down to our level, "and put the note there." She pointed to the lid of the glove box in the center of the hallstand. "Then I'm afraid I went back to bed." Her head drooped and I remembered the severity of her headache. When she looked up it was with a touching look of bewilderment. "I was so sure that Elinor would find it when she came back from the farm."

The extent of my relief surprised me, almost as if I had doubted her.

"You don't mean . . . Elinor, my dearest, you didn't see it? But how could that be? It was there." She laid her hand on the lid as if reproaching it. "And you didn't see it."

I tried to remember. Hurrying back from the farm, I had put the jug on the hall chair, pulled off the knitted jacket I was wearing, flung it onto a hook without a glance and made for the kitchen.

"An envelope? I don't remember . . ."

"No, dear. A sheet of notepaper, folded, with your name on it." She raised the lid of the glove box and looked inside. "Do you remember, Kelda, we used to pretend this was our private letter box when we were children? It was always a thrill to look in every time we passed, hoping to find a note."

"What were they about?" The silent black shape at the foot of the stairs stirred into life. "I've forgotten."

"Secrets, of course. We loved secrets."

They exchanged intimate looks, as if uncovering a store of occult knowledge, May smiling, Kelda grave.

"You're so very much at home here, Elinor—you've fitted in

so well with all our ways that I forgot you wouldn't know of our childish habit of leaving messages here, ordinary practical things on the lid and special ones inside."

Kelda came over to the hallstand.

"And sometimes when the real post came the letters were put here," she said, "and I've just remembered, we found one weeks after it was delivered." She went down on her knees and reached across the flat base with its metal drip tray for umbrellas. "There now!" From between the stand and the wall she plucked a folded paper. "You must have knocked it off, Elinor, when you hung up your coat."

I opened it, glanced at May's neat handwriting and handed the paper to Clem. He didn't take it. His anger had subsided but he looked glum and upset. May looked at him regretfully, penitently too, although there was no need—she had acted for the best.

"I should have made a point of telling Elinor in person as soon as she came in but my head ached so unbearably that I could only lie still and hope the pain would go. Mercifully I fell asleep and when I woke the trouble at Minhayton had gone from my mind. You must forgive me, Clem. I know that Elinor will. I'm so very sorry."

He did not forgive her. I positively felt his old prejudice hardening into outright hostility.

"If you're coming, Elinor," he said, "I'll wait for you outside."

How could he resist May's humility and pleading eyes? I put the question in a slightly different form when, arrayed for the third time in my yellow tussore, I got into the car.

"How could I resist? Easily. By simply not believing her. No, don't say another word about it. I know those two. The fact is they want me out of the way as much as they want to keep you there. The two things hang together and if we don't watch out, they'll succeed in both."

"But you must believe her. You saw the note. And if anyone is to blame it's me. I must have swept it out of sight with my jacket,

110

as May said. And I'm sorry to have been so frosty, Clem, when I opened the door."

Despite these two handsome apologies it took him longer than I would have expected to recover his good humor. He seemed preoccupied and disinclined to talk during the whole of the drive to Bidminster.

10

THE REVIVAL OF Bidminster's famous regatta, suspended since the outbreak of war, had attracted crowds of visitors. We watched the races from the grandstand in the riverside park until midafternoon, then climbed the steep streets to the privacy of the Tasses' garden.

"Clem's cheered up a bit," Mirabel remarked when he had gone indoors to fetch the tea things. "He's been like a bear with a sore head lately. It isn't like him. You should do something about it."

"Me? What can I do for goodness' sake?"

As it happened, there was no need for me to do anything. Clem was already deploying his own strategy, on his own ground and with powerful allies. It was simple, straightforward, and in the event entirely successful.

Mrs. Tass joined us and as she poured out tea, remarked in her mild way, "I've been thinking, Elinor, how sensible it would be if you were to spend a few days here. There'll be so much going on in town this next week. It would be a pity for you to miss the dance on Wednesday."

"Good idea!" Mirabel responded to her cue. "And it would save all that racketing back and forth in Clem's old bone-shaker."

Clem ignored the insult to his car. He sat at ease in his deck

112

chair, his face sun-browned, his fair hair glinting against the blue canvas. It struck me all at once how good-looking he was—and how self-confident.

"Thank you, I should love to if it won't put you out." Sunshine, pleasant company, the cool smell of the river, holiday crowds shuffling and talking on the path below, the skimming boats, the prospect of a dance, above all the absence of my aunts! "Only I'm not sure whether—"

"No trouble," Mirabel said. "The spare bed is all ready and made up."

"Clem can take you home to collect your things and pick you up in the morning."

"No." Clem got to his feet, a tall man, taller than ever when one looked up at him from a deck chair. "I'll take Elinor home now, wait while she packs and bring her back tonight."

"But I shall have to make arrangements . . ."

"Drink your tea and do as you're told," he said. "I'll give you five minutes."

Again we didn't talk much during the drive. This time was different. Unfamiliar emotions stirred in me. I stole occasional glances at his profile. Familiar as it was, I had never paid much attention to the details of his features: strong-boned, regular, the corners of his mouth now firmly turned down.

"Don't dither about trying to decide which frocks to bring," he said as he opened the car door for me. "Bring them all. It'll save time."

A mood of heady recklessness seized me. The tactful, considerate speech explaining my change of plan would also be a waste of time. I flung open the drawing room door.

"Mrs. Tass has invited me to stay for a few days," I announced clearly to May at the window and Kelda beyond in the conservatory. "Haven't time to explain. Clem's waiting for me. I'm going up to pack."

It took less than ten minutes. We left in a cloud of dust.

"Why are we stopping here?" I asked as Clem pulled up at Winkblade.

"Get out," he said.

Bemused, I obeyed. He took my hand. We went round the house to the garden, hushed in the long shadows of early evening. The syringa was in full bloom and the air smelt of orange blossom.

"It's like another world," I said, "but oughtn't we to . . ."

Without a word, without preamble or half measures or undue delicacy, he took me in his arms and kissed me, held me close, kissed me again. Breathless, I felt my bones melt, my entire being fall to pieces and reassemble itself transformed—and speechless. We gazed into each other's eyes. It was not the first time he had kissed me, but this had been a kiss to change the world: a world divested of all complications now that it contained no one but Clem and me, yet dazzling in its infinite possibilities.

"I love you," he said several times. "I must have loved you ever since Kelda's ghastly wedding. Then since you came back— talk about miracles!—I couldn't believe my eyes when I saw you at the gate, lovelier than ever, and since then it's got worse. You don't know how hard it's been, waiting and hoping to see some sign that you feel as I do. Then I decided not to wait any longer."

"It's wonderful," I breathed, "and here of all places."

"Yes, the place is right. I thought of that. Anyplace would have done for me and anytime. But for you there had to be flowers." Vaguely he included in our rapture the sunflowers by the wall, the lilies and canterbury bells. "And all that romantic dream of lovers and nightingales."

"Of course. We aren't the first, remember, to love each other in this beloved place."

"We're the only ones. This habit of dwelling on the past has got to stop. What happened is over and done with."

"Yes, I know," I murmured, turning my back on aspects of the past he knew nothing about: casting other people's guilt as well as other people's loves to the four winds.

"It's what's happening now that matters. You think it was a sort of fairy-tale world when those others were young. It wasn't like that—or like this."

This, I was aware, as he kissed me again, was undoubtedly the dire temptation May had warned me against. Poor untempted May! Poor Kelda! I shed them as well as all the problems that weighed them down and soared irresponsibly into a realm empty of relations. To think that Clem had been here all the time and I had seen him as not much more than a kind of brother! Cheek to cheek, we gazed entranced through the gap between the ash trees over the gold-tinged fields to the blue distant hills; but trees, fields, hills would never again be as they had been: Saury had become a place to be loved in, not to be looked at. From its margins Clem had moved with complete assurance to the center.

We were late for dinner and must have made something of an entrance. Looks were exchanged. They know, I thought, what we've been doing, and we didn't care.

"I can't tell you how happy it would make us," Mrs. Tass said as the blissful week came to an end, "if you and Clem were to marry. Our families were so close in the past. Your parents would have felt just as we do."

It was too soon to make plans when a lifetime of loving stretched before us, though naturally in such circumstances one's mind turns to embroidered nightdresses, Brussels lace, and one's mother's pearls. Mine also dwelt on the To Let sign outside a house on the corner of Priorsgate and Watt Lane. It was an oddly shaped little house improbably wedged between substantial town houses on one side and ancient timbered dwellings on the other.

"Four stories at least," Mirabel warned, sensing my interest as we passed one day. "Far too many stairs."

But its motley of windows peering down to the river over rooftops and the door set in a deep archway with flower tubs gave it a charm that took my fancy, and it was no more than five minutes' walk from the offices of Tass and Son.

Not until I stood once more in the hall at home did I come down to earth. As the sound of Clem's car died away my heart sank a little. But life at Hoodman House must surely be easier to endure now that my release was certain. My dutiful resolve to stay with my aunts as long as they needed me had been short-lived. In the first thrill of loving and being loved I simply forgot it. Ours was to be one of those effortless, inevitable love affairs as natural as breathing. It was as if our being drawn silently together at the wedding breakfast had destined us to have lunch, tea, and dinner together for the rest of our lives: a prosaic image doing little justice to the raptures of the days that followed. But to reduce them to simple prose is in itself a triumph for one whose reaction to other matters was over-romantic to say the least.

My aunts greeted me quietly. No doubt they guessed what had happened. It was not yet time to talk of leaving to be married, nor did I even hint at it; but it must be hard to share a house with someone walking on air without noticing the phenomenon. Having rather lost interest in them, I overlooked the possibility that their interest in me and in my future might actually have increased: that they might be observing me more intently and for more urgent reasons than I had ever observed them.

In this careless state of mind I paid little attention to an incident whose significance I should have recognized at once: the arrival one morning of a bulky parcel addressed to Mrs. Cade.

The postman dumped it on the table in the kitchen where Kelda and I were preparing lunch and went perspiring back to his handcart with an aggrieved air.

"Oh dear!" Kelda looked distressed. "I do hope . . ." She leaned over the parcel, keeping both hands on the table as if afraid to touch it.

"Shall I open it for you?"

"There's no need really. I know what it is." Nevertheless she wiped the knife she had been using to cut up stewing steak and slit the brown paper as grimly as if it covered a corpse. "It's May's paintings." She counted them. "All her work for the past six months."

"How dreadful for her!"

"For us all." Kelda was developing a frown between her brows. It deepened as she read the agent's letter. He was no longer able to sell work of this kind and requested that no more be sent. "The money wasn't much but it did help."

"I suppose you must break it to her."

"I shall have to—but not just yet."

We lifted the heavy package into a cupboard and closed the door on the kittens and ringleted children, the cozy nurseries and flower-filled gardens that no one wanted anymore. Unreal though they were, they had provided May's only link with the practical world, her only occupation.

The problem disturbed me but less than it would once have done, particularly as I soon found myself in the position of earning a little money for the first time in my life.

"We could do with a part-time secretary." Harriet broached the subject one evening when Clem and I dropped in on the Penfolds for coffee and a chat. By this time she was in my confidence to the extent of knowing about our financial problems. I daresay she and Clem had put their heads together. "Would you be interested, Elinor?"

Taken by surprise, I could only protest my lack of experience.

"Aidan could never face a trained secretary. She would terrify him. We want someone to come and go like one of us without irritating us to death and yet be more firmly committed than these volunteers, bless their hearts. Even two days a week would be enough to keep Aidan's papers in order."

At the time even two days would have been awkward for me to arrange and would have entailed long walks to and from the station, where there were only two trains a day. But the idea appealed to me and I went so far as to borrow a typewriter from

Tass and Son, buy a beginner's manual, and teach myself to type. Progress was slow and laborious but I planned to work hard and improve my skill while Clem was in Dorset.

This amateurish attitude was given a sudden jolt by the rejection of May's pictures and the loss of her tiny income. It was Willie Kimble, the world-weary taxi driver, who unexpectedly lent a helping hand by buying a small bus and running it four times a day between Saury village and Bidminster. By September I had become Aidan's part-time assistant, happily unaware that my wage of eighteen shilling for the few hours a week was far more than the going rate. I handed it over to Kelda as my contribution to the housekeeping and having thus cleared my conscience was able to leave most of my quarterly allowance in the bank.

I evolved a primitive method of filing Aidan's papers in cardboard boxes, copied letters, and, according to Harriet, exercised a soothing influence on Aidan and made life for her worth living.

I arrived at the house in Priorsgate one morning to find Aidan already submerged by the day's delivery of letters.

"Thank goodness you're here, Elinor. Here, read these for me."

He was collecting material for a series of articles entitled "The Aftermath" for the periodical he had launched. As a change from statistics and reasoned argument he was now concerned with the effect of war on individuals, both civilians and ex-servicemen, and had used the columns of a national paper to appeal for information. The response was more than he had bargained for. We had already read over two hundred letters from people in all walks of life who wrote of the practical and emotional effects on them of four years of war. There were heart-rending accounts of the loss of work from returning soldiers, loss of hope, loss of direction, and the loss of sons and husbands from bereaved women.

"All loss," I said despairingly when we had each read a new

batch and were comparing notes. "Has nothing good come out of it—nothing at all?"

"The strong characters who can react positively to experience may be able to answer that question"—Aidan looked gloomily over his spectacles—"the ones who've survived it, that is—but they're too busy to write to us. And most of the young men who would have taken a lead in our national affairs are dead."

"The cream of the country. That's what Mrs. Torgill calls them."

"And we're left with the skimmed milk. Middle-aged crocks like me."

He was still suffering the after-effects of gas, but there was no self-pity in his half smile, and in spite of his lined face and receding hair I did not think of him as middle-aged. Idealism, I suppose, is a youthful quality.

"But if the best are gone," I said, "some of the worst must be gone too."

"Can one ever fit human beings into such categories? But you're right, Elinor. We're inclined to think that the dead could never have done wrong."

My task was to group the letters under various headings and to address and post the cyclostyled letters of thanks while Mr. Penfold drafted others. We became absorbed. The simplest of the letters were the most poignant, particularly one written by a man about his wife. The couple had lost their only son at Vimy Ridge but his mother was still setting a place for him at table for every meal; still brushing his Sunday suit every Saturday night.

"I haven't the heart to reason with her," the husband wrote, "but I wonder if I should put a stop to it, for her own sake as well as my own. Sometimes the senselessness of it nearly drives me crazy."

"Reasoning wouldn't do any good. It has nothing to do with reason," Aidan said. "She has chosen the only way she knows of keeping in touch with the boy. If this fellow did put a stop to it, she might be the one to go crazy."

Laying a place at the table, brushing a Sunday suit, waiting under the cherry tree by the gate . . . I wondered if Aunt May would go crazy if she were deprived of her daily communication with Dick and immediately rejected so preposterous an idea. All the same, not for the first time, my attitude was less than wholly sympathetic. I felt a faint distaste, as on finding that flowers kept too long in a vase not only have lost their fragrance but also have begun to smell of decay.

"The woman is finding practical expression for an inexpressible emotion." Aidan laid down the letter and sought comfort in a generalization. "The laying out of food, the preparation of garments, the preservation and consequently the hallowing of a place—all religious ritual must have had its origin in such acts. The ritual outlives the need that inspires it."

"I find that almost as sad as the actual grief."

"Yes, yes, but inevitable. Intense grief must wear itself out or become something else," he concluded cryptically. Before I could ask him to elaborate, Harriet tapped on the door.

"Mrs. Brady has gone without her key and we'll both be out when she comes back to do the brasses this afternoon. Would you mind taking it to her, Elinor, when you go to the post office? It won't be far out of your way."

She gave me the direction. Mrs. Brady, the daily help, lived in a row of workmen's cottages by the riverside in the lower part of the town, a locality new to me. The railway had long since put paid to the river as a means of transport but warehouses still fronted the broad quay. The clattering hooves of cart horses, the bustle of loading, and beyond the stir of human life, the bright flow of the river were stimulating after a morning in the quiet study. Mrs. Brady was at her door taking in bread from a baker's boy as I threaded my way between trucks and drays and she saw me coming.

120

"Well now, I'm sorry, Miss Findon"—as I held out the key—"I clean forgot it and you've had to come all this way."

We chatted a few minutes on the doorstep. It was my first opportunity of getting to know Mrs. Brady, whom I had seen from time to time as she dusted the stairs or polished the front door knocker at the house in Priorsgate.

"I know someone who'd be pleased to see you, Miss Findon." She cast a meaningful glance over her shoulder. The door opened directly into her living room, where a bright fire burned in the grate. In an armchair beside it sat a little old woman wrapped in a shawl. "You pricked up your ears, didn't you, Auntie, when you heard me say Miss Findon." Mrs. Brady had raised her voice and now lowered it again to a conspiratorial undertone. "You'll come in for a minute, won't you? She'll be over the moon."

Mystified, I followed her into the room.

"Now"—Mrs. Brady enjoyed keeping me in suspense—"you won't know who this is."

The face above the shawl was colorless except for the brown eyes turned toward me and communicating some message I failed to understand. They scanned my face and person; the thin lips moved in a trembling smile; inspiration came to me.

"It must be—is it Annie?"

She beamed with pleasure. I took her hand and knelt by her side.

"My Aunt Annie"—Mrs. Brady watched our reunion with the pride of a successful impressario—"that nursed your father."

"Oh how pleased I am, how absolutely delighted to have found you."

"There now," said Mrs. Brady, highly gratified. She raised her voice to the level she evidently deemed suitable for the elderly, though Annie gave no sign of being deaf. "Now you'll be in your element, won't you? Yes, she is pleased."

"Why didn't you tell me, Mrs. Brady?"

"Your name didn't mean anything at first. It wasn't until yesterday that I mentioned the new young lady to Auntie . . ."

Here Annie took up the story. " 'Findon?' I says. 'Would that be one of the Findons from Saury? Then it's Mr. Vincent's girl,' I says."

"Mrs. Torgill told me that you were with your niece in Bidminster. I was determined to find you but never expected it to happen like this."

Mrs. Brady left us together and we spent a highly satisfactory half hour. No one in the world, now that my mother was gone from it, had known or cared for my father as Annie had done.

"And it was when *his* mother died," she said when I had tried to tell her this, "that I cared for your father and cherished him in his loneliness."

Inevitably, exploring the family history together, we drew nearer to the dangerous area of Annie's dismissal.

"Yes," she said, "I looked after them all as babies, fed them and bathed them and made them behave. We'd all been a bit nervous when Mr. Findon married again and I never felt the same about the second Mrs. Findon as I did about your grandmother, but to be fair, she was a good mistress and she begged me to stay on and help with the housekeeping and then the two babies. That's why it was such a shock . . . I couldn't hardly believe it when Lucy and Mabel got their notice, but I never thought it would happen to me."

It was Kelda who had broken the news.

"She came to me when I was making Mr. Findon's bed. We'd brought him a bed downstairs and put him in that poky little place next to the morning room. No bigger than a hen coop. He was an old man by that time, but he wasn't past going upstairs to bed as I told Miss Kelda. 'You'll make an invalid of him and shorten his life,' I said, 'when what he needs is stirring up and being kept busy.' " Annie momentarily lost the thread of her story and sought it in the heart of the fire, her eyes troubled as they must have been then, almost seven years ago, I calculated.

" 'I'm afraid you'll have to go, Annie,' " she said quite sharp. It was as if she was distracted and hardly thought what she was saying. She would never have been so abrupt if she'd been herself, not Miss Kelda. She was such a loving little thing and grew into a warm-hearted lovable young woman. It was as if she'd stuck a knife into me. 'Well, there it is then,' I said when I got hold of myself. 'If I must go, I'll go, but I'll finish making this bed first if there's no objection.' With that she burst out crying as if her heart would break. Not another word did she say but 'Oh Annie, Annie,' and stood there crying and then she went away."

"It must have hurt her very much. She didn't want you to go."

"Likely not," Annie said, "but Miss Kelda should have been used to not getting what she wanted by that time. And there was something wrong; something I couldn't fathom; and there's been something wrong there ever since."

Her look was one of appeal, as if she were passing on to me the burden of doubt and anxiety, as if I could put things right. If I had stayed she would have said more, but I had to leave, though reluctantly, and promised to come again. I walked slowly back across the quay. Annie had confirmed my theory as to the urgency with which my aunts had wanted the house to themselves in some crisis as unfathomable to her as it was to me. But she had also confronted me with new problems, chiefly to do with dates and the order of events before I had come to Saury.

My mind wandered. "She was such a loving little thing . . . a warm-hearted lovable young woman . . ." The picture was appealing, my mood mellow in the warmth of my own happiness. My heart softened toward Kelda. She had been so manifestly crushed by whatever it was she had done, was so deeply unhappy, that I wondered if perhaps she had atoned sufficiently and de-served—as do all repentant sinners—forgiveness.

123

But as I climbed the steps to the marketplace I found myself pondering less on what Annie had said than on what she had not said: a curious omission. She had talked only of Kelda and had never once mentioned May.

11

KELDA AND I spent most of our time in the barely furnished morning room or in the kitchen as we did the mending, peeled apples, or sliced onions or fueled the stove with wood and coal or washed dishes. There never seemed time to sit decorously in the conservatory as ladies living in the country might be expected to do. The sunless drawing room would not have been inviting even if it had not been almost exclusively May's. She sat now in total idleness neither sewing nor reading nor painting. With more experience I would surely have seen the danger of her condition, all physical activity suspended, the whole weight of existence borne by the mind.

I went to the drawing room one morning to clear the grate and there she was in the window bay. As usual a blank sheet of white drawing paper lay on the table in front of her. It would remain blank. The sight was so familiar that there should have been nothing remarkable in it. Perhaps it was the abrupt plunge from the relative brightness of the kitchen into the twilight gloom at the front of the house that stimulated my senses so that for the first time I recognized a curious quality in her stillness. It was not—if it ever had been—reposeful. It lacked any suggestion of relaxation. Waiting, if that was what she was doing, begets a certain tension even if prolonged beyond all reasonable limits. But she wasn't just waiting. There was something else.

How could inactivity be purposeful? There flashed upon me the conviction that her aloofness was no longer, as I had thought, an upward motion of the spirit. It was the outward sign of a deep preoccupation: she was lost in thought, her mind pursuing a positive direction. The possibility that instead of dwelling on the past she was occupied with some plan for the future was difficult to reconcile with her seeming passivity.

On tiptoe, I daresay, I stole reverently across the room, entering as it were her presence. She turned her head.

"It seems such a shame"—I indicated the discarded palette with its dried up paints—"not to go on painting, for yourself, I mean. I had the impression that the pictures weren't always the ones you would have chosen to paint, although"—I hastened to add with a mental snap of the fingers at Clem—"they were so charming. But now you can paint exactly as you wish. It would be"—I hit on the phrase with some satisfaction—"a new phase."

She had listened with her remote smile.

"How thoughtful you are, dear! We're so lucky to have you here, so blessed . . ." Her voice trailed away. The blessedness of having me at Hoodman House was one of her favorite themes and her themes were few.

It was hardly surprising that a growing sense of claustrophobia drove me to spend as much time as possible out of doors. I had soon learned my way about the district, a pleasant undramatic countryside of undulating fields and lanes. On the farther side of Packhorse Way a clear stream flowed between banks of loosestrife and meadowsweet. I had followed its course one morning, walking upstream until a heron rising in slow flight guided me to its source in a wide pool, its margin shaded here and there by willows and at one end by a spreading beech tree.

Lott's Pool? I took my bearings. Fed by an unseen spring, it lay in the shallow cradle of a field misted over in that summer season with the lacy white flowers of earthnut. To the south less than a quarter of a mile away between the two ash trees guarding its wicket gate glowed the red tiled roof of Winkblade.

Farther down, the stream ran clear over pebbles, but where it found its sluggish way from the pool, it was turgid and dull with the silt of fallen leaves. The banks were soft and muddy and it was only after a search that I found a stone big enough to hurl experimentally into the brighter water beyond the shade of the trees. From the heavy plop of its fall and the ominously slow widening of the circles it left, I judged that the pool was deep enough to treat with caution: certainly deep enough to drown in.

The mud on my shoes, the melancholy droop of trees, a puzzled awareness of the difference between people as they seemed and as they were, a recurring and faintly distressing conviction that the golden Edwardian past had been alloyed with baser metal—combined to give me a distaste for Lott's Pool.

More often on warm days I spent my spare time at Winkblade. It was there, one sunny morning in September, that I unexpectedly made new friends. I had been peering in at the empty rooms when I heard voices and, turning the corner to the front of the house, found company: a young woman sitting on the steps and watching a small boy as he gathered twigs and stacked them in a little handcart.

"There's a lady," he cried and pointed a twig at me.

"Don't point. It's rude." The reproving voice was easy and amused. She was a big handsome girl with rich red hair and was respectably dressed in a navy-blue serge skirt and a white blouse. But there was a touch of raffishness, a too luxurious idleness in the way she sat, knees wide apart, leaning back against the low balustrade by the top step. "He's not used to ladies, isn't Arthur."

Her red mouth with its big strong teeth was of the kind that never quite closes, so that she seemed always to be smiling; but the smile was not altogether pleasant. Her remark held overtones of mockery, not of Arthur but of ladies in general.

127

In contrast to his mother the little boy was instantly appealing: a slim fair-skinned child entirely without awkwardness, as if mind and limbs were so well coordinated that he could rely on them with perfect confidence.

"I'm gathering sticks for the fire at home." He had paused to look me over, his well-shaped head erect. "The cart's full. We'll be going home for dinner soon. The Tile Sheds, that's where we live." He remembered just in time not to point. "Over there."

"Then you're our nearest neighbors. I live at Hoodman House."

"I've seen you about." The woman's tone was faintly disagreeable. It diminished me. I saw myself moving unsuspectingly about the countryside being seen. And when she added, "One Sunday night, I saw you," I felt even more uncomfortable. Had she been here in the garden, spying on Clem and me?

"It was a lovely night," she said suggestively and instantly the remembered starlight became disreputable: seductive, lax.

For once I didn't linger in the garden.

"It would be Thyrza Beck," May said. Kelda was ironing in the kitchen. "She must be married. It's years since I saw her. She's been living in the west country, I believe. Her mother died last year and left her the house. She must just have come back."

"Clem said she used to tag along when you were all children."

"So Clem mentioned her, did he? She's a troublemaker and always was. Idle and brazen. There was something low about her even as a little girl. Oh, I don't mean because the family was poor; her mother was a nice enough woman. I mean by nature."

"And yet Arthur is a lovely little boy."

"Then he doesn't take after his mother. What did you say her name is now?"

"She didn't say."

Rather to my annoyance at first, Thyrza showed signs of infesting the garden at Winkblade. I had to remind myself that she had every bit as much right to be there as I had: more right in fact. Inevitably we chatted, and when I asked her married name, she said, "You have to be married to have a married name. My name's Beck."

"Mr. Tass—Clem—spoke of you," I said when I had recovered from my faux pas.

"I daresay he would," she said cryptically.

On Thyrza's part there was to be no raking up of childhood adventures in the garden: no affectionate reminiscences. Her backward glance was tinged with contempt—or disillusionment. Of my aunts she made short shrift.

"Just a bit too fond of themselves. And where has it got them? Not an inch past their own front door from what I hear."

She on the other hand had seen the world and liked what she saw.

"I may have made mistakes"—she showed her big teeth—"when I was young and knew no better, but we've done all right one way and another, Arthur and me, and that's more than can be said for some."

She had returned unwillingly to the Tile Sheds after various undisclosed adventures elsewhere.

"We had to live somewhere and the house is mine now. They never exactly turned me out but my father didn't want me at home because of my disgrace." Applied to Arthur, the word was absurd. She used it casually, as if disgrace were one of her attributes like the splendid red hair warming the stone wall against which she leaned, relaxed, indolent, knowing. She planned to have it cut short.

"Oh no, you mustn't." The universal bob had not yet come into its own. So far only bold pioneering females were laying their heads on the block. "It's beautiful."

"It'd be a change." But she seemed pleased by the compliment as with both hands she pushed up the heavy red-gold coils. The gesture was sensuous and feline.

129

There was nothing, nothing at all to do in Saury, she told me. In Bidminster there was a bit of life if you knew where to look for it. Plainly Thyrza did know. She had a friend who would always keep an eye on Arthur if she wanted to go out.

"He's no trouble."

We watched him strutting up and down the terrace with a stick tucked under his arm like an officer's cane. He was a self-sufficient child, attractive and endearing.

After that we met quite often. I soon got into the habit of telling Arthur about India, particularly the elephants. He was delighted with a photograph of me at his age with our Indian servants and with the picture of a snake charmer I gave him for his own. As I described the blue mountains with their peaks lost in haze and snow, the immense brilliant moon, the strange exotic scents, his mother, hands idle in her lap, eyes half shut, would listen with lips parted in the unfortunate smile that was half a sneer; but when she said once, "You've found a friend, Arthur, haven't you?" it was without mockery. We all three got on well together, though May gently reproved me for my choice of company when I told her of Thyrza's unmarried state.

There were several ways by which Thyrza could take Arthur to school in Saury, the lane past our house being much the longest. For some reason she began to use it, passing only a few yards from the bay window. May couldn't have missed seeing the flamboyant redhead, and Thyrza never hurried. Whether either ever acknowledged the other I couldn't say: as the day drew near for Clem's departure for Dorset I was spending less time at home than usual.

All the same I was distantly aware of some change in May's behavior toward me: an occasional sorrowful look, a sigh, a leaning toward me as if about to speak. But the impression was slight and I gave no thought to it.

Not until the morning when Clem was to leave. We had spent the previous evening together and there was nothing more to be said in the way of good-bye, but the faint hope that he might drive out to Saury before catching his train kept me on the qui vive. I was at the front gate when Thyrza sauntered into view. She stopped to wait for Arthur, who was picking up stones and stowing them carefully in his already overloaded pockets. I went out to speak to them.

"You aren't taking *all* the stones to show teacher, are you?"

He shook his head and laughed.

"No, only interesting ones, like this."

Before I could find out what made it interesting, the sound of a car, unmistakably Clem's Calcott, made us all three look up the lane. I rushed to open the field gate.

"I didn't think you'd have time."

"I haven't. I must be out of my mind. Actually I am, where you're concerned." He had climbed out, smiling, full of life; and then he saw Thyrza.

"Well, if it isn't Clem, after all these years!" Her tone as usual was bold but I saw in her face and felt in her manner some other quality less easy to define. Arthur stood beside her, all his attention directed to the car.

"Isn't he a lovely boy?" I whispered so that Arthur himself couldn't hear.

Clem ignored me. I saw with concern that he looked suddenly ill; all the color had drained from his face. I thought he would faint and looked round desperately for somewhere for him to sit down, only half aware that May had come out of the house and was watching from the path.

"Is something wrong? You'd better come inside." But he paid no attention and brushing me aside, took Thyrza by the arm and walked her away until they were out of earshot. Whatever they needed to discuss was plainly a private matter. I tried not to mind that it excluded me.

"Who is that gentleman?" Abruptly left on his own, Arthur showed no surprise. He must have been used to seeing his mother led away by gentlemen and his attention was not diverted from the car for more than a few seconds. But as the conversation went on—and on—he resumed his search for interesting stones.

"How strange of Clem! What can be the matter with him? He's going to miss that train." Grieved at the loss of precious minutes he should have been spending with me, I turned to May for comfort. "It's so unlike him to be so . . ." To be so upset as to forget me completely?

"I'm afraid, Elinor, darling, you may not know him as well as you think." There was more than regret in May's quiet voice. She could always infuse into the simplest remark a suggestion of special significance and this time had done it so successfully that I felt a chill of apprehension. "I've suspected all along that there may be a good deal you don't know about young men—or about women like Thyrza."

I stared at her in dismay, not that I had yet grasped her implication: simply it dismayed me that any connection should be suggested—of any kind—between Clem and any living creature but me. That there was some connection was beyond doubt. They were still there, facing each other. He was questioning her, I thought. She had lost her brassy swagger and looked unhappy. He glanced round, covertly, at May and me, turned his back squarely and seemed to reach into an inside pocket. Thyrza shook her head and moved away.

"You had better come indoors, Elinor." May took my arm and drew me into the hall.

"But I must speak to Clem."

"You can speak to him later—if you still want to."

"Of course I shall want to. What do you mean? What *is* wrong?"

"We'd better talk about this privately. In my room." She released my arm and took my hand in her cold one. Like an unhappy child I climbed the stairs in her wake. I remember that from the depths of my bewilderment there arose in me like a warning the knowledge that I was being led wherever she wanted: that she was irresistible.

"Just the two of us," she was saying, "no one else . . ." And I knew that she was replaying an old tune, that she had said the same thing to Kelda and Kelda had said the same thing to her a hundred times as they closeted themselves in this same room to whisper secrets to each other: unwholesome secrets. It was my turn now. A new cobweb was being spun. All this I knew yet had no power to resist.

She sat me in a low chair in the window where I looked through the trees toward Winkblade. With my whole soul I longed to look the other way—toward Clem—and yet I couldn't take my eyes off her as she stood, gazing over my shoulder and down toward the wild cherry tree where the farm track joined the road to Saury.

"Before you give your heart to any man, Elinor, you must be sure, as sure as you can be, that he is worthy of it. It must be someone whom you can trust without question. Then your love can be steadfast . . ."

As hers? Could any human being be more steadfast? The soulful eyes seemed to be seeking some object beyond the reach of mortal gaze, as if she could see almost into eternity. A sort of terror came over me.

". . . as his should be for you. A man who cannot restrain his physical nature will always lust after women like Thyrza Beck—and then abandon them to their shame as she has been abandoned."

"Lust?" I knew that she was talking about Clem, but he had become, in this conversation, unrecognizable. The urge to turn and be reassured that he was still as he used to be made my shoulder blades ache. But I didn't turn; he was no longer as he used to be. Nothing would ever be the same again.

"Fortunately," she smiled wanly, "for us it's no more than a word. We can't understand it or its power to change people into—

beasts. Women as well as men. The woman in such a case deserves every hour of the suffering she brings on herself."

She went on talking. Most of the words passed unapprehended through my mind. I was aware of May herself rather than what she said and of a level, controlled purposefulness in her conduct of the hateful scene.

"A woman of that sort . . . slut . . . degradation . . ." It was the vocabulary of outrage and disgust, except that the words had no life in them: no human coarseness. Like toads and vipers they fell from her lips but without disturbing their pure curves. Her unhurried voice never lost its sweetness. Indignation, moral anger, passion of any kind would have warmed the air. As it was I might have been listening to a recitation in a morgue. It was unbearable. I bowed my head.

"I've been trying to bring myself to the point of telling you for quite a while, ever since she took to flaunting the child in our faces. When you first mentioned her of course I didn't know, but as soon as I saw him, I realized. There couldn't be any mistake as to who the father is. Let me show you something."

She went to her bureau, pulled down the lid and took a packet from one of the pigeonholes. She kept her back to me while she shook out its contents. With an effort I turned and looked down from the window behind me. They were still there, not talking, just standing there, trapped in the crisis that kept me too a prisoner. Clem had picked up Arthur and was holding him close.

"Do you recognize this?" May held out a piece of pasteboard: a photograph, a little boy. Between his sailor collar and the upturned brim of his Breton straw hat I recognized Arthur's slim straight neck, the confident poise of his handsome head, his look of alert interest.

"Yes, it's Clem." May smiled as if with affection. "Just as I remember him—the baby of our little group. How sad! That he should have to grow up into that sort of man."

"I don't know what to do," I said. "I don't know what to say to him," and wished that I could fade out of sight, fade altogether out of life without saying another word. "I don't think Clem knew—about Arthur."

May sighed. "Only he could tell us that. It's fortunate under the circumstances that he's going away. It will save you from some unpleasantness."

From the superior height of her window she was watching them with detachment, but leaning against the curtain now that the awful words had ceased, as if wearied by the ordeal she had imposed upon herself. Thyrza and Clem had parted; she was going on to Saury; he was coming up the path. He knocked.

"You'd better let me go, Elinor."

"He came to say good-bye. You won't . . ."

"I won't intervene in any way. You know I wouldn't do that. I'll say you aren't well. He'll understand that you know and need time."

He knocked again. From behind the curtain I saw his face upturned to the windows, first to mine above the front door, then to May's. Except that his expression was serious he didn't look different.

"We were going to say good-bye," I said again and added miserably, "in any case."

She had gone. I heard them talking on the step. It took her longer than might have been expected to tell him that I wasn't well. At last he went quickly down the path, slammed the gate behind him, climbed into his car and drove off without a backward glance.

I came to life. It was absolutely necessary to get into my own room and shut the door before May came back. But she was already there on the landing.

"It was my duty to tell you." An artist might have taken her as his model for the angel in a more important annunciation. "My dear little sister. It was a dreadful thing to have to do."

"Yes," I said and wondered if I ought to thank her.

"May behaved perfectly." The remembered words took on a different coloring. The blow had been delivered with the cool resolution of a surgeon making an amputation. An operating theater is no place for mere womanly kindness: strength was needed and had been found. Afterward the patient may recover and be grateful to be alive, though maimed: but I felt no gratitude, saw no hope of recovery, felt only the keen wound of the knife.

"We won't speak of this to anyone. After all the Tasses are old friends. A thing like this—a rather sordid business, I'm afraid—would be very distressing for them."

"Kelda?"

"Kelda will have drawn her own conclusions. She'll keep them to herself. I do wish I hadn't been the one to tell you. We've been so close, so comfortable together. You can imagine how I feel."

She was wrong: I had no idea how she felt. From the depths of a new isolation and so with an altered vision, I looked at her and found that the inward light that for me had given her the luster of a being set apart, was gone. Instead I saw only the gleam of winter sun on ice.

I went into my room and shut the door. Except for the ache in my heart my faculties seemed paralyzed. I felt no resentment toward Clem; if what I had felt for him was love, I loved him still; and what else could it be but love, this longing for his tenderness, for his arms round me and his cheek against mine, this urgent need to talk to him with its counterbalancing dread of facing him. Most hurtful of all was the feeling of being shut out: my artless acceptance of the fact that he belonged to Thyrza and to Arthur, not to me. There were to be sharper pangs when the remembered ardour of his lovemaking seemed to take on the gloss of practised ease. He had been used to it, I thought, and forced myself to think of him with Thyrza in the ultimate physical closeness.

But for the present it was a feeling of helplessness that brought me to my knees to crouch with my head against the bed rail. There was nowhere else to go, nothing I could do, no future I could bear to think of. Without Clem there was no hope of escape. I would always be here, day after day, year after year. There were three of us now, three women who had lost the men they loved.

Instinctively I turned inward, curling in upon myself with head on knees in a forlorn attempt to occupy no space, as nearly as possible to disappear altogether. And—as if in response—I felt the house close in upon me as a carnivorous plant closes upon the victim it entraps and, taking its time, devours.

12

CLEM'S FIRST LETTER arrived two days later. He had written only a few lines to say that he was sorry not to have seen me. "A good thing we had already said good-bye, as it should be said the night before ..." He had despaired of his train but having driven too fast did just manage to catch it with half a minute to spare. He had rather specially wanted to talk to me but it could wait until later.

His second letter was chiefly about his work, his lodgings, and how much he looked forward to hearing from me. Ten days after that he wrote again, anxiously this time. He had expected my letter every day. It had suddenly occurred to him that my headache or whatever it was might have been the beginning of a real illness. He was worried ...

The next day I dragged myself to Bidminster and passing the house on the corner of Watt Lane, saw that the To Let notice had been taken down. It seemed the last straw, confirming that all was over. I answered none of Clem's letters, not from pique or resentment but from the continuing inability to decide what to say. Leaving love out of it, if that could be done, a friend who had been as good to me as Clem had been deserved to be written to. To cut myself off from him without explanation would be an uncivilized thing to do: to set down on paper the tangle of thoughts and feelings I tried endlessly to unravel was beyond me. I did try but no sooner had I opened my writing case than the shadow of Thyrza darkened the page.

As often as not I had only to glance out of the window to see her in the flesh. Since the day Clem left I had avoided her and kept firmly away from Winkblade. But Thyrza felt no obligation to avoid anyone. Scarcely a day passed without her walking past with Arthur, her hips swinging, her red hair blazing against the wayside hedge like a sudden fire threatening our dim cool drawing room.

"There goes Thyrza Beck," May would say unnecessarily and always sorrowfully, "displaying that child. But then one can't expect sensitivity from women of that stamp," or "She will pay for her sin as does every woman whose low instincts lead her astray."

She talked more than usual; at least she talked about Thyrza. I don't recall the range of her conversation being extended in other directions. There was a nerve-racking insistence in the way she reminded me of the retribution to be meted out to the likes of Thyrza, for it was not merely for Thyrza as an individual that she grieved, but also as one of the entire depraved sisterhood of fallen women.

It was as though she had forgotten how closely I was involved in Thyrza's situation; or perhaps she put too much faith in the efficacy of that surgical operation on my feelings for Clem she had felt it her duty to carry out. If she had known how I writhed at the very sight of Thyrza and the constant reminders of her illicit relationship and of her partner in it, could she have harped, though with every conceivable permutation of sorrow and regret, on so painful a theme?

Kelda didn't like it either. Rousing myself now and then from my own problems, I was aware of a change in Kelda; or an intensification of feeling, as if her spells of unhappiness had settled into constant pain. It almost seemed as if my own misery found its counterpart in hers and that made a bond between us. She was losing weight. Her black skirt and blouse hung gracelessly on her thin figure like the feathers of a moulting bird—the raven Clem had mentioned. And yet her face, cruelly challenged by her black cotton collar and pared of superfluous flesh, was taking on an added refinement. Whereas care and harassment had threatened to spoil her beauty, suffering was restoring it. But what on earth was she suffering from?

"Ought you perhaps to see a doctor?" I suggested when for the third morning in succession she ate no breakfast. "You don't look as well as you did—I mean in health."

The qualification was necessary because in other ways she looked better. If only she would leave off her dreary black and dress becomingly as she used to. I sighed for the silk and lace and beads and bows of that first vision at my bedside. How far away it seemed! How long ago!

"I'm well enough. As well as I shall ever be."

She picked up a basket of newly washed towels and went out to hang them in the yard. Unsmiling, with arms upstretched to the line, she had a martyred look, as if she too might be hung on a line for daws to peck at, especially in those penitential garments. The idea came unbidden, but with the conviction of a diagnosis made by instinct. A person doing penance for some past misdeed would look and behave very much as Kelda did. But when she came in again, folding a table cover as she walked, her face above the green cloth caught the sunlight and for the first time I saw that she was no less beautiful than May.

Paradoxically it was as the sisters appeared more alike that certain differences became more marked. I was finding in Kelda unsuspected reserves of sympathy or so I thought: it was as if she realized how much May's constant references to Thyrza's low character upset me. Once I saw in her eyes the look of distress she must be seeing in mine; and once when I was goaded into protesting, "Please, May, please don't," Kelda jumped up and left the room, as if she couldn't bear it either.

Despite her frequent comments on Thyrza, May had taken

no interest in Arthur. It was Kelda who spoke to him as he dawdled behind his mother to explore the resources of field and hedgerow. Once, at the edge of the field outside our backyard I found the two of them nibbling rock buns like old friends.

"It's Miss Findon," Arthur said as I joined them. "There are two Miss Findons but only one Mrs. Cade." He turned to Kelda with an enthusiasm that transformed the statistics into a compliment. He had certainly inherited the Tasses' natural charm. Kelda's expression touched me.

"Oh, Elinor," she said impulsively as he ran to catch up with his mother, "can it be a sin to give life to a child like that?"

"No, I don't think it can be."

No one in her senses could think of Clem as a sinner. It was just unfortunate for me that I had come into his life too late. How young he must have been when he and Thyrza were lovers!

"Seeing Arthur," Kelda murmured, "brings it all back, those old times when we were children at Winkblade. I haven't been there for years."

She took to walking up to the farm sometimes in the afternoon and because she looked lonely and sad I occasionally went with her. Indeed I owed her a debt of gratitude. A growing concern for her served to rouse me from my inertia. Thinking of her, I could—occasionally—stop thinking about myself.

We were at Winkblade one afternoon when Harriet Penfold arrived in the Sunbeam car she had triumphantly learned to drive. She wore a simple fawn linen costume and a cream tulle scarf tied round her hat and looked rich, successful, and full of life. I felt the contrast between the two women as I introduced them.

"I had a sudden urge to look at the dear old place again," Harriet said. "You know I've been here several times, with Clem, with Adrian, with Cameron the builder—all men. Feminine support is just what I need now. You must know the place very well, Mrs. Cade. I shall be glad of your advice. Is it a wise proposition to take it on, do you think?"

We stood on the worn terrace looking down across the garden and through the ash trees to the sloping fields beyond.

"It's so exactly what I've always wanted"—Harriet's voice had lost its briskness and become confidential—"that it almost frightens me. Do you know the feeling? That it's too good to be true and some dire thing might happen to take it from me? What am I talking about? Dire things don't happen in a place like this." She turned to Kelda, who smiled and made no reply. "It's not the place for evil spirits, is it? They wouldn't like it here, would they, Elinor?"

"I'm not sure about evil spirits but I know that nightingales never come here." My inept remark was made at random for something to say. It was impossible to share Harriet's jubilant mood. My own memories of Winkblade, though so short, were already poignant: Kelda's were much longer. What was she remembering?

"How did you know about the nightingales?" She had smiled suddenly, as a much younger Kelda must have smiled.

"My father told me. It was just an excuse," I explained to Harriet, "for lovers to meet. But nightingales don't come to Saury."

"They don't know what they're missing," she said.

When we had explored the house together and discussed its possibilities, we made a tour of the outbuildings.

"Of course you'll know about the oven." Harriet opened the bakehouse door. "It's an interesting feature and I haven't liked to tell Clem but I'm afraid these buildings will have to be taken down. We'll put a kitchen here and servants' quarters. It's a pity the oven will have to go."

Kelda had stayed outside and now with an abruptness barely redeemed by her apologetic, "I'm so sorry. Will you excuse me, Miss Penfold. I must go," she left us.

"Is your aunt unwell?" Harriet watched with concern as the thin black figure disappeared round the corner of the house.

"I sometimes wonder. She has seemed depressed lately and she may have sad memories of this place. They used the bake-house in their games, for treasure hunts and so on."

"I'm sorry. I didn't realize."

If the garden here at Winkblade held tender memories for Kelda those memories should rightly be of her husband. He too was entitled to make assignations with absentee nightingales even if he had arrived on the scene at a later stage. Not for the first time I strove to be fair to Mr. Cade. The conviction that in this flower-scented anchorage of lost youth he didn't quite fit was based on nothing more than a glimpse of him at his wedding—that source of headaches and unreliable impressions. To do him justice he had not burst into angry sobbing and fled upstairs on hearing that his bride was penniless. Once again I fished in the muddy waters of that appalling incident in an effort to remember what had been said: something about telling or not telling. How odd that the disclosure of their mutual poverty, if that was what the disclosure was about, should be made just then! Having won and been won under false pretenses, could they not have maintained the decep-tion a little longer, say until after the honeymoon? Had each burst simultaneously into confession; or, angling in murky waters I felt a pull on the line—had someone else told, felt it her duty to tell? "My dear little sister . . . a dreadful thing to have to do . . ."

I found myself standing absently beside the car. Harriet was pulling on her gloves.

"I was interested to meet your aunt. Such a beautiful sad face!" Her shrewd eyes had missed nothing. "Some deep wound unhealed, I suspect; and how isolating that deep black is! Why do people stay in mourning when the conventional time is over? Economy, like French peasants waiting for the next death?" And when I found no answer she went on thoughtfully, "Not in this case of course. You mustn't think me flippant. No, it's an assertion, a signal of some kind. But to whom? Who was it that hoisted a black flag and forgot to take it down? With tragic results, I'm afraid." She settled herself in her seat but seemed not quite ready to leave. "Remember, Elinor, that you have friends in Bidminster. If you need us, you have only to let us know . . ."

"I do know. But won't you come home with me and meet Aunt May?"

"Meeting Aunt May will be very interesting indeed—but no, it must be another time. I shall be back soon. It's hard to keep away. Shall I see you on Thursday as usual? Good. How is Clem?"

"Oh, very well." I managed a smile suitable to the occasion and waved her off, thankful that there were still some things she didn't know: not to mention the things I didn't know either. For a number of reasons I was increasingly intrigued by the relationship between Kelda and her husband. Was it remorse that kept her clothed forever in mourning; remorse for having deceived him into thinking she was still rich? But would not that act of deception be cancelled out by an identical one on his part? And here, to the mournful accompaniment of one of his songs, Aunt Claudia's voice intervened: Julius had been talented, a perfect gentleman and unworldly. Suppose he had never deliberately thought of money at all—artists often disregarded it, in which case he must have married for love and wouldn't care if Kelda hadn't a sou. Equally, if a woman loved a man sufficiently to mourn his death for the rest of her life, whether from grief or remorse, why had she reacted with such despair on discovering that he was poor? The two circumstances were irreconcilable. That business of telling or not telling had nothing to do with money or the lack of it.

I closed the garden gate. The mountain ash above me drooped crimson berries against a sky of china blue. A robin sang somewhere among its branches. No nightingale's song could have been sweeter or more hauntingly modulated to regret. Someday soon I must talk to Kelda. She needed help. It was the least I could do to find out what troubled her: my duty as a friend, a woman close to her. The word "sisterly" no longer appealed to me. It had acquired disturbing overtones. It wouldn't be easy to penetrate her extraordinary reticence, nor was I eager to begin. But when, half dazzled by the crimson and green and china blue, I came upon a sudden blackness and found it to be Kelda crouching in the hedge like a crippled bird, I hesitated no longer but went and knelt beside her and put my arms round her.

"Tell me what it is that makes you so unhappy. Let me help." She laid her head on my shoulder and drew a deep shuddering breath; and since he was uppermost in my mind I said, "Is it about Mr. Cade? You've never told me about him," and, gathering all my courage, "Do you want to tell me anything about what happened to him. I mean, how he died?"

She became quite still. I held my breath. Then she drew away from me, wiped her cheek with the back of her hand, and looked me in the face. Close as we were she seemed to recognize me with surprise across a wide tract of empty space.

"Julius? Nothing happened to him. He didn't die," and to make the situation for once perfectly clear she added, "Julius isn't dead."

It was as if a cupboard opened and a skeleton clattered out; except that a skeleton was evidently what Julius was not. Actually a skeleton would have surprised me less: it was the living breathing man that took my breath away. At first I could only think that Kelda had fallen victim to a hallucination similar to May's, identical in fact: each refusing to believe that the dead were dead. Both my aunts were mentally astray.

"But where is he?" I asked nervously.

"At St. Mark's Preparatory School for Boys near Dorking in Surrey."

The precision of Kelda's reply suggested that she was still in possession of her senses, but one could never tell; one simply couldn't be sure. All the same having got this information out, she seemed relieved and sat up, woebegone but dry-eyed and apparently reasonable.

"It's a long story. I won't inflict it on you."

"I wish you would." When she showed no immediate urge to do so I ventured, "How was it that everybody thought he was dead?"

"Everybody?" she said bitterly. "Whom do you mean? There was no one who mattered or cared or gave a thought to me and my affairs."

"You didn't *tell* people that your husband had died?"

"I told no one whether he was dead or alive. It was none of their business."

"But grandfather—and May?"

"Well yes, of course they knew."

Though convinced that she wanted and needed to unburden herself I hesitated to go on plying her with questions. Some notion of the truth was taking shape in my mind, but there was so much that challenged belief. And yet the bizarre affair could be reduced to simple terms. She had married, gone away with her husband, returned without him, dressed in widow's weeds, and shut herself away. Saury and Bidminster though balked by distance of a funeral would naturally assume that a funeral had taken place: she had loved him and when he left her had gone into mourning, as if he were dead. It was logical, if highly unusual.

"You agreed to part?"

"Oh no. It wasn't what Julius wanted." Her lips quivered. "But I had to come home." Then as if casting about for a reason she added, "They needed me."

"And yet," I suggested hesitantly, "Julius must have needed you too."

She nodded, drawing another sharp breath as if stabbed with sudden pain. "I had no choice. No choice. You don't understand. No one can possibly understand."

"You don't feel that you could tell me?"

"Oh Elinor, you don't know what you ask." Her look was so desperate that I leaned toward her and clasped her hands in mine.

146

"But I do want to help."

"And I love you for that. It's so long, so terribly long since anyone cared."

"Grandfather was old," I said, "and didn't realize what he was doing in asking you to come home."

"Father?"

"But when he died, did you not feel free to go back to your husband?"

"No." She spoke with a dull flat certainty. "No, I didn't feel free."

"Perhaps now that I'm here, you could go back to him." The offer was genuine but surprisingly distasteful to me.

"I shall never be free." She got up and stepped from under the sheltering bushes into the lane.

"It seems very hard." I too got up. Plucking a stem of convolvulus, I stared into its pale flower, and found the long delicate stamens pointing up at me with unexpected menace—"when you love him so much."

She laughed. There was no lightness in the sound, only despair.

"Love? Julius is a good kind man. He's my husband. I would rather be with him than drag on in misery here, but he knew all along that I didn't feel as he did. That was one thing I did tell him. He knows I never loved him—never."

That raven's croak was her last word as she hurried away, the emphatic blackness of her dress violating the green vista of the lane. So that was it. The one she loved really *was* dead: blown to pieces with the rest of his platoon when they walked across open ground into enemy gunfire. For of course it was Dick. I should have guessed. No one could resist him: she could barely speak of him; they had been close childhood friends, christened on the same day; had sung duets together, sweet as birds; he had given the squirrel to her, not to May.

In a matter of seconds—the convolvulus flower still trembled

147

from Kelda's abrupt movement—the entire view had altered. My aunts had been rivals and were rivals still, each exercising her claim on a dead man: May in her daily ritual dedicated to the pain of parting and the vain hope of reunion; Kelda draped in black to demonstrate her right to mourn for him.

Their suffocating intimacy took on a new dimension. To see reflected in one's mirror the other's face, to see the other, face-to-face, and recognize one's self, were tricks of nature that could do no harm when two people were bound by affection. But suppose into that bond there should be entwined strands of jealousy and the hatred that comes from it.

I felt the strange sadness of their story, though I was still far from knowing the whole of it.

13

"YOU'VE NEVER TALKED about it, have you—about loving Dick?"

"Never." As we talked her face was losing its haggard look. "Even before . . ." She stopped, as if a hand had been laid on her shoulder. There were still to be reserves of silence, areas I was not to tread. "I never talked about my feelings for Dick." With a smile of secret tenderness she added, "There was no need. He knew."

Everyone must have known, I thought, especially May.

"Even as children," I prompted, "you were particular friends."

"Always, from the beginning." The yearning sadness in her eyes almost brought tears to mine. "We knew each other so well. There was nothing about him that I didn't know and understand and love."

We were speaking quietly. I had followed her home and found her sitting at the kitchen table, head in hands. I made tea, the universal panacea, and boldly took up the threads where we had left them dangling; but all the time she spoke so low that I too dropped my voice to a near whisper. It was as though we were afraid of being overheard.

"And he . . . ?"

"He loved me, Elinor. Loved me, me!" Her voice faded in anguish.

"And yet somehow . . ."

Could he possibly have loved them both? Had he too seen them as two halves of a single entity and having felt compelled to choose one, chose May?

"It was on her seventeenth birthday that she showed me the ring. I wanted to die."

"I wonder why he . . . She must have been very lovely. But so were you."

"There was something about her, something I never had. I'm an ordinary person."

Gazing into my cup, I considered the extraordinariness of May.

"Do you think," I ventured, hoping in spite of all decency for a negative reply, "that he was happy? I mean having made the choice, did he ever seem to regret it?"

It occurred to me that the choice might not have been his.

"He was—unbelieving. He came to tell me about it. We met up there at Winkblade. 'What have I done, Kay?' he said. 'You've broken my heart,' I said. 'It was as if I was hypnotized,' he said, 'and now, how can I get out of it without hurting her?' "

So delicate as she seemed, floating above the coarse practicalities of a harsh world! Hurting May would seem to him like trampling on a lily. My tendency to depict her poetically persisted; but poetry has many moods.

"He told his parents that he had made a mistake. Mr. Tass was furious and insisted that the engagement was absolutely binding unless May wanted to release him. I believe he thought she would have a steadying effect on Dick. You see, he wasn't interested in the work he was doing, just filling in time. His father thought it was time he settled down and took on more responsibility. 'But I'll never marry her, Kay,' he said. 'I must have been mad.' "

150

He had lived recklessly, as if to make the most of his freedom before resigning himself to having to spend the rest of his life within the pure cool ambience of May.

"Sometimes I've asked myself, would it have been better to have him safely home and married to May—or worse. I suppose I could have borne it. But being tied down changed him, or perhaps it was a foreknowledge that he was going to die that made him want to live as fully as possible and do everything that offered. He lived quite wildly sometimes."

"I can understand that he wanted to cram in as much living as possible before it was too late," I said. "It's strange to have heard so much about him and never to have known him or even to have seen a photograph."

"We have several photographs and Mrs. Tass must have others."

"Was he like Clem?" I asked with some pain.

"Quite like him but more handsome, more charming."

"More everything."

"No. Clem is more stable, more unselfish and thoughtful. He'll make a better husband, Elinor, and I'm glad that the two families will be related at last. It was always meant to happen, only things went wrong."

She obviously didn't know that things had gone wrong again. May must have had some reason for not telling her. May, one could be sure, had always a reason for what she did or did not do, I thought, still smarting keenly from the wound she had so dutifully inflicted in telling me about Clem and Thyrza. It was on the tip of my tongue to confide in Kelda but the moment belonged to her: the need to tell was so undeniably hers that I held my tongue and afterward was glad of it; but on the subject of Julius, her reason for leaving him and the cloistered seclusion in which she had lived ever since, she was not to be drawn. Not that I probed. Like her I rated the lost idyll above the sober reality. Moreover I knew from Kelda's occasional pauses to listen for any sound outside the room

151

that our conversation was to be kept private: May was not to know that she was confiding in me.

Kelda fished out a chain from the neck of her blouse and opened a locket.

"Yes, I see what you mean." It was a face that defied the limitations of its small oval setting: young, half smiling, instinct with life. "What a shame! What a terrible waste!"

"That's why"—Kelda hesitated—"I haven't mentioned this, Elinor. One doesn't talk of such things and I wouldn't want you to have a wrong impression of Dick . . ."

"How could I?"

"You called it a terrible waste, his death, and so it was. But just recently, although the pain of it has been almost more than I could bear, there's been comfort in it too. I've brought myself to see it as a consolation that Dick's life is starting all over again in his son. In Arthur. So like him. It could be Dick himself at the same age." She became aware that a thunderbolt had struck me. "You didn't know of course. How could you? Arthur is Dick's son"—and misinterpreting my silence—"you mustn't condemn him. What he did—that's only part of a man's life, or a woman's either, not the whole of it."

"I don't condemn him." The surge of reviving happiness warmed my whole being. And yet it wasn't surprising, I daresay, that the joy and relief were modified by doubt. How could one know what to believe?

"I suppose you're quite sure that Arthur is Dick's son. I mean—there could have been someone else. How can one know such things?"

"Seeing Arthur would be proof enough. But I know it because Dick told me." It was touching to see her pride in their intimate comradeship.

"But didn't you mind, that he and Thyrza . . . ?"

"Of course I minded. It made me miserable. But I knew him so well, better than anyone else knew him. It wasn't lust." The word was May's. Kelda rejected it with contempt. "It was a kind of love. There are different kinds of love."

Having found a sympathetic listener, she had found her tongue too. Dick still occupied her heart and mind as when he was alive, and if I no longer saw him as the fallen hero but with a certain censorious coolness, at least I saw him as he had seemed to her. Vitality had flowed from him and spread itself abroad in sparkling waves. Being widespread it had been, as I can now see, of necessity shallow. Having been unfailingly successful in his relations with other people, he had never experienced suffering: never dreamed that he could inflict it but lived each moment of his life with zest; and that was a blessing, as his life was to be short; or perhaps the blessing lay in the shortness of it. Age might not have matured his essentially light nature. With time the charm might have worn thin especially if that time had been spent with May.

"He had other—adventures. He told me everything. Each one was perfect for him while it lasted. Yes, of course I minded but they had nothing to do with his love for me or mine for him. It was always there from the very beginning and nothing could change it."

She might have minded more, I guessed, but for the consoling thought that he was being repeatedly disloyal to May. Some faint notion came to me of Kelda's anguish when he engaged himself to the sister who had always taken first place, whom she had cherished, admired, deferred to but never understood. No one, I was to discover, had ever taken the measure of May, least of all me. On the other hand, May presumably hadn't taken the measure of Dick.

"May mustn't know," I said, "about Dick and Thyrza—and those others."

"We never talk about him. I didn't tell her."

"That was kind."

"It wasn't kindness."

She didn't elaborate and I said, awkwardly but with more

153

sincerity than she knew, "Thank you for telling me all this. It really has helped me to understand and I'm grateful."

Her warmth in speaking of Dick had brought color to her cheeks and softness to her voice; but in my newly restored energy I had raised mine. She looked anxiously over her shoulder. I went to the door and opened it cautiously. May was walking quietly away along the narrow passage. She didn't turn her head but with the smoothness that governed all her movements went into the drawing room.

Had she overheard? In hoping that she had not I was far from clear as to my true feelings. Suppose I were to feel it my duty to enlighten her about Dick, as she had so conscientiously enlightened me about Clem? It was out of the question. I couldn't stoop to it. As May had stooped? The derogatory word shocked me into facing the truth: that there had been no need to tell me. She could have left it to Clem to tell me himself. He had said in his letter that he "had rather specially wanted to talk to me," presumably about his first meeting with his nephew. Even if the meeting had been with his own son—as May believed—he would very likely have told me if I hadn't skulked in her room to avoid seeing him.

All the same, restored to happiness, I could be kind—and consistent; for there was no need to tell May either. She had suffered enough. Let her go on thinking the worst of Clem. It could do no harm to him—or to me. Nothing could harm us now: we were invulnerable.

But the shape of things had altered, as when a kaleidoscope is shaken and the pieces settle into new relationships. For instance, it had never occurred to me that I might rise above May and looking down, find her lacking in the compassion I could feel for her. Moreover the new pattern introduced a new enigma. Since Julius was alive and Kelda therefore absolved from guilt, why had the two parted—and so irrevocably? Why could Kelda never be free—and apparently never free from fear? She would never tell me: I must look elsewhere for the answers.

154

Almost without a sound May had closed the drawing room door. Eyes narrowed, I peered along the passage to the hall beyond, as if its dimness might coalesce into the silent forms of those others who had lived here, had gone up and down the stairs and in and out of the rooms. There must be someone, somewhere, who knew what had happened to condemn my aunts to an imprisonment they seemed powerless to escape.

Meanwhile in one area at least, and that the only one that mattered, nothing but openness was called for. I ran upstairs, found pen and paper and began my letter:

"Dearest, dearest Clem . . ."

It would be two days before I could hope for a reply, but the next morning brought a diversion in the shape of a visit from Sintram. Once again the yard bell rang unexpectedly, I opened the back gate and there he was, tall, gaunt, shabbier than ever. The brim of his hat had so nearly left its weather-stained crown that it took some skill to raise it. I invited him in. He clutched gratefully at the arm of the wooden bench by the back door but remained standing while I stood, and he sat down with obvious relief when I left him and went indoors.

Kelda had gone to the village. In view of the fuss caused by his earlier visit it was awkward to find Aunt May in the kitchen. I couldn't decide whether to mention his name in a perfectly normal way (it would be a step toward encouraging her interest in her fellow creatures) or whether to lure her out of the kitchen without mentioning him at all. While I dithered over the bread crock she said, "It's Sintram, isn't it? How ill he looks! Let me do that. You make the tea."

She sliced bread with the lofty grace that never deserted her, wielding the knife with unexpected precision. The kettle was on the boil. I carried out a steaming half-pint mug, the tea liberally sweetened.

"Don't get up."

His parched lips parted in something between a smile of apology and a gasp. He sat heavily, as if all his overtaxed muscles conspired to keep him there. The hot tea revived him a little. Someday, I thought, he'll sit down on that seat and never get up again; and I wished Kelda would come back.

Presently May appeared at the back door, a spectacle rare enough to create in a less limited audience a small sensation. She wore a blue summer dress with a deep bertha collar from which her slender neck rose stalklike to her face, as delicately tinted as a flower. In her hand she held the white kitchen plate. Like a beautiful ministering angel, I was still capable of thinking, though not long ago I would have omitted the word "like," she stepped down into the yard, put the plate on the seat at Sintram's side and went indoors again. Neither of them had spoken, and when I glanced at Sintram, interested as to the effect on him of such an apparition as must rarely come his way, I saw that his eyes were closed.

When I went inside May had already gone back to the drawing room. A sound from the yard drew me to the kitchen window in time to see Sintram making his way unsteadily to the gate. The plate of bread and cheese lay untouched.

Only the sudden worsening of his condition, or the primitive instinct of a sick animal to creep to a hiding place could account for his inability to eat. He had confessed to having walked ten miles fasting. I waited uneasily for a minute; then, feeling that he shouldn't be left alone, picked up the plate and ran after him.

At first there was no sign of him. If he had gone toward Saury he should still have been in sight; but there was, I now knew, another way of retreat from Hoodman House. Sure enough, having slithered down into Packhorse Way I saw him trudging toward the farmhouse.

"Wait! Please wait!"

He didn't turn. I caught up with him in the open glade where the steps led up to the garden.

"Are you ill? Why haven't you eaten anything? I've brought it . . ."

He stopped and looked down at me. His unshaven face, stern with suffering, softened. His eyes were mild.

"You're exhausted. You must try to eat, even if it isn't very tempting. You could have taken it with you."

Other tramps did so, wrapping food in cloth or paper and stowing it in filthy pockets; and now rather to my surprise he produced a folded sheet of newspaper and took the bread from the plate, his hands shaking.

"That's better. Now you're being sensible." Unconsciously I had adopted the tone of one of the nurses at Rosedown Hall when encouraging a very sick patient. I climbed the steps to push open the wicket gate. "You can rest in that corner by the wall."

"It won't be the first time." He followed with painful slowness. "The old place has been like a home to me, especially in bad weather."

"You can't possibly walk to Bidminster today."

"I'll sleep for an hour or two, then beg a lift on the Upper Saury road. There'll be a cart going most of the way." He laid the paper of food carefully on the wall and raised his ramshackle hat. "Thank you, Miss Elinor. You have been gracious to me. Very gracious."

"You'll eat it now? It worried me that you didn't seem to want it."

"A hungry man always wants food." He had never throughout the incident lost his dignity. His voice, though tremulous and hoarse, still held an authentic note of self-confidence, so that despite his dreadful clothes and failing strength he appeared undefeated. "I take it willingly and gratefully"—with a surge of spirit he lifted his head. His light hazel eyes lost their look of illness and glowed with intense earnestness—"from your hands."

Had it not seemed so improbable, I could have fancied that he stressed the word "your." While I boggled at the implication,

157

he went on: "However low a man may sink, he keeps some freedom of choice. When he can no longer exercise the right to
choose, he might as well starve to death. I have striven to turn from
evil. You should do the same—and you will."

"From evil? But I haven't . . . I don't know . . . what kind of
evil?"

"I can't help you. You must find out for yourself. Yes, you will
come to recognize it."

I wondered if through hunger and sickness and old age he
was wandering in mind now as well as body. All the same he
impressed me as possessing a peculiar insight such as the dying are
endowed with.

"From *your* hands." He couldn't have meant what I thought
he meant: he had simply intended a graceful old-world compliment to me. All the same—why had he left the food untouched?

I looked back before going down the slope. Instead of settling
in the sheltered corner by the well-head he had taken his packet
of bread and cheese and disappeared to some other resting place
of his own. He must know every nook and cranny of Winkblade
and its outbuildings. He had been coming here for years—and
years. He had known my aunts for most of their lives.

Goodness knows there was nothing in Sintram's appearance
to account for the impression he gave of wielding an almost
biblical authority: nothing of the sandaled prophet in his broken
boots and stained army greatcoat; no flowing locks. And yet in the
deep lane between tangled banks of bramble and briar I seemed to
have sunk to earth again from a loftier region where the flimsy
decencies of social life had been blown away to reveal like a brief
gap in clouds a moment of truth; a region where good and evil
could be confronted and recognized without qualification or com-
promise. It had been like the first awareness of returning sight to
someone blind.

The moment of perception was unexpectedly followed almost at once by another. The front door was ajar. I closed it behind

me and leaned against it, listening. Light filtered only feebly through the opaque panes and fell uncertainly on the empty pegs of the tall hallstand, on the lower stairs of the long flight, on the entrance to the passage to the morning room. No sound; no life.

May wasn't in her usual place. Like a starved plant seeking light I went to the window only to draw back, startled. On the table lay the usual sheet of drawing paper. Its virgin whiteness had been deeply scored by a frenzy of irregular zigzag black lines savagely drawn. I saw in them—or imagine I saw—a mindless ferocity that made me shiver, and in the ruined paper a purity wilfully despoiled. From what depths of frustration could so destructive a force erupt? The abnormality frightened me like an encounter with madness.

It was like a sudden glimpse, all the more startling for its unexpectedness, of the horrors that can lie beneath the surface of even the quietest of lives: as if in turning over the soil to plant snowdrops I had come upon the more ghastly whiteness of a skeleton hastily buried in too shallow a grave. The image came to me instinctively, bringing no warning that it might be prophetic.

Paradoxically I was rescued from such disagreeable thoughts by the very place that inspired them. The room itself intervened. Its unremarkable contents—occasional tables, sofa and chairs covered in faded once elegant fabrics, its unassertive greens and gray, its silent pot plants on lace mats—suggested a conventional propriety that couldn't fail to reassure. Appearances can count for a great deal. No wonder people set such store by them.

14
ϬϬϬϬϬϬ

"THERE MUST BE something more," Clem said. "Something we don't know."

The parlor at Winkblade shimmered in dusty shafts of sunlight. Since there was nowhere else to sit we were sitting on the floor facing the windows, our backs to the wall. From the garden came the moist smell of fallen leaves.

His response to my letter had been to come to me at once, bang on the door knocker, walk in and having located me in the kitchen, take me in his arms regardless of the basting spoon I was too agitated to put down. After the first exquisite reunion, we walked up to Winkblade where we could talk freely.

His cold anger against May made any attempt to excuse her a waste of breath. It was no time to labor the point that she had genuinely thought she was speaking the truth. All my sympathy was for Clem; and he, knowing how I had suffered, was remarkably restrained.

"I'm touched," he said grimly, "to think that May has treasured a photograph of me. Which one was it, by the way?"

"Sailor suit, straw hat, fishing net, head in the air."

"I don't remember that one."

Eventually, when our own affairs had been thoroughly gone

into, we arrived at the unhappy triangular relationship—quadrilateral if one included Julius—of our elders.

Clem had not been surprised to hear of Kelda's feeling for Dick: they had always been special friends. It had been taken for granted, mistakenly as we now knew, that their attachment was that of brother and sister, especially after Dick's engagement. On the other hand he had been completely bowled over by the totally unexpected meeting with his nephew.

"It fairly knocked the stuffing out of me," he said, "when I saw Arthur. Except that Arthur is still only seven and I was still in my cradle when Dick was that age, it was like seeing him again as I first remembered him. No, that's too simple. Very small children don't consciously see other people, but pictures of them must be imprinted on the mind like negatives waiting to be developed. Until I saw Arthur I didn't even know that I'd ever seen Dick looking like that. At any rate, can you imagine being jerked back without warning to being an infant and at the same time to be towering over your elder brother shrunk to half his proper size? Staggering! It made me so dizzy that I could hardly stand." He leaned forward, eyes narrowed in thought, remembering how time had abruptly reversed its onward flow and swept him back to childhood. "I hadn't the faintest idea that Dick had made love to Thyrza much less had a child by her, but afterward, thinking it over, I wasn't surprised. He was like that and so was she. Remember, he'd fallen into May's clutches before he was twenty. Once she had his ring on her finger there was no getting it off. Even if father relented, May never would. Not that there could be any excuse for letting Thyrza down like that, but he did at least provide for her and Arthur. She told me so."

"It's interesting that Kelda is the one who understands. She loves Arthur. Do you know, she's been ransacking the attics for toys and games for him and he's perfectly at ease with her. And it was Kelda that Dick confided in about Thyrza. I suppose he couldn't bear to tell May."

161

"And neither can you. You're becoming as devious as your extraordinary aunts. The sooner I can get you out of that house the better. We must get married as soon as ever we can! Incidentally that house you fancied is still empty. I've been trying to find out who's taken the lease but the agent muttered something about not giving his client's name at this stage. You can be looking at other houses while I'm away."

"And the client may change his mind, whoever he is. But what about Kelda? I can't leave without trying to sort things out for her. She's so unhappy."

"And that's another thing that gets under my skin." Clem's anger was mounting again. "How could she let us all think that Julius was dead? No, don't make excuses. It was bad enough to turn her back on him and write him off like a bad debt: but the faked widowhood was unforgivable."

"She didn't actively deceive or lie, did she? And I can see now that her mourning served a double purpose. It expressed her mood—grief for Dick—and it also . . ."

"Yes. The widow's weeds supplied a sufficient reason for her coming home and concealed the real reason, whatever it was. What's more, putting herself into black made her return home final. There could be no going back once the message got through to anyone interested, that poor old Julius had passed away."

"I thought of that. If May had simply needed her help with my grandfather, she could have gone back to Julius when grandfather died; but for some reason she felt unable to." And I told him how Kelda had looked and spoken when she said, "I shall never be free, never."

It was then that Clem made his remark about there being something else we didn't know.

"Some other skeleton in the cupboard. Not Julius."

I considered the unappealing possibility and rejected it as beyond belief: there couldn't be two of them.

"Why should she be afraid of May?" Clem too had been lost

in thought. "Jealousy, even hatred one could understand but not fear. Even allowing for May's special brand of hypnotism . . . Yes, you must admit it worked with you—and with Dick—and with me *once*"—Lott's Pool yawned again—"once and never again, and it must have worked many a time with Kelda. But why should it frighten her?"

"Are you saying that May must have forced her to come home?"

"People like Kelda can't be forced to leave their husbands, or to do anything else for that matter unless to resist would involve them in a catastrophe they couldn't face."

"What is the worst of sins?" It was May who had used the phrase.

"It depends," Clem said unhelpfully.

The Winkblade robin was singing in the rowan tree, its song sweet and sad; but we were too happy to believe in either sadness or evildoing, light-hearted enough to enjoy the melodrama we were creating. The sun was in our eyes. We huddled together more closely to escape the dazzle. In each broad shaft of light a myriad moving motes made ever-changing patterns in helpless obedience to some obscure design. Somewhere in the empty house a board creaked: a reminder of other presences. People we knew had walked and talked and loved and lain there.

"Whatever happened had already happened before the wedding," I said. "Because of it they had got rid of the servants."

"Or got rid of them because it was going to happen?"

"Yes! And somehow that's worse, like a crime deliberately planned. What could it be, for heaven's sake?"

"Not theft, nothing that enriched them, since they remained so obviously unenriched."

"We're assuming that they were both involved. Guilt would keep them together because they dared not separate."

"It's no use asking Kelda point blank?"

"No use at all."

"Then we must put our heads together."

In its literal form the suggestion was delightfully easy to put into practice. It was to our credit in the circumstances that we did apply our minds to the possible rescue of Kelda. After his return to Dorset the next day Clem would take the first opportunity of looking up Mr. Cade at St. Mark's Preparatory School . . .

"Dash it all," he said, "the man's been shamefully treated. We can at least find out how he feels about being played fast and loose with."

"And how he feels about Kelda?"

On the whole it seemed best not to noise his continued existence abroad. As Clem said, there was no point in exhuming a body until you knew what you were going to do with it; and it would be adding to Kelda's problems to make her the subject of gossip at this stage. The best course, if only we could contrive it, would be to get her away quietly before releasing the news—a small bombshell in Bidminster—that her widowhood had been predated.

We could treat the affair lightly because it was all so nebulous. If the only way to release Kelda was to exert pressure on May, it was a project fraught with innumerable difficulties, the chief one being our ignorance as to the circumstances that had overshadowed their lives. So long as the solution remained safely out of reach we enjoyed talking about it as we would have enjoyed any mortal thing now that we were together again. So that when Clem said, "You realize that we may be getting out of our depth. Strictly speaking it's none of our business and we may stir up more than we settle," the warning barely reached me, though it ought to have revived misgivings I had already felt: intimations that, with Clem close beside me, I was happy to forget.

"Whatever they're hiding it couldn't have been anything really bad. Not criminal, I mean." Once bitten, I had grown wary.

We cleaned the window, folded the rug, and tore ourselves

away, leaving the autumnal garden to the robin. In Packhorse Way we said a lingering good-bye.

"It won't be long." Clem held me close, his cheek against mine. "Then we'll be together all the time. I must talk to my father. He'll do all he can to help us and if the worst comes to the worst there's always my uncle in diamonds. You haven't forgotten Uncle Vernon."

"Certainly not. He's my chief reason for marrying you."

"We've been keeping him in cold storage for years. This may be the time to thaw him out and get to know the old boy. Let's invite him to the wedding."

As soon as the project in Dorset was finished we could make definite plans. Meanwhile Clem hoped to come home again on a flying visit after he had seen Mr. Cade.

I watched him out of sight, then clambered up the bank and made my way slowly to the front door. May was at her table, her hands idle. Nothing moved except the leaf shadows reflected in the tall windowpanes. In their wavering green light the contours of her neck and face lost definition as if seen through water. Impressions, half remembered, stirred in my mind and rose almost to the surface, only to drift away, leaving me haunted by a foreboding both sinister and sad. The effort to understand her strange personality had worn out my powers of perception. It was as if I could no longer see her at all, though every line of her face, every delicate tint of her skin, every light cadence of her voice, were to remain imprinted on my memory so that, mercifully, that is how I sometimes see her still: fair and pure as the Madonna in a Raphael painting.

I untied the belt of my knitted jacket and found in the pocket an unposted letter to Mrs. Burnett. I laid it on the lid of the glove box and gazed at it, at first absently as I undid my buttons, then with a dawning sense that it was signaling some kind of message. I went back to the door. From there the envelope was clearly visible, arrestingly white against the dark oak. I took off my jacket and put it on its usual hook where it hung inches clear of the box lid. Then I unhooked the jacket and like a person in a hurry flung it back on the hook, on another hook and another. The envelope lay untouched.

Warming to the experiment, I swished the jacket back and forth like a brush until the envelope was swept from the lid and fell on the metal drip tray. On hands and knees I explored with my right hand the space between the hallstand and the wall. It took some maneuvering to fix the envelope there but having done so, I stood up, stepped back a few paces and surveyed the effect.

"What *are* you doing?"

My pulse quickened but it was only Kelda. She had come along from the morning room.

"I'm going to post a letter," I said casually, reaching yet again for my jacket. "Do you want anything in the village?"

"No, I don't think so, but come here for a minute."

Retrieving my letter, I followed her to the morning room. On the table were strewn the contents of a letter case.

"I thought you might be interested." She had closed the door. She was a little flushed—with pleasure for a change. "You remember when we were talking about Arthur and how like Dick he is. Well, there's a photograph somewhere of Dick about the same age. Actually there's one of me too. Mr. Tass took them on the same day. We'd been fishing in Lott's Pool. I can't find the one of Dick, but here I am, with the basket."

The ivory-colored mount with its double rectangle of gilt lines enclosed a laughing little girl in a sailor blouse with long curling hair under the brim of a white sun hat.

"We didn't catch anything. There's nothing in that pool worth catching, only frogs. But Dick posed with his fishing net and his head in the air, as if he'd made a record catch. 'Pretend the basket's full, Kay,' he said when it was my turn." She turned over papers, dance programs, notebooks. "I wish I could find it."

I left her to look and, postponing my walk to the post office, went upstairs and sat down at my window. The sun was setting; its long rays had left even the topmost boughs of the trees opposite. I waited. Presently the front door opened and May came out. From above only the sculptured bands of her hair were visible, the gray folds of her dress and the white fringe of her shawl. My angle of vision afforded no clue of the woman herself but reduced her to a moving shape of gray and white. She closed the iron gate and walked steadily down the lane.

With a deliberation as smooth as her own I left my room and went into hers, to the bureau. It wasn't locked: she had never needed to fear the sacrilege of such an intrusion as this. Carefully, light-fingered as a professional thief, I took out the contents of each pigeonhole in turn.

It was there, the companion photograph to Kelda's, in a brown folder with others. I didn't look at them, only at the handsome boy putting on an act, the sham fisherman who had grown up to become a bogus hero: the conjuror whose tricks went wrong, the shallow lover who edged away from the two women who truly loved him, yet could not face the unpleasantness of breaking free of a woman incapable of love.

Contempt for Dick threatened the entire company of legendary lovers: Lancelot, Tristam, and all—they were swept away in the tide of a disillusionment far more wounding, a loss of faith that sickened me.

She had lied deliberately. "It's Clem," she had said, showing me Dick, knowing that when the photograph was taken Clem was an infant in his cot. It was the cruelest and most flagrant of her deceptions; but there had been others, all designed to separate me from Clem and keep me here at Hoodman House. I had ignored Clem's warnings. It had suited me to go on believing in her, to remain under her spell. Even now I shrank with a feeling of irreverence from any comparison between the shabbiness of her conduct and the pure image I had admired and loved.

In a dismal burst of spite I vowed to thwart her by leaving at once never to return. Then I remembered our plans for rescuing Kelda. However little she deserved our efforts, something must be done for Julius Cade. I saw him more clearly now as a victim of some such scheming as I had narrowly escaped but of a darker and more deadly kind: a web spun six years ago and strong enough to hold the three of them still entrapped.

The front door opened. May had come back. She herself made no sound. I heard only the click of the key as she turned it, locking us in. When I went downstairs she was sitting as before in the window. Its cold light fell on her face and found no imperfection in it. No impulse toward evil. And yet I knew now where the malign spirit of the house had its source. The discovery had done more than overturn an idol. In the heart of the worshipper something had died: a spark of spontaneous trust, a natural innocence.

She must have known that recent events had changed me: that Clem and I were happily reconciled; that Kelda had begun to confide in me. If that knowledge put me at risk I was still unaware of it. Otherwise I might have wondered if her stillness had become more purposeful, her long-lashed eyes more watchful, her egotism more dangerous.

15

THE DAYS PASSED slowly. There was nothing to be done until I heard from Clem. In this uneasy time my work as Mr. Penfold's part-time secretary was proving a godsend. My working days, Tuesdays and Thursdays, could be looked forward to as holidays when like a prisoner on parole I could shake off the restraints of the other five days. Those restraints had increased. I grew weary of the intensity with which I had once again taken to watching the faces of my aunts: faces so similar in all their features, alike in their power to conceal what lay within. Sometimes when I was alone, by a curious blending the two became in memory one face, one pale oval with blue eyes framed in honey-colored hair: sometimes as I lay awake they floated in the darkness, appearing in turn like opposite sides of a two-faced mask.

The house was so quiet that my natural tones like theirs became subdued. I found myself opening doors slowly to give an unseen listener time to steal away. We revolved each on her own axis, responding to a shared routine yet isolated.

To walk into Saury, wait for Willie Kimble's bus, picturesquely named the Valley Queen—for Willie, though he lacked sparkle, had romantic leanings—to chat with the passengers and hear the local news, was as exhilarating as going to a party. There was usually time for a fruitful word with Mrs. Torgill, the bus stop being, doubtless at her request, at her shop window. I had just arrived at her open door one Tuesday morning when she addressed me from her seat behind the counter.

"I was thinking now that Willie Kimble's running this bus we could have Annie out here for a day. It'd be like old times."

I agreed and remarked that they couldn't have seen much of each other since Annie left Saury.

"She did come once in a while by horse and trap and have her dinner. Then she'd go on to the Tile Sheds to Martha Beck's. They were old friends. But it was too cold for her, sitting in a draughty trap when her rheumatism got bad. She didn't even get to Martha's funeral."

Since my first visit I had popped into Mrs. Brady's several times when my transactions at the post office took me in that direction, and I put the suggestion to Annie that afternoon.

"There's nothing I'd like better." She perked up at once. "But it would be getting to the bus that would be awkward."

I assured her that I would borrow a bath chair and her niece could wheel her to the nearest point.

"There'd be a rare hoisting and a pushing and a pulling and keeping folks waiting, I doubt."

"Willie Kimble won't mind that."

"Well, he shouldn't," Annie conceded. "I went to school with his mother."

The enterprise was successfully carried out on the following Friday. I made a special trip to the village, helped Susan Torgill to install Annie in the room behind the shop, and stayed for a while to gossip.

Annie, I discovered, had been too sweeping in her assertion that she had never set foot in Hoodman House since her dismissal. It was when my grandfather was mentioned that she changed her tune a little.

170

"The last time I saw Mr. Findon would be about two months after I left."

"But I thought you said you never went back after you were given notice."

"Now so I did, but it's just come to me, that one other time. I had to pass the house, you see, to get to Tile Sheds. I used to dread seeing it after all that happened and this particular day it was like a house of the dead. Not a face at the front windows, nobody at the front door, not a sound from the backyard. If it hadn't been for the chimney smoke you'd have thought nobody lived there."

"There'd be just the old gentleman and Miss May," put in Mrs. Torgill. "That would be the winter Miss Kelda was in London, and a bitter cold winter it was. The pairs of socks our Susan put off her needles for the boys in the trenches would take some counting—and the mufflers."

"The day I'm telling you about it was fit to freeze you to death, a gray sky and that quietness everywhere before it snows. John Kimble—that was Willie's father—took me in the trap as far as the lane end. He was going on to Saury Mill and I had to walk the rest of the way to the Tile Sheds but I made the effort. If I hadn't seen Martha that day before the bad weather set in there wouldn't be another chance till spring. You know the state yon lane gets into."

Actually I didn't. The weather that summer had been fine and dry and I hadn't yet experienced a winter in Saury; but like all homely storytellers Annie gripped the attention. Hoodman House had never seemed less inviting, never more isolated or more forbiddingly secretive than now, as she described her last visit there.

"Somehow—it was just a feeling then but it turned out to be true—it seemed as if everything was coming to an end and this would be the last time I'd ever be there. And I thought 'Poor Mr. Findon! I wonder how he's faring, penned up in that little room downstairs?' He'd been failing when I left and I never really said good-bye, the way I was feeling. And he seemed confused, as if he didn't understand what was happening. He had a lost look, if you know what I mean."

I remembered it and his bewildered blue eyes as we clasped hands at the wedding, reaching for a moment across the gap between his generation and mine.

"As it turned out it was the last time I ever went that way. Whether it was the cold that got me or being upset at the way he was and finding everything so different, I don't know, but the very next day the rheumatism really got hold of me and laid me out and I've never been the same since."

There followed a sympathetic pause before Mrs. Torgill produced a number of suggested remedies: thermogene wrapped round the joints, a boiled onion for supper, Hoare's liniment.

"And plenty of rest, Annie. Every time you sit back in your chair it's worth a sovereign in your pocket. It's an affliction and no mistake and it gets us all in the end."

"Did you call to see my grandfather?"

"Not exactly call. I don't know what made me go in. If you'd asked me five minutes before if I'd ever set foot in Hoodman House again, I'd have sworn on the Bible that wild horses wouldn't drag me. But it was as if a guiding hand led me round to the side. You know how the field goes right up to the railings? It used to be the garden with flowerbeds and a statue and we used to serve tea there under a cedar tree. Well, lo and behold, there he was at the window in his dressing gown and propped up with pillows, just staring out. He saw me but he didn't take in who it was. I was in my hat and coat of course. 'It's Annie,' I said, only mouthing it so that no one else could hear. 'It's Annie.' After a bit he seemed to come to himself and lifted up his hand slowly, as if it was a day's work to do it and beckoned me to go in."

"That was touching," Mrs. Torgill sighed. "Really touching."

Annie had felt it so. Reluctantly and with scarcely a sound, she had opened the wicket and gone round to the back door, through the deserted kitchen and into my grandfather's room.

"Like a child he was and ever so pleased to see me, not that he quite recognized me. He was left too much alone. I always said it was a mistake to make an invalid of him and by that time his mind was wandering. He kept on saying the same thing over and over again." She groped for the rug, which was slipping from her knees. I tucked it round her. "A sort of fancy he had." She looked troubled.

"They do," Mrs. Torgill said comfortably, "have them, don't they, when they're old."

"What sort of fancy?" I asked.

" 'Have you everything you want, Mr. Findon, sir?' I asked him, which I don't expect he had. It was always Miss Kelda that saw to his needs. He didn't answer. 'My daughter May,' he says, as if he was speaking to a stranger, 'is in the drawing room and my other daughter is in London.' 'I know that, sir,' I said and then it came to him again who I was. 'But there's something you don't know, Annie.' He leaned his head close to mine and whispered, 'There's somebody upstairs, somebody else.' "

Annie too was whispering—with eerie effect. Sick fancy or not, the idea was chilling. And my grandfather, having got it into his head, could think of nothing else but went on repeating it. "But who can it be?" Annie had asked, humoring him. "I don't know," he had replied. "They don't tell me. They don't tell me anything."

As soundlessly as she had come Annie crept out of the house and since then had never darkened its doors again.

At that point the tireless Susan came in to make their tea and leaving them to their toasted tea cakes and seed cake, I went home, reflecting that my grandfather's hallucination was easily explained. Profound silence stimulates the imagination into creating sound. When there is no movement the mind invents it. Lack of sound and movement would otherwise become unbearable—as Hood-man House often seemed.

173

Somebody upstairs? Somebody *else*? There couldn't have been: he and May had been quite alone. From the hall I went slowly up the wide staircase to the first floor. Five bedrooms opened off the square landing: May's was as it must always have been, the prettiest, with china ornaments on the mantelpiece, a lace-draped dressing table and lace-curtained window, a chaise longue, and thanks to me, usually a fire; Kelda's room, on the west side, simply furnished with a sagging armchair upholstered in worn striped silk, a desk, the tin cash box she brooded over anxiously; and my own narrow room. The remaining two had been Mrs. Findon's bedroom and the guest room, unused for years, each with an immovable mahogany wardrobe, drawers, dressing table, and bed valances edged with yellowing crochet lace.

From the landing a narrow passage led to a winding attic stair. Except to take a quick peep into them on my first day I had not visited the attics. The two at the back had been maids' rooms. A large one at the front, running the whole width of the house, had been partitioned at one end to make a small apartment without a window. The main attic was light and airy with a window and a fanlight and was used as a dump for household relics: a trunk or two, a speckled swivel mirror, an orange box containing children's books and toys.

Here if anywhere I might expect to find my friend the stuffed squirrel. It wasn't in the box with the monkey-on-a-stick and the eyeless doll. With some eagerness I lifted the trunk lids, peered behind a crate of books, heaved out the reluctant drawers of a painted chest—to no avail. So thoroughly had I imbued it with life, so magically had it turned up to astonish the assembled children in the bakehouse that its failure to reappear seemed deliberate. I hoped for a reunion and was disappointed.

The fanlight in the sharply angled roof gave a bird's-eye view through trees into Packhorse Way; an arched window at floor level on the west wall overlooked the farm lane, the gate by the cherry tree, and the distant road to Saury. The fanlight had been fitted with a blind, the low window with a heavy velour curtain.

For some reason it was the cramped space beyond the partition that had been used as a bedroom, though it was windowless and dingy and with the door closed would be quite dark. Crowded into this tiny cell were a single iron bedstead with a soiled counterpane; a washstand with basin and ewer, and underneath, a china bucket and a pair of chamber pots; an upright cane chair; a chest by the bed and on it a wooden candlestick. As a servant's room it was a disgrace. No servant I had ever come across would have put up with it; no respectable employer would have offered it.

It was not just untidy but dirty. In its overcrowded state there would scarcely have been room to wield a dustpan but the experiment had not been tried, at least not for years. Gingerly examining the basin, bucket, and chamber pots, I was disgusted to find that they had been emptied but not washed or polished. In the ewer the decaying remains of a blue bottle floated in an inch or two of discoloured water. On the chest by the bed lay an empty black bottle of Dr. Haggie's Mixture. Its label proclaiming "Soothes all pain" was familiar. The mixture had been used surreptitiously— and compassionately—at Rosedown Hall. Its basic ingredient was laudanum.

Squeezing between bed and washstand I dislodged a pile of roughly folded sheets of grayish flannelette. The top one overhung the edge of the bed. I picked it up to refold it and hastily put it down again. It was covered with ugly brown stains and smelt unpleasantly.

Even allowing for the difficulty of cleaning such a room and for the abrupt departure of the servants, it was hard to account for such squalor. In fact I couldn't imagine Annie allowing stained sheets to be used or to be left in such a state. They should be burned at once. I went out, closing the door with a disapproving slam. The outer attic was filled with yellow light from the setting sun. On the bare floor a broad swathe in the dust showed that the box of oddments had recently been moved. Glancing back from the head of the winding stair, I traced the dust-free curve back to its starting point. In its former position the box must have blocked the door to the bedroom.

Exploring the family attic is supposed to be fun. Lost treasures may be unearthed: unrecognized old masters; silver goblets masquerading as pewter, priceless brooches fallen between floorboards, love letters smelling of lavender, missing wills. Hoodman House as usual failed to conform to the normal pattern. Its family secrets took no tangible form. All that I took with me down two flights of stairs was an impression of nastiness hastily shut away and for years ignored.

Safe in the kitchen, I remembered what it was that had roused my interest in the attics: my grandfather's conviction, though he and May were alone, that there was somebody else upstairs. Just an old man's delusion. Yet it caught the imagination, the idea of someone without form or identity, someone impossible to picture, who had used the room and had passed on: someone who had vanished into the past, leaving no trace.

16

"It was a weird experience," Clem wrote, "to be saying how-do-you-do to a man supposed to be dead for years. The last time I shook hands with him was at his wedding. He used to visit us quite often in Bidminster and he hadn't forgotten; and although obviously he wouldn't have recognized me (I've improved since then, as you pointed out), he remembered the silent younger Tass and was so pleased to see me that I felt ashamed. Why, for God's sake, was he allowed to fade out of our lives without anyone bothering to ask even how he died or, more accurately, didn't die?"

We both knew where to lay the blame and it was not upon the Tass family. A woman in widow's weeds without a husband in sight is indistinguishable from a bona fide widow; and Mrs. Tass had had little opportunity of talking to Kelda after her return home. I learned later that she had once called at Hoodman House to express her sympathy, an experience she never discussed with her family and never repeated. Whatever the coolness, evasiveness, or deliberate untruths she encountered can only be conjecture. Even so, after years of estrangement she had been the first to attempt to heal the breach by writing to Kelda when she heard from the Penfolds of my arrival. The letter had been ignored but this second rebuff had been countered: she had sent Clem, to my undying gratitude.

Now again it was Clem who acted as go-between. He had lost no time in finding St. Mark's Preparatory School for Boys, a country house near Dorking, and asking for Mr. Cade.

"One good thing to report. He is well looked after here. His rooms are comfortable and I had the impression he is well thought of. In fact he seems to have become a cherished institution, not surprising considering how much too good he is for the job he's doing. With his talents he could have gone much further but he was always a quiet, self-effacing chap and my guess is that the wretched affair of his marriage shattered what little confidence he had in himself. . . . St. Mark's provided him with a refuge where he could lick his wounds. 'I was too old for her,' he kept on saying. 'She was young and beautiful. What could she see in me? It was a dream.' "

A dream from which he had been as rudely awakened as any knight-at-arms left wandering on the cold hillside, la belle dame sans merci in his case having gone home to her sister. "But it wasn't the lack of money," Clem wrote. "That didn't help, but it was only a side issue. You'll gather that we didn't skirt round the problems. I told him that something seemed to have gone badly wrong at Hoodman House and that you and I were anxious to help Kelda. Incidentally he did remember you: the polite little girl with the big tired gray eyes. As a matter of fact, he's by no means penniless: not rich but quite able to support a wife in comfort, a lot more comfort than Kelda has known in recent years . . ."

Their few weeks together as man and wife had been over-shadowed by the news about Dick, but Kelda had given no sign of regretting her marriage. He had not expected anything more wholehearted and was modestly content. My heart warmed to Julius, who had tried so hard and so hopelessly to be worthy of his beautiful bride. If he had handled the catastrophe weakly, backing unhappily away instead of fighting to keep his prize, his weakness was rooted in humility. He could never believe in his own worth.

As for the catastrophe, it had taken the form of Aunt May's letter. He and Kelda had been contentedly at ease with each other in their little house in Chichester. Kelda was an experienced housekeeper; she had also helped him with his oratorio by trying out the solo parts: there were musical evenings and recitals for the troops. Then one morning had come the letter. He had found Kelda crouching, stricken, in an armchair, sick, pale, and incoherent. "I must go home, Julius," she said, "at once. They need me." Her account of the letter was confused. He gathered that both my grandfather and May were ill and offered to take her home there and then. Her refusal had been absolute, woundingly so.

"The crux of the whole rotten business must have been in that letter," Clem wrote. "I asked him if he had read it. Apparently not. When he tentatively showed signs of wanting to, Kelda tore it up, violently, and threw it in the fire. Julius thought her hysterical. She was subject to sudden moods of distress. Even on their wedding day there had been an unfortunate scene that left him bewildered and completely baffled. He accepted that she must leave, helped her to pack, took her to the station—and that was the last he saw of her. The letter she wrote a week later made it clear that she would never come back: their marriage was at an end.

"The sheer cruelty of it makes my blood boil." Clem's pen had developed a vicious point. "Believe me, it broke his heart. He isn't in good health. We've got to help him, Elinor. It's time someone intervened: someone strong-minded and sane, who won't stand any nonsense. Yes, you've guessed. I mean me. My plan is to use May's own method of getting Kelda away. When you've read to the end, do as Kelda did and burn this letter. Those two mustn't know that I've seen Julius, not yet. We must spring it on them suddenly before a counterattack can be launched. See you soon . . ."

I stirred the kitchen fire into a blaze and obediently tore each of the three sheets in half, consigned each piece to the flames, and waited until the last black and shriveled scrap fluttered up the chimney.

"Burning a love letter?" Aunt May's light voice made me turn. I had left the envelope on the table and now snatched it up defensively. The gesture didn't escape her. She raised her eyebrows, her expression wounded. I wondered if she had also noticed the Dorking postmark.

The keynote of the enterprise was to be its suddenness. Kelda must be hurried off before May could find excuses for keeping her. I resigned myself to waiting. Apart from writing to Clem to remind him that on Tuesday and Thursday mornings I was away from home, there was nothing I could do.

Except one small thing.

"By the way," Clem had warned me in his letter, "Cade doesn't know that Kelda has been draped in mourning all this time. Heaven knows what he would have made of it. The man has problems enough without seeing his wife masquerading as Hamlet in the trappings and the suits of woe. Before she leaves can you get her into something more normal?"

Some forethought would be needed if she was to appear before her husband suitably dressed. Had she sold the clothes she used to wear? Righteously donning an apron, I took a brush and dustpan upstairs to sweep the bedroom carpets, starting with Kelda's room. A swift peep into her wardrobe revealed in one half nothing but garments of familiar black. Hastily transferring the key to the other door, I opened it and saw crammed together in too small a space a mass of dresses, costumes, skirts, their faint perfume recalling a happier period in their owner's life. There must be a few things still wearable.

Three days passed; then events moved swiftly. Kelda answered the sharp rap on the front door.

"It's Clem," she called. I joined them in the hall. May emerged from the drawing room. Greetings were exchanged, with well-simulated astonishment on my part. Clem didn't beat about the bush.

"I have news for you, Kelda. You must prepare yourself." He looked stern, even grim and somehow conveyed the impression of having hurried all the way from the southern counties with a message burning on his lips. Kelda paled. I went to her side. "You'll never believe whom I've met—in Surrey." May stiffened into attention. Kelda gave a suppressed moan of distress. "Yes, Julius, poor fellow. It was a tremendous shock to me of course. I managed to keep from him the fact that we had all thought him dead. I hope he'll never find out about a situation so wounding to any human being and especially a man of his fine caliber—but I won't go into that. He sends you his love and kindest wishes." Clem didn't pause to elaborate but cut through the web of deceit and betrayal without mercy. "I'm afraid he isn't well—a sick man—not to mention his depressed state of mind. In short, your husband needs you. If you've an ounce of humanity left in you after neglecting him all these years you'll go to him at once." He paused before adding solemnly, "Before it's too late."

"Oh, Kelda," I urged, "you must go."

She had been not unnaturally thunderstruck, but now she roused herself and looked anxiously at May.

"I don't think I can . . ."

"*I* don't think you have a choice," Clem said. "I've come all this way to fetch you. Can you be ready"—he looked at his watch—"in an hour? We can catch the four o'clock from Bidminster. I know it's sudden but at least you have a chance now to put things right. Elinor, you'd better take Kelda upstairs and help her to pack. May here can scramble me up something to eat. I haven't had anything since breakfast."

Afterward I was able to tell him how splendidly he had managed the situation. Most effective of all had been his handling of the chief obstacle to Kelda's departure. "May here" reduced the loftier of my aunts to the status of a useful younger sister. Wordlessly she went to the kitchen. Clem followed and shut the door behind him, pausing only to say, "Kimble will be back in an hour, so look sharp."

"You can't go in those clothes." I hustled Kelda up to her room where she sank helplessly on the bed and watched as I threw open her wardrobe for the second time, snatched dresses from the rail and strewed them about the room.

"There's nothing," she wailed. "They're so old and old-fashioned. What will Julius think?"

"Judging from what Clem says he won't care. It's you he wants. Take that dress off. Hurry. Oh dear, you're so thin."

The dresses hung loose on her but it was gratifying to see how the mere effort of trying them on brought her back to life. I sorted out the simplest on the principle that they would have dated least, determined, if there was nothing fit to wear, to purloin one of May's dresses. Somehow she had contrived to remain well dressed in spite of her slender means.

Kelda's indecision was pitiful though hardly surprising in the circumstances. She fluttered from one garment to another, fumbled in drawers, shed tears and wasted time by taking down her hair and brushing it endlessly. The allocated hour sped on. Despair inspired me.

"What were you wearing that day when you left Chichester?" She stopped brushing and looked at me sharply. I had given myself away.

"You knew. You and Clem have arranged this."

"Yes, and we're determined that you're going, even if we have to tie you hand and foot and carry you there. Oh Kelda, don't waste any more time. If you can make him happy, you'll be happy too."

"You're very good to me, Elinor." Her eyes were wistful. "It's more than I ever hoped for, but you don't understand what has kept me away from him. That hasn't changed and never will."

"I know there's a shadow over your life and that you can't tell me. But being afraid all the time is making you old when you're still young and should have years of happiness ahead of you. Can't you start again? In any case it's your duty to go to Mr. Cade. You promised—I heard you—to cleave unto him forsaking all others. And we won't let any harm come to you, Clem and I. Leave everything to us." I spoke in absolute ignorance of her true plight but suddenly she capitulated.

"It was this." She pointed to a coat and skirt of deep blue. "And a white blouse with pink sprigs."

We found the blouse: I slipped it over her head; she twisted up her hair, stepped into the skirt, and stood smiling, transformed.

"Kelda! It's lovely. He'll see you just as you were, as if nothing had ever happened to spoil it. Only you'll need a warm coat."

Burrowing in the depths of the wardrobe I found one pushed away to the end of the rail: a heavy musquash with a deep collar. Though a ponderous garment, it would do for the journey and see her through the winter. It was a symptom of her nervous state that she recoiled when I hauled it out.

"No, not that. I hate it."

"It will have to do. There isn't time to find anything else."

I snapped the catches of the portmanteau together as Clem came leaping up the stairs to take it and tell us that the taxi was waiting.

"You won't be alone," Kelda gasped as she embraced her sister. "Elinor will take care of you while I'm away."

May kissed her gently on the forehead. Nothing had shaken—nothing could shake her remarkable poise.

"And there'll be so much to talk about when you come back," she said.

The softly spoken words were conventional, irreproachable, banal. All the same their implication bothered me.

From the door she watched us settling ourselves in the taxi, Kelda almost obliterated by the voluminous fur coat.

"She'll never let go of her," I whispered to Clem. "Never."

His mood too had changed. He looked tired and anxious, and when we had said good-bye on the platform of Bidminster station, he held me in his arms a moment longer.

"I'm not sure that this is such a good idea. I hate leaving you in that dreary place. It hadn't dawned on me that you would be alone."

"Alone? What about May?"

He hesitated.

"Promise you'll be careful, darling."

"What about?"

"God knows." He laughed unconvincingly. "The fact is I've always been wary of May . . ."

"I know." I patted his cheek soothingly. "And I promise to keep away from Lott's Pool."

The whistle blew; he joined Kelda in the compartment; the train pulled out. Feeling flat and lonely, I went back through the archway and down the steps to where Willie Kimble was waiting.

"Well, she's really gone this time and no messing about," he remarked as he opened the door for me. "Funny, it had gone right out of my mind. Then when I saw her this afternoon with her bag and that fur coat it all came back to me."

He took his place at the wheel. I pushed open the glass panel and leaned forward.

"What came back to you?"

The story that reached me over his left shoulder as we drove back to Saury kept me fully attentive and moving closer and closer to the edge of my seat.

17

"I WAS CALLED up the next day, you see," Willie began. "What with the rush of getting ready and saying good-bye to all the relations I never gave it another thought. Plenty more important things happened after that to put it out of my mind. Plenty! It was another three years before I got out of uniform and back home again." A wagon just ahead of us took his attention and I thought he had put it out of his mind yet again, whatever it was; but when the road was clear he went on: "Well, it was nothing much really, but I wondered about it at the time. It seemed funny. Come to think of it, it still seems funny."

"What seemed funny?" I demanded. "I suppose you mean 'odd.' " There could be little doubt of it as Willie hadn't much sense of humor.

"This is the first time I've driven Mrs. Cade anywhere since then. Oh, I've seen her about in Saury but never thought about it. It was helping her in with her bag—and that fur coat—that must have jerked my memory. Only she was Miss Findon then and I was driving my old dad's horse and cab; old Prince. It was the only cab for miles around and came in useful for funerals and weddings and catching trains, and old Prince . . ."

"You drove my aunt somewhere?" I intervened as he showed signs of remembering his old dad's horse in too much detail.

"When she wanted to be taken to the station, Dad had bronchitis pretty bad, so I had to do the job. He threatened me with death and destruction if I got a scratch on the bodywork, so I drove as if we were going to a funeral although there was a London train to catch at Bidminster. Miss Findon never said a word the whole of the way nor got agitated about missing the train. Most people would have. As things turned out it wouldn't have mattered."

"She was going to London?"

"Supposed to be," Willie said cryptically. "There'd been talk in the village that she'd be going to London to stay for a bit—and there'd have been more talk if they'd known what happened; only as I said there was never a chance to mention it. It was a bit late when I got home and Dad gave me a rough time, wanting to know where I'd been. Well, it was mother that did the talking. He couldn't get his breath with the bronchitis. Then my calling-up papers came the next morning."

How could I ever have thought him tight-lipped and reserved. His triumph in having recollected the incident—as yet undisclosed—had gone to his head. He rambled. Only gradually did the facts emerge.

On an autumn evening in 1915 he had taken Miss Findon to Saury station for the first lap of her journey to London. The branch line passed through Bays End and Hubblewick before reaching Bidminster where she would change to the main line. She was traveling on the late train, she told him when she booked the cab, because she hadn't been able to reserve a seat in a Ladies Only compartment on any other train: most London trains were heavily overcrowded in wartime. Her luggage, Willie understood, had been sent on in advance; she carried a small valise; he had handed it to her in her compartment and seen the local train pull out, relieved at not having missed it.

What could he find funny in either sense of the word in such an incident?

"I'll tell you," he said when I had put the question. "Seeing as I had the cab it seemed a shame not to make use of it. I was courting Mona at the time on the quiet, that's my wife, and her father had the forge about a mile out of Bays End on the Saury road. Anyway I sneaked off to see her. I didn't stay long but it was pitch dark when I set off for home and raining hard."

He had the road entirely to himself until about two miles short of Saury village, where he saw in the light from his oil lamps a movement on the right-hand side of the road ahead: a shape, a woman in a fur coat just turning into Packhorse Way.

"At first I thought it was some sort of animal with the rain across the lamplight shining on the fur. Then I saw the valise. It was Miss Findon all right. She must have got out of the train at Bays End. I'd have stopped to pick her up but by then she'd disappeared into the trees and there was no sign of her when I got to the lane end."

That would be the far end of Packhorse Way. I hadn't realized that it connected Winkblade and Hoodman House with the road from Saury to Bays End, which was unfamiliar to me though I had seen it from the train.

"It seemed wrong." Willie too was thinking of Packhorse Way. "A delicate lady like Miss Findon in her neat shoes and good clothes. She shouldn't have been trudging along that mucky old lane by herself in the dark."

"It's a short cut, I suppose, to our house."

"It misses the village, I'll admit, but it'll be more than a mile from the Bays End road to Hoodman by Packhorse Way. Even in daylight you've to bend double under the trees, and on a wet night it'd be like walking in a gutter. I wonder"—he was becoming thoughtful—"why she got out of the train at Bays End."

"She must have forgotten something," I said quickly. "I expect she traveled the next day instead. There's no danger of that

187

happening this time. I saw that she had everything she needed, and Mr. Tass is traveling with her, as you know."

"Then if she'd forgotten something it's a wonder she didn't go on a couple of stations to Bidminster and get a cab to take her home from there, considering the weather. It's not worth saving the fare if you get pneumonia." Willie had reverted to his usual sardonic tone, a little offended perhaps. My brisk suggestion had robbed his story of its appealing mystery.

He would have been gratified to know how intensely it interested me: how disturbing a picture he had drawn of a delicate, and in those days elegant young lady, neatly shod, valise in hand, groping her way through the mile-long darkness of Packhorse Way—and in her long loose fur coat. Somehow the musquash coat made the incident all the more outlandish. What a state she must have been in as she clambered up the steep embankment and came out at her own front gate: hat torn by branches, hair soaked, shoes and stockings sodden and thick with mud! Grandfather would be in his room downstairs at the back of the house. It would be May who opened the door, usually kept locked after dark. Imagination conjured up a companion picture of May: immaculate, composed, faintly smiling, *and not surprised.*

I came to myself with a positive jerk, so startlingly had intuition brought me to a discovery that reason, plodding behind, might eventually have made and now endorsed as true. May had been expecting her. Kelda had never intended to go to London. For some reason it had been necessary for her only to seem to go, and to come back, quietly, without knocking, knowing that May would be waiting . . .

It was still daylight when I got home and slipped into the hall as quietly as Kelda must have done. For all its lack of charm the house had been well built and of the best materials, weather-defying stone and solid oak. Not a board creaked under the thick carpet as I went noiselessly upstairs, imagining the drag on my shoulders of a heavy wet fur coat, the wretchedness of being mud stained, disheveled, tired—and sick with the dread of what lay ahead. On the square landing without pausing at my own door I turned right like a sleepwalker, went up the second flight of stairs and pushed open the door of the front attic.

The arched window was yellow with the afterglow of sunset. Almost at once it faded, leaving the room in sudden shade. So convinced was I of what had happened here that a mingling of pity and distaste set me shivering. The orange box had been pushed back across the door of the hateful little apartment at the far end. I slid it aside and although the very thought of going into the room again turned my stomach it seemed an inescapable duty to verify for my own sake as well as Kelda's that it had been as I suspected—a sick room, a prison cell, and something worse. My impression that it might also have become a torture chamber could be a nervous reaction, an over-excited fancy, like the recurring notion of a malevolent spirit now and then released from the bonds of civilized convention to flicker balefully about the house: but other factors more subtle and even more disagreeable hovered on the fringe of thought. Those lacerating comments on Thyrza and her sluttish morals could equally have applied to Kelda. Had they been so intended? Had there been times when the secret trembled on the verge of deliberate disclosure—to the terror of the person most desperately anxious to keep it hidden?

There was scarcely light enough to see by or space enough to move between the primitive furnishings: the narrow iron bed with its stained covers, the thin flock mattress, the upright wooden chair . . . Anger mounted within me. There had been no need for this. They could have done better, made other arrangements. They had behaved insanely. The problem that beset them had been as old as history. Millions of women must have faced it, few of them in more demeaning conditions; for I felt again—sensibility tuned to its highest pitch—that there lingered in the small enclosed place not merely the stale smells of an uncleaned sick room but the taint of an implacable cruelty. So it seemed to me then as

189

half faint with disgust I squeezed past the bed to the door and escaped into the lesser gloom of the main attic.

Looking back with the cooler judgment of hindsight, I can see how inevitably the circumstances of their life had led them to that desperate seclusion: their inseparable closeness, their self-sufficiency, their precocious authority when their mother died, their dependence on each other. These factors alone would have accounted for the plot they had hatched to escape social ruin. They would face catastrophe together in total secrecy; but it would also be in total ignorance. The innocence they shared with other young women of their time and class made them incompetent to deal with the realities involved. I have sometimes wondered how Kelda survived the ministrations of her sister.

But then I have wondered many other things besides. Even then, as gasping for purer air I reached up to open the fanlight in the outer room, I was conscious of evading more dangerous aspects of the affair. When Kelda heard of Dick's engagement to May, she had wanted to die. How had May felt when she knew that Kelda was carrying his child? Wanting to die seemed a natural if misguided response to bitter disappointment, more or less normal and much less complex than the probable reaction of May on finding herself relegated to second place by the sister she had always outshone.

No one will ever know what Kelda suffered during those months of confinement but it seems likely that May's heartlessness in trying to separate me from Clem would be far outstripped by her earlier ruthlessness in dealing with any threat to separate her from Dick.

Horrible as these conclusions were, their tally was not complete. Beyond them lurked a darker shadow. A birth is a beginning, not an end. That is to say, it should not be. The agony on the iron bed must have fulfilled its purpose: there had been an outcome. Of that outcome no trace remained. To know what had happened to

190

it had become, for reasons I could not have expressed, my responsibility.

The feverish mental activity roused by these thoughts drove me from the grisly scene. Groping my way down the darkening stairs, I was confronted by the figure of May. Twilight filled the house. She stood like a blue shadow, looking up at me as if with her unique capacity for remaining still, she rested between events. Her capacity for directing their course was also unique.

What, at her worst, would she be capable of?

18

PREOCCUPIED AS I was with past events I never dreamed—well, not then—that the question might have relevance to myself. It didn't occur to me that one act already accomplished might lead to another and similar one still to come. Although by this time my reverence for Aunt May had degenerated into suspicion and fear, it was of her personality that I was afraid, its intense inwardness, its unflagging selfishness. Since day after day she appeared to do almost nothing, I was not afraid of anything she might do. The possibility that a force too long contained might eventually explode should perhaps have occurred to me.

Meanwhile there were Kelda's letters. She wrote to me twice and to May regularly every week. It couldn't have been easy for her, especially as May never replied. Her first letter to me was disappointing. It contained nothing but a few simple facts: Julius had been very pleased to see her; his health was improving; she had been made to feel at home at St. Mark's. The second in answer to mine was only slightly more expansive. She was afraid I would have too much to do. I must just leave the rooms that were never used and not attempt to clean them. She felt guilty having everything done for her. But there were several references to Julius, to the boys, and to the headmaster and his wife, who were proving companionable. In conclusion Julius wished to be remembered to the little girl with the big gray eyes. As Mrs. Torgill would have done, I found this touching.

Correspondence with Clem was more satisfactory. Writing to him took up all my evenings. Our letters were long, detailed, and repetitive. Having dumped Kelda at St. Mark's he had hurried off to Dorset to make up for the time he had lost and was anxious to make the most of this opportunity to learn as much as he could about the restoration of a sixteenth-century manor house. If only I were nearer! What about accepting the Burnetts' open invitation to visit them at Rosedown?

I folded the letter with a sigh and put the finishing touches to May's breakfast tray. Living at Hoodman House had brought home to me rather strikingly the obvious fact that there are two spheres of existence, the outward and the inner. It was the outward life that May and I shared. I still took up her breakfast tray and lit her fire because a deliberate break in our routine would need to be explained and might precipitate the moment for candor between us: the moment I dreaded, balancing the urge to get it over against my uncertainty as to what there was to be candid about.

We were together at mealtimes and occasionally in the kitchen, where May shared the lighter chores but fortunately we were more often apart. On Tuesdays and Thursdays when my secretarial duties were over, I stayed on in town and spent a good deal of time with Harriet and Mirabel. What May did during my absence didn't interest me. There was no reason to think that she did anything at all.

Or so I thought until one wet afternoon when in an attempt to shake off a mood of loneliness and depression I set about rearranging my room. Clem had given me a set of half a dozen charming colored prints of old Bidminster. To make room for them I took down my father's cases of butterflies and his photographs of the school cricket team and rowing club and put them out on the landing. My narrow little room had become a refuge;

193

I had made curtains and covered the easy chair with a length of silk damask Mrs. Tass had given me; but there was no fireplace, and now that the year was closing in, the room was too cold for comfort.

Indeed, by the time everything was straight again my hands were so cold that I was tempted to leave the clutter on the landing and go down to the warm kitchen, but as it would take only a few minutes to clear up the mess and the light was already fading, I tucked three of the frames under one arm, picked up a silver-crested shield and a German beer mug, and took them up to the attic. I found it changed.

Cold and tired as I was, it took me a little while to realize that the change was a momentous one. The drama of my aunts' secret life had been brought up-to-date by the addition of an unexpected act. The inner door now stood open, frankly inviting an inspection of the room within. The bed had been stripped; the soiled covers had vanished; the toilet ware had been washed and polished; the air was still depressingly stale but the unpleasant smell had gone.

Gone too was my only evidence, slight as it had been, that there had ever been anything amiss there. It was now just a poky little room that might conceivably have been slept in by a disgruntled servant or a child when every other bed in the house was occupied: a perfectly innocent room. I was left with no basis for my suspicions beyond hearsay: a secondhand account of a dead man's hallucination that there was somebody upstairs; a taxi driver's glimpse of a lady vanishing in the dark. My theory disintegrated like a puffball.

A cup of tea revived me. The second brought enlightenment. Evidence and truth—I sat up, electrified—are not identical. More-over, destroying evidence is a sign of guilt; and for Aunt May who never soiled her hands to have spring-cleaned the awkward little room up two flights of stairs was not only a remarkable achievement in itself but also a clear signal of her urgent need to rectify a six-year-long neglect. There could be no more striking proof that I had been right. Was it also proof that she was aware of my suspicions?

She was changing. One evening at sunset I found her still in the drawing room and by the fire. She had deserted her post in the window and had not gone to the field gate at the sacred time. The habit had been broken; she never resumed the old regularity, and gradually the ritual ceased altogether. In my present mood I could have sworn that the faithful vigils had less to do with Dick than with Kelda: that their purpose had been to serve as reminders not so much that Dick was lost as that he had been hers—May's—to lose. They had become meaningless mechanical acts arising from a sterile imagination. She had waited under the cherry tree not because she hoped for Dick's return but because she had nothing better to do.

One by one her pillars of support were failing her: her painting; her memorial pilgrimages; most of all Kelda. I believe she missed her with a deep instinctive sense of deprivation. If, loving or hating, they had been as necessary to each other as the two hands of a clock, the clock had ceased to show the time.

One morning when I went into her room she was still lying under the covers and didn't move, although usually I found her sitting up to welcome me—and the breakfast tray—with a patient smile.

"May, are you awake?"

A feeble sigh from under the counterpane was her only response.

"You're not ill?"

With apparent effort she struggled into a sitting position.

"Oh no, I mustn't be ill and make more work for you. I'm just desperately tired and my whole body aches."

I lit her fire and brought a hot-water bottle. She stayed in bed all day, and the next—inanimate, staring at the window or the ceiling. On the third day with my help she dragged herself out of bed and into her easy chair.

"I'm being a dreadful nuisance." She leaned back her lovely head against the deep blue velvet and smiled. Mrs. Torgill's Susan would have found the smile angelic and the withholding of those heavenly wings a deplorable oversight. "But we mustn't worry Kelda. She would come home at once if she knew I was ill."

"We certainly mustn't worry Kelda. She has her husband to look after. I'll look after you."

Not surprisingly she recovered, sufficiently at least to come downstairs. Her protracted convalescence was spent by the drawing room fire. Swathed in lacy shawls of blue and white she made so ravishing an invalid that it seemed a pity no one but me could see her. The spectacle was worthy of a more appreciative audience.

Her physical beauty must always have been and was still invincible. Had there been the least hint of coarseness or meanness in it or any small irregularity in cheek or nose or lip; had her skin been sometimes tinged with sallowness or her hair with lankness like other people's, her power over those others would have been less, her relations with them happier as she touched common ground. But in its flawless delicacy it was unassailable. I say "it" because the effect was impersonal, the appearance distinct from its possessor. The face expressed nothing of the self within: in fact (I glanced at it from time to time, as a curator might glance at a piece of sculpture in his care) its range of expression was limited to a sweetness I was beginning to detest.

And yet there were times when, alone with her, I felt the magic work upon me again. Looking at her, one simply couldn't believe that she had ever thought an evil thought, much less performed an evil action. Kelda's misery faded from my mind. I had to remind myself that May had lied about the photograph; that she was an idle parasite battening on other people; on me; that she had ordered a little boy into Lott's Pool not caring if he drowned. These were the known evils.

Our conversation was achingly uninteresting. There was

nothing to talk about, much to avoid mentioning. It was a welcome change when one evening, as if making a kind effort to come down to my level and divert me a little, May introduced the topic of my own future.

"How well things have turned out for you! 'And so they lived happily ever after,' " she whimsically observed. "Just the fairy-tale ending we have always wanted for you. Isn't that what every woman hopes for? And what so many of us never have? The longed-for happiness a lifetime of waiting may never bring."

Since no reply could do justice to the layers of falsity implicit in such a speech, I made none.

"Comfort, security, family . . . You must seize your good fortune, dear. Think of it as a divine gift. I've been wanting to tell you, to beg you not to let our plight cloud your happiness in any way. We are used to being poor—and lonely. We shall simply take up the burden again." Her smile was brave. "Those early morning fires have helped me to face many a thankless day—but I shall soon get used to my empty grate. You must never think of us as in need of help. Life is an unequal struggle, Elinor. Some are favored, others must suffer. That's the bitter truth of it and nothing can be done about it."

Was the bitter truth faintly tinctured with the hope that something might after all be done about it?

"Still, I suppose you'll be waiting until Clem is in a position to support a wife."

I murmured something to the effect that there would be no need to wait. Her sigh could have been one of regret at the prospect of parting with me; but her next remark suggested regret of a different kind.

"But you won't think of marrying until Kelda is free to come home. Otherwise I should be quite alone. No, don't think I mind that. Sometimes I feel that this weary life will soon be over and I shall have slipped away to a happier world."

I hinted that a less fundamental change might be considered.

"The house is far too big for us. Don't you think it would be a good idea to sell it so that you can move into a smaller place? In Bidminster perhaps. Because," I added nervously, "Kelda may not come back."

Incredible as it seemed, the possibility had not occurred to her. She had been watching the firelight deepen the red glow of the ruby on her finger. I felt the shock that cleft her whole being and sharpened her voice.

"What are you saying? Of course she'll come back. This is her home."

"But her husband?"

"Kelda sacrificed all right to marriage long ago."

It was the most revealing statement I had ever heard her make: she added not a word. I asked no question; it was as if it were understood between us that I had no need to ask nor she to explain. In its finality the dire pronouncement doomed Kelda all over again to a lifetime of servitude. Its ruthlessness filled me with foreboding. I remember my conviction that we had come without warning to a turning point. The room vibrated with impending crisis.

The worst misfortune to befall me at Hoodman House—the worst so far—was that I had been infected by May's cast of mind. Clem had warned me that it might happen. Now, it was as if her thoughts, tortuous and tainted with self-interest, became mine. I knew them as if they were my own. She could not live alone. So long as *I* was there, Kelda might be permitted to stay with her husband. When I married, May would be isolated, uncared for, and penniless, a prospect she would find means of avoiding. Kelda would be brought back. But my departure would condemn them both to the poverty-stricken existence I had rescued them from: my only relations; my sole heirs if I should die before they did.

She had got up and stood with one hand resting on the marble mantelshelf. Had she changed before my eyes or was the change in me? As her eyes traveled slowly round the firelit room, reached the low stool and came to rest steadily on me, it was as if for the first time the silken softness had fallen away. She saw me not as a nonentity to be soothed or charmed or manipulated but as an object to be dealt with.

In the abnormal isolation and restraint of our companionship my responses had become overactive as from hothouse growth: except that beyond the small circle of firelight the house was, as always, cold. I was all at once overwhelmed by a longing for India: for its far distant heat and light, its color and clamor, the lost security of childhood.

If anything happened to me—the vague phrase was all I could bring myself to use—before I was married, how fortunate that would be for my aunts, particularly for May! Supported by her half share of all I possessed, how gracefully she would mourn! The interval before my marriage, which had promised to be merely long drawn out, now threatened to be dangerous.

I must make a will leaving everything to Clem. As if galvanized into instant action, I too got to my feet and escaped, though only to the kitchen. Silent and thoughtful, she watched me go.

The nursery supper of warm milk and bread and butter which was all we bothered with was soon prepared. I set it on two trays and took May's to the drawing room, mine to my room, so that we had no further talk that evening. Snug under my eiderdown with two plump pillows at my back, I sipped and munched, glad to be alone, if only to worry about my will. I would go to Bidminster the very next morning—and ask Mr. Tass's advice. Or better still, Harriet's.

How odd it would seem, a healthy young woman preoccupied with thoughts of death so soon before her wedding! I pictured Harriet's raised eyebrows, her clear eyes, as she shrewdly assessed my motives. "In case of an accident," I would say . . .

But if the will was intended to protect me from my aunts, they must also be told about it: May at any rate. "By the way," I would announce casually, "I've made a will leaving everything to

Clem." The prospect of making such an announcement with the unspoken corollary, "and so my death would be of no advantage to you," over the breakfast table or at any other time brought me to my senses. Did I seriously believe that my life was in danger? What utter nonsense! I slid the tray from my lap to the bedside table, got up, undressed, washed, and remade my rumpled bed, placing one pillow against the brass head rail, the other for my head.

As might have been expected, my dreams were unpleasant though too confused to recollect, except for the impression of darkness that engulfed my dreaming self in towering black wave after wave: a sensation of sinking, a dread of suffocation so intense that I struggled desperately to call out and woke, sweating with terror, to find May bending over me, the spare pillow in her hands a few inches from my face.

"You've had a nightmare," she said.

The distress of my dream faded into the bewilderment of seeing her there—and seeing nothing else but her face close to mine and the blank pallor of the pillow as she bent over me, obliterating the rest of the world. She had never been in my room before, so far as I knew.

"I couldn't breathe." I raised myself on my elbow. "It was like drowning."

"It didn't stop you from calling out—in the most bloodcurdling way." She stepped back and stood upright, a tall white column in her long-sleeved nightdress. "You really frightened me." Her smile, affectionate and teasing, faded. She became serious. "This pillow had fallen on your head, half over your face. You were struggling to get free of it. You mustn't ever leave it there again. If you don't need it, put it here"—she laid it at the foot of the bed—"or on a chair. You might have suffocated."

"I woke you. I'm sorry."

"I was lying awake. It was one of my bad times. I scarcely closed my eyes all night."

Beyond her the room took shape, its corners still deeply shadowed. Furniture loomed. The window was gray with the first reluctant light of a winter morning and streaked with rain.

"I'm worried about you." She laid a cool hand on my brow. "You're growing nervous. This is no time for you to have a breakdown, is it? I must take more care of you."

She glided noiselessly away. I watched her naked feet, first on the carpet, then on the floorboards by the door. She must have leapt from her bed without bothering with a wrap or slippers when she heard me shout—or scream. It must have been pretty loud to penetrate the thick wall and two closed doors. Her speed had been uncharacteristic. She had been kind too, unusually so, and sensible. Her warning had been effective: I actually saw myself in danger of a breakdown. It would account for all that morbid worrying over wills and the grisly possibility of an early death even before this morning's striking illustration of how easily one's life might be snuffed out by a homely goose-feather pillow.

But not the life of a healthy young woman. The pillow would have to be held down and pressed hard—for how long? Until breathing ceased. It would be different—a tremor ran through my body and roused me to complete wakefulness—in the case of a baby. Babies suffocated so easily.

How tall May had seemed, how overpowering in spite of her slimness as she had leaned over me, blotting out the room! How lucky—and surprising—that she had heard me despite the house's capacity for deadening all sounds!

It rained heavily all day. The rush and gurgle of water in our sturdy gutters and drainpipes seemed an intervention by nature to stop me from going to Bidminster. After the rain the weather turned mild for a few days, the sky low and overcast, the air enervating. The importance of making a will became less urgent: next week would be soon enough. I couldn't be bothered with housework or sewing for my trousseau but lounged about, yawning and fidgeting. Could this really be the onset of a breakdown?

To my surprise May kept her word. Taking more care of me involved being with me every hour of the day. Wherever I went, in desperate need of the solitude I had once found so dispiriting, she contrived to be there or to follow me. I would look up and find her eyeing me, anxiously. Her concern even led her to leave the house and join me in my walks.

"You must have fresh air. I'll come with you."

It was a novel experience to walk at her side, a figure of dateless elegance in her long mauve coat with a deep capelike collar of moleskin and a matching velvet hat. Normally we avoided the muddy field paths and kept to the lanes where she walked with energy and a surprisingly swinging stride. I was less grateful for her company than I might have been, her evident concern for me being a constant reminder that I must need it; and I took every opportunity of nipping out of the house on my own.

But evasive action didn't always work. One afternoon I left by the back gate, skirted the west wall and picked my way down the muddy slope into the obscurity of Packhorse Way, at this time of year a dank tunnel smelling of fungus and dead leaves. Looking up to the gray sky between the boughs of trees on its high bank was like looking up from a grave. It would be misty later on. I passed Winkblade on my right, crouched in its drab garden, its chimneys half shrouded in haze.

The fields lying open to the left were more tempting. I crossed the wet grass and stood between the willows on the edge of Lott's Pool. Its still waters, smooth and dark except where fallen leaves floated under naked branches, gave no outward sign of the hidden spring beneath. A more melancholy spot it would have been hard to find, but at least I was alone and free and out of sight of Hoodman House.

So that I was startled out of my skin by the feel of a presence right behind me and the grip of hands on my arm.

"You mustn't," she said, a deeper note than usual in her voice, "I know what you were going to do but you *must not do it.*"

She had come upon me without a sound, had materialized from the dead scene like an unwelcome guardian angel. I turned. She released me.

"You have everything to live for, darling. Think of Clem. Think of us."

I recovered myself.

"Whatever do you mean? I wasn't going to do anything. You surely didn't think I was going to throw myself in. Why on earth should I?"

"Why indeed?" Her smile was soothing. She linked her arm in mine. "Let's go home. Your feet must be wet. Mine certainly are."

Like an invalid or a lunatic I suffered myself to be led from the brink of a watery grave. Such was my mental comment afterward. At the time other thoughts absorbed me, chiefly the discovery that May, subtle manipulator that she was, had for once gone too far. She was losing her finesse. In the past she had found me so pliable that she was bound to underestimate my common sense; but I too could be subtle (I told myself) and quite astute enough to see the purpose behind her new-found concern for me.

"Poor little Elinor," she would sigh when my body was found. "I'm afraid this was not the first attempt. She had got into a low state of mind . . . ."

We walked quietly home but she kept my arm firmly linked in hers. We must have seemed—had there been anyone there to see us—two affectionate relations taking a winter walk for the sake of their health. As it happened there was someone out of doors besides ourselves. When we got to the wicket gate, instead of risking the dirt of Packhorse Way, May guided me up the steps to Winkblade and through the garden. And there in the farmyard at the back we met Arthur. He had evidently been exploring and popped his head round the bakehouse door.

203

"I heard you coming." He greeted me with the happy confidence of an old friend.

"What are you doing here?" I detached myself from May's custody and joined him. To my alarm I saw that he had managed to unbar the great oven door and swing it open.

"It's nice in here." He had become the host, showing me round. "This is where the old gentleman sometimes sleeps. He makes a fire to keep himself warm at night. He told me. I talked to him, you see," he told me in his most social manner. "The fire is good for his cough; but he only comes sometimes. I wish he would come again."

I slammed the door shut and replaced the bar.

"It's all right for you to play here but you must promise me never to get into the oven, not even for fun."

"But I could easily get out again. I'll show you."

I lifted him bodily and bundled him outside into the yard, explaining that it was true, there was no danger unless someone else barred the door from the outside, some other thoughtless child perhaps . . .

"And they might go away and leave you there."

May was waiting by the yard gate. She had withdrawn into her habitual stillness. Mauve, I thought, was not the color for her. The brim of her hat cast a slightly lurid shadow on the upper part of her face, leaving the closed lips and pale curve of her jaw open to the unfriendly daylight. She was looking—different. I groped for a more precise word. Ghastly? A sudden meeting with Dick's son, Dick's counterpart, must have been a shock. Had her thoughts turned not only to Dick but to Dick's other lost child?

"When a thing's dead it's nothing else but dead." It was here that she had made the eerie remark, as if even then she had some special knowledge of death. Impossible then; but the scope of her knowledge could well have increased in the intervening years. She seemed, under the lowering sky, portentous: an embodiment of the interwoven complexities of a past I had once thought of as idyllic.

204

I wondered if its glamour had already begun to fade, the seeds of darkness already sown, when Dick conjured up the mysterious squirrel and gave it to Kelda.

May's pronouncement about death had awed Clem on that occasion. She had no need even to speak to upset another small boy. Daunted by some quality of strangeness in the lady barring the gateway, Arthur suddenly lost his nerve.

"I'm going home." I caught the hint of a sob manfully suppressed. He hesitated, then lowered his head, butted his way past the purple coat and ran helter-skelter across the fields towards the Tile Sheds, ignoring the path.

"That isn't like him," I said. "He's such a well-behaved boy."

Divested of her outdoor things and particularly the purple-shadowing hat, May became her familiar languid self. But the damage had been done. Such peace of mind as I had kept was gone. There were times when I actually believed that she willed my death and would contrive it in such a way as to make it seem like suicide. I saw myself suffocated, drowned, shut away in a small space and inadvertently locked in. I wondered what had happened to the bottle of Dr. Haggie's medicine and remembered with relief that it had been empty. At other times such ideas seemed fantastic beyond belief: worse still, a sign that my nerves if not my mind were playing me false.

It was unfortunate that a feverish cold kept me indoors for a few days including the Tuesday when I would normally have gone to Bidminster. Had I gone, even if I had never reached the point of seeing a solicitor or consulting Harriet, the brief escape would have restored a sense of normality.

As it was, confined to the house and May's unrelieved company, burning and shivering, I scarcely knew myself. The over-riding memory of those miserable days is of my preoccupation with death, chiefly my own, but also the deaths of my parents in India and Surrey, of Dick and countless others on the Somme; and nearer at hand, of those shadowy forebears who had died here at

Hoodman House leaving an impalpable legacy of worn-out lives to deepen its brooding atmosphere. Especially and most distressingly at the foot of the attic stairs, which I could not bring myself to climb again, there seemed a positive taint in the air: due no doubt to unopened windows but at the time suggestive of a less rational explanation.

My cold took its course; my head cleared. A firm decision to pull myself together coincided with the arrival of a letter from Kelda and addressed to me. I read it at the breakfast table.

". . . has told me that you haven't been well . . . am writing at once to urge you not to give way to depression. I know only too well how easy it is and how dangerous to neglect one's health and get into a low state. I reproach myself for having let you work too hard and looking back, I realize that you needed more nourishing food. Remember when you feel low-spirited that the cause is physical. You have nothing to be unhappy about, everything to live for . . ."

"What has Kelda to say?"

"Oh, it's all about my health. She seems to think I'm run down. I'll write straight away and tell her that I'm perfectly well and that there's nothing wrong with my nerves."

The letter had confirmed my suspicions, but it was also the outcome of another lapse on May's part. She had wanted Kelda—and Julius—and later on the world at large to know that I might be tempted to put an end to myself. She had not foreseen that Kelda might write to me as she did, or if she had instructed her not to, had counted too confidently on Kelda's obedience.

My reply to Kelda left her in no doubt as to my state of health. I had never been fitter, stronger, more energetic, cheerful, and in love with life and with Clem; never more happily absorbed in embroidering pillow slips and guest towels for my bottom drawer.

I made a point of reading extracts from my letter to May before walking to the village where I posted it, held cheerful conversations with Mrs. Torgill, Susan, Mrs. Green and Mr. Car-shott, the butcher, and on my return home reported them in detail.

"They all said how well I looked."

There was a falseness in all this that plunged me again and deservedly into gloom. My voice, I thought, stitching industri-ously at lover's knots and fleur-de-lys, was like the mindless clack-ing of a rattle used to scare away birds, in an empty field, moreover, where no bird capable of flying elsewhere would dream of coming. By evening the need to bring the situation to an end had become unbearable.

May followed me to the kitchen when I went to prepare the supper.

"Let me cut the bread."

She used the knife efficiently, producing slices of immaculate thinness. Once before I had noticed the skill of her hands and had been struck by the contrast between her elegance and the homely meal she was preparing . . . The milk boiled over. My hand shook as I poured it into the blue striped kitchen cups. I had remembered the one person who didn't share the general admiration of May: one who wouldn't accept her charity, who left food untouched because she had touched it.

When we had gone to our rooms I sat by my uncurtained window to brush my hair. The night was starless, the shape of trees just visible against the dark sky, their leafless branches out-stretched above the deep gully of Packhorse Way. Year after year the old man had plodded up the sunken lane to emerge suddenly at my grandfather's gate on one of his calls before going on to rest at Winkblade. He had known the family—known my aunts for most of their lives and had seen them grow up. Whatever personal tragedy or fatal mistake had cast him upon the world, he was a man of honor. He had spoken of conscience, of principle, of avoiding evil, not glibly but with the blaze of sincerity in his eyes. He was not too proud to take food from Kelda or from me, only from May.

It would need more than personal dislike to make a hungry man refuse food: a deeper revulsion.

I stared out into the darkness of sky and trees and wondered where he was. The weather had been warm when he last called; it was winter now. He had been tired and ill. Very likely he too was dead, I thought drearily, and all that he had seen and thought and known had died with him.

19

THE STREET WAS unfamiliar, and in the gloom of a damp November afternoon there seemed little prospect of getting to know it: little prospect of any kind. The pall of soot and smoke from Bidminster's forest of chimneys was thickening into fog: a fog permeated by the reek of malt from the town brewery. Buildings were blurred in outline, sounds muffled, distances deceptive. The way ahead melted into shade from which shawled women with baskets emerged like spectral shapes and vanished into shop doorways.

Having climbed steeply for a few minutes I turned to look back. Below, a lamp lighter had started his round. One by one the roadside lamps turned yellow in the gathering dusk. There was light too from an occasional window but not enough to define the shabby shops and houses in between. Against one boarded-up shop front half a dozen men in caps and collarless shirts stood in a dispirited row with the enforced patience of the unemployed.

I went on up the hill. Where the wet pavement widened outside the Cross Keys public house a circle of boys squatted over a game of marbles. From somewhere behind me came the despairing warble of a woman singing for coppers.

"Maxwelltown braes are bonnie, Where early falls the de-ew . . ."

Dragging one leaden foot after the other, she appeared in the rectangle of light from a window of the Cross Keys, her ashen cheeks sunken under a once respectable hat of black grosgrain.

She broke off to thank me for the threepence I gave her and I took the opportunity of asking her to direct me.

"Up there, love, right at the top. God bless you, love. 'And 'twas there that Annie Laurie gi'd me her promise true.' "

Her voice, gallant and hopeless, died away as I climbed out of earshot.

The workhouse was an early Victorian building towering on the crest of the hill like a rock face, its rows of windows dimly lit.

Inside, the long corridor smelt of soap and carbolic and cooked turnips. There was no one about, but presently a porter appeared wheeling a trolley stacked with loaves. He was a lean, soft-footed man with russet-colored hair like a fox's pelt. He stopped when I asked him to direct me to the master's office and looked me over before answering, as if I might have designs on the place; or as if he might have designs on me. His lips were thin and his eyes pale as amber.

But he spoke civilly and his appearance was of no consequence except to increase my regret that Sintram should spend his days in such a place and to be dependent on people with whom he could have little in common. But I soon found that my judgment had been too hasty and my first rather unfavorable impression misleading. Mr. Tadworth, the master, was a man in his fifties with a gray moustache and a lined, thoughtful face. He seemed quite willing to be interrupted, and when I told him who I was assured me that the name Findon was well known in the town.

"Sintram? Oh yes, he's one of our regulars. He's been coming here for years since long before my time. Not the sort you'd be likely to forget either. One of life's tragedies is Sintram, meant for

210

better things. We see them here from time to time, the men who've gone to waste."

I explained that my grandfather had taken an interest in him.

"It's a few months since we saw him, and at that time he was very unwell. I wondered . . . Is he here?" And when Mr. Tadworth shook his head—"Do you know where he might be?"

He pinched his lips together, as if uncertain how to answer.

"I'll tell you what, Miss Findon, if you'd come here asking for him last week, you'd have found him in the hospital ward."

"Do you mean—he died?"

"It's a miracle if he isn't dead but I'm bound to say I don't know. The fact is he discharged himself when Matron's back was turned, got himself into his clothes and just vamoosed, nobody knows where. There was no need for it. He could have ended his days here clean and comfortable among friends. Everybody knew old Sintram. For a man in his way of life he was highly respected."

"Could he have gone to another institution?" I put the question with some hesitation, fearing that Mr. Tadworth's pride in his own establishment might be ruffled by it.

"He'd never make Anstey or Collenford, not with that chest. He could barely shuffle, never mind walk. But the old chap was a lone wolf and would always go his own way. He hated regulations. You could say he lived in a world of his own and carried it about with him. I'm a practical man, Miss Findon: you have to be in this job; but I'm a religious man too, and there've been times when for me—I'm only speaking for myself—Sintram would suddenly raise a curtain and give me a hint of something beyond it in a way that no person has ever done. Not for me, anyway."

"I know what you mean." I found his use of the past tense depressing. "Then you don't think . . . ?"

But the master had descended to more mundane issues.

"He would never turn up at Christmas and we always put on a good dinner second to none. Roast beef, plum pudding, nuts . . . But the pleasures of the table wouldn't mean much to Sintram."

He hesitated, then added in a lowered voice: "This is in confidence, Miss Findon. I've stretched the rules a bit but I feel as you do, that he's a special case. Just before you came I spoke to one of the staff. I'm sending him out to scout round and make a few inquiries. He may be able to pick up some trace of the old fellow"—and as I got up to go—"it's good of you to ask about him. There aren't many that would have bothered."

Anxious though I was for Sintram's well-being I felt guilty, knowing that I sought him for a purpose of my own in the frail hope that he could add if not the last vital chapter to the history of my aunts, then at least a significant paragraph or two. For the umpteenth time as I exchanged the soap and turnips for the heady vapors from the brewery I asked myself what it was that I wanted to know and why it mattered. But it did matter. My shoulders ached, my feet were cold, but for all the discomfort and disappointment I was possessed only by the need to know the truth. If a wrong had been done, I must find it out. Jealously suppressed, it had festered for years. To know was not to judge or blame but rather to lance an infected place and release the poison if only for Kelda's sake.

Sintram alone could have helped. I knew that those visionary eyes of his had penetrated May's dazzling shell and seen to the very heart within—if there was a heart; and now it was too late to ask him what he knew: he had dragged his worn-out body away to die in some ditch like a sick animal, his wisdom lost forever. No one in the village had seen him lately. My inquiries had worried Arthur, who had taken to watching out for him on the Upper Saury road. Annie had known him from his visits to Hoodman House but had not laid eyes on him since she left. The workhouse had been my last hope.

"Were you looking for a job, love?" A voice addressed me from the dusk. "At the workhouse?"

I recognized the street singer. She was leaning against the green doorpost of the Cross Keys, presumably waiting for the opening hour. Ought I—or ought I not—to have encouraged her weakness by giving her the threepenny bit? An answer in moral terms eluded me. There was no doubt that she needed what comfort she could find, and alternatives to the kind of comfort offered by the Cross Keys were not readily available.

"No, I was looking for someone, a tramp as a matter of fact, but he's gone away."

"You see them comin' and goin'." The woman's desperate plight had not entirely quenched a feminine interest in my clothes, my face, my errand. She was almost toothless and looked half starved but she was still young, about May's age. It wasn't fair. The spurt of indignation I felt was not on May's behalf. "All sorts you see. Some good, some bad."

"This is an old man with a dreadful cough, a gentleman once . . ."

"With a swanky way of talking as if he was somebody?"

"You know him? Sintram?"

"That's him. He's gone to his place in the country," she said, unaware of any irony in the stylish phrase.

"He told you?"

"That's what he said, the very words. He had to hold on to door handles to get down that hill but he wasn't drunk. I never saw him touch a drop. No, not yesterday. The day before it would likely be. Ee, God bless you."

Throwing morality to the winds, I had given her a shilling. Her blessing this time was heartfelt. I reciprocated it fully and hurried off to catch the five o'clock Valley Queen, the last of the day.

It was already leaving as I panted up the steep street. I must have exclaimed aloud in despair.

"Come on, miss. We can make it."

The husky voice, a man's, came from a few paces behind me. He broke into a run, overtook me, and leapt onto the bus. The driver stopped. I scrambled aboard and dropped into the front seat, hoping that Sintram's place in the country was the one I had in mind.

There was no trace of fog at Saury: the night sky was clear and pricked with stars. Even so it was too dark for Packhorse Way, though that would have been the quickest way. Instead I took the cart road and hurried past our own gate and on to Winkblade. Across the farmyard I made out the bakehouse door limned with candlelight from within, picked my way through rubble and bits of rotting timber thrown out by the builder, and knocked.

"Mr. Sintram? Are you there? It's only me, Elinor Findon."

From the opposite wall came a wave of warm air. In the great chimney breast the iron door stood wide open and a fire of faggots burned in the oven. He was sitting swathed in ragged blankets with his back against the wall to the right of the chimney and as near to it as he could get. He had taken off his boots and wrapped his feet in sheets of newspaper. On the floor beside him a candle burned in a chipped enamel saucer. The effect was unexpectedly cozy, his manner that of a gentleman at peace in his own sanctum.

"I heard that you had come to your place in the country."

"You'll excuse my not rising." On his own ground his courtesy was more assured, even lordly, but he spoke slowly, as though husbanding his breath. "It has taken some time to dispose my"—he indicated the tattered blankets—"draperies. Any movement may involve me in a major reconstruction."

"I'm so glad and relieved"—I found myself standing beside a small tin trunk and sat down on it—"that you have something to keep you warm. Do you keep some of your belongings here?"

"You are sitting on my wardrobe, linen room, and kitchen cupboard. No, don't get up. I have no other seat to offer you."

The bakehouse had been empty on the other two occasions when I had looked into it. He must have dragged the trunk from its hiding place in some other outhouse. The effort entailed, added to that of making his way here from Bidminster, must have taken all his strength. I never doubted that the effort had been worth while.

"I can see why you wanted to come."

His neck was thin and wrinkled as a fowl's, his face fleshless with pools of purple shadow under the cheekbones and in the eye sockets; his nose had become a pale prominence of bone out of harmony with the other features. Every word he spoke was deliberate as he planned the most economical use of his worn-out lungs. But against the rough wall his face, goatlike and gentle, was serene. I saw in it—or fancied I saw—a faint radiance, not from the candle or the firelight but from an inward source of light.

"You're happy," I said, marveling.

"Happy to have laid down my burden for the last time and come to the end of the road." His eyes were larger and clearer even than I had remembered them. The change was such as I had seen more than once at Rosedown Hall and I knew he was near his end. Apart from the sadness of his going, the prospect of his dying here in the tumbledown bakehouse did not distress me. It was where he wanted to be. The freedom of choice he valued so highly had been exercised for the last time.

"You were looking for me?"

"Yes. I wanted to talk to you but now that I've found you— like this—I won't intrude on you. But there are one or two things I can bring to make you more comfortable and I hope—for my grandfather's sake—you won't refuse." The reference to my grandfather was a sudden inspiration. "I never had a chance to do anything for him so you must let me help you a little instead."

But not too much. My yearning to turn the bakehouse into a model sickroom must be sternly repressed. He wouldn't stand for that or for being moved to one of the empty rooms in Hoodman House. I ached to clean up the place, not to mention the patient, but for the time being I could deal only with the essentials: fetch pillows and bedding, a spirit kettle, basin and bucket, soap, towels, a lamp, and resolve privately to fetch a doctor.

It took several trips, and by the time I had got him onto a mattress, propped him up with pillows, and replaced the filthy tattered blankets with whole clean ones, it was very late in the evening. Aunt May, reclining in her chair in a web of lacy shawls, had received the news and watched my comings and goings with mild surprise and the remark: "You always wanted to be a nurse and now you have two invalids on your hands. One of my headaches, I'm afraid. You won't mind if I go to bed early?"

I made myself a bowl of bread and milk and took some to my patient. He swallowed a spoonful or two but the exertion brought on such a paroxysm of coughing that we had to give up. When it was over I made him as comfortable as possible, found wood and replenished the fire, then hesitated as to whether to go at once for the doctor, or to stay.

He had fallen into a doze but as I stood, uncertain what to do, his eyes opened.

"You have done all this by yourself?" With difficulty he fetched another breath. "Miss Kelda?"

"She's gone away—to her husband in Surrey."

Feeble though he was, his understanding was clear and complete. His eyes were lit with instant perception. He nodded with what seemed approval.

"So, she's put things right."

"You knew that he was still alive?"

"That she had left him? Yes." His eyelids closed. It was a little while before they opened again and then to my dismay a tremor of concern caused him to catch his breath. I prepared for another outbreak of coughing and wondered if he would survive it, blaming myself for having disturbed his serenity. But he found his breath to say, "Then you're alone there—with the other one? The quiet one?"

"Aunt May? Yes."

He motioned me to come nearer. I knelt beside him.

216

"You mustn't talk. I wanted to ask you why you wouldn't take food from her but this isn't the time."

It was too late: his last ounce of strength must not be squandered on telling whatever it was that now moved him, much as I wanted to know. But it was obvious that his wish to tell was as strong as my wish to know: stronger, because he felt his time was growing short.

"You ought to know," he said. "I've never told, for my friend Findon's sake. He never knew." His eyes explored the candle-lit wall in front of him where my kneeling shadow waited like a silent witness. "It was here . . ."

The shadow moved as I bent my head nearer to his, and there in the very place where it had happened he told me what she had done. It took a little time and it was in every sense the midnight hour when he had finished. He shuddered, lay back, and closed his eyes.

I wiped the dew from his forehead. Much as I hated to leave him, there was no time to be lost in fetching the doctor: no time to brood on the fearful tale he had told.

Outside it was bitterly cold. I paused to button the high collar of my coat before picking my way across the littered yard—then started violently. In the darkness a figure had moved. A man was standing so close that my arm touched his coat. I smelt his breath, his skin.

"It's all right, miss." The husky voice spoke in my ear. "I'm from Bidminster Workhouse."

"Oh, you frightened me."

"Mr. Tadworth sent me out. I'm looking for one of our inmates that could be needing a bit of help."

"He's here. I'm afraid he's very ill."

In the glow of candle and firelight I recognized the russet-haired porter.

"Tench. Albert Tench. I saw you this afternoon, miss." He

217

bent his lean back over the mattress. "Now then, old lad. It's Albert come to see you."

Sintram opened his eyes and seemed to recognize him.

"If help's to be got, it'd better be quick." Tench's long narrow shadow leapt up the wall as he faced me. "It'll be best if I stay with him, seeing how things are, and you know the way better than what I do. It was a bit of luck catching that bus . . ."

We exchanged a few urgent sentences. He had left the workhouse before me and had inquired here and there in the immediate district until he met the street singer.

"She said a young lady, smartly dressed, had just asked her the same question. I soon caught you up. There weren't so many smart young ladies in Brewer's Lane."

Thanks to him we had ridden out on the same bus but somewhere between Saury and Winkblade he had lost me in the dark. I was wondering how that could have happened and how he had found me again and why he hadn't made himself known earlier when he said, "I didn't like to speak to you, miss. A strange man might not be welcome to a young lady on a dark road."

The unofficial nature of his visit may have colored my impression of the man. I thought him smooth and ingratiating and would have preferred a more straightforward companion: moreover he smelt of drink. But the night was cold, he was working overtime, and it wasn't his fault that he reminded me of a fox. He seemed intelligent and competent.

"I'm glad you're here. He'll feel safer with someone he knows."

I ran most of the way to Saury. Even so when we came back it was too late. I could only offer up a silent prayer of thankfulness that the old gentleman had not died alone.

20

THERE WAS NO sun, no ripple on Lott's Pool. Bare willow boughs stretched motionless over its gray surface. At the far side fallen beech leaves had carpeted the water so thickly that one could have mistaken it for solid ground and walked right in. A person—a small boy—could have waded in, stumbled, and been drowned. How could she send him into those treacherous depths to fish for a bracelet?

I was making too much of it. The depth couldn't be so very great and only seemed treacherous because in my present mood I saw treachery everywhere. In any case it was pointless to dwell on that minor act of cruelty when, as I now knew, it paled in comparison with a later one infinitely worse. But my mind slipped from the more evil act as, with the same instinct to escape, I had slipped out of the house: to gain time; to think. The confrontation was at hand, the hour had come; and here I was wasting time on this quite unnecessary ramble because I was too weak-minded to face up to what I must do.

A rustle, a movement behind me, an audible breath. Thyrza had crossed the grass to join me. She was walking home after taking Arthur to morning school. Together we stood at the water's edge. She too was in a thoughtful mood. Early as it was the news

219

of Sintram's death had spread through the village. She had been saddened by it and Arthur had cried bitterly for his friend.

"They'll have taken him back to Bidminster, I suppose," she said, "after all the trouble he took to get away from it."

"He won't mind now," I said.

"It makes you wonder what it's all for, life. And what happens to us after? They say we have to answer for our sins."

Her hair needed sunlight to burnish its rich sheen. Under the colorless sky it looked merely garish and gave a yellowish tint to her skin.

"Getting old," she said. "We all have to come to it, if we live."

"You must keep Arthur away from this pool," I said suddenly. "Clem nearly drowned in it when he was a boy."

"And you know why, I expect. Don't worry. Nobody's going to treat Arthur like a galley slave, not if I've got anything to do with it."

"You knew about it—the bracelet?"

"Yes, I knew."

"I've never thought to ask Clem what happened after he waded in." The sacrificial wading had impressed me to the exclusion of other aspects of the affair.

"Her ladyship"—Thyrza bared her big teeth though not in a smile—"stood on the bank over there like a statue just pointing and keeping her eyes fixed on the spot where it had fallen in, claiming she couldn't move or she'd forget where it was."

"And is it still there? Clem didn't find it, did he?"

"Oh, she got it back all right. Trust her."

"You were here?"

"Over there." Thryza indicated the beech tree. "I'd been watching through the leaves, thinking it would be me that would have to get Clem out somehow because she never would."

"But you were only a little girl."

"Not so little. I'm only three years younger than her. I was getting a bit worried when Dick came riding over the field on his bicycle. He saw the commotion, walked in, and yanked Clem out and then, when the water had settled, he went in again with the fishing net." Thryza had warmed to her narrative. " 'Got it,' he said when he'd practically stirred up the whole pond and out he came all covered with weeds and mud. She was standing there like a princess in her muslin dress, but he walked up to her mud and all, and put it on her wrist. A gold bracelet. She just smiled and twisted it round and then she reached up and kissed his cheek. He looked"—she searched for the word.

"Spellbound?"

"That's it. Oh, she could make people feel like that." Thyrza lost animation and glared sullenly at the leaden water. "Dick said something about King Arthur and the Lady of the Lake. It's in a poem by Lord Tennyson. I found that out afterward."

Comparing the two episodes, the legendary appearance of Excalibur and the reappearance of the bracelet, I discovered some resemblances but found the differences between them more striking.

"What I don't understand," I said, "is how a bracelet could get into the middle of a pool like this in the first place."

"That's easy." Thryza's eyes gleamed with the rekindled light of battle. "I threw it in."

Though I was disinclined just then to rejoice at anything, my reaction was in the nature of a small inward cheer.

"Why?" I asked.

"Because she was so damned selfish. Nobody else mattered. She had to be queen of all she surveyed. The catch of the bracelet had come loose and it fell on the grass. 'You'll lose it one of these days,' I told her. 'Kelda will give me hers,' she said as cool as a cucumber, 'and she can have this one.' She picked it up and that was when I snatched it out of her hand and threw it as far as it would go, and then I walked away and waited behind the tree to see what would happen." Thyrza's brow darkened. "And much good it did me. That kiss changed everything. He would never have thought of her in that way if she hadn't kissed him; he never had. She had him in her clutches from then on and nothing could save him. She held on like grim death."

"You really did love him, Thryza."

"Haven't I shown it? He loved me too. Yes, it's true. If it hadn't been for me throwing that bracelet into the pool, it might have been me, not her: he'd have married me. I know I'm ignorant but a girl can learn. I'd have found a way of getting more education for his sake and I could have learned to behave nicely and talk the way you do. We could have had a year or two of happiness and he'd have been loved the way he deserved." Her voice had sunk low, its timbre soft and warm. "Instead—look what he got; and look at me, always on the outside—on my own."

"You have Arthur," I reminded her, "and that's the best of all."

"You're right." She blinked away tears. "I wouldn't exchange him for a ruby ring, and when all's said and done, that's all she's got out of it."

"I see why you chose the name."

"It stuck in my mind—and Dick liked it, so we called him Arthur Richard."

"And he's the image of his father. It's as if Dick had come back and was starting life all over again."

She looked at me, surprised, and her face broke into a smile of rare happiness.

"That's a lovely thing to say."

"It was Kelda who said it."

"Poor Kelda!" she said. "I'm glad she got away."

If only I too could get away at once without ever seeing May again! The story Sintram had told left me with a horror that all the years since then have not dispelled. All I wanted was to sneak home, pack my things, and leave without a word. Only the thought of Kelda restrained me and the memory of a brief encounter with May earlier that morning.

For once I had not taken up her breakfast tray. The commotion of the previous night would have been sufficient excuse—I hadn't gone to bed at all—but the hypocrisy entailed in even so simple an act of service was now beyond me. I was still drowsing over my own untouched breakfast when I heard the postman drop a letter into the box. Almost at once May's door opened and a few minutes later she came into the kitchen with the letter in her hand.

"Kelda is coming home," she said.

I stared at her aghast. It was the very last thing I had expected; and yet as I sat drooping over the table, too dazed and weary to deal with this new problem, I knew that it had been inevitable. After all the trouble we had taken, Clem and I, to rescue Kelda, it had taken only one tug on the leash by a practiced hand to bring her back.

"You sent for her?"

"What else could I do?"

She held out the letter between two fingers, as if to drop it into the fire, then paused to pick up the poker and stir the black coals into flame.

"When is she coming?"

"She doesn't say."

Apparently changing her mind about the letter, May put it in her dressing gown pocket and turned, the poker in her hand. And suddenly, my natural resilience at a low ebb, I was afraid of her. "You're alone there with her?" I heard Sintram's labored voice again. "The quiet one. Be careful. If it was of any advantage to her to have you dead, she would kill you"—and as I gasped, incredulous—"she's done it before," he said. "I mean murder."

I dragged my gaze from the poker. It came to rest on the sharp blade of the bread knife. I thought of pillows and of people being stifled by them while sleeping and fought down a mounting hysteria. It was all so unlikely: simply not feasible. She wasn't

223

strong enough to kill a fly, much less an active, energetic girl. Then I remembered how resolute those frail white hands had proved, how helpless the victim whose life they had crushed out.

My chair scraped the quarry-tiled floor as I got slowly to my feet.

"Don't bother to make up the bed for Kelda," May said quietly, replacing the poker inside the fender. "You look tired. I'll go and get the things out of the airing cupboard."

I seized the opportunity to escape and walked over the wet fields to the pool, where Thyrza joined me. We were glad of each other's company and afterward I went home with her to the Tile Sheds and dried my feet at her fire, filling in time until I could force myself to go home.

The sky had been overcast by heavy clouds all day. By three o'clock when I walked down the lane from Winkblade a chilling mist had crept into the hollows and hung about the trees so that, half-concealed, they seemed to have withdrawn into a deliberate secrecy. It was more than usually quiet. I heard nothing but the light tread of my own feet and the occasional drip of moisture on leaves against a background of stillness so profound that it became impossible to ignore, a positive force challenging the nerves.

The house loomed without warning out of the mist. In the absence of sky it appeared taller than ever, more than ever ill-proportioned in its ungainly height under the sharp pitch of its roof. Except for a glow from the drawing room the windows were unlit. The hall too was dark. Without light from outside or lamplight within, the stained-glass window was almost colorless, its effect subdued, as an empty church at nightfall. The drawing room door, half open, might have been the entrance to a side chapel, the figure seated by the hearth its presiding saint. In what might have seemed an act of reverence I took off my earth-stained shoes as well as my hat and coat and went noiselessly in.

Standing just inside the door I took a deep breath and found courage at last to say what had to be said.

21

"THERE'S SOMETHING I must tell you. I've known it for a while, known it in my heart I mean, but I couldn't talk about it until I was certain because it changes everything."

She had not moved and might have been asleep but firelight shone on the eyes half turned toward me and made them glitter. Then with the slightest of movements she turned her head away toward the fire so that I saw only the curve of her cheek and the delicate ear, listening.

"I realize what a blow it must have been when you found out that Kelda was going to have Dick's baby. He never knew about it, did he? You wouldn't let Kelda tell him. You knew very well that if he had known he would have married her. He wouldn't have left her in the lurch as he did Thyrza. The baby would have given him the excuse he had been longing for, a reason for breaking his engagement to you."

Recalling the scene, I am more than ever convinced of the power of words. It was as though as I spoke they took command, formulating truths I had not known until they were expressed. I became aware of an unfamiliar quality in my voice, the level incontrovertible tone of someone acting as a mouthpiece for judgments I had no right to make; and pausing, became myself again only to feel the hatefulness of my involvement in the sordid story and the drag of its weight bearing me down.

"Even after the baby was born you couldn't feel safe until Kelda was married to someone else, although it meant living without her, or trying to. You must have regretted maneuvering her into marrying Mr. Cade when you realized there had been no need because Dick was dead—probably before the wedding."

The fitful light gave me courage to say what I could never have said to her face-to-face in daylight. Here in a room half lost in shadow she had become even less the woman than ever before, more completely the image. I addressed it as a lapsed believer might reproach the plaster Madonna in a candle-lit church, seeing only the folds of her skirt, the rosette on her shoe, the slender, nerveless hand.

"It had to be a secret between the two of you. It's a wonder Kelda didn't die, shut up in that horrible little room for months without a doctor or nurse, only you. And it was you who took the baby away and you who"—but that word would not be said; I drew back on the brink and afterward gave thanks with all my heart for the moment of cowardice—"disposed of it."

It was then that she moved, this time so violently that my heart thumped. She leaned forward, as if drawn, staring toward the concealing darkness on the other side of the room; then swung to face me. At the same moment a coal hissed and released a tongue of flame: a tip of light reddened her hand and the ring on her third finger—not the ruby but a broad gold band. It couldn't be. Seized with awful misgivings, I went nearer.

"Kelda!" I fell on my knees beside her. "I didn't know you had come. What have I said? Oh please, please forgive me. I would never have said it if I had known it was you. I won't say another word."

She thrust her face close to mine not in affection but as if to force her way into my very mind. I felt a fierce energy in her hands as she gripped my wrists—and in her voice.

226

"No, you must go on," and as I tried to draw back, alarmed, "somehow you've found it all out and I'm glad. Just to hear it spoken of after years of keeping it to ourselves makes me realize how insanely we behaved. Our life has been one long misery when it need not have been. But if you know everything—I don't know how you can: there was no one who could have told you, no one who knew, we saw to that. But if you do know, tell me this. Quick—before she comes back. There's something I've never known and now"—I felt the feverish quivering of her whole body—"I daren't ask."

"What can it be? How can I possibly know what you yourself don't know?"

"At the time—you were right—I almost died. Sometimes it seems as if I really did die and came back a different person. It was one long nightmare and we were so ignorant; we didn't know what to do; for days on end it was so bitterly cold and dark; and the birth was difficult; it was torture—a whole day of agony and part of the night. Just the two of us. We gave father something to make him sleep. I told you—it was madness. Then when somehow at last it happened, I just faded away into blackness. When I came to myself I was alone. May had taken it—the baby—away." Unconsciously her nails dug into my wrist. She nerved herself to go on. "So—I never knew, I've never been sure whether my baby ever lived."

"But surely"—I felt the desperate urgency of her need to know as vividly as if the event had just taken place: I also felt the need for caution.

"May told me he was stillborn. I have asked her—and asked—and every time she has given the same answer."

"Then how can you say you don't know."

"Because of something in her manner when she says it, so that it doesn't feel true. And because somewhere in my heart or mind, in the very depths of me, I seem to have a faint memory like hearing a voice far far away and long ago, ages and ages ago, a memory of a baby crying and of my whole body—and my soul—

yearning to reach and comfort it." As I listened in a ferment of indecision as to what to do, what to say, she let go of my wrist and drew away. Her voice hardened: "And because his being stillborn would have been so—convenient. Yes, it's shocking, isn't it? It would have solved so many problems. That's why I've never been able to believe it."

"You must have made plans for the baby," I interrupted hurriedly, still wondering how to deal with a development I couldn't have foreseen.

"May did all that. She wrote to a magazine and got addresses. She arranged for a foster mother, some woman in Wales, the farthest away we could find. May would take the baby and meet her at Crew—she said." Doubt clouded her eyes. "But then, as things turned out, it wasn't necessary and she—what was the word you used—disposed of it. She never told me how or where. I begged her not to tell me that: I don't know why because wherever I go I think, 'This may be the place. It may be here.' You can't imagine how terrible it has been."

"I have some idea of what you must have suffered."

"One struggles on; one awful thing after another I have grown used to or put behind me. But it has lain on my conscience all these years, more terrible than all the rest, that because of my sin she was driven to a worse sin. I can't rid myself of the thought . . . Oh, Elinor, it's more than a thought: I do believe she killed the baby. If she did, it was my fault; I turned my beloved sister into a murderess. How can I ever be happy again? You don't understand, nobody understands how we feel about each other. I know her faults as if they were my own and she knows mine. We've each made the other suffer, as if we had deliberately chosen the very means that would hurt the other most. But if she did what I'm almost sure she did, it was for my sake; and if she lied about it, that was for my sake too."

"I believe," I said at last, feeling both mentally and physically helpless as if entangled in the web of a gigantic and fiendishly

cunning spider, "that you have tortured yourself unnecessarily."
In my pity for her I cast truth to the winds, forgetting everything
but the need for consolation. "Why should May lie to you of all
people? As you've just said, it would be like lying to herself.
Besides"—if I too was driven to tamper with the truth there was
no point in being half-hearted about it—"you can't seriously believe that May would harm a newborn baby, her sister's baby. It
surprises me that you should ever have imagined such a thing."

I got up quickly, cutting short Kelda's confidence with an
abruptness that must have seemed insensitive: but there had
flashed into my mind another possibility: one whereby Kelda
could keep her faith in May, pitifully misplaced though it was, and
May could remain as she had always seemed, immaculate. It was
vital that I should talk to May alone, providential that I had seen
Kelda first.

"You really think . . . ," she had begun.

"You must be mistaken."

"She changed, you see. She's never been the same since that
night. You've seen the way she lives. It's as if when the baby died,
part of her died too."

"But isn't that what happened to you? You said yourself that
you were reborn as a different person. It didn't have to be guilt that
changed her; the stress of it all and the misery of knowing that
Dick preferred you would have been enough."

"Where are you going?"

"To fetch May. She'll know what to say to reassure you."

Marveling at my own duplicity, I went into the kitchen,
closed the door, and stood with my back against it. The lamp on
the dresser had been lit. Passing from darkness into light, I was
dazzled and momentarily confused by the fact that my aunts had
changed places. The drawing room was May's domain. Here
among the metal dish covers and saucepans the presiding figure
should have been Kelda's. But May in a white apron with her cuffs
turned back was preparing tea, like one of those Greek goddesses

229

who occasionally came down to mingle with human kind. A hollow clank from the hot-water pipe mocked my arrival, reducing me to the level of the messenger in a burlesque so that I started at a disadvantage. Moreover the nervous energy I had already expended was not to be recovered. My attack had been mistimed: a second onslaught was bound to be something of an anticlimax. It was all I could do to concentrate my aim and discharge the facts in sharp bursts like a rain of bullets, though without much hope that they would reach their target.

"Sit down," I said. "I have to talk to you."

Smiling, eyebrows raised, she complied, sitting upright in the windsor chair, hands clasped before her on the scrubbed deal table, the lamp behind her and behind the lamp the bland white faces of the ranked dinner plates. I sat down opposite and immediately got up again and went to the end of the long table so that she had to turn her head and I could see at least half of her face.

"There's not much time," I said.

Time would not have helped. Reproaches, appeals to conscience or insistence on the truth would have been a waste of breath, I thought, with a depth of cynicism I remember with dismay. The speech I had mistakenly made to Kelda would have been no more effective if made to May. Nevertheless the speed with which I came to the point was nothing short of callous.

"I've been talking to Kelda about her baby. No, she didn't tell me: I found out for myself. Kelda can't believe that it was stillborn even though you have kept on telling her that it was. You could have made her believe it from the beginning if you'd wanted to: you can make people believe anything; but you wanted to keep her unconvinced. That was part of the punishment, wasn't it? You deliberately made her think you were lying for her sake. Well, it worked. That's what she does think."

Her self-control was—pardonably—shaken but not too much and not unbecomingly. She had turned in her chair and now faced me with an air of troubled frankness. The faintest of bewildered frowns rippled across her forehead and left its smoothness unimpaired.

"So you have found it out: Kelda's sad little story. You should have come to me: we could have talked. Because you're wrong, Elinor. The poor little thing *was* stillborn and why you should think that I—"

"Kelda doesn't believe you but she believes *in* you—still—and loves you and believes that you love her. She thinks you killed the baby for her sake to save her from scandal and blames herself for exposing you to temptation and causing you to make so terrible a decision."

I paused to consider what to say next. It was proving much harder to be outspoken here in the glare of the unshaded lamp than it had been in the unlit drawing room; difficult as always not to be influenced by the sheer physical presence of Aunt May, her fragile beauty seeming all the more rare in its homely setting of buff-painted waterpipes and black-leaded range.

"I simply do not know"—she had got up, feeling no doubt the disadvantage of being talked down to, and raising her head, looked past me with the remote air she might have worn in speaking of a stranger—"how all this started. You've been meddling, I'm afraid, Elinor, in very personal and private affairs that are none of your business. When we took you in—to share our home—I could never have dreamed that you would speak to me as you have done. How could you, or Kelda either, think me capable of such"—she hesitated and was wise, perhaps, in her choice of a noncommittal word—"behavior."

"There's no point in pretending," I said. "Kelda only suspects that you killed the baby but I know you did, not to save her from scandal but out of hatred and jealousy and to make sure that Dick wouldn't break off his engagement and marry Kelda. You deliberately murdered it—up there at Winkblade." At the mention of the farmhouse she drew a quick breath. "You were seen."

The direct blow was unexpected. This time she was genu-

231

inely taken aback and sank down in her chair, as if struck by a sledgehammer.

"The baby was alive when you took it to Winkblade and that was where you strangled it. Not 'it.' Him. He was a living person. You murdered Dick's son."

Like Arthur, I thought: his half-brother. It was a relief to withdraw into silence and think of Arthur: an effort to return to my immediate companion. I fancied her cheeks and brow were paler now, more nearly as white as the plates behind her but that may have been imagination.

"When I took it there," she whispered, "I thought it was dead."

"Never mind what you thought. It's what you did that matters. You never intended to let it live." (Was there really a woman in Wales who was to be met at Crewe or was she an invention to hoodwink Kelda?) "You had meant to dig a grave but the ground was frozen hard. You remembered the old hiding place in the bakehouse . . ."

What need was there to remind her even if I could have borne to do so: how she had laid the baby on the ground while she struggled with the heavy iron door, how he had cried and gone on crying until she stopped the crying for good. It was the pitiful wailing that had alerted Sintram as he came out of the shed where he kept his store of brushwood. He heard the clang of the oven door as it swung back against the wall and stood for a minute, astounded, until the wailing stopped. From the doorway of the shed he had seen her move swiftly and silently away. "It was dark," I reminded him. "How could you be sure it was Aunt May?" "She had a lantern," he said. "I saw her face. God gave her the face of an angel. We cannot know his purpose."

When she had gone he went to investigate, and in the deep cavity that had once been Aladdin's cave he found the bundle wrapped in a piece of flannelette. The baby was dead with the marks of May's fingers already blue on its throat. Sickened, distressed, Sintram had gone away and found some other shelter from the bitter night. Two days later the weather changed: he came back; the bundle was gone . . .

"When the thaw came you went and dug the grave," I said; and she didn't deny it.

Somewhere in the garden? Near the sheltered arbor where Clem and I had made friends and later kissed and talked of marriage? Or in the rich soil of one of the flowerbeds where in summer lilies grew tall and marguerites leaned white-faced over the path? Or under the trees where Arthur had gathered twigs? Sintram hadn't told me where: he may not have known.

"If you'd really loved Dick you would have wanted his child to live," I said. "Why did you spend all those hours waiting for him at the gate? It can't have been because you really wanted him to come back."

"Oh yes, I did," she said.

"But not because you loved him. Was it because you wanted to tell him that you would never forgive him?"

"Yes," she said. "I would have given anything to tell him that."

A glance at her expression was enough to convince me that she was capable of all I had accused her of. It was not forlorn love or the hope of his return but bitter jealousy that had kept her brooding at the gate like a frustrated harpy dreaming of revenge.

"It was nothing but a hopeless daydream," I said, "and all the time Kelda was at your mercy. Whenever you chose you could expose her and disgrace her—or threaten to. Even at the wedding you hinted that you might tell. How stupid she has been! She should have known that you couldn't tell without letting it be known that Dick had preferred her to you. You would never have admitted that. And in spite of everything in the midst of all her misery it has been you she has always thought of. She blames herself for what you have become."

The pathos of Kelda's long-tried trust must surely have

touched her. She seemed deep in thought and when her lips parted it could be for no other purpose than to say that she was sorry—or so I thought. What she actually said was, "That horrible old man. He must have been there. It couldn't have been anyone else."

"He could have told the police," I said sharply, "but he never told a living soul, out of respect for my grandfather, until he told me."

"If he had told," she said, "no one would have believed him."

It was almost true: not long ago I would have said that no one could see her and believe ill of her. All the same—

"I believed him," I said, but she was pursuing her own line of thought and didn't seem to hear.

"At any rate he's dead now," she said.

"But I'm not dead."

Apart from the pallor she had shown no sign of distress but now as if swooping down from a great height she lost her bird's-eye view of me as an insignificant and tiresome creature and with a rush of intelligence became aware of me as she had never done before and also of my power to harm her. But I was growing weary of recrimination and in a reckless moment threw away any advantage I had gained.

"You kept Kelda's secret for your own sake as well as hers, but there's no reason why I should keep your secret, is there?"

The words were no sooner spoken than I recognized my blunder and knew what she would say.

"You'll have to keep it, for Kelda's sake."

I knew then that I was no match for her: there was no way of reaching her; I was too tired to go on trying. I could only bow my head and walk slowly to the door, not knowing where to go. Impossible to go back to Kelda. My aimless feet moved like somebody else's feet across the red tiles. Why had they brought me here to Hoodman House? I hadn't wanted to come. At the door I stopped and spoke without turning.

"I didn't want to know the truth about you. I would rather not have known. I'd rather go on thinking of you as you seemed, as I thought of you when I first came: beautiful and loving and sad." Just for a moment I did remember. "You were an example I could look up to. You drew my thoughts upward like a vision. That's what you were meant to be like. And now you're dragging me down as you've dragged Kelda down. You've killed my love for you. You murdered the baby but you can destroy people without strangling them, without laying a finger on them, just by being yourself, not better than the rest of us as I used to think but worse, worse than I could ever have dreamed." I stared down at the tiles as if seeing beneath them the infernal pit, feeling for an instant its consuming heat, smelling its foul stench. "I feel so miserable I could die."

I leaned my head against the door frame, my hand on the brass knob. The feel of its cold metal recalled me to my physical surroundings and the unsolved problem of Kelda waiting for the release I had promised: behind me May, silent, self-contained, immovable; myself between them, ineptly trying to balance the scales. Justice, I have since learned, is a human concept: in nature there is none; but it seemed to me then unfair that in addition to all the other advantages May had been endowed with she should also be by far the cleverer.

Then she spoke, her voice gentle as ever and with its own irresistible sweetness. Her words amazed me.

"What shall I do?" she said.

Humbly, in a few words, I told her.

"Then her mind will be at rest," I concluded. "She will be free of it."

"And she will go back to Julius." A quiver of feeling animated May's lovely features and made them lovelier. "What about me?"

"You'll be free too"—and moved by some impulse too complex to be described except as other than hostile, I added—"we'll find a way for you to manage, I promise you"—and led the way along the passage.

235

The performance was almost faultless. Had I not known that it was also false throughout I might have lapsed once more into helpless admiration.

Kelda lay as I had left her in the deep chair. She turned her head but made no other movement, only her eyes followed May, who went softly across the room, stood for a moment on the hearth rug, then sank to her knees and laid her head in her sister's lap. Fascinated, I watched Kelda put out a weary hand and stroke the shining hair.

"It's all over, dearest." Smooth and sweet, May's voice flowed like honey. "The misunderstanding—the torment we have both suffered. You mustn't blame yourself." This was a master stroke, encompassing reproach and forgiveness in a single breath. "I should not have lied to you. Yes, I lied and felt all along that you knew I was lying. No, don't interrupt, I know. You don't have to remind me that we used never to need to lie to each other. This was the only time and I had to do it because I knew the truth would hurt you more—at least I thought I knew."

She lifted her head. Her face had a warmth I had not seen there before. It came from the fire which colored her cheeks and sparkled in her eyes, giving the illusion of active emotion.

"But I can see now that I was mistaken. The truth would have hurt you less than what you imagined. No, I won't talk about that—if you could misjudge me so cruelly, it must have been my fault. The truth is that your baby did live but only for a little while. I held it in my arms, pretending—just for a minute or two that it was mine"—a wistful sadness seeped into the room—"and Dick's." She paused: the imaginative touch had been a risk; Kelda had stiffened. "Then I saw you on that dreadful little bed. Your eyes were closed; you were the color of death. I put the baby down while I tried to revive you and almost forgot it—until it gave a dreadful choking sound—its little legs curled up and its face—its face turned darker and it . . ." She put her hands over her face then went bravely on . . . "And it was dead. I thought you were both dead. I was beside myself but I knew that the first and most important thing I could do for you was to keep your secret. So I wrapped the baby in a sheet—you know all this—and ran all the way to Winkblade—and back—and to my joy—you'll never know, darling, how wonderful it was, I'm not good at expressing my feelings—but to see you there with your eyes open." Her lips parted in a heavenly smile; tears shone on Kelda's cheeks: their hands met. "But as I came down the lane I had made up my mind to tell you that the baby was stillborn. Otherwise, it wasn't only that we were breaking the law in not registering it—you remember, we talked about that—but I knew that you would have reproached yourself for not having a doctor or a midwife to do all the right things and perhaps keep it alive, as I've reproached myself endlessly for my ignorance and helplessness—all these years; but it was something I could do for you, to bear the remorse myself and relieve you of it . . . It was a mistake of course. We should have shared it as we have shared so much—everything. After all its death was an act of nature, I've tried to tell myself that a thousand times."

"Yes. Yes." In the relief of yielding up the responsibility for the baby's death to nature, Kelda leaned forward and laid her wet cheek against her sister's. "And I'm so ashamed, terribly ashamed to have imagined . . . of the thoughts I have harbored . . . You did all you could. There was nothing else you could do."

May rose from the hearth rug, smoothed her saintly white apron, glided to the mahogany side table where the family Bible rested and laid on it her left hand, the ruby like a dark blot on its delicate pallor.

"No, don't!" Kelda exclaimed. "No, please. There's no need."

"But you must believe me, absolutely," May said with what seemed passionate earnestness. "I have told you the truth. There has been too much deception and there must be no more. I swear that your baby lived—and died—and that when it was dead I took it to Winkblade and hid its little body and afterward buried it."

What does it matter, I thought with my newly acquired and dreadful cynicism? Perjury, blasphemy were only additional straws; but the sudden leap of flames that reddened the white apron and cast on her hands and neck a ruddy glow put me uncomfortably in mind of the mediaeval burning of witches or worse still of a longer-lasting bonfire to which she was presumably already consigned; if, that is, she remained to the end unrepentant.

"It's all over," she said.

"I've been out of my senses," Kelda said, "as if a demon had got into me and filled my mind with evil thoughts. There's no other explanation." She got up and stretched her arms as if waking into life. "And if it hadn't been for Elinor . . ."

"Dear little Elinor," May said.

I started. The words released me from the entranced state in which from my viewpoint just inside the door I had listened and watched. They stood now with their arms round each other, equal in height, their two heads inclined at the same slight angle as they regarded me. "Dear little Elinor . . ." The tenderness had roused echoes of our first meeting when they had perched on either side of my bed like cooing doves. Half awake, not knowing one from the other, I had sensed in the two silk-clad and perfumed figures a single identity charged with a twofold power. It had taken me years to identify them as separate beings and know the essence of each, to distinguish the loving and the heartless, the weaker from the stronger. The better from the worse? I had begun to outgrow the arrogance and folly of exercising that kind of judgment.

They had moved to the window and were standing together in the bay. Beyond the uneven circle of the firelight the room was lightless as the mist outside so that they could be seen only as two female forms, their faces barely visible, motionless, speechless; yet in their unalterable closeness they seemed once more indivisible, absorbed in secret communication by means of their own voiceless language. What had I done? This was not what I had intended, this dreadful welding of the two once more into one. Kelda would never be free: she would never go back to Julius. The renewed bond of sisterly love would be stronger and more lasting even than the canceled bond of fear.

Simultaneously they turned.

"You'll never know how grateful we are," Kelda said.

"And now," said May, "everything will be as it used to be. We can begin all over again."

A frisson crept down my spine.

Afterward we drew the curtains and had tea by the fire; ate buttered toast and sponge cake and talked a little with the cozy decorum appropriate to ladies living quietly in the country.

22

Now that the secrets of Hoodman House had passed into my keeping it may be imagined that I also held my aunts in the palm of my hand: imagined, that is, by someone who didn't know them. In reality it was as if I no longer mattered. The clarification I had taken so much trouble to bring about (bogus though it was) had united them even more closely—and more exclusively. In spite of their gratitude to dear little Elinor no further effort was made to have her there on equal terms; certainly not as a younger sister: barely even as a half niece; rather as an outsider politely tolerated, barely noticed.

Not that any hint of estrangement ruffled the surface of our daily life, which was smoother and more amiable than before. I could truthfully claim that things were no worse. In any case my own personal happiness would have immunized me against any conceivable worsening.

All the same at least one of my forebodings had proved well founded. As if to atone for having misjudged her sister (as she thought) Kelda was more devoted to her than ever. No mention was made of a return to Surrey. Julius once more languished alone. Clem and I privately seethed and boiled with indignation and hatched wild schemes for restoring his wife to him but without enthusiasm on Clem's part: he had given up Kelda as a hopeless case. He was of course at a disadvantage: I hadn't told him Kelda's secret. It was too discreditable to Dick; and since one secret hung upon the other I didn't tell him May's either; not then at any rate—not until years later. What's more, infected by the atmosphere of Hoodman House, I had now a guilty secret of my own to hide, namely my part in conspiring with May to deceive Kelda about the baby's death. I had hushed up a crime and so become an accessory after the fact.

Knowing the truth could only have made Kelda more miserable, but it might have encouraged her to break away. As a result of my meddling Julius had been replaced on the shelf—permanently it seemed—though Clem and I had told the Tasses that he was alive and the news was passed on to their circle of friends. Every plan for his rescue must meet with the same insuperable obstacle. It had thwarted higher powers than ours. As Clem said, God had attempted to join Julius and Kelda in holy matrimony but May had preempted him. From infancy Kelda had been hers.

We were not absolutely without hope. For one thing, we were determined to have Julius at our wedding. Though his appearance would be fraught with indescribable awkwardness, it would establish him once more as a real live husband; and his friends in Bidminster could be relied on to welcome him with sufficient warmth to shame Kelda into recognizing her duty. Besides, however uncomfortable poor Julius might feel at my wedding I could harden my heart, having endured—and survived—all the discomforts of attending his.

For the time being the deadlock must be accepted. Clem and I announced our engagement in December and planned to be married in June. During the winter and spring I spent almost as much time with the Tasses as with my aunts. Otherwise the situation was unchanged. My aunts' financial problems remained unsolved. I still paid my share, more than a third, of the housekeeping expenses, but my contribution would cease when I married. Altogether our wedding would mark an epoch, not only for my aunts and ourselves but also for Mirabel. To everybody's surprise Uncle Vernon had promised to come and having seen his only remaining nephew married, would whisk off his only niece to the long promised new life in Kimberley.

Meanwhile if the outer world had not yet broken in on Hoodman House there were signs that in favorable circumstances its inmates might break out. When they actually did, it was with a degree of social ease that did credit to the family.

Early in March Harriet sent out invitations to an At Home to be held in the Assembly Rooms in Bidminster.

"We have so much hospitality to return," she told me, "and Aidan wants to show his gratitude to all you people who have helped him with his work during the winter. I particularly wanted to sound you out as to whether your aunts would come. We'll be neighbors some day, quite soon. It's high time we got to know each other."

An invitation was sent and accepted without any hesitation that I was aware of. I was spending a few days with the Tasses at the time and when we arrived at the Assembly Rooms my aunts had not yet appeared. A string quartet was playing light music; waitresses in black dresses and muslin caps and aprons offered refreshments; since most of the guests knew one another there was a lively buzz of conversation in which I took care not to become involved but waited near the door in readiness to introduce my aunts to their hosts; and perhaps, I was kind enough to think, ease their return to Bidminster after so long an absence.

Vigilance was unnecessary. There was no danger of missing their arrival. A rapid dying away of conversation directed all eyes to the entrance. They were there, Kelda in golden yellow, May in silvery gray, both wearing long fur soles. (Were they new? There was certainly no whiff of mothballs. How had they come by them? I was altogether too much impressed to care.)

"Miss Penfold, you have met my aunt Mrs. Cade. This is Aunt May, Miss Findon . . ."

Even while making the introductions I was engaged in an interesting discovery. There had been gossip about the Findons: their rise and fall; their debts; their neglect of social obligations; their eccentricities; the oddity of a prolonged and ostentatious engagement to a dead man; a marriage that was barely a marriage; a widowhood that was no such thing; there had been hurt feelings and malice without a doubt. None of these demerits, it seemed, could withstand the united confidence of two remarkably beautiful women. In all conscience I could not be proud of them but I was proud of the impression they made.

They both wore the straighter, simpler dresses with the scooped-out neckline then in vogue but somehow with the effect of having considered no fashion but their own; as if a mere mode required no more than a passing acknowledgment from two women entirely confident of their own position, experience, and taste.

"Gosh!" Prosaic as ever, Mirabel had joined me whilst Harriet chatted to Kelda and her brother took charge of Aunt May. "I must say they've worn well, those two."

The compliment was pitifully inadequate. What my aunts possessed, I thought, watching them fairly steadily throughout the evening, was a superiority of style: an air of having dropped in from a loftier sphere briefly to enjoy such limited attractions as Bidminster had to offer, the enjoyment being dependent on the brevity: a style unlikely to make them popular despite May's unsurpassable sweetness of manner.

It was not her way, nor was it necessary, to talk much. Whether or not she listened to Aidan, who had led her to an alcove and was presumably initiating her in the cause of world peace, she appeared to be listening, until Harriet intervened and took her away to meet other guests, with a reproving frown at her brother, who stumbled apologetically to his feet and wiped his pale scholarly brow with his handkerchief. The room was warm.

With admirable forbearance in overlooking past affronts, Mrs. Tass took Kelda under her wing, but I did notice that Aunt Claudia's politeness was on the frosty side.

Having arrived late, my aunts were the first to go, leaving a certain flatness in the atmosphere such as afflicts spectators when a procession has passed and the music of the band has died away.

Harriet must have been pleased with her success in making friends with her future neighbors. She was often at Winkblade as the days lengthened and the alterations went ahead and she occasionally called at Hoodman House. One day not long after the At Home we had another visitor. It was early afternoon. I happened to be taking the air at our front door. Except for the bleating of sheep and the occasional crow of a cock two fields away it was very quiet and I heard the car as soon as it turned off the Upper Saury road. By the time it passed the Tile Sheds I knew that it wasn't Clem's Calcott and assuming it to be Harriet's Sunbeam, I pulled on a jacket, ran up the lane to Winkblade, and was surprised to find Aidan.

He had had himself driven out from town and apart from the driver had come alone. The workmen were taking their mid-day break at the front of the house and he had the wide farmyard to himself, looking in his felt hat and warm overcoat rather out of place as he vaguely took stock of the piles of rubble and discarded picks and shovels. It couldn't be his first visit, but so far as I knew he had never before been there on his own. I felt pleased at this initiative, especially as he had lately seemed even more than usually out of touch with the practical world. The disorder in his study had become almost unmanageable; the letters he dictated were sometimes confused and he would break off to gaze out of the window while I waited, pencil poised, for him to finish the sentence. Sheer tiredness, I supposed; and too little relaxation. He was

244

the victim of his own enthusiasm. It was possible to be *too* dedicated.

"You've chosen a lovely day."

He ought to have seen me coming, a young woman of normal size and the only human being in sight but he gave a violent start as I spoke.

"Ah, Miss Findon! Elinor! Ah yes!"—and he dutifully scanned the surrounding scene, as if newly aware of the ewes and lambs in the nearest fields, the tentative sunlight, the softness of spring in the air.

"A good deal seems to have been done." He had worked his way round to the empty space where horses and cattle had once been housed and to the litter of worm-eaten timber and broken tiles. "Or"—with a gleam of his old humor—"undone."

As he seemed to have no urgent purpose in being there or indeed any purpose at all, I took it upon myself to show him round, reminded him of the layout of kitchen, scullery, and servants' bedrooms and, warming to the task, led him indoors, into every room, every cupboard, every nook and cranny. At each revelation he nodded intelligently if dreamily and we emerged at last to find the men back at work.

"I'm afraid we're in the way." He stood, hands clasped behind his back in the manner, not entirely convincing, of a country gentleman enjoying the leisurely contemplation of his estate. The driver opened the car door but Aidan seemed not quite ready to leave, and, casually, as if merely to make the most of the country air, he walked as far as the end of the wall. I felt obliged to follow. Beyond the bare elms at the bottom of the field—and almost as high—rose the walls of the house and higher still, its narrow chimneys.

"Hoodman House?" He spoke with an air of discovery. "An interesting name. Now let me see. How does it go? 'What devil wasn't that thus hath cozened you at hoodman blind?'" And as I looked startled: "What does it mean? Blindman's buff. But not of

the innocent nursery kind. Some diabolical misleading or deception. I'm sorry. The lines are wildly inappropriate to the present
inhabitants." He laughed. "The house was probably called after its
first owner or possibly the field where it was built. Hoodman
Meadow perhaps."

"My aunts will know. Have you time," I found myself saying,
"to call?"

I had always thought of him as rather a shy man and was
taken aback when he smiled acceptance of the invitation. He was
evidently too polite to refuse and told the driver to follow with the
car in a quarter of an hour.

Kelda, who had taken advantage of the fine weather to beat
the kitchen mats in the backyard, was even more taken aback and
did not appear; but May, seated at the drawing room window with
a book, was graciously welcoming. Her health had improved in
recent months but without adding an ounce to her weight or
stealing the transparent delicacy from her skin or the pensive
softness from her eyes. I had rarely seen Aidan either in a purely
social setting or without his sister and was agreeably surprised to
find him so affable, amusing, even witty in a quiet way. When
punctually the car drew up to the gate, he stayed on for a few more
minutes, hoped that Miss Findon would one day be interested in
inspecting the progress being made at Winkblade and took himself
off. May resumed her reading of *Mazzini: Patriot and Prophet,* an
odd choice, I thought—until I noticed a gap at the end of the book
shelf nearest to her chair.

It was disappointing to find that this short break from work
had little effect on Aidan's mental health. His powers of concentration showed no improvement. On the following Tuesday and
again on the Thursday he actually left me to my own devices in
the office and went for a walk "to clear" his head.

Shortly after that I went to Rosedown Hall to spend a fortnight with the Burnetts and returned on a Monday in the second
week of April. Clem met me at the station and drove me home. We

arranged to meet the next day at Winkblade where the interior work had just begun.

Packhorse Way was at its best with the blackthorn in bloom and the trees still bare of leaves so that sun and wind could dry out the puddles and harden the winter's mud. To go to Winkblade that way instead of by the farm road saved no more than three minutes at the most but when Clem was waiting every minute counted, especially after a fortnight's absence. We would light a fire in the empty sitting room and talk for as long as he could be free about the wedding and our new home. The house on the corner of Watt Lane was to be ours after all, thanks to Mr. Tass, who had taken the lease in what Clem called a thoroughly underhand manner— and had astonished us with the news on the day we announced our engagement.

I skimmed up the lane between white spikes of blossom and clumps of wild daffodils, took the garden steps two at a time and came to a halt at the wicket gate. Something was wrong. Except for the birds there was neither sound nor movement; no crash of bricks or men's voices or the stamp of Clydesdales or the throb of motor engines. No sign of Clem either.

I found him sitting glumly on a pile of stones, once the wall of a dairy.

"Where is everybody?"

"Laid off." He had got up. We confronted each other, our usual embrace forgotten, he gloomy, I apprehensive.

"Laid off? What does it mean? She hasn't changed her mind about the kitchen *again?*"

"I've a strong feeling that she's changed her mind about more than that."

"You don't mean—the whole thing? But she can't."

Harriet must have got up early that morning. She had telephoned both Clem and Cameron, the builder. They had met for a hasty consultation. For the time being work on Winkblade was to stop. Cameron had already moved his men to another property.

"What on earth did she say?"

"It didn't amount to much more than 'Down tools.' Naturally I asked her what it was all about but she just said something about a major change of plan and she would discuss it with me at a more convenient time."

"Is she going to make it even bigger? Add another wing perhaps?"

"If you ask me"—Clem picked up a lump of sandstone and hurled it in despair onto a pile of similar fragments that had once formed the stable and hayloft—"she's going to back out altogether."

"But why? She loves Winkblade?"

"Or did love it. It was a whim. And she happens to be rich enough to indulge her whims, I suppose."

Fortunately a contract had been signed. Except for the loss of time there would be no financial loss to either the architect or the builder—only to Harriet herself. She would surely not leave the place in its present ravaged condition. Only the west wing was untouched and the bakehouse. One of my secret pleasures was to leave a stone jar of wild flowers on its tiny window ledge in memory of Sintram, even though I never replenished the jar without remembering that he was not the only one to die there.

We kindled a fire and ate our lunch to the accompaniment of a wide-ranging exchange of theories as to what had got into Harriet, who until now had given no hint of any possible change of plan. Afterward I went back to Bidminster with Clem. In any case Tuesday was normally one of my working days. My holiday was to have lasted another week; but it would have been torment to wait so long to hear Harriet's reason for so startling a decision.

Mrs. Brady was dusting the stairs when I let myself in.

"Thank goodness you're back, Miss Findon," she breathed in a heavy whisper. "I've been on pins and needles here. I'll tell you what—there's something going on up there." She came close and hissed the words between clenched teeth with a significant glance up at the first-floor landing and a slow deliberate nod.

Spurred by so dramatic a greeting, I went quickly upstairs to the study and was a little disappointed. Harriet, mounted on a pair of steps with a scarf tied round her head, was handing down piles of paper to her brother from a high cupboard. The something that was going on appeared to be no more than a spring cleaning. Such was my first impression. A row of strong cardboard boxes and several wooden crates already labeled Luggage in Advance told a different story.

"Elinor!" She came carefully down the steps. "Sit down, dear. We have something to tell you."

She and I sat at the table. Aidan, who hadn't spoken, went to his desk and sank down in his swivel chair.

"You're not leaving?"

"I'm afraid we are. It's too bad to spring it on you without warning like this. I should have written to you in Surrey but it was only last week that it became a serious possibility and we didn't finally make up our minds until Sunday."

"Do you mean that you're going for good? Oh, I'm so sorry."

"I'm afraid so." Harriet's tone was indeed regretful but even more noticeably it was firm. I glanced at her brother. With his left elbow on the desk, brow in hand, he was flicking over the pages of a pamphlet: "What Have We Learned from War." His expression was not cheerful.

"Aidan," his sister nevertheless said with determined enthusiasm, "has received a most wonderful offer from the League of Nations Council. He's been chosen to convene a panel of British delegates to form part of a standing committee on social questions. It's to be established by the beginning of September when the Assembly meets for the disarmament conference in Geneva. We must go to London at once. There'll be so much preliminary work to be done. It's a most heartening sign of confidence in Aidan's campaign."

"You will go too—to Geneva?"

"Oh yes, we'll settle there for a while. This opening will at most certainly lead to a permanent appointment of some kind, in an editorial capacity probably."

"And Winkblade?"

She untied the scarf and loosened her hair with her fingers, as if she had a headache. For all her enthusiasm I detected a look of weariness in her eyes.

"It was evidently not meant to be. I suppose it's providential that this offer came before we moved there."

"I can't tell you how sorry I am that you have to go. But of course the work will be interesting—and important—much more important than anything in Bidminster."

Aidan had still not uttered a word but now gave a wry smile and a slight shake of his head. His sister's voice became firmer.

"It means exchanging a soapbox for the international stage." The remark was directed less to me than to the swivel chair. "There will be ministers and secretaries of state from all the European countries and from America. Aidan will have his finger on the pulse of the civilized world. The opportunity isn't to be missed. He can't refuse."

"I suppose not."

The responsibility of keeping his finger on so erratic a pulse seemed already to have had a devitalizing effect on Aidan. He was making a half-hearted attempt to arrange the various leaflets on his desk in some sort of order—"After Armageddon," "A World Parliament," "The Economics of Victory." I was going to miss them.

"Let me help with the packing. I know where everything is—or should be. And you must have worked very hard yesterday."

Harriet was glad to take a break and went to her room to put her feet up.

"You must find it encouraging," I said as I took her place on the steps. "I mean you've often told me you didn't feel that you were making any progress. You were wrong, weren't you? You're helping to change the climate of thought"—it was a phrase he had sometimes used—"and now you'll be doing what matters more than anything in the world."

"Yes," he said. "Thank you, Elinor. You're very kind."

"He's so doleful about it," I said at the Tasses' tea table later in the afternoon. "One would think he didn't want to go and was being pushed into it by Harriet. And yet they seemed to be really happy here—not to mention her beloved Winkblade."

"Yes," said Mirabel weightily. "That's the point. Winkblade."

"What do you mean?" Clem demanded.

"I've got eyes in my head." She added hot water to the teapot with a mysterious smile. "There could be good reasons why Winkblade might have to go west. I must say it wouldn't worry me to give it up, if it was mine. I never could see what people saw in the place. Personally I never enjoyed those days in the country. Some people might like tramping about in long grass and getting their stockings wet and mud on their shoes but it never appealed to me. And that rickety old house! I used to want to tidy it up and make it fit to sit down in, but the others would just drift away. I didn't know what they were up to half the time—quoting poetry and making ivy wreaths and pretending to have adventures. Then later on they would just stand about looking beautiful—some of them . . ."

"Alas, the Romantic movement passed Mirabel by," said Mr. Tass.

"Luckily for us." Clem took a second slice of his cousin's raisin cake. "Mirabel is a realist and sees things and people as they really are. As she says, she has eyes in her head."

"I hope so," said Mirabel as if she could say more.

"Had there been any talk of the Penfolds leaving Bidminster?" Mrs. Tass turned to me.

"Not at all. It seems to have been sprung upon them quite suddenly, this Geneva business."

251

"Geneva my foot," said Mirabel inelegantly.

To do her justice she had indeed seen more than the rest of us. My excuse for not having tumbled to the truth must be my absence in Surrey while Mirabel had continued to address envelopes for Aidan as well as keeping her finger on the pulse of social Bidminster.

It was not until the following Sunday that I understood what was going on. It was Harriet herself who enlightened me. She had driven out to Winkblade for the last time. They were to leave Bidminster at the end of the week. Hearing the car, I walked up to join her as I often did and found her on the stone seat by the front door. As usual she was quietly and expensively dressed in country clothes: a costume of Otterburn tweed in a rich weave of rust and warm brown; a Henry Heath hat and soft leather brogues. But with the sun in her face as she turned to greet me she looked older, less self-assured. Without its familiar quizzical expression her face seemed to have sagged: the downward crevices from nose to chin had deepened. "Yes," with her usual astuteness she had read my mind. "I feel spent and weary. Come and comfort me."

"I'm glad you're seeing the countryside at its best."

I joined her on the seat. Leaf buds were swelling on willow and birch, lilac and rowan, so that the garden seemed to hover on the verge of bursting into life: the green pasture beyond the wicket gate was speckled with ewes and lambs.

"This is the way I shall remember it." She pulled off her hat and lifted her face. "How blissfully sweet it smells!"

"I believe this must be as my father remembered it in India when he was homesick for England. I didn't know then . . ."

How could I have known the evanescent charm of an English spring: its endlessly varied greens and melting blues; its shifting light and shade; and at the heart of the enchantment a haunting sadness. The threat of mortality?

"It's sad that so many people have loved Winkblade and left it—and have never come back."

"Don't say that. It wrings my heart. I love this sheltered old house—the quiet fields—the way the view unfolds without making demands on one's attention . . . There's everything here I have ever wanted." Her voice trembled but she added lightly, "except the nightingale of course."

"The blackbirds are every bit as good. Why don't you stay?"

"I want to tell you why." She laid her hand on mine. "You're good at keeping secrets. Oh yes, I felt it at once when we met again that day at the Tasses. You know a good deal that you don't tell. Well, here's something else you must keep to yourself."

But it was a full minute before she spoke again.

"It's Aidan. I have to get him away."

"And he doesn't want to go?"

"You think I'm being cruel and domineering."

"No, I don't, because you don't want to go either. Whatever reason you have for leaving must be an unselfish one."

"I knew you'd comfort me. I *think* I'm acting for his good. I'm almost sure. But sometimes we claim to be acting for the best when we're really only doing what makes us happier ourselves."

"But it isn't making you happier, is it?"

"No. I'm thoroughly miserable. But not as miserable as I would be if . . . Of course I can't tell Aidan what to do. He has quite as much strength of mind as I have—as a rule. But I can influence him. Without my persuasion he would have turned down this offer as he did before."

I was surprised to learn that a similar offer had been made more than a year ago before they ever came to Bidminster and had been rejected without hesitation.

"Aidan's lungs were still in bad shape then. You know he was gassed and invalided out of the army. All we wanted was a peaceful quiet life. We were in complete agreement about that except that I wanted it for ourselves and Aidan wanted to spread peace to all mankind. You've seen how single-minded he is—and dedicated—at least until now . . ."

253

"If I had a brother I should want him to be like Aidan."

"And if you saw your brother in danger of ruining his life, you'd do everything in your power to stop him, wouldn't you?"

"Yes, of course. But it's hard to imagine Aidan doing anything wrong or foolish or likely to ruin his life. He isn't like that." I racked my brain for some clue as to what form his weakness or folly might take. For a man of his age Aidan Penfold had an endearing innocence and unworldliness that made me think of him as vulnerable rather than reckless or wrongheaded. Something of this I ventured to say.

"Vulnerable. Yes, he could be deeply, cruelly hurt."

So far I could only suppose that Aidan might be going to sacrifice the rest of his fortune on some quixotically generous project: endow a hospital for the wounded, finance a vast crusade for world peace—so leaving himself penniless and perhaps endangering his sister's fortune too. But what had that to do with leaving Bidminster?

"You're thinking of what other people could do to him?" I thought of the ingratitude a benefactor might find in those he tried to help or how he might even be tricked and cheated in the process. "Yes, I know—I have found out that lives can be ruined." I turned to face her and caught a look almost of terror in her eyes. "Only—no one could really hurt him. He's so good. He treats people so well and brings out the good in everyone."

"You believe there is good in everyone, Elinor? Has that been your experience?" The urgency in her voice put an end to any attempt to be merely comforting. Nothing but the truth would do. "Is that what Hoodman House has taught you?"

At the very name a sudden anxiety seized me, bringing the recollection of old terrors: of forms half seen, like the shadows of leaves on dark windowpanes; of silences, whispers, sobs of pain; of horror at the top of a narrow flight of stair; unmentionable acts suppressed, to be disinterred only in imagination and so distorted beyond belief. I felt again my own shuddering recoil from wicked-

254

ness suddenly released like forked lightning to flicker through the house and scorch a frenzy of black zigzag lines on white paper.

With relief I breathed the scented air of the garden like healing balm. Then the willow shook out its branches above the clumps of white narcissi growing in its shade. Was that the place, under the willow? The burial place? Had it moldered there, the small body whose soul was so briefly enclosed in the soft flesh? Or was it there in the depths of the old well shaft—or in the lily bed beside the wicket gate? Even the garden had been desecrated. There is no refuge from evil, I thought. It seeps from the past and spreads into every corner of the earth however lovely.

Harriet was speaking.

"If you were Aidan's sister, Elinor, would you want him to marry your Aunt May?"

Lying in anxious thought on my bed and staring at the high blank ceiling, I reproached myself for having left Harriet more abruptly than was kind. Sympathy—comfort—had been needed in huge consoling draughts. I saw myself in retrospect as all agape, flabbergasted, thrown completely off balance and powerless to help. Why had it never occurred to me that May might marry? It was the obvious solution to her most pressing problem—poverty. How could I have been so dense? The answer was equally obvious: because I had been indoctrinated to see her as the personification of chaste undying fidelity to Dick. Hope stirred. Perhaps, being so thoroughly used to it, she would sustain her impersonation of a woman forever faithful to her first love. The faint hope died. She would do as always what suited her best.

My startled "No. No. Never" had probably been more comforting than an hour of soothing talk. It had confirmed Harriet's instinct to hustle Aidan out of harm's way.

"He can't want to marry her," I gasped.

"But he does. He's in love with her—completely, madly. She's taken possession of him. He's never loved like this before."

She had been staring down at the hat inverted in her lap, head bowed, but now she turned to me with desperation in her voice. "Am I wrong in being afraid for him? Is there the least hope that she will make him happy? If there is, I'll withdraw and contradict everything I've said. You must advise me, Elinor."

"It would be a disaster," I said. "We can't let it happen."

"How can it be stopped? I've done all I can in urging him to go away for at least a year until he can be absolutely sure of his feelings. But I do believe it's too late. He'll come back, I'm sure of it. What's more I believe he'll speak to her before we go: tomorrow perhaps. That's why he's so nervous and overwrought. He has no high opinion of himself and he'll be terribly cast down if she refuses. But whether she refuses or accepts, in his present state of mind he'll make a botch of this new assignment. It's such a shame. Oh Elinor, do you think she'll have him?"

"There's no telling what she'll do." Inscrutable, self-possessed, purposeful, what was she planning now? Now that Sintram was dead I knew better than any living person, even Kelda, the depths of her nature—but not the heights. Might not Aidan bring out the best in her as he did in others? Here imagination failed me but a sense of urgency brought me to my feet. Without a notion as to how they could be saved I felt responsible for the Penfolds. There must be some way.

If Harriet felt that I was deserting her, she gave no sign.

"I hope I haven't offended you, Elinor. Miss Findon is your aunt. I had no right to ask you to sit in judgment on a person so close to you. But it has been a help to talk. I feel calmer. You're going? I'll stay a little longer and let Winkblade soothe me for the last time."

Was it likely, I demanded of the unresponsive ceiling, that with Kelda safe at home once more May would be content to go on living at Hoodman House for the rest of her life? Subsisting, not living. Since their debut at the Assembly Rooms my aunts had appeared (yes, that was the word) several times in Bidminster. It was May who had seemed the more suited to company. Feeling no need to put herself out for other people, she could neither be wearied nor made uncomfortable by them and being indifferent to the admiration she aroused, felt no obligation to respond to it. But for even the simplest social activities money is needed—more money than between them my aunts possessed. From sheer necessity if not from self-interest she would marry Aidan.

And then—the new train of thought brought me to a sitting position—Kelda would go back to Julius. By this time my disapproval of Kelda was almost as strong as my disapproval of May; on the other hand, my sympathy for Julius had also grown stronger. He deserved to be happy. It was definitely his turn. Yet it would be a pity if his happiness could be secured only by the sacrifice of poor bewitched Aidan and, for that matter, of his sister. Difficult as it was to imagine Aidan as May's husband, it was harder still to envisage Harriet snugly instated as her sister-in-law. Sadly I removed Aidan from the sacrificial altar and placed poor doomed Julius there instead. He was accustomed to suffering.

It was absurd to think that any decision of mine could affect the outcome but some notion of how May might be influenced was taking shape. There had crept into my mind the memory of something Mirabel had told me: an intriguing scrap of information about Dick. It was Dick who had started the rumor that Julius was well off. "He'd make a rich husband for some poor girl," he had said; and had said it to May. As to why he had seen fit to lie about such a thing, the only reason Mirabel could find was that he had wanted it to be true. (By this time the heroic image of Lancelot in shining armor was so irreversibly tarnished that to add lying to his other shortcomings barely raised a sigh.) But however flimsy his hold on reality, he certainly knew May. Had that particular lie been a desperate—a hopeless—move to tempt her into marrying someone else, so setting him, Dick, free? It hadn't worked, though May had found the information useful. A rich husband for Kelda would solve other problems, besides making it impossible for her ever to marry Dick.

Wealth had not tempted May, as Dick had forlornly hoped, but might not the lack of it deter her? There was no time to be lost if Aidan intended to propose tomorrow. That very evening as we lingered over supper:

"Isn't it a pity," I said, "that the Penfolds will be leaving? I believe it will mean a real sacrifice on Aidan's part."

"In what way?" Kelda asked, her eyes on May.

"Perhaps that isn't the right word." (I was certainly over-using it) "I meant that it is a wrench for him to leave the work he loves and take on a more demanding post. Harriet is afraid he will risk his health."

"Presumably he will be well paid for the risk," May remarked, her eyes on Kelda.

"I don't think so—even if he is appointed as editor of the various publications, and it's not at all certain he will take that on. At first he will only have his expenses and you know how un-worldly he is. Very likely he'll refuse even those and give the rest of his own money to promoting the cause of world peace." I sighed regretfully and placed my saucer on my plate as a prelude to clearing the table. "What's left of his own money, that is"—and into the silence following this remark I casually dropped another. "There can't be much of it left," and reached for the tray. "In the end he may be entirely dependent on his sister," and boldly borrowing a weapon from the enemy arsenal I concluded, "fortu-nately they are all in all to each other—as you two are. Just as close. Nothing will ever part them either. That's rather beautiful, isn't it?"

I could do no more and having stacked the tray withdrew to the kitchen, deeply dissatisfied with my puny effort to rescue Aidan from his folly; knowing too, and knowing that May knew, that however depleted his resources might be they would still far exceed seventy-five pounds a year.

The next afternoon he called; was alone with May for a quarter of an hour in the drawing room; emerged into the hall where I happened to be arranging—and rearranging—a bowl of spring flowers. Kelda came along the passage to wish him good-bye and incidentally to retrieve from under his arm one of the sofa cushions.

"Good gracious! I'm so sorry! I didn't realize . . ."

I reminded him that Clem and I would be at the station on Thursday to see them off. He nodded. The glazed, absent, unseeing look was beyond interpretation. Joy? Distress? Only the enchantment declared itself plainly.

Kelda and I went with him to the car but he had eyes only for May in the window, her hand raised—in promise—or farewell? We joined her to watch his progress down the lane.

"He asked me to marry him," May said.

Kelda's expression, like her sister's, was ambiguous. Did it express hope—or dread? For seconds her fate hung in the balance together with that of Aidan, Harriet, and gentle, lonely Julius.

"And you—accepted?" I was absolutely compelled to ask.

May turned her limpid eyes from the wild cherry blossom overhanging the distant gate. The faintly puckered eyebrows, the almost imperceptible shake of the head conveyed reproach. She laid her left hand on her lap and gazed down at the ruby's undimmed glow.

"How could I accept? It was painful to have to explain to Aidan that my girlish attachment to Dick had led me into an engagement far too soon and that it has held me prisoner all these years. However much to my own disadvantage I still cannot feel free of it. But he understood. We have so much in common, Aidan and I, especially a foolish unworldliness . . ."

"So you sent him away." Kelda's voice was steady, her face impassive, so that again it was impossible to define the words as a question, affirmation, or accusation.

"For the time being," said May whose foolish unworldliness

259

had not apparently blinded her to the advantage of keeping the option open.

Clem and I saw the Penfolds off at Bidminster station. It was not a time for conversation, but Harriet and I did manage a few whispered remarks.

"You know?" And when I nodded, "He will go on hoping. I can only pray that it won't distract him too much from all the work he's undertaken to do."

"Or worry you too much."

"You'll think of me sometimes when you go to Winkblade? My Paradise Lost."

"Of course I will. Always."

"I had so looked forward to settling at last but it wasn't to be. Who knows where we shall finally come to rest."

"You always wanted to go to Timbuktu," I reminded her.

"Winkblade has cured me of that. There are so many things to regret as we get older. Be happy, Elinor, while you're young. I can't tell you how disappointed I am at missing the wedding."

Doors were banging. Clem offered a hand to help her into the compartment.

"I've become a fatalist," she said as she stooped to kiss me good-bye. "It irks me to say so. You know how I've always liked taking charge. I do resent handing things over to the so-called Higher Powers"—the train moved—"but this particular crisis is beyond me. Fate must do its best."

"Let's hope the poor old chap will come to his senses and see May as she really is," Clem said as we left the station. "After all, Dick did."

"Only when it was too late."

"Oh, he'd have got out of it somehow, eventually. Dick always did."

Certainly in Dick's case fate had intervened and in the shape of a world war. One could only hope that in Aidan's the intervention would be of a less disastrous kind.

23

THE DEPARTURE OF the Penfolds left a gap in our lives soon to be filled by Uncle Vernon: filled to overflowing. As Clem said, we weren't prepared for Uncle Vernon, rightly implying that we should have looked to our defenses and braced ourselves against a siege. Not only did he take possession of our immediate circle: in the manner of a successfully invading army he occupied the entire town. He had left it as a youth in 1889 to seek his fortune and had only once come home on a short visit twenty years ago, so that there had been time for even those who knew him best to forget him a little and to be found defenseless against his impact. The warm sunny June that was to have been devoted to wedding preparations was dominated instead by Uncle Vernon. Every sentimental memory has to jostle for position or be ruthlessly thrust aside by rival memories of his thrusting, self-assertive, domineering personality, his loud rasping voice.

The statutory fairy godparent at a wedding is supposed to appear at the last minute in a clap of thunder and a puff of smoke. Characteristically Uncle Vernon arrived a week earlier than expected, preceded by a shower of telegrams, and went straight to his sister's, though mercifully not to stay there. Instead, the management of the Royal County Hotel, where he had reserved the judges' suite for a month, was thrown into disarray and had to take on extra staff. Every morning for the whole of his visit a small hopeful queue of the unemployed was to be seen at its kitchen entrance.

Knowing nothing of the telegrams, I came on him unexpectedly in the sitting room in Battle Street. He had only just arrived and was alone with Mrs. Tass. He sat in the middle of the sofa, occupying all of it, though he was not a big man—of middle height, thick-shouldered, short-necked, with a square chin jutting forward like a cliff above the collar of his shirt and loosely knotted red silk tie. He was then in his fifties, with a thick thatch of graying hair, a tough tawny skin, and small sharp blue eyes. He rose as I came in, and Mrs. Tass took the opportunity of closing the window, his voice being clearly audible on the pavement outside.

"Ah, here comes the young lady," he boomed, completely drowning her introduction. "So this is Mirabel."

His handshake was cordial but hard; the small blue eyes were kind; but their sharpness was misleading. Where people were concerned there was a good deal he failed to see and, being slightly deaf, failed to hear. He saw his fellow creatures only in a sweeping generalized way so that despite Mrs. Tass's, "No, no, dear, this is Clem's Elinor," he was several times to address me as Mirabel and his niece as Elinor before falling back on the safely nameless "Young lady."

Mrs. Tass already looked tired and was content to leave the brunt of the conversation to me until Mirabel came back from the Edstones.

"Ha! So this is the young lady," Uncle Vernon said, clasping her hand.

"Your niece. Belle's daughter. Mirabel." Mrs. Tass sought to make it clear.

It was an important moment for Mirabel, the first step toward her long-anticipated emergence into a new life, a new home, a new country. She was unusually quiet—with Uncle Vernon everyone

262

was unusually quiet—and a little disappointed perhaps at his repetition of "Belle's daughter," as if trying to place her clearly in his mind. But the awkwardness passed; he talked about Belle—loudly and at length, absorbed in childhood recollections and heedless of his sister's occasional gentle corrections: "No, no, Vernon. It wasn't like that. That was before Father died, and don't you remember, he had the dog shot . . ." and at last Mr. Tass and Clem came home to take on what already seemed the burden of their visitor.

But he had enjoyed himself. When Mrs. Tass pointed out that if he was to dine at the hotel it was time to leave, he looked startled, consulted a gold half hunter and bade us all put on our things and come with him.

"No, no, Vernon dear. Another time would be delightful, but this is your first day. You must be tired."

"Tired?" he roared in disbelief, and indeed I never saw a human being less subject to tiredness; his energy and strength were inexhaustible; and he genuinely wanted our company. That—as he reminded us at the top of his voice—was what he had come for.

And that we all found endearing, the only endearing thing about him. For that, all was forgiven. His disregard of other people's tastes and wishes, his pigheaded insistence on his own way, and his boring conversation were redeemed by his love of company and boyish zest for outings of almost any kind—luncheon, tea and dinner parties, excursions to old haunts by limousine, charabanc, open carriage or—on one occasion—hay wagon.

"We must all go," he would say, having planned some new scheme, "and bring your friends."

It has remained a family saying and never fails to conjure up a vision of Uncle Vernon, gold watch in hand, Panama hat pulled low on his brow, marshaling us in and out of car, boat, or train; or barking at waiters, porters, conductors, guards, as he pulled out a wallet stuffed with banknotes and amply replenished each day.

"Vernon was always a leader." Mrs. Tass sighed.

She was looking thinner. It was my turn now—too often—to dab her temples with eau de Cologne.

"Don't forget he employs hundreds of natives," Mirabel said, "and goodness knows how many engineers and clerks. He's got used to bossing people about." As his future housekeeper she felt obliged to make excuses for Uncle Vernon.

"No need to remind us," Clem said. "There isn't much we don't know about the Bluetzberg Mine."

In little over a week there had been ample opportunity to become familiar with its location, history, engineering techniques, workforce, transport, output, and reputation as well as with the daily fluctuations in value of shares in De Beer's Consolidated. To be fair, Uncle Vernon showed the same tireless interest in Bidminster as he expected us to show in the Bluetzberg; but he could do nothing alone. Whether visiting old friends, his old school, the office he had left thirty-three years ago when he went off to seek and find his fortune, the field where he had played cricket, a back street where a man he knew had kept racing pigeons—a small party must go with him like an entourage attendant on royalty. As individuals we didn't interest him; our remarks were drowned out by his own, our inclinations ignored.

"Where is everybody?" was always his first utterance, and "Where are you off to now?" if someone showed signs of escaping.

He talked a good deal about Stokeland Abbey, a country house he had admired as a boy.

"We'll spend a day there," he threatened, "and see how a gentleman ought to live. What would it cost, Clem, to buy a place like that?"

Clem looked alarmed and answered vaguely.

"Don't forget, Vernon," his sister reminded him one morning as I tried to sneak away to do some shopping, "that Elinor is going to be married in less than a month. She has a thousand things to do. And Mirabel . . ."

She and I exchanged glances, uneasily. Mirabel too, poised

on the brink of her great adventure, had a thousand things to do, or should have had; but so far not a word had been said about her future as Uncle Vernon's housekeeper, though words had been said on every other subject under the sun. Mirabel had become strangely subdued. It would have been more like her to open up the subject in her usual forthright sensible way; not that it should be necessary to remind a man of anything so momentous as a promise to take his niece into his home and become as a father to her. Could he conceivably have forgotten?

"He can't have," I told Clem in one of our too few private conversations. "It's not the sort of thing one could forget. The longer things go on in this uncertain way the more difficult it will be for her to ask him. I daren't even mention it to her but surely someone will have to speak to him about it."

"Father won't do it. He doesn't want Mirabel to leave. Mother won't dare. Don't look at me. My spirit is crushed. I have a theory that he remembers but hasn't got it clear which young lady he's supposed to take and can't stop talking long enough to find out. Why don't *you* ask him his intentions toward Mirabel? At least he'll know then that it's the other young lady he's saddled with."

"It puzzles me that he's so vague about other people because at heart he is very much a family man. He told me so. In any case it's obvious. He loves to be the center of a group . . ."

"I had noticed."

". . . and really cares about the old days in Bidminster."

"Could he have taken a dislike to Mirabel?"

"How could he? He doesn't notice people sufficiently to take a dislike to them, and since he came Mirabel has been much less noticeable than usual."

It was unlike her to slip in and out of rooms without drawing attention to herself by some practical remark or firmly stated opinion; or for that matter to slip out of the house whenever she had the chance. What was she doing? Our dresses for the wedding were almost finished: there need be no more fittings; she hadn't mentioned her packing or talked of shopping with South Africa in mind. Yet if she had been accumulating clothes over a long period, she hadn't told me.

"She goes to the Edstones quite often," I said. "Mrs. Edstone is tremendously grateful. She dreads Mirabel's going away."

Clem and I had also visited Paul Edstone several times and meant to look after him when Mirabel left. His condition was slowly improving. The spasmodic twitching and shaking were purely physical symptoms: Paul's mind was unimpaired; but his helplessness embarrassed and distressed him. Nevertheless he hadn't escaped Uncle Vernon, who had insisted on taking him with us to Stokeland Abbey and had hired a charabanc so that Paul could have a whole long seat to himself. The outing had been a success.

"He is kind, Clem, you must admit."

"Oh yes. Kind, deafening, and inescapable. There are times when I wonder if it's Uncle Vernon I'm going to marry. Frankly it will be a disappointment to find him waiting at the altar instead of you."

"He told me that he envies us. I believe he's lonely."

Conversation with Uncle Vernon was scarcely worthy of the name, since it consisted of scrappy comments and interjections hurled into the mere seconds dividing one of his speeches from the next: but when one succeeded in talking to him on anything like equal terms, sooner or later he would refer to the importance of family connections.

"Worldly success has come to me," I remember him saying, "but what use is it to a man if he has no family connections to share it with?" and though the words were boomed forth as if the Tasses' sitting room were the limitless veldt, they conveyed genuine feeling, and I felt sorry for him. "That's why," he bellowed, "I'm enjoying this trip so much. It's doing me good to be among my own kith and kin."

It was surely time to remind him that he would be taking one of these priceless assets home with him, but by this time the subject had become so delicate that no one dared to breathe a word of it. Mirabel herself was, as so often at that time, absent.

"We're very glad to be of use, sir," Clem said. "And you have another relative whom you still haven't met."

"Who's that then? Why aren't they here? He—or she?"

"He," Clem said, "and I think you'd like him."

"Then bring him along. Bring him to lunch at my hotel tomorrow."

"I'm not sure about lunch, but Elinor and I could bring him to meet you in your sitting room tomorrow morning. Shall we say at eleven?"

Making the acquaintance of their illegitimate grandson had been a deeply moving experience for Dick's parents. They had lost no time in visiting Thyrza at the Tile Sheds and offering the support and comfort they would have given to Dick's widow. On their advice she had changed her name to Tass by deed poll, for Arthur's sake. But she was both too proud and too sensible to take advantage of all the help they offered.

"It wouldn't do," she confided to me. "I'm not their sort, but I must say it's a relief to know there's somebody to help with Arthur and take care of him if anything happens to me. Mr. Tass has offered to pay for his education. The money Dick left wouldn't run to that. They want me to take him on regular visits and when he's older he can go on his own. It isn't me they want."

She underestimated their regard for her. They appreciated the tact with which she left Arthur alone with them, occupied herself in town, and collected him when it was time to catch the early evening Valley Queen back to Saury. She never wore out her welcome by overstaying, never called except at the appointed times. As she herself had said, Thyrza could learn. She had taken to reading, was careful in her speech, and had quite lost her bold manner.

"Dick could have done worse," Clem said. "He should have married her."

I agreed that of the three rivals for his love Thyrza was the worthiest by far, but refrained from adding that in my opinion she would have been too good for him.

On the morning after Clem's promise to Uncle Vernon I waited with Arthur in the foyer of the hotel while Clem went upstairs for a preliminary word with him. Arthur, in fine feather after his ride from the Tile Sheds in his uncle's motor car, wore a sailor suit with a broad collar and spotless white bands and cord. He had had his hair cut and sat smartly erect on the oak settle in perfect confidence as to his appearance.

"What is the gentleman's name?"

"You can call him Uncle Vernon. We all do. He was your father's uncle and that means he's really your great-uncle."

"Then I'll call him Great-uncle Vernon, shall I? It isn't rude, is it? Mother said . . ."

"No, of course it isn't rude. Just rather a lot to say every time."

"When you marry Uncle Clem, will you be my aunt?"

"Yes," I cried, suddenly delighted. "I'll be your Aunt Elinor."

We beamed at each other. Clem beckoned from the turn in the stairs. Arthur adjusted his garters, polished the toe of his right boot on the back of his left black-ribbed stocking, and that of the left on his right stocking—and thus prepared, blithely mounted the stairs.

Inevitably those two strong characters took to each other, each too confident to waste a moment on self-doubt. Arthur was so conspicuously a family connection of whom any man could be proud and so blatantly proud in his turn of a great-uncle with hundreds of black men at his command and an inexhaustible supply of diamonds that they positively basked in each other's goodwill.

"When you're older you can come and see me in South

Africa." Was that what he had said—or written—to Mirabel long ago? And had he forgotten?

"How much older?" Arthur asked.

"About ten years. What about some ice cream at Pirelli's?"

"We must all go," Clem said, "and take our friends."

There being none of these available we remained a quartet. Uncle Vernon had to content himself with bestowing a double cornet on a shoeless urchin squatting on the pavement.

There were other times when from the sharp little blue eyes another and more likeable Uncle Vernon peeped out; as when Mrs. Tass, who couldn't bring herself to broach the awkward topic of their niece's future, boldly reminded him that a whirl of social activities was not quite the thing for a bride in the last weeks before her wedding.

"Elinor has a good many things to think about and mustn't be over-tired."

"Elinor!" Pleased for once to be able to identify me as not being Mirabel, he looked me up and down. "Our bride-to-be—and a very pretty bride she'll be. I like good looks in a woman. You and Belle were good-looking girls, Janet . . ."

"And Mirabel is very like her mother," Mrs. Tass managed to interject, but Uncle Vernon had swept on. "But nearly all the women here seem poorly and pale. Not enough good food. They tell me the bread wasn't fit to eat during the war. But that's over now. What about a good dinner at my hotel this evening? Prime beef and a good red wine. You must all come."

I thanked him but declined on the grounds that I really must go home for a few days.

"Go home?" Uncle Vernon rasped, as if wondering for the first time where I lived.

"Elinor has scarcely seen her aunts for the past ten days."

"Her aunts? How many aunts has she got?" He thought of them, I swear, as fish who had evaded his net—so far. "Where do they live? They can join us for dinner. I'll send a car for them. Saury, you say. Isn't that where old Findon lived?"

"Elinor is his granddaughter, Vernon. You hadn't forgotten? And her aunts still live there. You remember the two little Findon girls, Vincent's half-sisters?"

"Why haven't I met them? Vincent went into the army, didn't he?" For once he had got it right but not for long. "So you're his granddaughter, young lady."

"Daughter," I said.

"And you'll be marrying my nephew. So these aunts of yours . . ."

He had established a connection, a family connection. There would be no escape for my aunts.

It was at this awkward time, three weeks before the wedding, that Kelda took to her bed. When she failed to appear at breakfast time I went up to her room and found her barely able to lift her head from the pillow.

"Keep away from me," she said. "If it's anything infectious you must go to the Tasses. I'd never forgive myself if your wedding had to be postponed. In fact I think you ought to go in any case and let May look after me."

For the past few weeks, indeed for months, I had paid little attention to Kelda and was shocked to see how wretchedly thin and pale she was, quite lost in the folds of her white nightdress, eyes dull, hair lank, her expression heavy and apathetic. I went to the village for the doctor who came at once and prescribed a week in bed and complete freedom from any mental stress.

"Mrs. Cade is suffering from exhaustion. These trembling fits she complains of—and the general debility—does she eat enough? She looks half starved. Has she been overworking—or worrying at all? She needs rest and light nourishing food: milk, eggs, lean meat, and a glass of claret with her midday meal. Get in touch with me

270

if there's no improvement. Otherwise I'll call today week. Remember, Miss Findon, no worry or excitement of any kind."

Seven years of suffering had taken their toll. It seems likely that Kelda never fully recovered from the physical and mental ordeal of her nightmarish confinement with its tragic aftermath, followed by an unwilling marriage, the twofold guilt of leaving Julius and causing May (as she had rightly suspected) to commit a horrible crime. Years of emotional servitude to May, the sheer toil of managing a big house on her own, her anxiety about money . . . to this burden of woes my marriage could be the last straw. I was deserting her.

When the doctor had gone she lay back on her pillow weeping the weak tears of utter defeat, gradually drifted into sleep and woke to weep again. I pitied her deeply, even while fuming over her weakness and folly. There had been no need to leave Julius a second time and she should certainly have gone back to him once the uncertainty of her baby's fate had been (with a significant rearrangement of the facts) cleared up. She owed May nothing— not another hour of her life.

Nevertheless she needed looking after. There were meals to prepare. My enemy the kitchen range must be faced. There were sticks to chop and coal scuttles to fill. Passing the hall mirror on my way upstairs for the twentieth time, I caught sight of my face, as pale and almost as weary as Kelda's, and I too wept.

"You're wearing yourself out," May said, coming out of the drawing room. "There's no need. All Kelda needs is rest. Let me look after her."

Considering the way in which she had looked after Kelda in the attic room, I had no faith in May's prowess as a nurse; but I was wrong. With her usual economy of movement and absence of emotional involvement she did all that was necessary and nothing more. I watched her pour milk from jug to saucepan, then unscrew the tight lid of a honey jar with unexpected ease. There was strength in those long tapering fingers, I reminded myself with a shudder, and May could always do what the occasion demanded.

Clem came that evening and rapidly taking in the situation, ordered me to pack my things and be ready to go back to Bidminster.

"Pack everything. I'll come for you tomorrow. No arguments. We'll get someone from the village to come and look after the house. Can you think of anyone?"

How simple it all was after all! I thought at once of Mrs. Torgill's Susan. Clem drove down to the village and was back in half an hour, having engaged her to come as a daily help for the next three weeks.

"That will see them over the wedding. After that they can . . . make their own arrangements. Thank God we persuaded you to be married from our house. From tomorrow you'll have nothing to do, my darling, but let me look after you—for the rest of our lives."

May was told of the new arrangement.

"There'll be no extra expense for you," Clem said. "Elinor and I will take care of that."

"You're very good to us." In May's sad little smile gratitude was mingled with and almost overshadowed by regret. "We have managed so long without help, Kelda and I."

Clem left early. I went straight to bed, slept a long dreamless sleep, woke with a start to find that it was nine o'clock and rushed to Kelda's room. A breakfast tray with a half-empty cup and some curling slices of bread and butter stood on her side table. Kelda was asleep. May drank a cup of tea with me in the morning room while I had breakfast. Susan had already taken charge in the kitchen. Liberated from the tyranny of the range, I planned my day and presently went upstairs to pack.

My stay at Hoodman House had come to an end. It had lasted just over a year. There was neither time nor room in my heart for any other emotion than gratitude that I need not spend another hour in the house I still partly owned. From the beginning when

I had leaned forward to catch a first glimpse of it from Willie Kimble's taxi, its chilling influence had drifted across the fields like a warning that the house itself would never welcome me; and such human welcome as I had found had come, not from natural kindness or family affection, but from calculation. Not that the cold logic of making ends meet was by any means the worst aspect of human behavior I had encountered during the past thirteen months.

I repacked the dresses, skirts, and blouses, unsuitable and little worn, that Mrs. Burnett and I had chosen for my debut in Bidminster, working swiftly and systematically, resolved to leave nothing behind, not a glove nor a handkerchief nor even a hairpin. I had to remind myself as I closed the trunk lid and fastened the clasps with a prayer of gratitude for my own happy escape that other people's problems were far from being solved.

How would my aunts live? What was to be done about the house? What of Julius—and what of Aidan, lost in hopeless longing for May? And if it should prove not to be hopeless and he married her, how much worse that would be! And what of Harriet's pining for Winkblade? And what of Winkblade itself, ravaged, deserted, doomed to stand empty until it fell at last into ruin?

Bending over my half-filled valise, I heard a knock at the front door, and forgetting Susan, ran down to answer it. A chauffeur in uniform had set down on the step a hamper, a crate of wine bottles, and a basket of fruit—and was standing aside to make way for Uncle Vernon. In his cream linen jacket, red tie and Panama, he advanced heavily up the path, hat-brim and chin jutting forward in a two-pronged attack. In one hand he held an immense sheaf of roses, in the other a cigar.

"Ah, there you are, young lady," he said, his brazen voice subdued to a decent concern. "Clem tells me you have illness in the house. How is the old lady?"—and when I failed momentarily to identify the old lady, he added—"your aunt, isn't it?"

"How kind! How very kind! All these things! Do come in."

He was already in the hall. Already its dim recesses vibrated to the grating timbre of his voice, the air swooned in the aroma of his cigar. He threw it away into the garden just in time, as if in preparation even before he saw her.

May had seen him from the drawing room window and had silently appeared, framed in the doorway. She wore the old blue summer dress with the deep bertha collar and stood half turned so that light from the room behind fell on her hair. Viewed from the twilight of the hall she seemed to have emanated there, insubstantial as a vision. She had never looked lovelier.

"It's Vernon, isn't it? Janet's brother." Her sweetness of manner held an unusual warmth. "You'll have forgotten me but I haven't forgotten you. Our families have always been friends. Such very old friends. I'm May." She took a step forward and as a white-crested wave advances caressingly upon a granite rock, held out her hand. "You haven't changed. I'm so very glad to see you after all these years."

With fateful accuracy the right chord had been touched. His small blue eyes glinted with tears. He took her slender white fingers in his hard brown generous hand. He was speechless. And so was I, as it dawned on me with the miraculous promise of approaching sunrise that in this meeting—heaven sent—might lie the solution to all our problems.

24

UNCLE VERNON AND Aunt May announced their engagement a week later: a seven days' wonder—an error of taste according to Aunt Claudia, who arrived in time to share in the general astonishment.

"They should have waited. At her age, not to mention his, a few more days would not have made any difference. This was to have been your special time. All the congratulations and good wishes should be for you and Clem. Personally I shan't say a word to them until you have left on your honeymoon."

If the more dramatic event threatened to reduce our wedding to an anticlimax, Clem and I were the last to complain.

"God bless Uncle Vernon!" was Clem's comment. "He's taken those two off your hands at one fell swoop. You won't have to worry about them anymore."

A very short inward debate convinced me that there was no need to worry about Uncle Vernon either. He was too complacent, too unobservant to see more than the outward luster of the latest gem he had acquired, and with that luster no fault could be found. Having no dreams that wealth could not fulfill, he was immune from any rude awakening: too thick-skinned to be hurt; too earthbound ever to be disillusioned; too rich, far too rich to be treated with anything but respect by a wife as clever as May. All the same I developed a reluctant sympathy for him as for one scarcely bad enough to deserve his fate. And as one problem after another melted away, I liked him more than had once seemed possible, especially as for the next fortnight he was less in evidence. He made at least one trip to London and presumably spent the rest of his time with his fiancée. When he did appear in Battle Street it was less forcefully; he was occasionally silent for minutes at a time, not so much tamed as dazzled by a bright light. The relief was temporary but it gave us time to recover.

Recovery was most strikingly manifest in Kelda, who had ceased to weep and had risen from her bed within a few days of Uncle Vernon's first call.

"Good food," he told me. "That was all she needed—and red wine. There's iron in claret, you know. I've sent another couple of cases."

"I'm sure it helped."

He rambled off to his hotel absentmindedly, his powerful energy for the time being directed elsewhere.

"He's not a bad old stick," Mirabel said as we went upstairs one morning to try on our wedding dresses. "But I couldn't, you know." She sat down on the dressing-table stool and stretched her arms above her head like a schoolgirl on holiday. Her eyes shone. She was radiant with relief. "Couldn't have gone."

"I felt that from the first—that you didn't take to him."

"Take to him! As a matter of fact to be honest it wasn't just his awfulness and the fact that he would be impossible to live with. No, I knew even before he came that I didn't want to go to South Africa. It was something to think about when there was nothing else to look forward to—that's all. It never seemed real. In fact I don't know where I got hold of the idea in the first place. I thought he said something to mother when she was ill about promising to look after me, or perhaps he wrote it. If he did, I can't find the letter."

"He hasn't mentioned it?"

"No. I've been holding my breath for fear that he would suddenly produce a ticket and say 'Be ready in two days' time.' It would be just like him. But now—now I'm safe, thanks to May. Gosh, she's welcome to him—and won't she make a stir in Kimberley, swanning round in all those diamonds. Not to mention Stokeland Abbey. You didn't know? He's probably going to buy it. A foothold in the old country, he calls it. I expect they'll stay there from time to time. Money!"

We stared at each other in dismay.

"So we won't really be . . . ?"

"Getting rid of them? No such luck. I wonder how the marriage will turn out. A bit of a risk, I should say. You know, there's a streak of cruelty there, real cruelty."

I had underestimated Mirabel: she knew nothing of the crime in the bakehouse and couldn't know what May was capable of— she must have felt it intuitively. But I was on the wrong tack, judging by her next remark.

"Oh yes, she'll have to watch out. It won't be all beer and skittles. Perhaps it'll do her good. She's had her own way all her life but believe me, she's met her match this time in more ways than one. I've been talking to Aunt Janet about Uncle Vernon's first wife, Dilys. She died young. They were married for just over a year. You know Aunt Janet: she never says a wrong word about anyone, although she did admit that Uncle Vernon hasn't improved. That's as far as she would go; but I did worm out of her that she and mother had been worried about Dilys when he brought her to England that one time he came home."

Whatever Dilys had been like before her marriage she had seemed to her sisters-in-law less like a happy wife than a frightened white mouse: frail, scared-looking . . .

"And they weren't really surprised that she didn't last long. She simply wasn't up to it."

277

Mirabel's terse manner of alluding to the challenge of being married to Uncle Vernon was all too effective. Poor Dilys!

"If she was a sensitive person his sheer awfulness as you call it might have broken her heart," I suggested, but Dilys, white as a mouse when last seen, had long since faded out of the picture and was in any case a side issue. "You said cruelty. It couldn't have been as bad as that."

"You weren't there that time he talked about the natives. It made me sick—well, all of us. 'Flog them,' he said. 'That's the only way to treat the scum. Treat them well and you lose their respect. They get above themselves. Yes' "—Mirabel achieved a passable imitation of Uncle Vernon's intimidating boom—" 'I've taken the whip to one of the lazy devils myself, many a time.' He enjoyed doing it, Elinor, enjoyed remembering it. He's no better than that slave driver in *Uncle Tom's Cabin*. 'Give them a kick in the right place,' he said, 'and there's no more trouble.' "

Horrible as this descent into barbarism might be, it presumably affected only the wretched natives. He was unlikely to inflict physical violence on Aunt May. I said so.

"You're probably right. But a person who can be cruel in one way will be cruel in another. Women should be careful whom they marry. She'd better watch out."

"She's good at that," I said but with a momentary loss of confidence in May's ability to hold her own, a suspicion that her barbed but delicate weapons would glance off Uncle Vernon's thick skin. He wouldn't even notice them. With the sensation, odd in the circumstances, of clutching at straws, I reminded Mirabel that he had in his way been kind to us all. We had neither of us hesitated to accept his gift of a diamond bracelet.

"He's thrown his money about and enjoyed finding ways of spending it," she conceded, and added in defiance of accepted wisdom, "diamonds aren't everything."

I helped her into her dress: pale pink voile over satin of a deeper pink.

278

"You look lovely, like a June rose."

She was slimmer than she had been when I first knew her and there was some other more subtle difference. She was smiling now in unashamed pleasure at her reflection in the long glass.

"I was thinking," she said, "Paul won't be at the wedding. It's such a shame that he misses out on everything. But of course I could go there afterward, couldn't I, just to show them my dress and flowers?"

"But why shouldn't he be at the wedding? Perhaps he would be uncomfortable in church but he must come to the reception. We were counting on it. It will be quite informal with everything in the garden (if only it's fine!) and he needn't feel conspicuous."

"Do you think so, really, Elinor? He is getting better, you know. It's going to take time, but he talks to me quite freely now and the doctor thinks it a good sign that he can speak about his experience in the trenches and all the horrible things that happened there."

"And that's another reason why you want to stay in Bidminster, isn't it? Paul needs you."

"Well . . ."

"We must have him at the wedding. Leave it to Uncle Vernon. He'll arrange everything." I slipped into my white satin underdress.

"Mm." Mirabel fell back a few paces to admire when the overdress of deeply scalloped lace was in place. "Three cheers for Miss Byrd, I must say. But the effect does rather depend on the girl inside too. No, not the veil. Not while you have the dress on. That's unlucky."

"Nothing can go wrong now." It was tempting fate to say so, but in marrying Uncle Vernon May would secure my future as well as her own. She no longer needed to lure me to my death. I could dismiss and even smile at so improbable a scenario. Here in Mrs. Tass's guest room where sunshine sparkled on silver-topped toilet bottles and the crystal vase of Dorothy Perkins roses, in this

279

safe bower of satin, tulle, and lace there could be no doubt that everything had turned out right in the end. I pushed open the window and leaned out.

"Orange blossom!" Mirabel sniffed appreciatively. "Just in time for the wedding."

The bush, sheltered by the north wall, was in full bloom, its long branches laden with waxlike flowers, their scent hauntingly sweet. At Winkblade too the syringa would be in bloom, drawing its fragrance from soil where lay the moldering remains of a murdered baby. There could be no happy ending to such a story, no end to any story, and what seemed the beginning was merely the point at which one stumbled into a series of events already shaped by what had gone before. Wherever people lived they left some residue of suffering. Not a moment passed unthreatened by distress. Panic seized me.

"Do you ever feel . . . ? I mean, suppose something does go wrong."

"Somebody's walking over your grave," Mirabel said. "What about a nice cup of coffee?"

We eased the dresses into their cotton covers and hung them in the wardrobe, laid the veil reverently in its box, and went downstairs.

25

"My dear Elinor," wrote Harriet, "How can I thank you for writing so promptly to tell me the unexpected news? I am still breathless with relief. It seemed best to tell Aidan at once, though it took courage, I can tell you. After the first shock of disappointment he has seemed calmer, has slept better, and is altogether more like his old self. The episode has been out of character. I am deeply thankful it's over—and it may not be long before he sees it in the same light. Already he has confessed to it as 'a last act of madness' before settling into middle age. I could never have hoped for so blessed a solution as her marrying somebody else. In other circumstances Aidan would have remained dangling on a thread of hope. As it is he will cherish her memory as a dream of all that is beautiful and good whereas no mortal woman even of the most blameless kind could sustain such a role in the reality of marriage. I take back all I said about the Higher Powers. They know what they are doing, wouldn't you say?

"We must go to Geneva as planned but I can now think of Winkblade again as our permanent home. Its nearness to Hoodman House is no longer a problem. *And* I shall be at your wedding on Wednesday, my dear. Aidan of course will not be there. I have booked a room at the Royal County and will take the opportunity of getting to know Clem's amazing uncle . . ."

By the time I had read the letter to Clem at the top of my voice above the noise of the engine as we drove to Saury, she would already be in Bidminster.

"A brand snatched from the burning," Clem said. "Aidan's a lucky fellow. He might have owned a diamond mine and then there'd have been no saving him." At Winkblade he pulled up. "Do you mind if I mooch about here for a bit while you talk to the aunts?"

It was to Aunt May that I would be talking. She had particularly wanted to see me alone and this was the last opportunity, late afternoon of the day before the wedding. I hadn't wanted to come but an unusual sound as I went up the path changed my mood. The front door stood open. The sound came from somewhere in the depths of the house. As delightful as it was unexpected, Kelda was singing, her voice a mezzosoprano true and sweet. I found her in the morning room retrimming a hat for the next day.

"Elinor! Oh Elinor!"

"Something has happened to you. You look—transfigured."

"Yes, everything has changed." She was tremulous with happiness. The table was littered with ribbons and wire and sheets of music. "I've been looking over some of his songs, Julius's, it's been so long. But you don't know—I haven't seen you to tell you. I came to a decision. Or rather it came to me in the most wonderful way. It must have been taking shape in my mind for a long time without my knowing it but then—it was while I was in bed, on the third day . . . I'd been sleeping a good deal. It was afternoon when I woke. The curtains weren't quite drawn and the sun was on my window. It shone directly on my face. I heard a voice, heard it distinctly in the room and yet it was inside my head. Oh Elinor, it was Julius speaking to me in the depths of my doubt and misery. 'Trust me, Kelda,' he said. The words went to my very heart. I knew at once what I must do . . ."

"Go back to him."

"Yes, yes, but first I must tell him everything, every single thing that happened. About Dick, about the baby . . . I couldn't wait. I got up and wrote to him, wrote it all down; and when I saw the whole sad chapter of my life in words on the paper in front of me, it seemed to have passed away from me. A marvelous feeling of peace came over me. I just added, 'Forgive me, Julius, my dear good husband'—and lay down again and slept."

"He has had the letter?"

"And replied." From under the ribbons and wire she pulled out a sheet of notepaper. "I'm the most blessed among women, Elinor. He writes with such love and understanding. He says if only he had known, how much he could have helped me. It's far more than I deserve to have found such a husband in spite of my wickedness and stupidity. Thank God I've come to my senses and realized his true worth: I'm going to spend the rest of my life making it up to him."

"This happened before May told you that she and Uncle Vernon were engaged."

"Oh yes. I'd made up my mind that I must go. Then when she told me, it seemed to set the stamp of approval on my decision. She will be safe and happy and well looked after. You know how frail she is, how much she needs to be looked after."

"You have always looked after her." It was the nearest I could get to agreeing. As I spoke May called from upstairs.

"Is that you, Elinor? Come up, dear, will you?"

"I'll be back in a minute. Do you know what she wants me for?"

Kelda shook her head, smiled, and twisted wire, humming.

With a touch of formality May indicated the window where a second chair had been placed opposite hers. The movement of her hand was of a regal kind. A long string of pearls encircled her throat and hung in a lustrous loop over the heavy silk of her white blouse.

"I wanted to have a few minutes alone, Elinor darling. We have been so close"—her smile was tenderly reminiscent of our past closeness—"and there won't be time tomorrow for all I want to say. It may be that we shall see very little of each other after that. By the time you come back from your honeymoon Vernon and I will have left. We shall stay in London for a while and be quietly married there."

She was looking at me thoughtfully, as if measuring my strength against hers, and as the object of the interview did not immediately transpire, I asked her what she would be wearing the next day. She opened the wardrobe and displayed a dress of pale aquamarine moiré. Involuntarily I thought of my first visit on the occasion of Kelda's wedding—and of May in misty blue and a wide gauzy hat, behaving perfectly. Our association had begun and would end with a wedding. Of the first the least said the better. The outcome had been unhappy and there had been the unpleasantness in the conservatory, which I had unwillingly over-heard. They had seemed as potent as spells, those phrases about telling . . . or not telling.

I don't know why—perhaps from wondering what May was up to this time—but the two threads of thought became entwined in the realization that it was I who now held it in my power to tell a damaging secret: a secret far worse than anything Kelda had to conceal. It was now May whose fortunes could be wrecked by a word or two from me. From the truth about May even Uncle Vernon would recoil. It was over May's head that the sword now hung. It dawned on me that if I had until now forgotten and so far failed to wield the sword, May had not forgotten, and I guessed that henceforth my goodwill would be a precious commodity she would be at pains to keep. Sure enough . . .

"I've been wanting to tell you how grateful I am for all you have done for us. You have worked for us, nursed us when we were ill, helped us with money, and not least"—her small deprecatory gesture was an appeal for tolerance—"you have put up with our peculiar ways and forgiven us our—various lapses. Loyalty! That is the keynote of your character, dear. Your father, our beloved brother, would be proud of you if only he could know what your loyalty and discretion have meant to us, what a tower of strength you have been. And will always be."

Realizing the significance of the last four words with their slightly interrogative inflection, I said nothing. It was unnecessary to point out that since towers do sometimes under certain pressure collapse, even loyalty and discretion as phenomenal as mine could not be absolutely relied on.

"That's why I want to give you a very special gift." She reached for a walnut box placed in readiness on the windowsill.

"But you've already . . ."

"Yes, I know. But your wedding present (my grandmother's silver tea service, mine by rights in any case) was from both Kelda and me. This is from me, from my heart, as a kind of pledge. Yes, that is the word. It has been a pledge, a sacred symbol and will keep its mystical power to bind me to someone I love; this time to you, my dear little sister."

Surely she couldn't intend . . . I felt a growing conviction that she did intend . . . My worst fears were confirmed as from the walnut box she took a small jewel case and opened it.

"The most precious thing I can give you as a memento."

And there it was glowering up at me from the black velvet with all the disturbing associations of the past year in its blood-red depths.

"For you, dear." She held it out.

"But you can't give that away," I protested, eyeing it nervously.

"Only to you."

We could neither of us resist a glance at its successor; it obliterated the third finger of her left hand as far as the first knuckle: Uncle Vernon's diamond, of the first water, brilliant cut, colorless, clear, pellucid, without depth and of such hardness that nothing could mar its surface. I thought it suitable. In contrast Clem's modest little ring on my own finger faded almost out of sight.

"I don't think you should part with this when it has meant so much to you. Suppose . . . suppose Dick did come back one day. You've always believed that he might." A fortnight ago it had been her reason for refusing Aidan, I recalled.

She shook her fair head.

"It was a wish, a dream. It helped me through a dark time, a valley of shadows. But that is over now. Reality has taken its place." Unconsciously, I daresay, she touched the pearl necklace with her diamond-laden hand. "You won't refuse to take it, Elinor, knowing what it means."

"A pledge means a promise," I said. "Are you asking me to make a promise?"

"I don't need to," she said. Was there a hint of desperation in the soft voice, a sharply watchful glint in the soulful eyes?

Somehow the little box got itself into my hand. We exchanged affectionately worded good wishes for each other's happiness, I made my escape and forgetting my promise to go back to Kelda, slipped out through the front door. Before disappearing into the shade of Packhorse Way I looked up at May's window and saw her there for almost the last time, slim and white and enigmatic as she had been when I first came.

Halfway up the lane I turned aside into open pasture and wound my way between gorse bushes until the daisies and buttercups gave way to coarse damp grass, my feet squelched in mud, and I stood among tall reeds at the edge of Lott's Pool. I knew what I was going to do but waited a little, feeling myself changed, savoring a new strength. The sun behind me cast my shadow on the water so that it was as if a stranger stood there, a creature taller, darker, older than myself. Standing among the cool reeds, I felt the first thrill of an unfamiliar pride. I alone, witchlike in my unholy knowledge, knew all the secrets and could use them or not as I chose. Beyond my shadow the pool sparkled dangerously; air and water blazed with diabolical fire.

It lasted no more than a minute, my trespass into forbidden territory. A cloud came; sky and pool darkened; the air felt cool. I was myself again, but not as I had once been. Hoodman House had changed me for the worse: it had initiated me in the power of evil. Its chill threatened my soul. Here on the very brink I must draw back. It was better not to know the dark side of other people's lives, better to leave the past alone. Knowledge might be a weapon, but it was a burden too, like a sharing of guilt. Best to leave still waters undisturbed.

All the same, in sudden revulsion from the person I might easily have become, I hurled the box into the water as far as it would go and with it every illusion I had cherished concerning the two whose property it had been, whose shallow vows the ring had sealed. Being small and light the box failed to travel far but with a little plop it struck the water and sank out of sight. Ripples appeared and spread and died away, leaving the surface smooth again.

As for May, she could rely on my discretion, but there was no need to tell her so. She would never be sure. My return to virtue had its limitations. One foot has remained on the primrose path.

"What on earth are you doing?" Clem had come up behind me.

"Just getting rid of something I didn't want. It's a very satisfying thing to have done."

"A wedding present, I presume. Shall I go and fetch some of the others while you're in the mood? A surplus toast rack or two?"

He had put his arm round my waist and was smiling down at me. With a keener perception than ever before of his goodness and dearness, I clung to him, recognizing in him my rescue, my salvation, my return to light and warmth.

"I love you, Clem. I love you."

"Then let's get married," he said. "Tomorrow?"

We crossed the field to Winkblade where Clem had left the car, taking our time. The next time we met it would be in public and in a new relationship, closer, happier, but different.

"Let's take a last look at Hoodman," I said, simply as an excuse to prolong the tranquil evening walk: not even the mellowing effect of mutual love could make me sentimental about Hoodman House.

Yet as we walked down the dusty lane toward it, my mood changed. The evening light fell kindly on its graceless roof and plain walls. Half screened by the fresh foliage of early summer, it appeared less dominant, less hostile an intruder on the countryside. For the first time I thought of it as my grandfather's home. When his daughters left—and until it was sold—for a little while he would come into his own again. He had been reckless, ill-advised, and not always honest, but I remembered him as the old man who had held my hand: a victim, not the cause, of Hoodman's sinister deceptions.

Whatever evil power had crept into the place, time—with a little help from Clem and me—had exorcised, I thought, embracing in my own happiness the entire scene: on our left the sloping fields enclosed within ancient hedgerows under a mild sky; on our right a bank of wild flowers topped by the dense growth of thorn and bramble concealing Packhorse Way. To the rare concurrence of the time, the place, and the loved one was added the light fragrance of flowering honeysuckle.

From these comfortable thoughts Clem's voice roused me abruptly.

"Who's that?"

I became aware that as we had walked down the farm lane, a man had been walking up it from the direction of Saury. We might have converged on the house at the same moment had not

288

Clem and I already slowed almost to a halt. Our intention had been to scramble through the well-worn gap in the trees opposite the front gate and go back to the car by Packhorse Way. We had got as far as the field end but were still screened from the house not more than twenty yards away.

Meanwhile the man had been walking steadily despite the upward slope and would soon be upon us on his way, presumably, to the Tile Sheds and the Upper Saury road. To avoid the awkwardness of appearing and instantly disappearing under his very nose we stopped by mutual consent, withdrew behind the hedge, and as Clem put it, "loitered with intent to see without being seen."

Through the twisted thorns the advancing figure seemed at first only partly human, a moving shape patterned with green leaves; but his long loping stride brought him rapidly nearer, and standing on tiptoe, I found a breach in the hedge through which I could see him more clearly.

At a distance of about a hundred yards below the house the lane widened to take in the semblance of a footpath, a trodden way stolen from an unfenced barley field and leading to the house. It was all that the Findons had salvaged for their own use when the adjoining land was sold.

Having reached it, the stranger swerved without hesitation to the right. He wasn't making for the Tile Sheds. There could be no doubt as to his destination. A man calling at this time in the evening? It was so rare an event that for a wild instant I thought of Dick, come home at last at what must surely be the most inconvenient of all possible times.

A quick glance at Clem reassured me. Of course it wasn't Dick. For all his faults—and they were many—Dick's bearing and walk would have been different. This man was narrow-shouldered, forward-leaning, downward-looking, each foot inward-turning, as if his boots pinched: a tall thin man in a cheap navy blue serge suit and trilby hat.

With barely a pause he unlatched the gate and went up the path. We were near enough to have heard his footsteps on the flags but he trod as soft-footed as a creature of the woods. It was the stealthy softness of his tread like that of a fox creeping toward a hen roost that stirred a memory and gave me my first clue to his identity.

But his summons as he raised the knocker and rapped three times seemed loud enough in the surrounding silence to wake the dead. A blackbird burst from the lilac and flew toward us, calling in alarm. The door opened. The caller removed his hat. His hair was russet-colored.

"You know him?" Clem had felt my sudden rigidity.

"Ssh!"

"Miss Findon?" The voice was husky, its tone bland. "Miss May Findon?"—and with the unswerving confidence of a man who knew exactly what he was about, with the inflexible purpose of Nemesis itself, I have since thought, he stepped inside.

"He's been here before?"

"No, not exactly."

"He seems to know his way about."

"His name is Tench. Albert Tench. He's a porter at the workhouse."

"Ah, the fellow you told me about. He looked after Sintram's funeral arrangements and so on?"

My acquaintance with Tench had been slight, beginning in the workhouse corridor when he had directed me to Mr. Tadworth's office in the late afternoon and ending in the small hours of the next morning when I had left him waiting at Winkblade for the ambulance that would take Sintram's body back to Bidminster . . .

"What the dickens does he want with May?"

"I don't know."

It was true when I spoke, but it seems to me even without the benefit of hindsight that in a flash, no more than seconds later, I guessed why he had come. He didn't know May, had never even seen her. "Miss May Findon?" he had needed to ask whichever of my aunts had opened the door. There was only one possible connection. It was to be found not in the first or last of my encounters with Tench but in the interval between, when I had been alone with Sintram in the bakehouse.

Details of the scene came back to me: the strange brilliance of the old man's eyes as he gasped out the truth about May; his labored breathing; the ache in my knees as I knelt on the stone floor beside my shadow cast by red firelight on the wall; the heat from the oven. I had been obliged to open the door—and leave it ajar.

And later, as I stood buttoning my coat against the cold outside, he had been there, Tench. I remembered my start of fear when he moved, close beside me in the dark, and my impression that he had not just arrived but had been there for—I didn't know how long. Why should a man stand about in the dark on a chilly November night when he had found what he was looking for and could have come in at once out of the cold?

"You're shivering. Do we have to go on skulking here in this furtive way?" Clem put his arm round me but he made no move to go. "Why should he particularly want to see May? Evidently Kelda wouldn't do."

Of the many factors that distinguished May from others, even from Kelda, there was one known only to me. Or so I had thought. Sintram had passed it on to me with almost his last breath. The thick stone wall of the bakehouse had enclosed us with whatever ill-boding influence remained of the crime committed there, in an isolation as profound as in a tomb. Except for the open door . . .

If Tench had overheard—a story of child murder might well have held his attention to the exclusion of discomforts worse than the cold—he had kept it to himself, so far as I knew. It was possible that he had wrung more details from the dying Sintram when they were alone together; but he had evidently not been impelled by conscience to bring the criminal to justice. It was seven months since Sintram's death, and in all that time Tench had given no sign. The poverty-stricken Miss Findon had been of no interest to him.

The chateleine of Stokeland Abbey was a different matter. The last edition of Bidminster's weekly *Gazette* had given two columns to the romantic tale of Vernon Bowland's return and forthcoming marriage: a tale powerful enough to infect even the carbolic-laden workhouse corridors with the temptation of new horizons.

"He could be looking for work," I said, unconvinced. "He knew that Sintram used to do odd jobs."

"You may be right. All the same if you're in no particular hurry I think perhaps we should hang about until he's gone. As a matter of fact—I've never said this before for fear of making you nervous—but it's a good thing you're all leaving. I've always thought it a crazy idea for women to live here on their own. Anything could happen and not a soul would know about it."

"I suppose so." I felt that Clem had summed up the history of Hoodman House pretty well. Considering his antipathy for May, his concern for her did him credit. Even when I reminded him that Kelda was there too—we could now hear her filling the coal scuttle in the backyard—he thought we should go so far as to knock, if only to establish a presence in the neighborhood.

Simple courtesy required no less, especially as I had promised Kelda that I would go back, but there were suddenly so many reasons why it didn't seem a good idea that I abandoned all attempts to explain and said, "No, I don't want to," at the same time urging him to the gap where we could slither down into Packhorse Way. And just in time! We were halfway down the steep bank when we heard the door open; and surging up again with one accord, we saw Tench already latching the gate behind him. He looked at his watch and took himself off down the lane at a good pace.

"That's all right then. Let's go." Clem took my arm and added casually, "Of course they could both be lying there unconscious—or even . . . Do you want to make sure?"

"No. I'm quite sure they're all right."

He grinned, probably interpreting my firmness as a rebuke to his nonsense. He would have been surprised to know on what grounds my assurance was based. If I had guessed his mission correctly, under no circumstances would Tench do violence to May. He wouldn't want any harm to come to her. Her preservation into old age would suit him much better and might indeed have become his chief aim in life. In spite of everything, I quailed for her.

Yet it was all surmise. Tench was just as likely to be collecting contributions for the workhouse summer outing or seeking casual work in the fresh air as a change from pushing trolleys round aseptic corridors and serving up boiled turnip. Another second and we would have left; my suspicions would never have been confirmed; the incident would have taken on in retrospect a less lurid coloring and been forgotten.

Poised awkwardly on the sloping bank, I glanced up over my shoulder at the tall house. Seen from below the level of the lane, it shut out the entire sky. A change in its façade caught my attention. I turned to look. The bay window of May's room had grown white; she was there; I could see the pearls, luminous against her silk blouse. She stood in profile apparently watching Tench as he made his way to the Saury road. An unaccountable impulse to make some gesture, some signal of acknowledgment, kept me there despite my eagerness to go. If she turns this way, I thought, I'll wave.

But when she did turn, having evidently watched Tench out of sight, I didn't wave. She wouldn't have seen me, as with the fixity of total abstraction she stared ahead into the impassive trees.

Their green shade gave a deathly pallor to her face. With trance-like slowness she raised her hands to her head; and then—the change made me gasp—in a sudden frenzy of violence clutched at her hair and tore at its smoothly sculptured bands, her fingers hooked and urgent like white claws. Combs must have been dislodged, hairpins scattered. One long lock fell over her shoulder giving her a wayward lopsided look.

The onslaught ended; the whole elaborate edifice tumbled. From its disorder emerged a rough symmetry of thick waves, framing her white face, which seemed diminished, its proportions altered—and covering her shoulders so that she looked less tall as she moved close to the window and laid her palms, fingers fully extended, flat against the pane. The droop of her head as she leaned her brow on the cold glass was more eloquent than language.

That last sight of her at Hoodman House was appropriate, for all its transforming strangeness. I had so often seen her at a window silently looking out. It was as if she had always seen the world through glass, impervious to reality like a beautiful object encased, to be looked at but never touched, never wanting to be touched. Had I just seen the first menacing crack in the protective glass? It occurred to me that Tench might have succeeded where those who knew her best had failed; had found in her a sensitive nerve and made her feel not love, of course, nor pity, nor remorse—but the chill onset of despair.

My tears surprised me. I hoped Clem wouldn't notice them. They would have been so difficult to explain.

26

§§§§§§

PICTURES OF OUR wedding are preserved for posterity in the family album. The various groups were taken in the Tasses' garden with the yew hedge as their backdrop. It has grown taller and thicker since then and the dresses have, alas, dated. Did Mirabel and I actually *choose* those regrettable shoes? And why does the eye invariably glide over the other faces and come to rest upon one, heart-melting in its beauty, and that not the face of the bride?

The album, needless to say, omits much more than it records. A wedding day, supposed to be the happiest in a woman's life, must for that very reason set the nerves on edge; and weddings in the Findon family seem to attract more than their share of additional stress. If the lean shadow of Albert Tench threatened the otherwise unalloyed bliss of my own wedding day, how much more darkly it must have fallen on May's! I wasn't there to see, thank goodness. No doubt she behaved perfectly as usual under the strain of an anxiety remarkably similar to that she had inflicted on Kelda at her wedding.

As a matter of fact in my own case Tench was more than a shadow. He was there, at St. Bartholomew's church, in person. When Clem and I emerged from the Norman doorway and paused to savor the relief of having survived the ceremony without mishap, almost the first person I saw in the churchyard was Tench. Leaning against one of the flat-topped tombs, he established a modest presence unremarkable as that of the other interested spectators but plainly visible to the bridal party, relations, and friends.

He was wearing the blue serge suit he had worn the previous evening, soon to be discarded for a less plebeian and more expensive style of dress. From the upstairs window of our house on the corner of Watt Lane I can keep my finger on the pulse of Bidminster, as Harriet would say, and Tench is often to be seen in the town and at all hours. Since he left the workhouse he has apparently not needed to take another job. His taste is for tweeds, well cut and of good quality, their checks a trifle louder than necessary—and comfortable leather brogues. With an expensive camera slung over his shoulder he has the leisurely look of a permanent holiday maker, has put on weight—and has exerted it successfully.

Stokeland Abbey is even more isolated than Hoodman House and May must often be alone there except for the servants. She no longer accompanies Uncle Vernon when he goes back to South Africa for the winter. He seems not to mind; and Tench probably prefers to keep her within easy reach. We exchange visits, though the intervals between them, always long, have lengthened. Outwardly she is little changed, though thinner. One would say that as Tench waxes, May wanes. One might put it like that. But a well-informed observer would be more cautious in assessing the odds between the two. Sometimes as Tench saunters down Priorsgate to the Royal Hotel where he likes to lunch and dine, I have felt an impulse (easily suppressed) to warn him to tread softly as he used to do for fear of falling into the mire he has helped to create. He may not have taken the full measure of his adversary. No one has ever quite measured up to May . . .

Are all photographs so deceptive, so reassuring in their limitations? The album can give no more than a hint of the reality it is supposed to reproduce anymore than it can restore the warmth of a cloudless day, the scents of roses and orange blossom, the rapture of the bride and groom, the quiet happiness of others. For me the highlights of the day are recorded only in the memory. One is a picture of two people side by side on the white seat under the copper beech: a light-haired woman no longer very young and a gray-haired man, her husband. They sit quietly, hand in hand in the shade, looking out on a sunlit garden in a mutual contentment, an intimate understanding long withheld.

The other is a more dramatic scene enacted at the front of the house. We are on the point of leaving. The car is at the door. Guests throng the pavement, among them a dignified young woman with splendid red hair and with her a small boy of precocious poise and charm. But for once the poise has faltered. The paper parcel he clutches is a source of trouble to him. A wedding gift? His mother urges him toward us; he advances, then retreats, blushing. It will soon be too late.

"Nothing was good enough for you," his mother whispers, "except this and now he isn't sure if it's quite the thing."

Confetti is thrown; last embraces are undergone. At the eleventh hour, in desperation, he rushes forward and thrusts the package into my hand, his face haggard with anxiety. Anxious-eyed, he watches me undo the wrappings to reveal, of all unexpected things, a red squirrel with a hazelnut between its paws.

My delighted surprise and the warmth of my hug restore him. From head to foot he is suffused with satisfaction.

"Mrs. Cade gave it to me. It was given to her once and I'm giving it to you. It's my best thing but I don't mind so much now because Great-uncle Vernon has given me a dog."

Dogs have come and gone. The squirrel has outlasted them all. Its attitude—bolt upright on the topmost bookshelf—might well be one of surprise at having lasted so long. The glass dome is a replacement. I never heard what happened to the old one.

Alive, the creature must have been beautiful. Buried, it would have enriched the earth. Stuffed, it lacks both the grace of life and the dignity of death. Victorian relics may be all the rage just now but few of us have inherited our great-great-grandparents' passion for decorating rooms with dead animals. Why then do I keep it when its belated cremation would be so easy to arrange? A quick blaze of dried fur and dessicated paws and it would be all over.

But not yet. It isn't true, as May has found to her cost, that a dead thing is nothing else but dead. Between the squirrel and me there has existed from the beginning a kind of camaraderie. Certain gaps in its history still intrigue me. And sometimes when a trick of light revives the startled watchfulness of its glassy eye, it puts me on my guard and warns me of the perils that lurk unseen in even the quietest of lives.